THEODORE STURGEON

Theodore Sturgeon was born on February 26, 1918, in Staten Island, New York, and died in Eugene, Oregon, on May 8, 1985. He lived in New York City, upstate New York, and Los Angeles. He is the author of *More Than Human,* winner of the International Fantasy Award; *Venus Plus X; To Marry Medusa,* which was also published under the title *The Cosmic Rape; The Dreaming Jewels;* and numerous other books and stories. He won the Hugo and Nebula Awards for his short story "Slow Sculpture" and the World Fantasy Life Achievement Award.

Also by THEODORE STURGEON

The Dreaming Jewels
More than Human
I, Libertine
Venus Plus X
To Marry Medusa
Some of Your Blood
Godbody

The Complete Stories of Theodore Sturgeon:
Volume I: *The Ultimate Egoist*
Volume II: *Microcosmic God*
Volume III: *Killdozer!*
Volume IV: *Thunder and Roses*
Volume V: *The Perfect Host*
Volume VI: *Baby Is Three*
Volume VII: *A Saucer of Loneliness*

SELECTED STORIES
THEODORE STURGEON

SELECTED STORIES

THEODORE STURGEON

VINTAGE BOOKS
A DIVISION OF RANDOM HOUSE, INC.
NEW YORK

FIRST VINTAGE BOOKS EDITION, NOVEMBER 2000

Copyright © 2000 by the Theodore Sturgeon Literary Trust

All rights reserved under International and Pan-American
Copyright Conventions. Published in the United States
by Vintage Books, a division of Random House, Inc.,
New York, and simultaneously in Canada by Random
House of Canada Limited, Toronto.

Vintage and colophon are registered trademarks
of Random House, Inc.

Library of Congress Cataloguing
in Publication Data is on file.

Vintage ISBN: 978-0-375-70375-1

www.vintagebooks.com

Printed in the United States of America

CONTENTS

SELECTED STORIES
THEODORE STURGEON

THUNDER AND ROSES

When Pete Mawser learned about the show, he turned away from the GHQ bulletin board, touched his long chin, and determined to shave. This was odd, because the show would be video, and he would see it in his barracks.

He had an hour and a half. It felt good to have a purpose again—even shaving before eight o'clock. Eight o'clock Tuesday, just the way it used to be. Everyone used to catch that show on Tuesday. Everyone used to say, Wednesday morning, "How about the way she sang 'The Breeze and I' last night?" "Hey, did you hear Starr last night?"

That was a while ago, before all those people were dead, before the country was dead. Starr Anthim, institution, like Crosby, like Duse, like Jenny Lind, like the Statue of Liberty.

(Liberty had been one of the first to get it, her bronze beauty volatilized, radioactive, and even now being carried about in vagrant winds, spreading over the earth—)

Pete Mawser grunted and forced his thoughts away from the drifting, poisonous fragments of a blasted Liberty. Hate was first. Hate was ubiquitous, like the increasing blue glow in the air at night, like the tension that hung over the base.

Gunfire crackled sporadically far to the right, swept nearer.

3

Pete stepped out of the street and made for a parked ten-wheeler. There's a lot of cover in and around a ten-wheeler.

There was a Wac sitting on the short running-board.

At the corner a stocky figure backed into the intersection. The man carried a tommy gun in his arms, and he was swinging to and fro with the gentle, wavering motion of a weathervane. He staggered toward them, his gun muzzle hunting. Someone fired from a building and the man swiveled and blasted wildly at the sound.

"He's—blind," said Pete Mawser, and added, "He ought to be," looking at the tattered face.

A siren keened. An armored jeep slewed into the street. The full-throated roar of a brace of .50-caliber machine guns put a swift and shocking end to the incident.

"Poor crazy kid," Pete said softly. "That's the fourth I've seen today." He looked down at the Wac. She was smiling.

"Hey!"

"Hello, Sarge." She must have identified him before, because now she did not raise her eyes or her voice. "What happened?"

"You know what happened. Some kid got tired of having nothing to fight and nowhere to run to. What's the matter with you?"

"No," she said. "I don't mean that." At last she looked up at him. "I mean all of this. I can't seem to remember."

"You . . . well, gee, it's not easy to forget. We got hit. We got hit everywhere at once. All the big cities are gone. We got it from both sides. We got too much. The air is becoming radioactive. We'll all—" He checked himself. She didn't know. She'd forgotten. There was nowhere to escape to, and she'd escaped inside herself, right here. Why tell her about it? Why tell her that everyone was going to die? Why tell her that other, shameful thing: that we hadn't struck back?

But she wasn't listening. She was still looking at him. Her eyes were not quite straight. One held his but the other was slightly shifted and seemed to be looking at his temples. She was smiling again. When his voice trailed off she didn't prompt him. Slowly he moved away. She did not turn her head, but kept looking up at where he had been, smiling a little. He turned away, wanting to run, walking fast.

(How long can a guy hold out? When you're in the Army they

try to make you be like everybody else. What do you do when everybody else is cracking up?)

He blanked out the mental picture of himself as the last one left sane. He'd followed that one through before. It always led to the conclusion that it would be better to be one of the first. He wasn't ready for that yet.

Then he blanked that out, too. Every time he said to himself that he wasn't ready for that yet, something within him asked, "Why not?" and he never seemed to have an answer ready.

(How long could a guy hold out?)

He climbed the steps of the QM Central and went inside.

There was nobody at the reception switchboard. It didn't matter. Messages were carried by guys in jeeps, or on motorcycles. The Base Command was not insisting that anybody stick to a sitting job these days. Ten desk men would crack up for every one on a jeep, or on the soul-sweat squads. Pete made up his mind to put in a little stretch on a squad tomorrow. Do him good. He just hoped that this time the adjutant wouldn't burst into tears in the middle of the parade ground. You could keep your mind on the manual of arms just fine until something like that happened.

He bumped into Sonny Weisefreund in the barracks corridor. The tech's round young face was as cheerful as ever. He was naked and glowing, and had a towel thrown over his shoulder.

"Hi, Sonny. Is there plenty of hot water?"

"Why not?" grinned Sonny. Pete grinned back, cursing inwardly. Could anybody say anything about anything at all without one of these reminders? Sure there was hot water. The QM barracks had hot water for three hundred men. There were three dozen left. Men dead, men gone to the hills, men locked up so they wouldn't—

"Starr Anthim's doing a show tonight."

"Yeah. Tuesday night. Not funny, Pete. Don't you know there's a war—"

"No kidding," Pete said swiftly. "She's here—right here on the base."

Sonny's face was joyful. "Gee." He pulled the towel off his shoulder and tied it around his waist. "Starr Anthim here! Where are they going to put on the show?"

"HQ, I imagine. Video only. You know about public gatherings." And a good thing, too, he thought. Put on an in-person show, and some torn-up GI would crack during one of her numbers. He himself would get plenty mad over a thing like that—mad enough to do something about it then and there. And there would probably be a hundred and fifty or more like him, going raving mad because someone had spoiled a Starr Anthim show. That would be a dandy little shambles for her to put in her memory book.

"How'd she happen to come here, Pete?"

"Drifted in on the last gasp of a busted-up Navy helicopter."

"Yeah, but why?"

"Search me. Get your head out of that gift horse's mouth."

He went into the washroom, smiling and glad that he still could. He undressed and put his neatly folded clothes down on a bench. There were a soap wrapper and an empty toothpaste tube lying near the wall. He went and picked them up and put them in the catchall. He took the mop which leaned against the partition and mopped the floor where Sonny had splashed after shaving. Got to keep things squared away. He might say something if it were anyone else but Sonny. But Sonny wasn't cracking up. Sonny always had been like that. Look there. Left his razor out again.

Pete started his shower, meticulously adjusting the valves until the pressure and temperature exactly suited him. He didn't do anything slapdash these days. There was so much to feel, and taste, and see now. The impact of water on his skin, the smell of soap, the consciousness of light and heat, the very pressure of standing on the soles of his feet—he wondered vaguely how the slow increase of radioactivity in the air, as the nitrogen transmuted to Carbon Fourteen, would affect him if he kept carefully healthy in every way. What happens first? Do you go blind? Headaches, maybe? Perhaps you lose your appetite. Or maybe you get tired all the time.

Why not look it up?

On the other hand, why bother? Only a very small percentage of the men would die of radioactive poisoning. There were too many other things that killed more quickly, which was probably just as well. That razor, for example. It lay gleaming in a sunbeam, curved and clean in the yellow light. Sonny's father and grandfather had used it, or so he said, and it was his pride and joy.

Pete turned his back on it and soaped under his arms, concentrating on the tiny kisses of bursting bubbles. In the midst of a recurrence of disgust at himself for thinking so often of death, a staggering truth struck him. He did not think of such things because he was morbid, after all! It was the very familiarity of things that brought death-thoughts. It was either "I shall never do this again" or "This is one of the last times I shall do this." You might devote yourself completely to doing things in different ways, he thought madly. You might crawl across the floor this time, and next time walk across on your hands. You might skip dinner tonight, and have a snack at two in the morning instead, and eat grass for breakfast.

But you had to breathe. Your heart had to beat. You'd sweat and you'd shiver, the same as always. You couldn't get away from that. When those things happened, they would remind you. Your heart wouldn't beat out its *wunklunk, wunklunk* any more. It would go *one-less, one-less*, until it yelled and yammered in your ears and you had to make it stop.

Terrific polish on that razor.

And your breath would go on, same as before. You could sidle through this door, back through the next one and the one after, and figure out a totally new way to go through the one after that, but your breath would keep on sliding in and out of your nostrils like a razor going through whiskers, making a sound like a razor being stropped.

Sonny came in. Pete soaped his hair. Sonny picked up the razor and stood looking at it. Pete watched him, soap ran into his eye, he swore, and Sonny jumped.

"What are you looking at, Sonny? Didn't you ever see it before?"

"Oh, sure. Sure. I was just—" He shut the razor, opened it, flashed light from its blade, shut it again. "I'm tired of using this, Pete. I'm going to get rid of it. Want it?"

Want it? In his foot locker, maybe. Under his pillow. "Thanks no, Sonny. Couldn't use it."

"I like safety razors," Sonny mumbled. "Electrics, even better. What are we going to do with it?"

"Throw it in the . . . no." Pete pictured the razor turning end over end in the air, half open, gleaming in the maw of the catchall.

"Throw it out the—" No. Curving out into the long grass. You might want it. You might crawl around in the moonlight looking for it. You might find it.

"I guess maybe I'll break it up."

"No," Pete said. "The pieces—" Sharp little pieces. Hollow-ground fragments. "I'll think of something. Wait'll I get dressed."

He washed briskly, toweled, while Sonny stood looking at the razor. It was a blade now, and if you broke it, there would be shards and glittering splinters, still razor sharp. You could slap its edge into an emery wheel and grind it away, and somebody could find it and put another edge on it because it was so obviously a razor, a fine steel razor, one that would slice so— "I know. The laboratory. We'll get rid of it," Pete said confidently.

He stepped into his clothes, and together they went to the laboratory wing. It was very quiet there. Their voices echoed.

"One of the ovens," said Pete, reaching for the razor.

"Bake ovens? You're crazy!"

Pete chuckled. "You don't know this place, do you? Like everything else on the base, there was a lot more went on here than most people knew about. They kept calling it the bake shop. Well, it *was* research headquarters for new high-nutrient flours. But there's lots else here. We tested utensils and designed beet peelers and all sorts of things like that. There's an electric furnace in here that—" He pushed open a door.

They crossed a long, quiet, cluttered room to the thermal equipment. "We can do everything here from annealing glass, through glazing ceramics, to finding the melting point of frying pans." He clicked a switch tentatively. A pilot light glowed. He swung open a small, heavy door and set the razor inside. "Kiss it good-bye. In twenty minutes it'll be a puddle."

"I want to see that," said Sonny. "Can I look around until it's cooked?"

"Why not?"

(Everybody around here always said "Why not?")

They walked through the laboratories. Beautifully equipped, they were, and too quiet. Once they passed a major who was bent over a complex electronic hook-up on one of the benches. He was watching a little amber light flicker, and he did not return their salute. They tiptoed past him, feeling awed at his absorption, envying it. They saw the models of the automatic kneaders, the vitaminizers, the remote-signal thermostats and timers and controls.

"What's in there?"

"I dunno. I'm over the edge of my territory. I don't think there's anybody left for this section. They were mostly mechanical and electronic theoreticians. The only thing I know about them is that if we ever needed anything in the way of tools, meters, or equipment, they had it or something better, and if we ever got real bright and figured out a startling new idea, they'd already built it and junked it a month ago. Hey!"

Sonny followed the pointing hand. "What?"

"That wall section. It's loose, or . . . well, what do you know?"

He pushed at the section of wall, which was very slightly out of line. There was a dark space beyond.

"What's in there?"

"Nothing, or some semiprivate hush-hush job. These guys used to get away with murder."

Sonny said, with an uncharacteristic flash of irony, "Isn't that the Army theoretician's business?"

Cautiously they peered in, then entered.

"Wh . . . *hey!* The door!"

It swung swiftly and quietly shut. The soft click of the latch was accompanied by a blaze of light.

The room was small and windowless. It contained machinery—a "trickle" charger, a bank of storage batteries, an electric-powered dynamo, two small self-starting gas-driven light plants and a Diesel complete with sealed compressed-air starting cylinders. In the corner was a relay rack with its panel-bolts spot-welded. Protruding from it was a red-top lever. Nothing was labeled.

They looked at the equipment wordlessly for a time and then Sonny said, "Somebody wanted to make awful sure he had power for something."

"Now, I wonder what—" Pete walked over to the relay rack. He looked at the lever without touching it. It was wired up; behind the handle, on the wire, was a folded tag. He opened it cautiously. "To be used only on specific orders of the Commanding Officer."

"Give it a yank and see what happens."

Something clicked behind them. They whirled. "What was that?"

"Seemed to come from that rig by the door."

They approached it cautiously. There was a spring-loaded solenoid attached to a bar which was hinged to drop across the inside of the secret door, where it would fit into steel gudgeons on the panel.

It clicked again. "A Geiger," said Pete disgustedly.

"Now why," mused Sonny, "would they design a door to stay locked unless the general radioactivity went beyond a certain point? That's what it is. See the relays? And the overload switch there? And this?"

"It has a manual lock, too," Pete pointed out. The counter clicked again. "Let's get out of here. I got one of those things built into my head these days."

The door opened easily. They went out, closing it behind them. The keyhole was cleverly concealed in the crack between two boards.

They were silent as they made their way back to the QM labs. The small thrill of violation was gone and, for Pete Mawser at least, the hate was back, that and the shame. A few short weeks before, this base had been a part of the finest country on earth. There was a lot of work here that was secret, and a lot that was such purely progressive and unapplied research that it would be in the way anywhere else but in this quiet wilderness.

Sweat stood out on his forehead. They hadn't struck back at their murderers! It was quite well known that there were launching sites all over the country, in secret caches far from any base or murdered city. Why must they sit here waiting to die, only to let the enemy—"enemies" was more like it—take over the continent when it was safe again?

He smiled grimly. One small consolation. They'd hit too hard: that was a certainty. Probably each of the attackers underestimated what the other would throw. The result—a spreading transmutation of nitrogen into deadly Carbon Fourteen. The effects would not be limited to the continent. What ghastly long-range effect the muted radioactivity would have on the overseas enemies was something that no one alive today could know.

Back at the furnace, Pete glanced at the temperature dial, then kicked at the latch control. The pilot winked out and then the door swung open. They blinked and started back from the raging heat within, then bent and peered. The razor was gone. A pool of brilliance lay on the floor of the compartment.

"Ain't much left. Most of it oxidized away," Pete grunted.

They stood together for a time with their faces lit by that small shimmering ruin. Later, as they walked back to the barracks, Sonny broke his long silence with a sigh. "I'm glad we did that, Pete. I'm awful glad we did that."

At a quarter to eight they were waiting before the combination console in the barracks. All hands except Pete and Sonny and a wiry-haired, thick-set corporal named Bonze had elected to see the show on the big screen in the mess hall. The reception was better there, of course, but, as Bonze put it, "you don't get close enough in a big place like that."

"I hope she's the same," said Sonny, half to himself.

Why should she be? thought Pete morosely as he turned on the set and watched the screen begin to glow. There were many more of the golden speckles that had killed reception for the past two weeks. Why should anything be the same, ever again?

He fought a sudden temptation to kick the set to pieces. It, and Starr Anthim, were part of something that was dead. The country was dead, a real country—prosperous, sprawling, laughing, grabbing, growing and changing, leprous in spots with poverty and injustice, but healthy enough to overcome any ill. He wondered how the murderers would like it. They were welcome to it, now. Nowhere to go. No one to fight. That was true for every soul on earth now.

"You hope she's the same," he muttered.

"The show, I mean," said Sonny mildly. "I'd like to just sit here and have it like . . . like—"

Oh, thought Pete mistily. Oh—that. Somewhere to go, that's what it is, for a few minutes. "I know," he said, all the harshness gone from his voice.

Noise receded from the audio as the carrier swept in. The light on the screen swirled and steadied into a diamond pattern. Pete adjusted the focus, chromic balance, and intensity. "Turn out the lights, Bonze. I don't want to see anything but Starr Anthim."

It *was* the same, at first. Starr Anthim had never used the usual fanfares, fade-ins, color, and clamor of her contemporaries. A black screen, then *click*, a blaze of gold. It was all there, in focus; tremendously intense, it did not change. Rather, the eye changed to take it in. She never moved for seconds after she came on; she was there, a portrait, a still face and a white throat. Her eyes were open and sleeping. Her face was alive and still.

Then, in the eyes which seemed green but were blue flecked with gold, an awareness seemed to gather, and they came awake. Only then was it noticeable that her lips were parted. Something in the eyes made the lips be seen, though nothing moved yet. Not until she bent her head slowly, so that some of the gold flecks seemed captured in the golden brows. The eyes were not, then, looking out at an audience. They were looking at me, and at *me*, and at ME.

"Hello—you," she said. She was a dream, with a kid sister's slightly irregular teeth.

Bonze shuddered. The cot on which he lay began to squeak rapidly. Sonny shifted in annoyance. Pete reached out in the dark and caught the leg of the cot. The squeaking subsided.

"May I sing a song?" Starr asked. There was music, very faint. "It's an old one, and one of the best. It's an easy song, a deep song, one that comes from the part of men and women that is mankind—the part that has in it no greed, no hate, no fear. This song is about joyousness and strength. It's—my favorite. Isn't it yours?"

The music swelled. Pete recognized the first two notes of the introduction and swore quietly. This was wrong. This song was not for . . . this song was part of—

Sonny sat raptly. Bonze lay still

Starr Anthim began to sing. Her voice was deep and powerful, but soft, with the merest touch of vibrato at the ends of the phrases. The song flowed from her without noticeable effort, seeming to come from her face, her long hair, her wide-set eyes. Her voice, like her face, was shadowed and clean, round, blue and green but mostly gold:

"When you gave me your heart, you gave me the world,
    You gave me the night and the day,

And thunder, and roses, and sweet green grass,
The sea, and soft wet clay.

"I drank the dawn from a golden cup,
From a silver one, the dark,
The steed I rode was the wild west wind,
My song was the brook and the lark."

The music spiraled, caroled, slid into a somber cry of muted, hungry sixths and ninths; rose, blared, and cut, leaving her voice full and alone:

"With thunder I smote the evil of earth,
With roses I won the right,
With the sea I washed, and with clay I built,
And the world was a place of light!"

The last note left a face perfectly composed again, and there was no movement in it; it was sleeping and vital while the music curved off and away to the places where music rests when it is not heard.

Starr smiled.

"It's so easy," she said. "So simple. All that is fresh and clean and strong about mankind is in that song, and I think that's all that need concern us about mankind." She leaned forward. "Don't you see?"

The smile faded and was replaced with a gentle wonder. A tiny furrow appeared between brows; she drew back quickly. "I can't seem to talk to you tonight," she said, her voice small. "You hate something."

Hate was shaped like a monstrous mushroom. Hate was the random speckling of a video plate.

"What has happened to us," said Starr abruptly, impersonally, "is simple, too. It doesn't matter who did it—do you understand that? *It doesn't matter.* We were attacked. We were struck from the east and from the west. Most of the bombs were atomic— there were blast bombs and there were dust bombs. We were hit by about five hundred and thirty bombs altogether, and it has killed us."

She waited.

Sonny's fist smacked into his palm. Bonze lay with his eyes open, quiet. Pete's jaw hurt.

"We have more bombs than both of them put together. We *have* them. We are not going to use them. *Wait!*" She raised her hands suddenly, as if she could see into each man's face. They sank back, tense.

"So saturated is the atmosphere with Carbon Fourteen that all of us in this hemisphere are going to die. Don't be afraid to say it. Don't be afraid to think it. It is a truth, and it must be faced. As the transmutation effect spreads from the ruins of our cities, the air will become increasingly radioactive, and then we must die. In months, in a year or so, the effects will be strong overseas. Most of the people there will die, too. None will escape completely. A worse thing will come to them than anything they gave us, because there will be a wave of horror and madness which is impossible to us. We are merely going to die. They will live and burn and sicken, and the children that will be born to them—" She shook her head, and her lower lip grew full. She visibly pulled herself together.

"Five hundred and thirty bombs—I don't think either of our attackers knew just how strong the other was. There has been so much secrecy." Her voice was sad. She shrugged slightly. "They have killed us, and they have ruined themselves. As for us—we are not blameless, either. Neither are we helpless to do anything— yet. But what we must do is hard. We must die—without striking back."

She gazed briefly at each man in turn, from the screen. "We must *not* strike back. Mankind is about to go through a hell of his own making. We can be vengeful—or merciful, if you like—and let go with the hundreds of bombs we have. That would sterilize the planet so that not a microbe, not a blade of grass could escape, and nothing new could grow. We could reduce the earth to a bald thing, dead and deadly.

"No, it just won't do. We can't do it.

"Remember the song? *That* is humanity. That's in all humans. A disease made other humans our enemies for a time, but as the generations march past, enemies become friends and friends ene- mies. The enmity of those who have killed us is such a tiny, tempo- rary thing in the long sweep of history!"

Her voice deepened. "Let us die with the knowledge that we have done the one noble thing left to us. The spark of humanity can still live and grow on this planet. It will be blown and drenched, shaken and all but extinguished, but it will live if that song is a true one. It will live if we are human enough to discount the fact that the spark is in the custody of our temporary enemy. Some—a few—of his children will live to merge with the new humanity that will gradually emerge from the jungles and the wilderness. Perhaps there will be ten thousand years of beastliness; perhaps man will be able to rebuild while he still has his ruins."

She raised her head, her voice tolling. "And even if this is the end of humankind, we dare not take away the chances some other life form might have to succeed where we failed. If we retaliate, there will not be a dog, a deer, an ape, a bird or fish or lizard to carry the evolutionary torch. In the name of justice, if we must condemn and destroy ourselves, let us not condemn all life along with us! We are heavy enough with sins. If we must destroy, let us stop with destroying ourselves!"

There was a shimmering flicker of music. It seemed to stir her hair like a breath of wind. She smiled.

"That's all," she whispered. And to each man there she said, "Good night—"

The screen went black. As the carrier cut off—there was no announcement—the ubiquitous speckles began to swarm across it.

Pete rose and switched on the lights. Bonze and Sonny were quite still. It must have been minutes later when Sonny sat up straight, shaking himself like a puppy. Something besides the silence seemed to tear with the movement.

He said softly, "You're not allowed to fight anything, or to run away, or to live, and now you can't even hate any more, because Starr says 'no.'"

There was bitterness in the sound of it, and a bitter smell to the air.

Pete Mawser sniffed once, which had nothing to do with the smell. He froze, sniffed again. "What's that smell, Son'?"

Sonny tested it. "I don't— Something familiar. Vanilla— no . . . no.

"Almonds. Bitter—*Bonze!*"

Bonze lay still with his eyes open, grinning. His jaw muscles were knotted, and they could see almost all his teeth. He was soaking wet.

"Bonze!"

"It was just when she came on and said 'Hello—you,' remember?" whispered Pete. "Oh, the poor kid. That's why he wanted to catch the show here instead of in the mess hall."

"Went out looking at her," said Sonny through pale lips. "I can't say I blame him much. Wonder where he got the stuff."

"Never mind that." Pete's voice was harsh. "Let's get out of here."

They left to call the meat wagon. Bonze lay watching the console with his dead eyes and his smell of bitter almonds.

Pete did not realize where he was going, or exactly why, until he found himself on the dark street near GHQ and the communications shack. It had something to do with Bonze. Not that he wanted to do what Bonze had done. But then he hadn't thought of it. What would he have done if he'd thought of it? Nothing, probably. But still—it might be nice to be able to hear Starr, and see her, whenever he felt like it. Maybe there weren't any recordings, but her musical background was recorded, and the Sig might have dubbed the show off.

He stood uncertainly outside the GHQ building. There was a cluster of men outside the main entrance. Pete smiled briefly. Rain, nor snow, nor sleet, nor gloom of night could stay the stage-door Johnny.

He went down the side street and up the delivery ramp in the back. Two doors along the platform was the rear exit of the communications section.

There was a light on in the communications shack. He had his hand out to the screen door when he noticed someone standing in the shadows beside it. The light played daintily on the golden margins of a head and face.

He stopped. "Starr Anthim!"

"Hello, soldier. Sergeant."

He blushed like an adolescent. "I—" His voice left him. He swallowed, reached up to whip off his hat. He had no hat. "I saw the show," he said. He felt clumsy. It was dark, and yet he was very conscious of the fact that his dress shoes were indifferently shined.

She moved toward him into the light, and she was so beautiful that he had to close his eyes. "What's your name?"

"Mawser. Pete Mawser."

"Like the show?"

Not looking at her, he said stubbornly, "No."

"Oh?"

"I mean . . . I liked it some. The song."

"I . . . think I see."

"I wondered if I could maybe get a recording."

"I think so," she said. "What kind of a reproducer have you got?"

"Audiovid."

"A disk. Yes; we dubbed off a few. Wait, I'll get you one."

She went inside, moving slowly. Pete watched her, spellbound. She was a silhouette, crowned and haloed; and then she was a framed picture, vivid and golden. He waited, watching the light hungrily. She returned with a large envelope, called good night to someone inside, and came out on the platform.

"Here you are, Pete Mawser."

"Thanks very—" he mumbled. He wet his lips. "It was very good of you."

"Not really. The more it circulates, the better." She laughed suddenly. "That isn't meant quite as it sounds. I'm not exactly looking for new publicity these days."

The stubbornness came back. "I don't know that you'd get it, if you put on that show in normal times."

Her eyebrows went up. "Well!" she smiled. "I seem to have made quite an impression."

"I'm sorry," he said warmly. "I shouldn't have taken that tack. Everything you think and say these days is exaggerated."

"I know what you mean." She looked around. "How is it here?"

"It's O.K. I used to be bothered by the secrecy, and being buried miles away from civilization." He chuckled bitterly. "Turned out to be lucky after all."

"You sound like the first chapter of *One World or None*."

He looked up quickly. "What do you use for a reading list—the Government's own '*Index Expurgatorius*'?"

She laughed. "Come now—it isn't as bad as all that. The book was never banned. It was just—"

"Unfashionable," he filled in.

"Yes, more's the pity. If people had paid more attention to it when it was published, perhaps this wouldn't have happened."

He followed her gaze to the dimly pulsating sky. "How long are you going to be here?"

"Until . . . as long as . . . I'm not leaving."

"You're not?"

"I'm finished," she said simply. "I've covered all the ground I can. I've been everywhere that . . . anyone knows about."

"With this show?"

She nodded. "With this particular message."

He was quiet, thinking. She turned to the door, and he put out his hand, not touching her. "Please—"

"What is it?"

"I'd like to . . . I mean, if you don't mind, I don't often have a chance to talk to— Maybe you'd like to walk around a little before you turn in."

"Thanks, no, Sergeant. I'm tired." She did sound tired. "I'll see you around."

He stared at her, a sudden fierce light in his brain. "I know where it is. It's got a red-topped lever and a tag referring to orders of the commanding officer. It's really camouflaged."

She was quiet so long that he thought she had not heard him. Then, "I'll take that walk."

They went down the ramp together and turned toward the dark parade ground.

"How did you know?" she asked quietly.

"Not too tough. This 'message' of yours; the fact that you've been all over the country with it; most of all, the fact that somebody finds it necessary to persuade us not to strike back. Who are you working for?" he asked bluntly.

Surprisingly, she laughed.

"What's that for?"

"A moment ago you were blushing and shuffling your feet."

His voice was rough. "I wasn't talking to a human being. I

was talking to a thousand songs I've heard, and a hundred thousand blond pictures I've seen pinned up. You'd better tell me what this is all about."

She stopped. "Let's go up and see the colonel."

He took her elbow. "No. I'm just a sergeant, and he's high brass, and that doesn't make any difference at all now. You're a human being, and so am I, and I'm supposed to respect your rights as such. I don't. You're a woman, and—"

She stiffened. He kept her walking, and finished, "—and that will make as much difference as I let it. You'd better tell me about it."

"All right," she said, with a tired acquiescence that frightened something inside him. "You seem to have guessed right, though. It's true. There are master firing keys for the launching sites. We have located and dismantled all but two. It's very likely that one of the two was vaporized. The other one is—lost."

"Lost?"

"I don't have to tell you about the secrecy," she said disgustedly. "You know how it developed between nation and nation. You must know that it existed between State and Union, between department and department, office and office. There were only three or four men who knew where all the keys were. Three of them were in the Pentagon when it went up. That was the third blast bomb, you know. If there was another, it could only have been Senator Vandercook, and he died three weeks ago without talking."

"An automatic radio key, hm-m-m?"

"That's right. Sergeant, must we walk? I'm so tired—"

"I'm sorry," he said impulsively. They crossed to the reviewing stand and sat on the lonely benches. "Launching racks all over, all hidden, and all armed?"

"Most of them are armed. Enough. Armed and aimed."

"Aimed where?"

"It doesn't matter."

"I think I see. What's the optimum number again?"

"About six hundred and forty; a few more or less. At least five hundred and thirty have been thrown so far. We don't know exactly."

"Who are *we?*" he asked furiously.

"Who? Who?" She laughed weakly. "I could say, 'The Government,' perhaps. If the President dies, the Vice President takes over, and then the Speaker of the House, and so on and on. How far can you go? Pete Mawser, don't you realize yet what's happened?"

"I don't know what you mean."

"How many people do you think are left in this country?"

"I don't know. Just a few million, I guess."

"How many are here?"

"About nine hundred."

"Then as far as I know, this is the largest city left."

He leaped to his feet. *"NO!"* The syllable roared away from him, hurled itself against the dark, empty buildings, came back to him in a series of lower-case echoes: nononono . . . nono—n . . .

Starr began to speak rapidly, quietly. "They're scattered all over the fields and the roads. They sit in the sun and die in the afternoon. They run in packs, they tear at each other. They pray and starve and kill themselves and die in the fires. The fires—everywhere, if anything stands, it's burning. Summer, and the leaves all down in the Berkshires, and the blue grass burnt brown; you can see the grass dying from the air, the death going out wider and wider from the bald spots. Thunder and roses . . . I saw roses, new ones, creeping from the smashed pots of a greenhouse. Brown petals, alive and sick, and the thorns turned back on themselves, growing into the stems, killing. Feldman died tonight."

He let her be quiet for a time. "Who is Feldman?"

"My pilot." She was talking hollowly into her hands. "He's been dying for weeks. He's been on his nerve ends. I don't think he had any blood left. He buzzed your GHQ and made for the landing strip. He came in with the motor dead, free rotors, giro. Smashed the landing gear. He was dead, too. He killed a man in Chicago so he could steal gas. The man didn't want the gas. There was a dead girl by the pump. He didn't want us to go near. I'm not going anywhere. I'm going to stay here. I'm tired."

At last she cried.

Pete left her alone, and walked out to the center of the parade ground, looking back at the faint huddled glimmer on the bleachers. His mind flickered over the show that evening, and the way she had sung before the merciless transmitter. "Hello—you." "If we must destroy, let us stop with destroying ourselves!"

The dimming spark of humankind—what could it mean to her? How could it mean so much?

"*Thunder and roses.*" Twisted, sick, nonsurvival roses, killing themselves with their own thorns.

"And the world was a place of light!" Blue light, flickering in the contaminated air.

The enemy. The red-topped lever. Bonze. "They pray and starve and kill themselves and die in the fires."

What creatures were these, these corrupted, violent, murdering humans? What right had they to another chance? What was in them that was good?

Starr was good. Starr was crying. Only a human being could cry like that. Starr was a human being.

Had humanity anything of Starr Anthim in it?

Starr *was* a human being.

He looked down through the darkness for his hands. No planet, no universe, is greater to a man than his own ego, his own observing self. These hands were the hands of all history, and like the hands of all men, they could by their small acts make human history or end it. Whether this power of hands was that of a billion hands, or whether it came to a focus in these two—this was suddenly unimportant to the eternities which now infolded him.

He put humanity's hands deep in his pockets and walked slowly back to the bleachers.

"Starr."

She responded with a sleepy-child, interrogative whimper.

"They'll get their chance, Starr. I won't touch the key."

She sat straight. She rose, and came to him, smiling. He could see her smile because, very faintly in this air, her teeth fluoresced. She put her hands on his shoulders. "Pete."

He held her very close for a moment. Her knees buckled then, and he had to carry her.

There was no one in the Officers' Club, which was the nearest building. He stumbled in, moved clawing along the wall until he found a switch. The light hurt him. He carried her to a settee and put her down gently. She did not move. One side of her face was as pale as milk.

There was blood on his hands.

He stood looking stupidly at it, wiped it on the sides of his trousers, looking dully at Starr. There was blood on her shirt.

The echo of no's came back to him from the far walls of the big room before he knew he had spoken. Starr wouldn't do this. She couldn't!

A doctor. But there was no doctor. Not since Anders had hung himself. Get somebody. *Do* something.

He dropped to his knees and gently unbuttoned her shirt. Between the sturdy, unfeminine GI bra and the top of her slacks, there was blood on her side. He whipped out a clean handkerchief and began to wipe it away. There was no wound, no puncture. But abruptly there was blood again. He blotted it carefully. And again there was blood.

It was like trying to dry a piece of ice with a towel.

He ran to the water cooler, wrung out the bloody handkerchief and ran back to her. He bathed her face carefully, the pale right side, the flushed left side. The handkerchief reddened again, this time with cosmetics, and then her face was pale all over, with great blue shadows under the eyes. While he watched, blood appeared on her left cheek.

There must be *somebody*— He fled to the door.

"Pete!"

Running, turning at the sound of her voice, he hit the doorpost stunningly, caromed off, flailed for his balance, and then was back at her side. "Starr! Hang on, now! I'll get a doctor as quick as—"

Her hand strayed over her left cheek. "You found out. Nobody else knew, but Feldman. It got hard to cover properly." Her hand went up to her hair.

"Starr, I'll get a—"

"Pete, darling, promise me something?"

"Why, sure; certainly, Starr."

"Don't disturb my hair. It isn't—all mine, you see." She sounded like a seven-year-old, playing a game. "It all came out on this side, you see? I don't want you to see me that way."

He was on his knees beside her again. "What is it? What happened to you?" he asked hoarsely.

"Philadelphia," she murmured. "Right at the beginning. The mushroom went up a half mile away. The studio caved in. I came to the next day. I didn't know I was burned, then. It didn't show. My left side. It doesn't matter, Pete. It doesn't hurt at all, now."

He sprang to his feet again. "I'm going for a doctor."

"Don't go away. Please don't go away and leave me. Please don't." There were tears in her eyes. "Wait just a little while. Not very long, Pete."

He sank to his knees again. She gathered both his hands in hers and held them tightly. She smiled happily. "You're good, Pete. You're so good."

(She couldn't hear the blood in his ears, the roar of the whirlpool of hate and fear and anguish that spun inside him.)

She talked to him in a low voice, and then in whispers. Sometimes he hated himself because he couldn't quite follow her. She talked about school, and her first audition. "I was so scared that I got a vibrato in my voice. I'd never had one before. I always let myself get a little scared when I sing now. It's easy." There was something about a windowbox when she was four years old. "Two real live tulips and a pitcherplant. I used to be sorry for the flies."

There was a long period of silence after that, during which his muscles throbbed with cramp and stiffness, and gradually became numb. He must have dozed; he awoke with a violent start, feeling her fingers on his face. She was propped up on one elbow. She said clearly, "I just wanted to tell you, darling. Let me go first, and get everything ready for you. It's going to be wonderful. I'll fix you a special tossed salad. I'll make you a steamed chocolate pudding and keep it hot for you."

Too muddled to understand what she was saying, he smiled and pressed her back on the settee. She took his hands again.

The next time he awoke it was broad daylight, and she was dead.

Sonny Weisefreund was sitting on his cot when he got back to the barracks. He handed over the recording he had picked up from the parade ground on the way back. "Dew on it. Dry it off. Good boy," he croaked, and fell face downward on the cot Bonze had used.

Sonny stared at him. "Pete! Where've you been? What happened? Are you all right?"

Pete shifted a little and grunted. Sonny shrugged and took the audiovid disk out of its wet envelope. Moisture would not harm it particularly, though it could not be played while wet. It was made of a fine spiral of plastic, insulated between laminations. Electrostatic pickups above and below the turntable would fluctuate with changes in the dielectric constant which had been impressed by the recording, and these changes were amplified for the video. The audio was a conventional hill-and-dale needle. Sonny began to wipe it down carefully.

Pete fought upward out of a vast, green-lit place full of flickering cold fires. Starr was calling him. Something was punching him, too. He fought it weakly, trying to hear what she was saying. But someone else was jabbering too loud for him to hear.

He opened his eyes. Sonny was shaking him, his round face pink with excitement. The audiovid was running. Starr was talking. Sonny got up impatiently and turned down the audio gain. "Pete! Pete! Wake up, will you? I got to tell you something. Listen to me! Wake up, will yuh?"

"Huh?"

"That's better. Now listen. I've just been listening to Starr Anthim—"

"She's dead," said Pete. Sonny didn't hear. He went on explosively, "I've figured it out. Starr was sent out here, and all over, to *beg* someone not to fire any more atom bombs. If the government was sure they wouldn't strike back, they wouldn't have taken the trouble. Somewhere, Pete, there's some way to launch bombs at those murdering cowards—and I've got a pret-ty shrewd idea of how to do it."

Pete strained groggily toward the faint sound of Starr's voice. Sonny talked on. "Now, s'posing there was a master radio key, an automatic code device something like the alarm signal they have on ships, that rings a bell on any ship within radio range when the operator sends four long dashes. Suppose there's an automatic code machine to launch bombs, with repeaters, maybe, buried all over the country. What would it be? Just a little lever to pull; thass all. How would the thing be hidden? In the middle of a lot of other equipment, that's where; in some place where you'd expect to find crazy-looking secret stuff. Like an experiment station. Like right here. You beginning to get the idea?"

"Shut up. I can't hear her."

"The hell with her! You can hear her some other time. You didn't hear a thing I said!"

"She's dead."

"Yeah. Well, I figure I'll pull that handle. What can I lose? It'll give those murderin' . . . *what?*"

"She's dead."

"Dead? Starr Anthim?" His young face twisted, Sonny sank down to the cot. "You're half asleep. You don't know what you're saying."

"She's dead," Pete said hoarsely. "She got burned by one of the first bombs. I was with her when she . . . she— Shut up, now, and get out of here and let me listen!" he bellowed hoarsely.

Sonny stood up slowly. "They killed her, too. They killed her. That does it. That just fixes it up." His face was white. He went out.

Pete got up. His legs weren't working right. He almost fell. He brought up against the console with a crash, his outflung arm sending the pickup skittering across the record. He put it on again and turned up the gain, then lay down to listen.

His head was all mixed up. Sonny talked too much. Bomb launchers, automatic code machines—

"You gave me your heart," sang Starr. *"You gave me your heart. You gave me your heart. You—"*

Pete heaved himself up again and moved the pickup arm. Anger, not at himself, but at Sonny for causing him to cut the disk that way, welled up.

Starr was talking, stupidly, her face going through the same expression over and over again. *"Struck from the east and from the Struck from the east and from the—"*

He got up again wearily and moved the pickup.

"You gave me your heart. You gave me—"

Pete made an agonized sound that was not a word at all, bent, lifted, and sent the console crashing over. In the bludgeoning silence he said, "I did, too."

Then, "Sonny." He waited.

"Sonny!"

His eyes went wide then, and he cursed and bolted for the corridor.

The panel was closed when he reached it. He kicked at it. It flew open, discovering darkness.

"Hey!" bellowed Sonny. "Shut it! You turned off the lights!"

Pete shut it behind him. The lights blazed.

"Pete! What's the matter?"

"Nothing's the matter, Son'," croaked Pete.

"What are you looking at?" said Sonny uneasily.

"I'm sorry," said Pete as gently as he could. "I just wanted to find something out, is all. Did you tell anyone else about this?" He pointed to the lever.

"Why, no. I only just figured it out while you were sleeping, just now."

Pete looked around carefully while Sonny shifted his weight. Pete moved toward a tool rack. "Something you haven't noticed yet, Sonny," he said softly, and pointed. "Up there, on the wall behind you. High up. See?"

Sonny turned. In one fluid movement Pete plucked off a fourteen-inch box wrench and hit Sonny with it as hard as he could.

Afterward he went to work systematically on the power supplies. He pulled the plugs on the gas engines and cracked their cylinders with a maul. He knocked off the tubing of the Diesel starters—the tanks let go explosively—and he cut all the cables with bolt cutters. Then he broke up the relay rack and its lever. When he was quite finished, he put away his tools and bent and stroked Sonny's tousled hair.

He went out and closed the partition carefully. It certainly was a wonderful piece of camouflage. He sat down heavily on a workbench nearby.

"You'll have your chance," he said into the far future. "And by heaven, you'd better make good."

After that he just waited.

THE GOLDEN HELIX

I

Tod awoke first, probably because he was so curious, so deeply alive; perhaps because he was (or had been) seventeen. He fought back, but the manipulators would not be denied. They bent and flexed his arms and legs, squeezed his chest, patted and rasped and abraded him. His joints creaked, his sluggish blood clung sleepily to the walls of his veins, reluctant to move after so long.

He gasped and shouted as needles of cold played over his body, gasped again and screamed when his skin sensitized and the tingling intensified to a scald. Then he fainted, and probably slept, for he easily reawoke when someone else started screaming.

He felt weak and ravenous, but extraordinarily well rested. His first conscious realization was that the manipulators had withdrawn from his body, as had the needles from the back of his neck. He put a shaky hand back there and felt the traces of spot-tape, already half-fused with his healing flesh.

He listened comfortably to this new screaming, satisfied that it was not his own. He let his eyes open, and a great wonder came over him when he saw that the lid of his Coffin stood open.

He clawed upward, sat a moment to fight a vicious swirl of vertigo, vanquished it, and hung his chin on the edge of the Coffin.

27

The screaming came from April's Coffin. It was open too. Since the two massive boxes touched and their hinges were on opposite sides, he could look down at her. The manipulators were at work on the girl's body, working with competent violence. She seemed to be caught up in some frightful nightmare, lying on her back, dreaming of riding a runaway bicycle with an off-center pedal sprocket and epicyclic hubs. And all the while her arms seemed to be flailing at a cloud of dream-hornets round her tossing head. The needle-cluster rode with her head, fanning out behind the nape like the mechanical extrapolation of an Elizabethan collar.

Tod crawled to the end of his Coffin, stood up shakily, and grasped the horizontal bar set at chest level. He got an arm over it and snugged it close under his armpit. Half-suspended, he could then manage one of his feet over the edge, then the other, to the top step. He lowered himself until he sat on it, outside the Coffin at last, and slumped back to rest. When his furious lungs and battering heart calmed themselves, he went down the four steps one at a time, like an infant, on his buttocks.

April's screams stopped.

Tod sat on the bottom step, jackknifed by fatigue, his feet on the metal floor, his knees in the hollows between his pectorals and his shoulders. Before him, on a low pedestal, was a cube with a round switch-disc on it. When he could, he inched a hand forward and let it fall on the disc. There was an explosive tinkle and the front panel of the cube disappeared, drifting slowly away as a fine glittering dust. He lifted his heavy hand and reached inside. He got one capsule, two, carried them to his lips. He rested, then took a beaker from the cube. It was three-quarters full of purple crystals. He bumped it on the steel floor. The beaker's cover powdered and fell in, and the crystals were suddenly a liquid, effervescing violently. When it subsided, he drank it down. He belched explosively, and then his head cleared, his personal horizons expanded to include the other Coffins, the compartment walls, the ship itself and its mission.

Out there somewhere—somewhere close, now—was Sirius and its captive planet, Terra Prime. Earth's first major colony, Prime would one day flourish as Earth never had, for it would be a

planned and tailored planet. Eight and a half light-years from
Earth, Prime's population was composed chiefly of Earth immi-
grants, living in pressure domes and slaving to alter the atmosphere of the planet to Earth normal. Periodically there must be
an infusion of Earth blood to keep the strain as close as possible
on both planets, for unless a faster-than-light drive could be developed, there could be no frequent interchange between the worlds.
What took light eight years took humans half a lifetime. The solution was the Coffins—the marvelous machine in which a man
could slip into a sleep which was more than sleep while still on
Earth, and awake years later in space, near his destination, subjectively only a month or so older. Without the Coffins there could be
only divergence, possibly mutation. Humanity wanted to populate
the stars—but with humanity.

Tod and his five shipmates were hand-picked. They had supe-
riorities—mechanical, mathematical, and artistic aptitudes. But
they were not all completely superior. One does not populate a
colony with leaders alone and expect it to live. They, like the rest
of their cargo (machine designs, microfilms of music and art, technical and medical writings, novels and entertainment) were neither advanced nor extraordinary. Except for Teague, they were the
tested median, the competent; they were basic blood for a mass,
rather than an elite.

Tod glanced around the blank walls and into the corner where
a thin line delineated the sealed door. He ached to fling it open
and skid across the corridor, punch the control which would slide
away the armor which masked the port, and soak himself in his
first glimpse of outer space. He had heard so much about it but he
had never seen it—they had all been deep in their timeless sleep
before the ship had blasted off.

But he sighed and went instead to the Coffins.

Alma's was still closed, but there was sound and motion, in
varying degrees, from all the others.

He glanced first into April's Coffin. She seemed to be asleep
now. The needle-cluster and manipulators had withdrawn. Her
skin glowed; it was alive and as unlike its former monochrome
waxiness as it could be. He smiled briefly and went to look at
Teague.

Teague, too, was in real slumber. The fierce vertical line

between his brows was shallow now, and the hard, deft hands lax and uncharacteristically purposeless. Tod had never seen him before without a focus for those narrow, blazing green eyes, without decisive spring and balance in his pose. It was good, somehow, to feel that for all his responsibilities, Teague could be as helpless as anyone.

Tod smiled as he passed Alma's closed Coffin. He always smiled at Alma when he saw her, when he heard her voice, when she crossed his thoughts. It was possible to be very brave around Alma, for gentleness and comfort were so ready that it was almost not necessary to call upon them. One could bear anything, knowing she was there.

Tod crossed the chamber and looked at the last pair. Carl was a furious blur of motion, his needle-cluster swinging free, his manipulators in the final phase. He grunted instead of screaming, a series of implosive, startled gasps. His eyes were open but only the whites showed.

Moira was quite relaxed, turned on her side, poured out on the floor of the Coffin like a long golden cat. She seemed in a contented abandonment of untroubled sleep.

He heard a new sound and went back to April. She was sitting up, cross-legged, her head bowed apparently in deep concentration. Tod understood: he knew that sense of achievement and the dedication of an entire psyche to the proposition that these weak and trembling arms which hold one up shall *not* bend.

He reached in and gently lifted the soft white hair away from her face. She raised the albino's fathomless ruby eyes to him and whimpered.

"Come on," he said quietly. "We're here." When she did not move, he balanced on his stomach on the edge of the Coffin and put one hand between her shoulder-blades. "Come on."

She pitched forward but he caught her so that she stayed kneeling. He drew her up and forward and put her hands on the bar. "Hold tight, Ape," he said. She did, while he lifted her thin body out of the Coffin and stood her on the top step. "Let go now. Lean on me."

Mechanically she obeyed, and he brought her down until she sat, as he had, on the bottom step. He punched the switch at her feet and put the capsules in her mouth while she looked up at him numbly, as if hypnotized. He got her beaker, thumped it, held it until its foaming subsided, and then put an arm around her shoulders while she drank. She closed her eyes and slumped against him, breathing deeply at first, and later, for a moment that frightened him, not at all. Then she sighed. "Tod. . . ."

"I'm here, Ape."

She straightened up, turned and looked at him. She seemed to be trying to smile, but she shivered instead. "I'm cold."

He rose, keeping one hand on her shoulder until he was sure she could sit up unassisted, and then brought her a cloak from the clips outside the Coffin. He helped her with it, knelt and put on her slippers for her. She sat quite still, hugging the garment tight to her. At last she looked around and back; up, around, and back again. "We're—there!" she breathed.

"We're *here*," he corrected.

"Yes, here. Here. How long do you suppose we . . ."

"We won't know exactly until we can take some readings. Twenty-five, twenty-seven years—maybe more."

She said. "I could be old, old—" She touched her face, brought her fingertips down to the sides of her neck. "I could be forty, even!"

He laughed at her, and then a movement caught the corner of his eye. "Carl!"

Carl was sitting sidewise on the edge of his Coffin, his feet still inside. Weak or no, bemused as could be expected, Carl should have grinned at Tod, should have made some healthy, swaggering gesture. Instead he sat still, staring about him in utter puzzlement. Tod went to him. "Carl! Carl, we're here!"

Carl looked at him dully. Tod was unaccountably disturbed. Carl always shouted, always bounced; Carl had always seemed to be just a bit larger inside than he was outside, ready to burst through, always thinking faster, laughing more quickly than anyone else.

He allowed Tod to help him down the steps, and sat heavily while Tod got his capsules and beaker for him. Waiting for the liquid to subside, he looked around numbly. Then drank, and almost toppled. April and Tod held him up. When he straightened again, it was abruptly. "Hey!" he roared. "We're here!" He looked up at them. "April! Tod-o! Well what do you know—how are you, kids?"

"Carl?" The voice was the voice of a flute, if a flute could whisper. They looked up. There was a small golden surf of hair tumbled on and over the edge of Moira's Coffin.

Weakly, eagerly, they clambered up to Moira and helped her out. Carl breathed such a sigh of relief that Tod and April stopped to smile at him, at each other.

Carl shrugged out of his weakness as if it were an uncomfortable garment and went to be close to Moira, to care about Moira and nothing else.

A deep labored voice called, "Who's up?"

"Teague! It's Teague . . . all of us, Teague," called Tod. "Carl and Moira and April and me. All except Alma."

Slowly Teague's great head rose out of the Coffin. He looked around with the controlled motion of a radar sweep. When his head stopped its one turning, the motion seemed relayed to his body, which began to move steadily upward. The four who watched him knew intimately what this cost him in sheer willpower, yet no one made any effort to help. Unasked, one did not help Teague.

One leg over, the second. He ignored the bar and stepped down to seat himself on the bottom step as if it were a throne. His hands moved very slowly but without faltering as he helped himself to the capsules, then the beaker. He permitted himself a moment of stillness, eyes closed, nostrils pinched; then life coursed strongly into him. It was as if his muscles visibly filled out a little. He seemed heavier and taller, and when he opened his eyes, they were the deeply vital, commanding light-sources which had drawn them, linked them, led them all during their training.

He looked toward the door in the corner. "Has anyone—"

"We were waiting for you," said Tod. "Shall we . . . can we go look now? I want to see the stars."

"We'll see to Alma first." Teague rose, ignoring the lip of his Coffin and the handhold it offered. He went to Alma's. With his height, he was the only one among them who could see through the top plate without mounting the steps.

Then, without turning, he said, "Wait."

The others, half across the room from him, stopped. Teague

turned to them. There was no expression on his face at all. He stood quite motionless for perhaps ten seconds, and then quietly released a breath. He mounted the steps of Alma's Coffin, reached, and the side nearest his own machine sank silently into the floor. He stepped down, and spent a long moment bent over the body inside. From where they stood, tense and frightened, the others could not see inside. They made no effort to move closer.

"Tod," said Teague, "get the kit. Surgery *Lambda*. Moira. I'll need you."

The shock of it went to Tod's bones, regenerated, struck him again; yet so conditioned was he to Teague's commands that he was on his feet and moving before Teague had stopped speaking. He went to the after bulkhead and swung open a panel, pressed a stud. There was a metallic whisper, and the heavy case slid out at his feet. He lugged it over to Teague, and helped him rack it on the side of the Coffin. Teague immediately plunged his hands through the membrane at one end of the kit, nodding to Moira to do likewise at the other. Tod stepped back, studiously avoiding a glance in at Alma, and returned to April. She put both her hands tight around his left biceps and leaned close. *"Lambda. . . ."* she whispered. "That's . . . parturition, isn't it?"

He shook his head. "Parturition is Surgery *Kappa*," he said painfully. He swallowed. *"Lambda's* Caesarian."

Her crimson eyes widened. "Caesarian? *Alma?* She'd never need a Caesarian!"

He turned to look at her, but he could not see, his eyes stung so. "Not while she lived, she wouldn't," he whispered. He felt the small white hands tighten painfully on his arm. Across the room, Carl sat quietly. Tod squashed the water out of his eyes with the heel of his hand. Carl began pounding knuckles, very slowly, against his own temple.

Teague and Moira were busy for a long time.

II

Tod pulled in his legs and lowered his head until the kneecaps pressed cruelly against his eyebrow ridges. He hugged his shins, ground his back into the wall-panels, and in this red-spangled blackness he let himself live back and back to Alma and joy, Alma and comfort, Alma and courage.

He had sat once, just this way, twisted by misery and anger, blind and helpless, in a dark corner of an equipment shed at the spaceport. The rumor had circulated that April would not come after all, because albinism and the Sirius Rock would not mix. It turned out to be untrue, but that did not matter at the time. He had punched her, punched *Alma!* because in all the world he had been given nothing else to strike out at, and she had found him and had sat down to be with him. She had not even touched her face, where the blood ran; she simply waited until at last he flung himself on her lap and wept like an infant. And no one but he and Alma ever knew of it. . . .

He remembered Alma with the spaceport children, rolling and tumbling on the lawn with them, and in the pool; and he remembered Alma, her face still, looking up at the stars with her soft and gentle eyes, and in those eyes he had seen a challenge as implacable and pervasive as space itself. The tumbling on the lawn, the towering dignity—these co-existed in Alma without friction. He remembered things she had said to him; for each of the things he could recall the kind of light, the way he stood, the very smell of the air at the time. "Never be afraid, Tod. Just think of the worst possible thing that might happen. What you're afraid of will probably not be *that* bad—and anything else just has to be better." And she said once, "Don't confuse logic and truth, however good the logic. You can stick one end of logic in solid ground and throw the other end clear out of the cosmos without breaking it. Truth's a little less flexible." And, "Of *course* you need to be loved, Tod! Don't be ashamed of that, or try to change it. It's not a thing you have to worry about, ever. You are loved. April loves you. And I love you. Maybe I love you even more than April, because she loves everything you are, but I love everything you were and ever will be."

And some of the memories were deeper and more important even than these, but were memories of small things—the meeting of eyes, the touch of a hand, the sound of laughter or a snatch of song, distantly.

Tod descended from memory into a blackness that was only loss and despair, and then a numbness, followed by a reluctant awareness. He became conscious of what, in itself, seemed the merest of trifles: that there was a significance in his pose there against the bulkhead. Unmoving, he considered it. It was comfortable, to be so turned in upon oneself, and so protected, unaware . . . and Alma would have hated to see him this way.

He threw up his head, and self-consciously straightened from his fetal posture. *That's over now,* he told himself furiously, and then, dazed, wondered what he had meant.

He turned to look at April. She was huddled miserably against him, her face and body lax, stopped, disinterested. He thumped his elbow into her ribs, hard enough to make her remember she had ribs. She looked up into his eyes and said, "How? How could . . ."

Tod understood. Of the three couples standard for each ship of the Sirian project, one traditionally would beget children on the planet; one, earlier, as soon as possible after awakening; and one still earlier, for conception would take place within the Coffin. But—not *before* awakening, and surely not long enough before to permit of gestation. It was an impossibility; the vital processes were so retarded within the Coffin that, effectively, there would be no stirring of life at all. So—"How?" April pleaded. "How could. . . ."

Tod gazed upon his own misery, then April's, and wondered what it must be that Teague was going through.

Teague, without looking up, said, "Tod."

Tod patted April's shoulder, rose and went to Teague. He did not look into the Coffin. Teague, still working steadily, tilted his head to one side to point. "I need a little more room here."

Tod lifted the transparent cube Teague had indicated and looked at the squirming pink bundle inside. He almost smiled. It was a nice baby. He took one step away and Teague said, "Take 'em all, Tod."

He stacked them and carried them to where April sat. Carl rose and came over, and knelt. The boxes hummed—a vibration which could be felt, not heard—as nutrient-bearing air circulated inside and back to the power-packs. "A nice normal deliv— I mean, a nice normal batch o' brats," Carl said. "Four girls, one boy. Just right."

Tod looked up at him. "There's one more, I think."

There was—another girl. Moira brought it over in the sixth box. "Sweet," April breathed, watching them. "They're sweet."

Moira said, wearily, "That's all."

Tod looked up at her.

"Alma . . . ?"

Moira waved laxly toward the neat stack of incubators. "That's all," she whispered tiredly, and went to Carl.

That's all there is of Alma, Tod thought bitterly. He glanced across at Teague. The tall figure raised a steady hand, wiped his face with his upper arm. His raised hand touched the high end of the Coffin, and for an instant held a grip. Teague's face lay against his arm, pillowed, hidden and still. Then he completed the wiping motion and began stripping the sterile plastic skin from his hands. Tod's heart went out to him, but he bit the insides of his cheeks and kept silent. *A strange tradition*, thought Tod, *that makes it impolite to grieve. . . .*

Teague dropped the shreds of plastic into the disposal slot and turned to face them. He looked at each in turn, and each in turn found some measure of control. He turned then, and pulled a lever, and the side of Alma's Coffin slid silently up.

Good-bye. . . .

Tod put his back against the bulkhead and slid down beside April. He put an arm over her shoulders. Carl and Moira sat close, holding hands. Moira's eyes were shadowed but very much awake. Carl bore an expression almost of sullenness. Tod glanced, then glared at the boxes. Three of the babies were crying, though of course they could not be heard through the plastic incubators. Tod was suddenly conscious of Teague's eyes upon him. He flushed, and then let his anger drain to the capacious inner reservoir which must hold it and all his grief as well.

When he had their attention, Teague sat cross-legged before them and placed a small object on the floor.

Tod looked at the object. At first glance it seemed to be a metal spring about as long as his thumb, mounted vertically on a black base. Then he realized that it was an art object of some kind, made of a golden substance which shimmered and all but flowed. It was an interlocked double spiral; the turns went round and up, round and down, round and up again, the texture of the gold clearly indicating, in a strange and alive way, which symbolized a rising and falling flux. Shaped as if it had been wound on a cylinder and the cylinder removed, the thing was formed of a continuous wire or rod which had no beginning and no end, but which turned and rose and turned and descended again in an exquisite continuity. . . . Its base was formless, an almost-smoke just as the gold showed an almost-flux; and it was as lightless as ylem.

Teague said, "This was in Alma's Coffin. It was not there when we left Earth."

"It must have been," said Carl flatly.

Teague silently shook his head. April opened her lips, closed them again. Teague said, "Yes, April?"

April shook her head. "Nothing, Teague. Really nothing." But because Teague kept looking at her, waiting, she said, "I was going to say . . . it's beautiful." She hung her head.

Teague's lips twitched. Tod could sense the sympathy there. He stroked April's silver hair. She responded, moving her shoulder slightly under his hand. "What is it, Teague?"

When Teague would not answer, Moira asked, "Did it . . . had it anything to do with Alma?"

Teague picked it up thoughtfully. Tod could see the yellow loom it cast against his throat and cheek, the golden points it built in his eyes. "Something did." He paused. "You know she was supposed to conceive on awakening. But to give birth—"

Carl cracked a closed hand against his forehead. "She must have been awake for anyway two hundred and eighty days!"

"Maybe she made it," said Moira.

Tod watched Teague's hand half-close on the object as if it might be precious now. Moira's was a welcome thought, and the welcome could be read on Teague's face. Watching it, Tod saw the complicated spoor of a series of efforts—a gathering of emotions, a determination; the closing of certain doors, the opening of others.

Teague rose. "We have a ship to inspect, sights to take, calculations . . . we've got to tune in Terra Prime, send them a message if we can. Tod, check the corridor air."

"The stars—we'll see the stars!" Tod whispered to April, the heady thought all but eclipsing everything else. He bounded to the corner where the door controls waited. He punched the test button, and a spot of green appeared over the door, indicating that with their awakening, the evacuated chambers, the living and control compartments, had been flooded with air and warmed. "Air okay."

"Go on then."

They crowded around Tod as he grasped the lever and pushed. *I won't wait for orders*, Tod thought. *I'll slide right across the corridor and open the guard plate and there it'll be—space, and the stars!*

The door opened.

There was no corridor, no bulkhead, no armored port-hole, no—

No *ship!*

There was a night out there, dank, warm. It was wet. In it were hooked, fleshy leaves and a tangle of roots; a thing with legs which hopped up on the sill and shimmered its wings for them; a thing like a flying hammer which crashed in and smote the shimmering one and was gone with it, leaving a stain on the deckplates. There was a sky aglow with a ghastly green. There was a thrashing and a scream out there, a pressure of growth, and a wrongness.

Blood ran down Tod's chin. His teeth met through his lower lip. He turned and looked past three sets of terrified eyes to Teague, who said, "Shut it!"

Tod snatched at the control. It broke off in his hand. . . .

How long does a thought, a long thought, take?

Tod stood with the fractured metal in his hand and thought:

We were told that above all things we must adapt. We were told that perhaps there would be a thin atmosphere by now, on Terra Prime, but that in all likelihood we must live a new kind of life in pressure-domes. We were warned that what we might find would be flash-mutation, where the people could be more or less than human. We were warned, even, that there might be no life on Prime at all. But look at me now—look at all of us. We weren't meant to adapt to this! And we can't . . .

Somebody shouted while somebody shrieked, each sound a word, each destroying the other. Something thick as a thumb, long as a hand, with a voice like a distant airhorn, hurtled through the door and circled the room. Teague snatched a folded cloak from the clothingrack and, poising just a moment, batted it out of the air. It skittered, squirming, across the metal door. He threw the cloak on it to capture it. "Get that door closed."

Carl snatched the broken control lever out of Tod's hand and tried to fit it back into the switch mounting. It crumbled as if it were dried bread. Tod stepped outside, hooked his hands on the edge of the door, and pulled. It would not budge. A lizard as long as his arm scuttled out of the twisted grass and stopped to stare at him. He shouted at it, and with forelegs much too long for such a creature, it pressed itself upward until its body was forty-five degrees from the horizontal, it flicked the end of its long tail upward, and something flew over its head toward Tod, buzzing angrily. Tod turned to see what it was, and as he did the lizard struck from one side and April from the other.

April succeeded and the lizard failed, for its fangs clashed and it fell forward, but April's shoulder had taken Tod on the chest and, off balance as he was, he went flat on his back. The cold, dry, pulsing tail swatted his hand. He gripped it convulsively, held on tight. Part of the tail broke off and buzzed, flipping about on the ground like a click-beetle. But the rest held. Tod scuttled backward to pull the lizard straight as it began to turn on him, got his knees under him, then his feet. He swung the lizard twice around his head and smashed it against the inside of the open door. The part of the tail he was holding then broke off, and the scaly thing thumped inside and slid, causing Moira to leap so wildly to get out of its way that she nearly knocked the stocky Carl off his feet.

Teague swept away the lid of the Surgery *Lambda* kit, inverted it, kicked the clutter of instruments and medicaments aside and clapped the inverted box over the twitching, scaly body.

"April!" Tod shouted. He ran around in a blind semicircle, saw her struggling to her feet in the grass, snatched her up and bounded inside with her. "Carl!" he gasped. "Get the door. . . ."

But Carl was already moving forward with a needle torch. With two deft motions he sliced out a section of the power-arm which was holding the door open. He swung the door to, yelling, "Parametal!"

Tod, gasping, ran to the lockers and brought a length of the synthetic. Carl took the wide ribbon and with a snap of the wrists broke it in two. Each half he bent (for it was very flexible when moved slowly) into a U. He placed one against the door and held out his hand without looking. Tod dropped the hammer into it. Carl tapped the parametal gently and it adhered to the door. He turned his face away and struck it sharply. There was a blue-white flash and the U was rigid and firmly welded to the door. He did the same thing with the other U, welding it to the nearby wall plates. Into the two gudgeons thus formed, Moira dropped a lux-alloy bar, and the door was secured.

"Shall I sterilize the floor?" Moira asked.

"No," said Teague shortly.

"But—bacteria . . . spores . . ."

"Forget it," said Teague.

April was crying. Tod held her close, but made no effort to stop her. Something in him, deeper than panic, more essential than wonderment, understood that she could use this circumstance to spend her tears for Alma, and that these tears must be shed now or swell and burst her heart. *So cry,* he pled silently, *cry for both of us, all of us.*

With the end of action, belated shock spread visibly over Carl's face. "The ship's gone," he said stupidly. "We're on a planet." He looked at his hands, turned abruptly to the door, stared at it and began to shiver. Moira went to him and stood quietly, not touching him—just being near, in case she should be needed. April grew gradually silent. Carl said, "I—" and then shook his head.

Glick. Shh. Clack, click. Methodically Teague was stacking the scattered contents of the medical kit. Tod patted April's shoulder and went to help. Moira glanced at them, peered closely into Carl's face, then left him and came to lend a hand. April joined them, and at last Carl. They swept up, and racked and stored the clutter, and when Teague lowered a table, they helped get the dead lizard on it and pegged out for dissection. Moira cautiously disentangled the huge insect from the folds of the cloak and clapped a box over it, slid the lid underneath to bring the feebly squirming thing to Teague. He studied it for a long moment, then set it down and peered at the lizard. With forceps he opened the jaws and bent close. He grunted. "April. . . ."

She came to look. Teague touched the fangs with the tip of a scalpel. "Look there."

"Grooves," she said. "Like a snake."

Teague reversed the scalpel and with the handle he gingerly pressed upward, at the root of one of the fangs. A cloudy yellow liquid beaded, ran down the groove. He dropped the scalpel and slipped a watch-glass under the tooth to catch the droplet. "Analyze that later," he murmured. "But I'd say you saved Tod from something pretty nasty."

"I didn't even think," said April. "I didn't . . . I never knew there was any animal life on Prime. I wonder what they call this monster."

"The honors are yours, April. You name it."

"They'll have a classification for it already!"

"Who?"

Everyone started to talk, and abruptly stopped. In the awkward silence Carl's sudden laugh boomed. It was a wondrous sound in the frightened chamber. There was comprehension in it, and challenge, and above all, Carl himself—boisterous and impulsive, quick, sure. The laugh was triggered by the gush of talk and its sudden cessation, a small thing in itself. But its substance was understanding, and with that an emotional surge, and with that, the choice of the one emotional expression Carl would always choose.

"Tell them, Carl," Teague said.

Carl's teeth flashed. He waved a thick arm at the door. "That isn't Sirius Prime. Nor Earth. Go ahead, April—name your pet."

April, staring at the lizard, said, "*Crotalidus*, then, because it has a rattle and fangs like a diamondback." Then she paled and turned to Carl, as the full weight of his statement came on her. "Not—*not Prime?*"

Quietly, Teague said, "Nothing like these ever grew on Earth. And Prime is a cold planet. It could never have a climate like that," he nodded toward the door, "no matter how much time has passed."

"But what . . . where . . ." It was Moira.

"We'll find out when we can. But the instruments aren't here—they were in the ship."

"But if it's a new . . . another planet, why didn't you let me sterilize? What about airborne spores? Suppose it had been methane out there or—"

"We've obviously been conditioned to anything in the atmosphere. As to its composition—well, it isn't poisonous, or we wouldn't be standing here talking about it. Wait!" He held up a hand and quelled the babble of questions before it could fully start. "Wondering is a luxury like worrying. We can't afford either. We'll get our answers when we get more evidence."

"What shall we do?" asked April faintly.

"Eat," said Teague. "Sleep." They waited. Teague said, "Then we go outside."

III

There were stars like daisies in a field, like dust in a sunbeam, and like flying, flaming mountains; near ones, far ones, stars of every color and every degree of brilliance. And there were bands of light which must be stars too distant to see. And something was stealing the stars, not taking them away, but swallowing them up, coming closer and closer, eating as it came. And at last there was only one left. Its name was Alma, and it was gone, and there was nothing left but an absorbent blackness and an aching loss.

In this blackness Tod's eyes snapped open, and he gasped, frightened and lost.

"You awake, Tod?" April's small hand touched his face. He took it and drew it to his lips, drinking comfort from it.

From the blackness came Carl's resonant whisper, "We're awake. Teague? . . ."

The lights flashed on, dim first, brightening swiftly, but not so fast as to dazzle unsuspecting eyes. Tod sat up and saw Teague at the table. On it was the lizard, dissected and laid out as neatly as an exploded view in a machine manual. Over the table, on a gooseneck, was a floodlamp with its lens masked by an infrared filter. Teague turned away from the table, pushing up his "black-light" goggles, and nodded to Tod. There were shadows under his eyes, but otherwise he seemed the same as ever. Tod wondered how many lonely hours he had worked while the two couples slept, doing that meticulous work under the irritating glow so that they would be undisturbed.

Tod went to him. "Has my playmate been talking much?" He pointed at the remains of the lizard.

"Yes and no," said Teague. "Oxygen-breather, all right, and a true lizard. He had a secret weapon—that tail-segment he flips over his head toward his victims. It has primitive ganglia like an Earth salamander's, so that the tail-segment trembles and squirms, sounding the rattles, after he throws it. He also has a skeleton that—but all this doesn't matter. Most important is that he's the analog of our early Permian life, which means (unless he's an evolutionary dead-end like a cockroach) that this planet is a billion years old at the least. And the little fellow here—" he touched the flying thing—"bears this out. It's not an insect, you know. It's an arachnid."

"With *wings?*"

Teague lifted the slender, scorpion-like pincers of the creature and let them fall. "Flat chitinous wings are no more remarkable a leg adaptation than those things. Anyway, in spite of the ingenuity of his engineering, internally he's pretty primitive. All of which lets us hypothesize that we'll find fairly close analogs of what we're used to on Earth."

"Teague," Tod interrupted, his voice lowered, his eyes narrowed to contain the worry that threatened to spill over, "Teague, what's happened?"

"The temperature and humidity here seem to be exactly the same as that outside," Teague went on, in precisely the same tone as before. "This would indicate either a warm planet, or a warm season on a temperate planet. In either case it is obvious that—"

"But, *Teague*—"

"—that a good deal of theorizing is possible with very little evidence, and we need not occupy ourselves with anything else but that evidence."

"Oh," said Tod. He backed off a step. "Oh," he said again, "sorry, Teague." He joined the others at the food dispensers, feeling like a cuffed puppy. *But he's right*, he thought. *As Alma said . . . of the many things which might have happened, only one actually has. Let's wait then, and worry about that one thing when we can name it.*

There was a pressure on his arm. He looked up from his thoughts and into April's searching eyes. He knew that she had heard, and he was unreasonably angry at her. "Damn it, he's so cold-blooded," he blurted defensively, but in a whisper.

April said, "He has to stay with things he can understand, every minute." She glanced swiftly at the closed Coffin. "Wouldn't you?"

There was a sharp pain and a bitterness in Tod's throat as he thought about it. He dropped his eyes and mumbled, "No, I wouldn't. I don't think I could." There was a difference in his eyes as he glanced back at Teague. *But it's so easy, after all, for strong people to be strong,* he thought.

"Teague, what'll we wear?" Carl called.

"Skinflex."

"Oh, no!" cried Moira. "It's so clingy and hot!"

Carl laughed at her. He swept up the lizard's head and opened its jaws. "Smile at the lady. She wouldn't put any tough old skinflex in the way of your pretty teeth!"

"Put it down," said Teague sharply, though there was a flicker of amusement in his eyes. "It's still loaded with God-knows-what alkaloid. Moira, he's right. Skinflex just doesn't puncture."

Moira looked respectfully at the yellow fangs and went obediently to storage, where she pulled out the suits.

"We'll keep close together, back to back," said Teague as they helped each other into the suits. "All the weapons are . . . were . . . in the forward storage compartment, so we'll improvise. Tod, you and the girls each take a globe of anesthene. It's the fastest anesthetic we have and it ought to take care of anything that breathes oxygen. I'll take scalpels. Carl—"

"The hammer," Carl grinned. His voice was fairly thrumming with excitement.

"We won't attempt to fasten the door from outside. I don't mean to go father than ten meters out, this first time. Just—you, Carl—lift off the bar as we go out; get the door shut as quickly as possible, and prop it there. Whatever happens, do not attack anything out there unless you are attacked first, or unless I say so."

Hollow-eyed, steady, Teague moved to the door with the others close around him. Carl shifted the hammer to his left hand, lifted the bar and stood back a little, holding it like a javelin. Teague, holding a glittering lancet lightly in each hand, pushed the door open with his foot. They boiled through, stepped aside for Carl as he butted the rod deep into the soil and against the closed door. "All set."

They moved as a unit for perhaps three meters, and stopped.

It was daytime now, but such a day as none of them had dreamed of. The light was green, very nearly a lime-green, and the shadows were purple. The sky was more lavender than blue. The air was warm and wet.

They stood at the top of a low hill. Before them a tangle of jungle tumbled up at them. So vital, so completely alive, it seemed to move by its own power of growth. Stirring, murmuring, it was too big, too much, too wide and deep and intertwined to assimilate at a glance; the thought, *this is a jungle,* was a pitiable understatement.

To the left, savannah-like grassland rolled gently down to the choked margins of a river—calmfaced, muddy, and secretive. It too seemed astir with inner growings. To the right, more jungle. Behind them, the bland and comforting wall of their compartment.

Above—

It may have been April who saw it first; in any case, Tod always associated the vision with April's scream.

They moved as she screamed, five humans jerked back then like five dolls on a single string, pressed together and to the compartment wall by an overwhelming claustrophobia. They were ants under a descending heel, flies on an anvil . . . together their backs struck the wall, and they cowered there, looking up.

And it was not descending. It was only—big. It was just that it was there, over them.

April said, later, that it was like a cloud. Carl would argue that it was cylindrical, with flared ends and a narrow waist. Teague never attempted to describe it, because he disliked inaccuracies, and Moira was too awed to try. To Tod, the object had no shape. It was a luminous opacity between him and the sky, solid, massive as mountains. There was only one thing they agreed on, and that was that it was a ship.

And out of the ship came the golden ones.

They appeared under the ship as speckles of light, and grew in size as they descended, so that the five humans must withstand a second shock: they had known the ship was huge, but had not known until now how very high above them it hung.

Down they came, dozens, hundreds. They filled the sky over the jungle and around the five, moving to make a spherical quadrant from the horizontal to the zenith, a full hundred and eighty degrees from side to side—a radiant floating shell with its concave surface toward, around, above them. They blocked out the sky and the jungle-tops, cut off most of the strange green light, replacing it with their own—for each glowed coolly.

Each individual was distinct and separate. Later, they would argue about the form and shape of the vessel, but the exact shape of these golden things was never even mentioned. Nor did they ever agree on a name for them. To Carl they were an army, to April, angels. Moira called them (secretly) "the seraphim," and to Tod they were masters. Teague never named them.

For measureless time they hung there, with the humans gaping up at them. There was no flutter of wings, no hum of machinery to indicate how they stayed aloft, and if each individual had a device to keep him afloat, it was of a kind the humans could not recognize. They were beautiful, awesome, uncountable.

And nobody was afraid.

Tod looked from side to side, from top to bottom of this incredible formation, and became aware that it did not touch the ground. Its lower edge was exactly horizontal, at his eye level. Since the hill fell away on all sides, he could see under this lower edge, here the jungle, there down across the savannah to the river. In a new amazement he saw eyes, and protruding heads.

In the tall grass at the jungle margin was a scurry and cease, scurry and cease, as newtlike animals scrambled not quite into the open and froze, watching. Up in the lower branches of the fleshy, hook-leaved trees, the heavy scaly heads of leaf-eaters showed, and here and there was the armed head of a lizard with catlike tearing tusks.

Leather-winged fliers flapped clumsily to rest in the branches, hung for a moment for all the world like broken umbrellas, then achieved balance and folded their pinions. Something slid through the air, almost caught a branch, missed it and tumbled end-over-end to the ground, resolving itself into a broad-headed scaly thing with wide membranes between fore and hind legs. And Tod saw his acquaintance of the night before, with its serrated tail and needle fangs.

And though there must have been eater and eaten here, hunter and hunted, they all watched silently, turned like living compass-needles to the airborne mystery surrounding the humans. They crowded together like a nightmare parody of the Lion and the Lamb, making a constellation, a galaxy of bright and wondering eyes; their distance from each other being, in its way, cosmic.

Tod turned his face into the strange light, and saw one of the golden beings separate from the mass and drift down and forward and stop. Had this living shell been a segment of curving mirror, this one creature would have been at its focal point. For a moment there was complete stillness, a silent waiting. Then the creature made a deep . . . *gesture.* Behind it, all the others did the same.

If ten thousand people stand ten thousand meters away, and if, all at once, they kneel, it is hardly possible to see just what it is they have done; yet the aspect of their mass undergoes a definite change. So it was with the radiant shell—it changed, all of it, without moving. There was no mistaking the nature of the change, though its meaning was beyond knowing. It was an obeisance. It was an expression of profound respect, first to the humans themselves, next, and hugely, to something the humans represented. It was unquestionably an act of worship.

And what, thought Tod, *could we symbolize to these shining ones?* He was a scarab beetle or an Egyptian cat, a Hindu cow or a Teuton tree, told suddenly that it was sacred.

All the while there flooded down the thing which Carl had tried so ineptly to express: *"We're sorry. But it will be all right. You will be glad. You can be glad now."*

At last there was a change in the mighty formation. The center rose and the wings came in, the left one rising and curling to tighten the curve, the right one bending inward without rising. In a moment the formation was a column, a hollow cylinder. It began to rotate slowly, divided into a series of close-set horizontal rings. Alternate rings slowed and stopped and began a counter-rotation, and with a sudden shift, became two interlocked spirals.

Still the over-all formation was a hollow cylinder, but now it was composed of an upward and a downward helix.

The individuals spun and swirled down and down, up and up, and kept this motion within the cylinder, and the cylinder quite discrete, as it began to rise. Up and up it lifted, brilliantly, silently, the living original of that which they had found by Alma's body . . . up and up, filling the eye and the mind with its complex and controlled ascent, its perfect continuity; for here was a thing with no beginning and no end, all flux and balance where each rising was matched by a fall and each turn by its counterpart.

High, and higher, and at last it was a glowing spot against the hovering shadow of the ship, which swallowed it up. The ship left then, not moving, but fading away like the streamers of an aurora, but faster. In three heartbeats it was there, perhaps it was there, it was gone.

Tod closed his eyes, seeing that dynamic double helix. The tip of his mind was upon it; he trembled on the edge of revelation. He *knew* what that form symbolized. He knew it contained the simple answer to his life and their lives, to this planet and its life and the lives which were brought to it. If a cross is more than an instrument of torture, more than the memento of an event; if the *crux ansata,* the Yin-and-Yang, David's star and all such crystallizations were but symbols of great systems of philosophy, then this dynamic intertwined spiral, this free-flowing, rigidly choreographed symbol was . . . was—

Something grunted, something screamed, and the wondrous answer turned and rose spiraling away from him to be gone in three heartbeats. Yet in that moment he knew it was there for him when he had the time, the phasing, the bringing-together of whatever elements were needed. He could not use it yet but he had it. He had it.

Another scream, an immense thrashing all about. The spell was broken and the armistice over. There were chargings and fleeings, cries of death-agony and roaring challenges in and over the jungle, through the grasses to the suddenly boiling river. Life goes on, and death with it, but there must be more death than life when too much life is thrown together.

IV

It may be that their five human lives were saved, in that turbulent reawakening, only by their alienness, for the life around them was cheek-and-jowl with its familiar enemy, its familiar quarry, its familiar food, and there need be no experimenting with the five soft containers of new rich juices standing awestruck with their backs to their intrusive shelter.

Then slowly they met one another's eyes. They cared enough for each other so that there was a gladness of sharing. They cared enough for themselves so that there was also a sheepishness, a troubled self-analysis: *What did I do while I was out of my mind?*

They drew together before the door and watched the chase and slaughter around them as it subsided toward its usual balance of hunting and killing, eating and dying. Their hands began to remember the weapons they held, their minds began to reach for reality.

"They were angels," April said, so softly that no one but Tod heard her. Tod watched her lips tremble and part, and knew that she was about to speak the thing he had almost grasped, but then Teague spoke again, and Tod could see the comprehension fade from her and be gone. "Look! Look there!" said Teague, and moved down the wall to the corner.

What had been an inner compartment of their ship was now an isolated cube, and from its back corner, out of sight until now, stretched another long wall. At regular intervals were doors, each fastened by a simple outside latch of parametal.

Teague stepped to the first door, the others crowding close. Teague listened intently, then stepped back and threw the door open.

Inside was a windowless room, blazing with light. Around the sides, machines were set. Tod instantly recognized their air-cracker, the water-purifiers, the protein-converter and one of the auxiliary power-plants. In the center was a generator coupled to a light-metal fusion motor. The output buses were neatly insulated, coupled through fuseboxes and resistance controls to a "Christmas tree" multiple outlet. Cables ran through the wall to the Coffin compartment and to the line of unexplored rooms to their left.

"They've left us power, at any rate," said Teague. "Let's look down the line."

Fish, Tod snarled silently. *Dead man! After what you've just seen you should be on your knees with the weight of it, you should put out your eyes to remember better. But all you can do is take inventory of your nuts and bolts.*

Tod looked at the others, at their strained faces and their continual upward glances, as if the bright memory had magnetism for them. He could see the dream fading under Teague's untimely urgency. *You couldn't let us live with it quietly, even for a moment.* Then another inward voice explained to him, *But you see, they killed Alma.*

Resentfully he followed Teague.

Their ship had been dismantled, strung out along the hilltop like a row of shacks. They were interconnected, wired up, restacked, ready and reeking with efficiency—the lab, the library, six chambers full of mixed cargo, then—then the noise Teague made was as near to a shout of glee as Tod had ever heard from the man. The door he had just opened showed their instruments inside, all the reference tapes and tools and manuals. There was even a dome in the roof, and the refractor was mounted and waiting.

"April?" Tod looked, looked again. She was gone. "April!"

She emerged from the library, three doors back. "Teague!"

Teague pulled himself away from the array of instruments and went to her. "Teague," she said, "every one of the reels has been read."

"How do you know?"

"None of them are rewound."

Teague looked up and down the row of doors. "That doesn't sound like the way they—" The unfinished sentence was enough. Whoever had built this from their ship's substance worked according to function and with a fine efficiency.

Teague entered the library and picked a tape-reel from its rack. He inserted the free end of film into a slot and pressed a button. The reel spun and the film disappeared inside the cabinet.

Teague looked up and back. Every single reel was inside out on the clips. "They could have rewound them," said Teague, irritated.

"Maybe they wanted us to know that they'd read them," said Moira.

"Maybe they did," Teague murmured. He picked up a reel, looked at it, picked up another and another. "Music. A play. And here's our personal stuff—behavior film, training records, everything."

Carl said, "Whoever read through all this knows a lot about us."

Teague frowned. "Just us?"

"Who else?"

"Earth," said Teague. "All of it."

"You mean we were captured and analyzed so that whoever they are could get a line on Earth? You think they're going to attack Earth?"

"'You mean . . . You think . . .'" Teague mimicked coldly. "I mean nothing and I think nothing! Tod, would you be good enough to explain to this impulsive young man what you learned from me earlier? That we need concern ourselves only with evidence?"

Tod shuffled his feet, wishing not to be made an example for anyone, especially Carl, to follow. Carl flushed and tried to smile. Moira took his hand secretly and squeezed it. Tod heard a slight exhalation beside him and looked quickly at April. She was angry. There were times when he wished she would not be angry.

She pointed. "Would you call *that* evidence, Teague?"

They followed her gesture. One of the tape-readers stood open. On its reelshelf stood the counterpart of the strange object they had seen twice before—once, in miniature, found in Alma's Coffin; once again, huge in the sky. This was another of the miniatures.

Teague stared at it, then put out his hand. As his fingers touched it, the pilot-jewel on the tape-reader flashed on, and a soft, clear voice filled the room.

Tod's eyes stung. He had thought he would never hear that voice again. As he listened, he held to the lifeline of April's presence, and felt his lifeline tremble.

Alma's voice said:

"They made some adjustments yesterday with the needle-clusters

*in my Coffin, so I think they will put me back into it . . . Teague, oh,
Teague, I'm going to die!*

"*They brought me the recorder just now. I don't know whether
it's for their records or for you. If it's for you, then I must tell
you . . . how can I tell you?*

"*I've watched them all this time . . . how long? Months . . . I
don't know. I conceived when I awoke, and the babies are coming
very soon now; it's been long enough for that; and yet—how can I
tell you?*

"*They boarded us, I don't know how, I don't know why, nor
where . . . outside, space is strange, wrong. It's all misty, without
stars, crawling with blurs and patches of light.*

"*They understand me; I'm sure of that—what I say, what I
think. I can't understand them at all. They radiate feelings—sorrow,
curiosity, confidence, respect. When I began to realize I would die,
they gave me a kind of regret. When I broke and cried and said I
wanted to be with you, Teague, they reassured me, they said I would.
I'm sure that's what they said. But how could that be?*

"*They are completely dedicated in what they are doing. Their
work is a religion to them, and we are part of it. They . . . value us,
Teague. They didn't just find us. They chose us. It's as if we were the
best part of something even they consider great.*

"*The best . . . ! Among them I feel like an amoeba. They're
beautiful, Teague. Important. Very sure of what they are doing. It's
that certainty that makes me believe what I have to believe; I am
going to die, and you will live, and you and I will be together. How
can that be? How can that be?*

"*Yet it is true, so believe it with me, Teague. But—find out how!*

"*Teague, every day they have put a machine on me, radiating. It
has to do with the babies. It isn't done to harm them. I'm sure of
that. I'm their mother and I'm sure of it. They won't die.*

"*I will. I can feel their sorrow.*

"*And I will be with you, and they are joyous about that. . . .*

"*Teague—find out how!*"

Tod closed his eyes so that he would not look at Teague, and
wished with all his heart that Teague had been alone to hear that
ghostly voice. As to what it had said, the words stood as a frame
for a picture he could not see, showing him only where it was, not
what it meant. Alma's voice had been tremulous and unsure, but

he knew it well enough to know that joy and certitude had lived with her as she spoke. There was wonderment, but no fear.

Knowing that it might be her only message to them, should she not have told them more—facts, figures, measurements?

Then an old, old tale flashed into his mind, an early thing from the ancient Amerenglish, by Hynlen (Henlyne, was it? no matter) about a man who tried to convey to humanity a description of the superbeings who had captured him, with only his body as a tablet and his nails as a stylus. Perhaps he was mad by the time he finished, but his message was clear at least to him: *"Creation took eight days."* How would he, Tod, describe an association with the ones he had seen in the sky outside, if he had been with them for nearly three hundred days?

April tugged gently at his arm. He turned toward her, still avoiding the sight of Teague. April inclined her shining white head to the door. Moira and Carl already stood outside. They joined them, and waited wordlessly until Teague came out.

When he did, he was grateful, and he need not say so. He came out, a great calm in his face and voice, passed them and let them follow him to his methodical examination of the other compartments, to finish his inventory.

Food stores, cable and conduit, metal and parametal rod and sheet stock, tools and tool-making matrices and dies. A hangar, in which lay their lifeboat, fully equipped.

But there was no long-range communication device, and no parts for one.

And there was no heavy space-drive mechanism, nor tools to make one, nor fuel if they should make the tools.

Back in the instrument room, Carl grunted. "Somebody means for us to stick around."

"The boat—"

Teague said, "I don't think they'd have left us the boat if Earth was in range."

"We'll build a beacon," Tod said suddenly. "We'll get a rescue ship out to us."

"Out where?" asked Teague drily.

They followed his gaze. Bland and silent, merciless, the decay chronometer stared back at them. Built around a standard radioactive, it had two dials—one which measured the amount of energy radiated by the material, and one which measured the lost mass. When they checked, the reading was correct. They checked, and the reading was 64.

"Sixty-four years," said Teague. "Assuming we averaged as much as one-half light speed, which isn't likely, we must be thirty light-years away from Earth. Thirty years to get a light-beam there, sixty or more to get a ship back, plus time to make the beacon and time for Earth to understand the signal and prepare a ship. . . ." He shook his head.

"Plus the fact," Tod said in a strained voice, "that there is no habitable planet in a thirty-year radius from Sol. Except Prime."

Shocked, they gaped silently at this well-known fact. A thousand years of scrupulous search with the best instruments could not have missed a planet like this at such a distance.

"Then the chronometer's wrong!"

"I'm afraid not," said Teague. "It's sixty-four years since we left Earth, and that's that."

"And this planet doesn't exist," said Carl with a sour smile, "and I suppose that is also that."

"Yes, Teague," said Tod. "One of these two facts can't exist with the other."

"They can because they do," said Teague. "There's a missing factor. Can a man breathe under water, Tod?"

"If he has a diving-helmet."

Teague spread his hands. "It took sixty-four years to get to this planet *if*. We have to find the figurative diving-helmet." He paused. "The evidence in favor of the planet's existence is fairly impressive," he said wryly. "Let's check the other fact."

"How?"

"The observatory."

They ran to it. They sky glowed its shimmering green, but through it the stars had begun to twinkle. Carl got to the telescope first, put a big hand on the swing-controls, and said, "Where first?" He tugged at the instrument. "Hey!" He tugged again.

"Don't!" said Teague sharply. Carl let go and backed away. Teague switched on the lights and examined the instrument. "It's already connected to the compensators," he said. "Hmp! Our hosts are most helpful." He looked at the setting of the small motors which moved the instrument to cancel diurnal rotation effects. "Twenty-eight hours, thirteen minutes plus. Well, if that's correct for this planet, it's proof that this isn't Earth or Prime—if we needed proof." He touched the controls lightly. "Carl, what's the matter here?"

Carl bent to look. There were dabs of dull silver on the threads of the adjusting screws. He touched them. "Parametal," he said. "Unflashed, but it has adhered enough to jam the threads. Take a couple days to get it off without jarring it. Look here— they've done the same thing with the objective screws!"

"We look at what they want us to see, and like it," said Tod.

"Maybe it's something we want to see," said April gently.

Only half-teasing, Tod said, "Whose side are you on, anyway?"

Teague put his eye to the instrument. His hands, by habit, strayed to the focusing adjustment, but found it locked the same way as the others. "Is there a Galactic Atlas?"

"Not in the rack," said Moira a moment later.

"Here," said April from the chart table. Awed, she added, "Open."

Tensely they waited while Teague took his observation and referred to the atlas and to the catalog they found lying under it. When at last he lifted his face from the calculations, it bore the strangest expression Tod had ever seen there.

"Our diving-helmet," he said at last, very slowly, too evenly, "—that is, the factor which rationalizes our two mutually exclusive facts—is simply that our captors have a faster-than-light drive."

"But according to theory—"

"According to our telescope," Teague interrupted, "through which I have just seen Sol, and these references so thoughtfully laid out for us . . ." Shockingly, his voice broke. He took two deep breaths, and said, "Sol is two-hundred and seventeen light-years away. That sun which set a few minutes ago is Beta Librae." He studied their shocked faces, one by one. "I don't know what we shall eventually call this place," he said with difficulty, "but we had better get used to calling it home."

They called the planet Viridis ("the greenest name I can think of," Moira said) because none among them had ever seen such a green.

It was more than the green of growing, for the sunlight was green-tinged and at night the whole sky glowed green, a green as bright as the brightest silver of Earth's moon, as water molecules, cracked by the star's intense ultraviolet, celebrated their nocturnal reunion.

They called the moons Wynken, Blynken, and Nod, and the sun they called—the sun.

They worked like slaves, and then like scientists, which is a change of occupation but not a change of pace. They built a palisade of a cypress-like, straight-grained wood, each piece needle-pointed, double-laced with parametal wire. It had a barred gate and peepholes with periscopes and permanent swivel-mounts for the needle-guns they were able to fabricate from tube-stock and spare solenoids. They roofed the enclosure with parametal mesh which, at one point, could be rolled back to launch the lifeboat.

They buried Alma.

They tested and analyzed, classified, processed, researched everything in the compound and within easy reach of it—soil, vegetation, fauna. They developed an insect-repellent solution to coat the palisade and an insecticide with an automatic spray to keep the compound clear of the creatures, for they were numerous, large, and occasionally downright dangerous, like the "flying caterpillar" which kept its pseudopods in its winged form and enthusiastically broke them off in the flesh of whatever attacked them, leaving an angry rash and suppurating sores. They discovered three kinds of edible seed and another which yielded a fine hydrocarbonic oil much like soy, and a flower whose calyces, when dried and then soaked and broiled, tasted precisely like crab-meat.

For a time they were two separate teams, virtually isolated from each other. Moira and Teague collected minerals and put them through the mass spectroscope and the radioanalyzers, and it fell to April to classify the life-forms, with Carl and Tod competing mightily to bring in new ones. Or at least photographs of new ones. Two-ton *Parametrodon*, familiarly known as Dopey—a massive herbivore with just enough intelligence to move its jaws—was hardly the kind of thing to be carried home under one's arm, and *Felodon*, the scaly carnivore with the catlike tusks, though barely as long as a man, was about as friendly as a half-starved wolverine.

Tetrapodys (Tod called it "Umbrellabird") turned out to be a rewarding catch. They stumbled across a vine which bore foul-smelling pods; these the clumsy amphibious bats found irresistible. Carl synthesized the evil stuff and improved upon it, and they smeared it on tree-boles by the river. *Tetrapodys* came there by the hundreds and laid eggs apparently in sheer frustration. These eggs were camouflaged by a frilly green membrane, for all the world like the ground-buds of the giant water-fern. The green shoots tasted like shallots and were fine for salad when raw and excellent as onion soup when stewed. The half-hatched *Tetrapodys* yielded ligaments which when dried made excellent self-baited fish hooks. The wing-muscles of the adult tasted like veal cutlet with fish-sauce, and the inner, or main shell of the eggs afforded them an amazing shoe-sole—light, tough, and flexible, which, for some unknown reason, *Felodon* would not track.

Pteronauchis, or "flapping frog," was the gliding newt they had seen on that first day. Largely nocturnal, it was phototropic; a man with a strong light could fill a bushel with the things in minutes. Each specimen yielded twice as many, twice as large, and twice as good frog-legs as a Terran frog.

There were no mammals.

There were flowers in profusion—white (a sticky green in that light), purple, brown, blue, and, of course, the ubiquitous green. No red—as a matter of fact, there was virtually no red anywhere on the planet. April's eyes became a feast for them all. It is impossible to describe the yearning one can feel for an absent color. And so it was that a legend began with them. Twice Tod had seen a bright red growth. The first time he thought it was a mushroom, the second it seemed more of a lichen. The first time it was surrounded by a sea of crusher ants on the move—a fearsome carpet which even *Parametrodon* respected. The second time he had seen it from twenty meters away and had just turned toward it when not one, but three *Felodons* came hurtling through the undergrowth at him.

He came back later, both times, and found nothing. And once Carl swore he saw a brilliant red plant move slowly into a rock crevice as he approached. The thing became their *edelweiss*—very nearly their Grail.

Rough diamonds lay in the streambeds and emeralds glinted

in the night-glow, and for the Terran-oriented mind there was incalculable treasure to be scratched up just below the steaming humus: iridium, ruthenium, metallic neptunium 237. There was an unaccountable (at first) shift toward the heavier metals. The ruthenium-rhodium-palladium group was as plentiful on Viridis as the iron-nickel-cobalt series on Earth; cadmium was actually more plentiful here than its relative, zinc. Technetium was present, though rare, on the crust, while Earth's had long since decayed.

Vulcanism was common on Viridis, as could be expected in the presence of so many radioactives. From the lifeboat they had seen bald-spots where there were particularly high concentrations of "hot" material. In some of these there was life.

At the price of a bout of radiation sickness, Carl went into one such area briefly for specimens. What he found was extraordinary—a tree which was warm to the touch, which used minerals and water at a profligate pace, and which, when transplanted outside an environment which destroyed cells almost as fast as they developed, went cancerous, grew enormously, and killed itself with its own terrible viability. In the same lethal areas lived a primitive worm which constantly discarded segments to keep pace with its rapid growth, and which also grew visibly and died of living too fast when taken outside.

The inclination of the planet's axis was less than 2°, so that there were virtually no seasons, and very little variation in temperature from one latitude to another. There were two continents and an equatorial sea, no mountains, no plains, and few large lakes. Most of the planet was gently rolling hill-country and meandering rivers, clothed in thick jungle or grass. The spot where they had awakened was as good as any other, so there they stayed, wandering less and less as they amassed information. Nowhere was there an artifact of any kind, nor any slightest trace of previous habitation. Unless, of course, one considered the existence itself of life on this planet. For Permian life can hardly be expected to develop in less than a billion years; yet the irreproachable calendar inherent in the radioactive bones of Viridis insisted that the planet was no more than thirty-five million years old.

V

When Moira's time came, it went hard with her, and Carl forgot to swagger because he could not help. Teague and April took care of her, and Tod stayed with Carl, wishing for the right thing to say and not finding it, wanting to do something for this new strange man with Carl's face, and the unsure hands which twisted each other, clawed the ground, wiped cruelly at the scalp, at the shins, restless, terrified. Through Carl, Tod learned a little more of what he never wanted to know—what it must have been like for Teague when he lost Alma.

Alma's six children were toddlers by then, bright and happy in the only world they had ever known. They had been named for moons—Wynken, Blynken, and Nod, Rhea, Callisto, and Titan. Nod and Titan were the boys, and they and Rhea had Alma's eyes and hair and sometimes Alma's odd, brave stillness—a sort of suspension of the body while the mind went out to grapple and conquer instead of fearing. If the turgid air and the radiant ground affected them, they did not show it, except perhaps in their rapid development.

They heard Moira cry out. It was like laughter, but it was pain. Carl sprang to his feet. Tod took his arm and Carl pulled it away. "Why can't I do something? Do I have to just *sit* here?"

"Shh. She doesn't feel it. That's a tropism. She'll be all right. Sit down, Carl. Tell you what you can do—you can name them. Think. Think of a nice set of names, all connected in some way. Teague used moons. What are you going to—"

"Time enough for that," Carl grunted. "Tod . . . do you know what I'll . . . I'd be if she—if something happened?"

"Nothing's going to happen."

"I'd just cancel out. I'm not Teague. I couldn't carry it. How does Teague do it? . . ." Carl's voice lapsed to a mumble.

"Names," Tod reminded him. "Seven, eight of 'em. Come on, now."

"Think she'll have eight?"

"Why not? She's normal." He nudged Carl. "Think of names. I know! How many of the old signs of the zodiac would make good names?"

"Don't remember 'em."

"I do. Aries, that's good. Taurus. Gem—no; you wouldn't want to call a child 'Twins.' Leo—that's *fine!*"

"Libra," said Carl, "for a girl. Aquarius, Sagittarius—how many's that?"

Tod counted on his fingers. "Six. Then, Virgo and Capricorn. And you're all set!" But Carl wasn't listening. In two long bounds he reached April, who was just stepping into the compound. She looked tired. She looked more than tired. In her beautiful eyes was a great pity, the color of a bleeding heart.

"Is she all right? Is she?" They were hardly words, those hoarse, rushed things.

April smiled with her lips, while her eyes poured pity. "Yes, yes, she'll be all right. It wasn't too bad."

Carl whooped and pushed past her. She caught his arm, and for all her frailty, swung him around.

"Not yet, Carl. Teague says to tell you first—"

"The babies? What about them? How many, April?"

April looked over Carl's shoulder at Tod. She said, "Three."

Carl's face relaxed, numb, and his eyes went round. "Th— what? Three so far, you mean. There'll surely be more. . . ."

She shook her head.

Tod felt the laughter explode within him, and he clamped his jaws on it. It surged at him, hammered in the back of his throat. And then he caught April's pleading eyes. He took strength from her, and bottled up a great bray of merriment.

Carl's voice was the last fraying thread of hope. "The others died, then."

She put a hand on his cheek. "There were only three. Carl . . . don't be mean to Moira."

"Oh, I won't," he said with difficulty. "She couldn't . . . I mean it wasn't her doing." He flashed a quick, defensive look at Tod, who was glad now he had controlled himself. What was in Carl's face meant murder for anyone who dared laugh.

April said, "Not your doing either, Carl. It's this planet. It must be."

"Thanks, April," Carl muttered. He went to the door, stopped, shook himself like a big dog. He said again, "Thanks," but this time his voice didn't work and it was only a whisper. He went inside.

Tod bolted for the corner of the building, whipped around it and sank to the ground, choking. He held both hands over his mouth and laughed until he hurt. When at last he came to a limp silence, he felt April's presence. She stood quietly watching him, waiting.

"I'm sorry," he said. "I'm sorry. But . . . it *is* funny."

She shook her head gravely. "We're not on Earth, Tod. A new world means new manners, too. That would apply even on Terra Prime if we'd gone there."

"I suppose," he said, and then repressed another giggle.

"I always thought it was a silly kind of joke anyway," she said primly. "Judging virility by the size of a brood. There isn't any scientific basis for it. Men are silly. They used to think that virility could be measured by the amount of hair on their chests, or how tall they were. There's nothing wrong with having only three."

"Carl?" grinned Tod. "The big ol' swashbuckler?" He let the grin fade. "All right, Ape. I won't let Carl see me laugh. Or you either. All right?" A peculiar expression crossed his face. "What was that you said? April! Men never had hair on their chests!"

"Yes they did. Ask Teague."

"I'll take your word for it." He shuddered. "I can't imagine it unless a man had a tail too. And bony ridges over his eyes."

"It wasn't so long ago that they had. The ridges, anyway. Well—I'm glad you didn't laugh in front of him. You're nice, Tod."

"You're nice too." He pulled her down beside him and hugged her gently. "Bet you'll have a dozen."

"I'll try." She kissed him.

When specimen-hunting had gone as far as it could, classification became the settlement's main enterprise. And gradually, the unique pattern of Viridian life began to emerge.

Viridis had its primitive fish and several of the mollusca, but the fauna was primarily arthropods and reptiles. The interesting thing about each of the three branches was the close relationship between species. It was almost as if evolution took a major step with each generation, instead of bumbling along as on Earth, where certain stages of development are static for thousands, millions of years. *Pterodon*, for example, existed in three varieties, the simplest of which showed a clear similarity to *pteronauchis*, the gliding newt. A simple salamander could be shown to be the common ancestor of both the flapping frog and massive *Parametrodon*, and there were strong similarities between this salamander and the worm which fathered the arthropods.

They lived close to the truth for a long time without being able to see it, for man is conditioned to think of evolution from simple to complex, from ooze to animalcule to mollusc to ganoid; amphibid to monotreme to primate to tinker . . . losing the significance of the fact that all these co-exist. Was the vertebrate eel of prehistory a *higher* form of life than his simpler descendant? The whale lost his legs; this men call recidivism, a sort of backsliding in evolution, and treat it as a kind of illegitimacy.

Men are oriented out of simplicity toward the complex, and make of the latter a goal. Nature treats complex matters as expediencies and so is never confused. It is hardly surprising, then, that the Viridis colony took so long to discover their error, for the weight of evidence was in error's favor. There was indeed an unbroken line from the lowest forms of life to the highest, and to assume that they had a common ancestor was a beautifully consistent hypothesis, of the order of accuracy an archer might display in hitting dead center, from a thousand paces, a bowstring with the nock of his arrow.

The work fell more and more on the younger ones. Teague isolated himself, not by edict, but by habit. It was assumed that he was working along his own lines; and then it became usual to proceed without him, until finally he was virtually a hermit in their midst. He was aging rapidly; perhaps it hurt something in him to be surrounded by so much youth. His six children thrived, and, with Carl's three, ran naked in the jungle armed only with their sticks and their speed. They were apparently immune to practically everything Viridis might bring against them, even *Crotalidus'* fangs, which gave them the equivalent of a severe bee-sting (as opposed to what had happened to Moira once, when they had had to reactivate one of the Coffins to keep her alive).

Tod would come and sit with him sometimes, and as long as there was no talk the older man seemed to gain something from the visits. But he preferred to be alone, living as much as he could with memories for which not even a new world could afford a substitute.

Tod said to Carl, "Teague is going to wither up and blow away if we can't interest him in something."

"He's interested enough to spend a lot of time with whatever he's thinking about," Carl said bluntly.

"But I'd like it better if he was interested in something here, now. I wish we could . . . I wish—" But he could think of nothing, and it was a constant trouble to him.

Little Titan was killed, crushed under a great clumsy *Parametrodon* which slid down a bank on him while the child was grubbing for the scarlet cap of the strange red mushroom they had glimpsed from time to time. It was in pursuit of one of these that Moira had been bitten by the *Crotalidus*. One of Carl's children was drowned—just how, no one knew. Aside from these tragedies, life was easy and interesting. The compound began to look more like a *kraal* as they acclimated, for although the adults never adapted as well as the children, they did become far less sensitive to insect bites and the poison weeds which first troubled them.

It was Teague's son Nod who found what was needed to bring Teague's interest back, at least for a while. The child came back to the compound one day, trailed by two slinking *Felodons* who did not catch him because they kept pausing and pausing to lap up gouts of blood which marked his path. Nod's ear was torn and he had a green-stick break in his left ulna, and a dislocated wrist. He came weeping, weeping tears of joy. He shouted as he wept, great proud noises. Once in the compound he collapsed, but he would not lose consciousness, nor his grip on his prize, until Teague came. Then he handed Teague the mushroom and fainted.

The mushroom was and was not like anything on Earth. Earth has a fungus called *schizophyllum*, not uncommon but most strange. Though not properly a fungus, the red "mushroom" of Viridis had many of the functions of *schizophyllum*.

Schizophyllum produces spores of four distinct types, each of which grows into a genetically distinct, completely dissimilar plant. Three of these are sterile. The fourth produces *schizophyllum*.

The red mushroom of Viridis also produced four distinct heterokaryons or genetically different types, and the spores of one of these produced the mushroom.

Teague spent an engrossing earth-year in investigating the other three.

VI

Sweating and miserable in his integument of flexskin, Tod hunched in the crotch of a finger-tree. His knees were drawn up and his head was down; his arms clasped his shins and he rocked slightly back and forth. He knew he would be safe here for some time—the fleshy fingers of the tree were clumped at the slender, swaying ends of the branches and never turned back toward the trunk. He wondered what it would be like to be dead. Perhaps he would be dead soon, and then he'd know. He might as well be.

The names he'd chosen were perfect and all of a family: Sol, Mercury, Venus, Terra, Mars, Jupiter . . . eleven of them. And he could think of a twelfth if he had to.

For what?

He let himself sink down again into the blackness wherein nothing lived but the oily turning of *what's it like to be dead*?

Quiet, he thought. *No one would laugh.*

Something pale moved on the jungle floor below him. He thought instantly of April, and angrily put the thought out of his mind. April would be sleeping now, having completed the trifling task it had taken her so long to start. Down there, that would be Blynken, or maybe Rhea. They were very alike.

It didn't matter, anyway.

He closed his eyes and stopped rocking. He couldn't see anyone, no one could see him. That was the best way. So he sat, and let time pass, and when a hand lay on his shoulder, he nearly leaped out of the tree. "Damn it, Blynken—"

"It's me. Rhea." The child, like all of Alma's daughters, was large for her age and glowing with health. How long had it been? Six, eight . . . nine Earth years since they had landed.

"Go hunt mushrooms," Tod growled. "Leave me alone."

"Come back," said the girl.

Tod would not answer. Rhea knelt beside him, her arm around the primary branch, her back, with his, against the trunk. She bent her head and put her cheek against his. "Tod."

Something inside him flamed. He bared his teeth and swung a heavy fist. The girl doubled up soundlessly and slipped out of the tree. He stared down at the lax body and at first could not see it for the haze of fury which blew and whirled around him. Then his vision cleared and he moaned, tossed his club down and dropped after it. He caught up the club and whacked off the tree-fingers which probed toward them. He swept up the child and leapt clear, and sank to his knees, gathering her close.

"Rhea, I'm sorry, I'm sorry . . . I wasn't . . . I'm not—*Rhea!* Don't be dead!"

She stirred and made a tearing sound with her throat. Her eyelids trembled and opened, uncovering pain-blinded eyes. "Rhea!"

"It's all right," she whispered, "I shouldn't've bothered you. Do you want me to go away?"

"No," he said. "No." He held her tight. *Why not let her go away?* a part of him wondered, and another part, frightened and puzzled, cried, *No! No!* He had an urgent, half-hysterical need to explain. *Why explain to her, a child? Say you're sorry, comfort her, heal her, but don't expect her to understand.* Yet he said, "I can't go back. There's nowhere else to go. So what can I do?"

Rhea was quiet, as if waiting. A terrible thing, a wonderful thing, to have someone you have hurt wait patiently like that while you find a way to explain. Even if you only explain it to yourself . . . "What could I do if I went back? They—they'll never—they'll laugh at me. They'll all laugh. They're laughing now." Angry again, plaintive no more, he blurted, "April! *Damn* April! She's made a eunuch out of me!"

"Because she had only one baby?"

"Like a savage."

"It's a beautiful baby. A boy."

"A man, a real man, fathers six or eight."

She met his eyes gravely. "That's silly."

"What's happening to us on this crazy planet?" he raged. "Are we evolving backward? What comes next—one of you kids hatching out some amphibids?"

She said only, "Come back, Tod."

"I can't," he whispered. "They'll think I'm . . . that I can't . . ." Helplessly, he shrugged. "They'll laugh."

"Not until you do, and then they'll laugh *with* you. Not at you, Tod."

Finally, he said it, "April won't love me; she'll never love a weakling."

She pondered, holding him with her clear gaze. "You really need to be loved a whole lot."

Perversely, he became angry again. "I can get along!" he snapped.

And she smiled and touched the nape of his neck. "You're loved," she assured him. "Gee, you don't have to be mad about that. I love you, don't I? April loves you. Maybe I love you even more than she does. She loves everything you are, Tod. I love everything you ever were and everything you ever will be."

He closed his eyes and a great music came to him. A long, long time ago he had attacked someone who came to comfort him, and she had let him cry, and at length she had said . . . not exactly these words, but—it was the same.

"Rhea."

He looked at her. "You said all that to me before."

A puzzled small crinkle appeared between her eyes and she put her fingers on it. "Did I?"

"Yes," said Tod, "but it was before you were even born."

He rose and took her hand, and they went back to the compound, and whether he was laughed at or not he never knew, for he could think of nothing but his full heart and of April. He went straight in to her and kissed her gently and admired his son, whose name was Sol, and who had been born with hair and two tiny incisors, and who had heavy bony ridges over his eyes. . . .

"A fantastic storage capacity," Teague remarked, touching the top of the scarlet mushroom. "The spores are almost microscopic. The thing doesn't seem to want them distributed, either. It positively hoards them, millions of them."

"Start over, please," April said. She shifted the baby in her arms. He was growing prodigiously. "Slowly. I used to know something about biology—or so I thought. But *this*—"

Teague almost smiled. It was good to see. The aging face had not had so much expression in it in five Earth-years. "I'll get as basic as I can, then, and start from there. First of all, we call this thing a mushroom, but it isn't. I don't think it's a plant, though you couldn't call it an animal, either."

"I don't think anybody ever told me the real difference between a plant and an animal," said Tod.

"Oh . . . well, the most convenient way to put it—it's not strictly accurate, but it will do—is that plants make their own food and animals subsist on what others have made. This thing does both. It has roots, but—" he lifted an edge of the skirted stem of the mushroom—"it can move them. Not much, not fast; but if it wants to shift itself, it can."

April smiled, "Tod, I'll give you basic biology any time. Do go on, Teague."

"Good. Now, I explained about the heterokaryons—the ability this thing has to produce spores which grow up into four completely different plants. One is a mushroom just like this. Here are the other three."

Tod looked at the box of plants. "Are they really all from the mushroom spores?"

"Don't blame you," said Teague, and actually chuckled. "I didn't believe it myself at first. A sort of pitcher plant, half full of liquid. A thing like a cactus. And this one. It's practically all underground, like a truffle, although it has these cilia. You wouldn't think it was anything but a few horsehairs stuck in the ground."

"And they're all sterile," Tod recalled.

"They're not," said Teague, "and that's what I called you in here to tell you. They'll yield if they are fertilized."

"Fertilized how?"

Instead of answering, Teague asked April, "Do you remember how far back we traced the evolution of Viridian life?"

"Of course. We got the arthropods all the way back to a simple segmented worm. The insects seemed to come from another worm, with pseudopods and a hard carapace."

"A caterpillar," Tod interpolated.

"Almost," said April, with a scientist's nicety. "And the most primitive reptile we could find was a little gymnoderm you could barely see without a glass."

"Where did we find it?"

"Swimming around in—oh! In those pitcher plant things!"

"If you won't take my word for this," said Teague, a huge enjoyment glinting between his words, "you'll just have to breed these things yourself. It's a lot of work, but this is what you'll discover.

"An adult gymnoderm—a male—finds this pitcher and falls in. There's plenty of nutriment for him, you know, and he's a true amphibian. He fertilizes the pitcher. Nodules grow under the surface of the liquid inside there—" he pointed "—and bud off. The buds are mobile. They grow into wrigglers, miniature tadpoles. Then into lizards. They climb out and go about the business of being—well, lizards."

"All males?" asked Tod.

"No," said Teague, "and that's an angle I haven't yet investigated. But apparently some males breed with females, which lay eggs, which hatch into lizards, and some find plants to fertilize. Anyway, it looks as if this plant is actually the progenitor of all the reptiles here; you know how clear the evolutionary lines are to all the species."

"What about the truffle with the horsehairs?" asked Tod.

"A pupa," said Teague, and to the incredulous expression on April's face, he insisted, "Really—a pupa. After nine weeks or so of dormance, it hatches out into what you almost called a caterpillar."

"And then into all the insects here," said April, and shook her head in wonderment. "And I suppose that cactus-thing hatches out the nematodes, the segmented ones that evolve into arthropods?"

Teague nodded. "You're welcome to experiment," he said again, "but believe me—you'll only find out I'm right: it really happens."

"Then this scarlet mushroom is the beginning of everything here."

"I can't find another theory," said Teague.

"I can," said Tod.

They looked at him questioningly, and he rose and laughed. "Not yet. I have to think it through." He scooped up the baby and then helped April to her feet. "How do you like our Sol, Teague?"

"Fine," said Teague. "A fine boy." Tod knew he was seeing the heavy occipital ridges, the early teeth, and saying nothing. Tod was aware of a faint inward surprise as the baby reached toward April and he handed him over. He should have resented what might be in Teague's mind, but he did not. The beginnings of an important insight welcomed criticism of the child, recognized its hairiness, its savagery, and found these things good. But as yet the thought was too nebulous to express, except by a smile. He smiled, took April's hand, and left.

"That was a funny thing you said to Teague," April told him as they walked toward their quarters.

"Remember, April, the day we landed? Remember—" he made a gesture that took in a quadrant of sky— "Remember how we all felt . . . good?"

"Yes," she murmured. "It was like a sort of compliment, and a reassurance. How could I forget?"

"Yes. Well . . ." He spoke with difficulty but his smile stayed. "I have a thought, and it makes me feel like that. But I can't get it into words," After a thoughtful pause, he added, "Yet."

She shifted the baby. "He's getting so heavy."

"I'll take him." He took the squirming bundle with the deep-set, almost humorous eyes. When he looked up from them, he caught an expression on April's face which he hadn't seen in years. "What is it, Ape?"

"You—*like* him."

"Well, sure."

"I was afraid. I was afraid for a long time that you. . . . he's ours, but he isn't exactly a pretty baby."

"I'm not exactly a pretty father."

"You know how precious you are to me?" she whispered.

He knew, for this was an old intimacy between them. He laughed and followed the ritual: "How precious?"

She cupped her hands and brought them together, to make of them an ivory box. She raised the hands and peeped into them, between the thumbs, as if at a rare jewel, then clasped the magic tight and hugged it to her breast, raising tear-filled eyes to him. "That precious," she breathed.

He looked at the sky, seeing somewhere in it the many peak moments of their happiness when she had made that gesture, feeling how each one, meticulously chosen, brought all the others back. "I used to hate this place," he said. "I guess it's changed."

"You've changed."

Changed how? he wondered. He felt the same, even though he knew he looked older. . . .

The years passed, and the children grew. When Sol was fifteen Earth-years old, short, heavy-shouldered, powerful, he married Carl's daughter Libra. Teague, turning to parchment, had returned to his hermitage from the temporary stimulation of his researches on what they still called "the mushroom." More and more the colony lived off the land and out of the jungle, not because there was any less to be synthesized from their compact machines, but out of preference; it was easier to catch flapping frogs or umbrella-birds and cook them than to bother with machine settings and check-analyses, and, somehow, a lot more fun to eat them, too.

It seemed to them safer, year by year. *Felodon,* unquestionably the highest form of life on Viridis, was growing scarce, being replaced by a smaller, more timid carnivore April called *Vulpidus* (once, for it seemed not to matter much any more about keeping records) and everyone ultimately called "fox," for all the fact that it was a reptile. *Pterodon* was disappearing too, as were all the larger forms. More and more they strayed after food, not famine-driven, but purely for variety; more and more they found themselves welcome and comfortable away from the compound. Once Carl and Moira drifted off for nearly a year. When they came back they had another child—a silent, laughing little thing with oddly long arms and heavy teeth.

The warm days and the glowing nights passed comfortably and the stars no longer called. Tod became a grandfather and was proud. The child, a girl, was albino like April, and had exactly April's deep red eyes. Sol and Libra named her Emerald, a green name and a ground-term rather than a sky-term, as if in open expression of the slow spell worked on them all by Viridis. She was mute—but so were almost all the new children, and it seemed not to matter. They were healthy and happy.

Tod went to tell Teague, thinking it might cheer the old one up a little. He found him lying in what had once been his laboratory, thin and placid and disinterested, absently staring down at one of the arthropodal flying creatures that had once startled them so by zooming into the Coffin chamber. This one had happened to land on Teague's hand, and Teague was laxly waiting for it to fly off again, out through the unscreened window, past the unused sprays, over the faint tumble of rotted spars which had once been a palisade.

"Teague, the baby's come!"

Teague sighed, his tired mind detaching itself from memory episode by episode. His eyes rolled toward Tod and finally he turned his head. "Which one would that be?"

Tod laughed. "My grandchild, a girl. Sol's baby."

Teague let his lids fall. He said nothing.

"Well, aren't you glad?"

Slowly a frown came to the papery brow. "Glad." Tod felt he was looking at the word as he had stared at the arthropod, wondering limply when it might go away. "What's the matter with it?"

"What?"

Teague sighed again, a weary, impatient sound. "What does it look like?" he said slowly, emphasizing each one-syllabled word.

"Like April. Just like April."

Teague half sat up, and blinked at Tod. "You don't mean it."

"Yes, eyes red as—" The image of an Earth sunset flickered near his mind but vanished as too hard to visualize. Tod pointed at the four red-capped "mushrooms" that had stood for so many years in the test-boxes in the laboratory. "Red as those."

"Silver hair," said Teague.

"Yes, beau—"

"All over," said Teague flatly.

"Well, yes."

Teague let himself fall back on the cot and gave a disgusted snort. "A monkey."

"Teague!"

"Ah-h-h . . . go 'way," growled the old man. "I long ago

resigned myself to what was happening to us here. A human being just can't adapt to the kind of radioactive ruin this place is for us. Your monsters'll breed monsters, and the monsters'll do the same if they can, until pretty soon they just won't breed any more. And that will be the end of that, and good riddance. . . ." His voice faded away. His eyes opened, looking on distant things, and gradually found themselves focused on the man who stood over him in shocked silence. "But the one thing I can't stand is to have somebody come in here saying, 'Oh, joy, oh happy day!' "

"Teague . . ." Tod swallowed heavily.

"Viridis eats ambition; there was going to be a city here," said the old man distinctly. "Viridis eats humanity; there were going to be people here." He chuckled gruesomely. "All right, all right, accept it if you have to—and you have to. But don't come around here celebrating."

Tod backed to the door, his eyes horror-round, then turned and fled.

VII

April held him as he crouched against the wall, rocked him slightly, made soft unspellable mother-noises to him.

"Shh, he's all decayed, all lonesome and mad," she murmured. "Shh. Shh."

Tod felt half-strangled. As a youth he had been easily moved, he recalled; he had that tightness of the throat for sympathy, for empathy, for injustices he felt the Universe was hurling at him out of its capacious store. But recently life had been placid, full of love and togetherness and a widening sense of membership with the earth and the air and all the familiar things which walked and flew and grew and bred in it. And his throat was shaped for laughter now; these feelings hurt him.

"But he's right," he whispered. "Don't you see? Right from the beginning it . . . it was . . . remember Alma had six children, April? And a little later, Carl and Moira had three? And you, only one . . . how long is it since the average human gave birth to only one?"

"They used to say it was humanity's last major mutation," she admitted, "Multiple births . . . these last two thousand years. But—"

"Eyebrow ridges," he interrupted. "Hair. . . that skull, Emerald's skull, slanting back like that; do you see the tusks on that little . . . *baboon* of Moira's?"

"Tod! *Don't!*"

He leaped to his feet, sprang across the room and snatched the golden helix from the shelf where it had gleamed its locked symbolism down on them ever since the landing. "Around and down!" he shouted. "Around and around and down!" He squatted beside her and pointed furiously. "Down and down into the blackest black there is; down into *nothing*." He shook his fist at the sky. "You see what they do? They find the highest form of life they can and plant it here and watch it slide down into the muck!" He hurled the artifact away from him.

"But it goes up too, round and up. Oh, Tod!" she cried. "Can you remember them, what they looked like, the way they flew, and say these things about them?"

"I can remember Alma," he gritted, "conceiving and gestating alone in space, while they turned their rays on her every day. You know *why?*" With the sudden thought, he stabbed a finger down at her. "To give her babies a head-start on Viridis, otherwise they'd have been born normal here; it would've taken another couple of generations to start them downhill, and they wanted us all to go together."

"No, Tod, no!"

"Yes, April, yes. How much proof do you need?" He whirled on her. "Listen—remember that mushroom Teague analyzed? He had to *pry* spores out of it to see what it yielded. Remember the three different plants he got? Well, I was just there; I don't know how many times before I've seen it, but only now it makes sense. He's got four mushrooms now; do you see? Do you see? Even back as far as we can trace the bugs and newts on this green hell-pit, Viridis won't let anything climb; it must fall."

"I don't—"

"You'll give me basic biology any time," he quoted sarcastically. "Let me tell you some biology. That mushroom yields three plants, and the plants yield animal life. Well, when the animal life fertilized those heterowhatever—"

"Heterokaryons."

"Yes. Well, you don't get animals that can evolve and improve. You get one pitiful generation of animals which breeds back into a mushroom, and there it sits hoarding its spores. Viridis wouldn't let one puny newt, one primitive pupa build! It snatches 'em back, locks 'em up. That mushroom isn't the beginning of everything here—*it's the end!*"

April got to her feet slowly, looking at Tod as if she had never seen him before, not in fear, but with a troubled curiosity. She crossed the room and picked up the artifact, stroked its gleaming golden coils. "You could be right," she said in a low voice. "But that can't be all there is to it." She set the helix back in its place. "They *wouldn't.*"

She spoke with such intensity that for a moment that metrical formation, mighty and golden, rose again in Tod's mind, up and up to the measureless cloud which must be a ship. He recalled the sudden shift, like a genuflection, directed at them, at *him*, and for that moment he could find no evil in it. Confused, he tossed his head, found himself looking out the door, seeing Moira's youngest ambling comfortably across the compound.

"They *wouldn't?*" he snarled. He took April's slender arm and whirled her to the door. "You know what I'd do before I'd father another one like *that?*" He told her specifically what he would do. "A lemur next, hm? A spider, an oyster, a jellyfish!"

April whimpered and ran out. "Know any lullabies to a tapeworm?" he roared after her. She disappeared into the jungle, and he fell back, gasping for breath. . . .

Having no stomach for careful thought nor careful choosing, having Teague for an example to follow, Tod too turned hermit. He could have survived the crisis easily perhaps, with April to help, but she did not come back. Moira and Carl were off again, wandering; the children lived their own lives, and he had no wish to see Teague. Once or twice Sol and Libra came to see him, but he snarled at them and they left him alone. It was no sacrifice. Life on Viridis was very full for the contented ones.

He sulked in his room or poked about the compound by himself. He activated the protein converter once, but found its products tasteless, and never bothered with it again. Sometimes he would stand near the edge of the hilltop and watch the children playing in the long grass, and his lip would curl.

Damn Teague! He'd been happy enough with Sol all those years, for all the boy's bulging eyebrow ridges and hairy body. He had been about to accept the silent, silver Emerald, too, when the crochety old man had dropped his bomb. Once or twice Tod wondered detachedly what it was in him that was so easily reached, so completely insecure, that the suggestion of abnormality should strike so deep.

Somebody once said, *"You really need to be loved, don't you, Tod?"*

No one would love this tainted thing, father of savages who spawned animals. He didn't deserve to be loved.

He had never felt so alone. *"I'm going to die. But I will be with you too."* That had been Alma. Huh! There was old Teague, tanning his brains in his own sour acids. Alma had believed something or other . . . and what had come of it? That wizened old crab lolling his life away in the lab.

Tod spent six months that way.

"Tod!" He came out of sleep reluctantly, because in sleep an inner self still lived with April where there was no doubt and no fury; no desertion, no loneliness.

He opened his eyes and stared dully at the slender figure silhouetted against Viridis' glowing sky. "April?"

"Moira," said the figure. The voice was cold.

"Moira!" he said, sitting up. "I haven't seen you for a year. More. Wh—"

"Come," she said. "Hurry."

"Come where?"

"Come by yourself or I'll get Carl and he'll carry you." She walked swiftly to the door.

He reeled after her. "You can't come in here and—"

"Come on." The voice was edged and slid out from between clenched teeth. A miserable part of him twitched in delight and told him that he was important enough to be hated. He despised himself for recognizing the twisted thought, and before he knew what he was doing he was following Moira at a steady trot.

"Where are—" he gasped, and she said over her shoulder, "If you don't talk you'll go faster."

At the jungle margin a shadow detached itself and spoke. "Got him?"

"Yes, Carl."

The shadow became Carl. He swung in behind Tod, who suddenly realized that if he did not follow the leader, the one behind would drive. He glanced back at Carl's implacable bulk, and then put down his head and jogged doggedly along as he was told.

They followed a small stream, crossed it on a fallen tree, and climbed a hill. Just as Tod was about to accept the worst these determined people might offer in exchange for a moment to ease his fiery lungs, Moira stopped. He stumbled into her. She caught his arm and kept him on his feet.

"In there," she said, pointing.

"A finger tree."

"You know how to get inside," Carl growled.

Moira said, "She begged me not to tell you, ever. I think she was wrong."

"Who? What is—"

"Inside," said Carl, and shoved him roughly down the slope.

His long conditioning was still with him, and reflexively he sidestepped the fanning fingers which swayed to meet him. He ducked under them, batted aside the inner phalanx, and found himself in the clear space underneath. He stopped there, gasping.

Something moaned.

He bent, fumbled cautiously in the blackness. He touched something smooth and alive, recoiled, touched it again. A foot.

Someone began to cry harshly, hurtfully, the sound exploding as if through clenched hands.

"April!"

"I told them not to. . . ." and she moaned.

"April, what is it, what's happened?"

"You needn't . . . be," she said, sobbed a while, and went on, " . . . angry. It didn't live."

"What didn't . . . you mean you . . . April, you—"

"It wouldn't've been a tapeworm," she whispered.

"Who—" he fell to his knees, found her face. "When did you—"

"I was going to tell you that day, that very same day, and when you came in so angry at what Teague told you, I specially wanted to, I thought you'd . . . be glad."

"April, why didn't you come back? If I'd known. . . ."

"You *said* what you'd do if I ever . . . if you ever had another . . . you meant it, Tod."

"It's this place, this Viridis," he said sadly. "I went crazy."

He felt her wet hand on his cheek.

"It's all right. I just didn't want to make it worse for you," April said.

"I'll take you back."

"No, you can't. I've been . . . I've lost a lot of . . . just stay with me a little while."

"Moira should have—"

"She just found me," said April. "I've been alone all the— I guess I made a noise. I didn't mean to. Tod . . . don't quarrel. Don't go into a lot of . . . It's all right."

Against her throat he cried. *"All right!"*

"When you're by yourself," she said faintly, "you think; you think better. Did you ever think of—"

"April!" he cried in anguish, the very sound of her pale, pain-wracked voice making this whole horror real.

"Shh, sh. Listen," she said rapidly. "There isn't time, you know, Tod. Tod, did you ever think of us all, Teague and Alma and Moira and Carl and us, what we are?"

"I know what I am."

"*Shh.* Altogether we're a leader and mother; a word and a shield; a doubter, a mystic. . . ." Her voice trailed off. She coughed and he could feel the spastic jolt shoot through her body. She panted lightly for a moment and went on urgently, "Anger and prejudice and stupidity, courage, laughter, love, music . . . it was all aboard that ship and it's all here on Viridis. Our children and theirs—no matter what they look like, Tod, no matter how they live or what they eat—they have that in them. Humanity isn't just a way of walking, merely a kind of skin. It's what we had together and what we gave Sol. It's what the golden ones found in us and wanted for Viridis. You'll see. You'll see."

"Why Viridis?"

"Because of what Teague said—what you said." Her breath puffed out in the ghost of a laugh. "Basic biology . . . ontogeny follows phylogeny. The human fetus is a cell, an animalcule, a gilled amphibian . . . all up the line. It's there in us; Viridis makes it go backward."

"To what?"

"The mushroom. The spores. We'll be spores, Tod. Together . . . Alma *said* she could be dead, and together with Teague! That's why I said . . . it's all right. This doesn't matter, what's happened. We live in Sol, we live in Emerald with Carl and Moira, you see? Closer, nearer than we've ever been."

Tod took a hard hold on his reason. "But back to spores—why? What then?"

She sighed. It was unquestionably a happy sound. "They'll be back for the reaping, and they'll have us, Tod, all we are and all they worship: goodness and generosity and the urge to build; mercy; kindness.

"They're needed too," she whispered. "And the spores make mushrooms, and the mushrooms make the heterokaryons; and from those, away from Viridis, come the life-forms to breed us—*us*, Tod! into whichever form is dominant. And there we'll be, that flash of old understanding of a new idea . . . the special pressure on a painter's hand that makes him a Rembrandt, the sense of architecture that turns a piano-player into a Bach. Three billion extra years of evolution, ready to help wherever it can be used. On every Earth-type planet, Tod—millions of us, blowing about in the summer wind, waiting to give. . . ."

"Give! Give what Teague is now, rotten and angry?"

"That isn't Teague. That will die off. Teague lives with Alma in their children, and in theirs . . . she *said* she'd be with him!"

"Me . . . what about me?" he breathed. "What I did to you. . . ."

"Nothing, you did nothing. You live in Sol, in Emerald. Living, conscious, alive . . . with me. . . ."

He said, "You mean . . . you could talk to me from Sol?"

"I think I might." With his forehead, bent so close to her, he felt her smile. "But I don't think I would. Lying so close to you, why should I speak to an outsider?"

Her breathing changed and he was suddenly terrified. "April, don't die."

"I won't," she said. "Alma didn't." She kissed him gently and died.

It was a long darkness, with Tod hardly aware of roaming and raging through the jungle, of eating without tasting, of hungering without knowing of it. Then there was a twilight, many months long, soft and still, with restfulness here and a promise soon. Then there was a compound again, found like a dead memory, learned again just a little more readily than something new. Carl and Moira were kind, knowing the nature of justice and the limits of punishment, and at last Tod was alive again.

He found himself one day down near the river, watching it and thinking back without fear of his own thoughts, and a growing wonder came to him. His mind had for so long dwelt on his own evil that it was hard to break new paths. He wondered with an awesome effort what manner of creatures might worship humanity for itself, and what manner of creatures humans were to be so worshipped. It was a totally new concept to him, and he was completely immersed in it, so that when Emerald slid out of the grass and stood watching him, he was frightened and shouted.

She did not move. There was little to fear now on Viridis. All the large reptiles were gone, and there was room for the humans, the humanoids, the primates, the . . . children. In his shock the old reflexes played. He stared at her, her square stocky body, the silver hair which covered it all over except for the face, the palms, the soles of the feet. *"A monkey!"* he spat, in Teague's tones, and the shock turned to shame. He met her eyes, April's deep glowing rubies, and they looked back at him without fear.

He let a vision of April grow and fill the world. The child's rare red eyes helped (there was so little, so very little red on Viridis). He saw April at the spaceport, holding him in the dark shadows of the blockhouse while the sky flamed above them. *We'll go out like that soon, soon, Tod. Squeeze me, squeeze me . . . Ah*, he'd said, *who needs a ship?*

Another April, part of her in a dim light as she sat writing; her hair, a crescent of light loving her cheek, a band of it on her brow; then she had seen him and turned, rising, smothered his first word with her mouth. Another April wanting to smile, waiting; and April asleep, and once April sobbing because she could not find a special word to tell him what she felt for him . . . He brought his mind back from her in the past, from her as she was, alive in his mind, back to here, to the bright mute with the grave red eyes who stood before him, and he said, "How precious?"

The baby kept her eyes on his, and slowly raised her silken hands. She cupped them together to make a closed chamber, looked down at it, opened her hands slightly and swiftly to peer inside, rapt at what she pretended to see; closed her hands again to capture the treasure, whatever it was, and hugged it to her breast. She looked up at him slowly, and her eyes were full of tears, and she was smiling.

He took his grandchild carefully in his arms and held her gently and strongly. Monkey?

"April," he gasped. "Little Ape. Little Ape."

Viridis is a young planet which bears (at first glance) old life-forms. Come away and let the green planet roll around its sun; come back in a while—not long, as astronomical time goes.

The jungle is much the same, the sea, the rolling savannahs. But the life. . . .

Viridis was full of primates. There were blunt-toothed herbi-vores and long-limbed tree-dwellers, gliders and burrowers. The fish-eaters were adapting the way all Viridis life must adapt, becoming more fit by becoming simpler, or go to the wall. Already the sea-apes had rudimentary gills and had lost their hair. Already tiny forms competed with the insects on their own terms.

On the banks of the wandering rivers, monotremes with opposed toes dredged and paddled, and sloths and lemurs crept at night. At first they had stayed together, but they were soon too numerous for that; and a half dozen generations cost them the power of speech, which was, by then, hardly a necessity. Living was good for primates on Viridis, and became better each genera-tion.

Eating and breeding, hunting and escaping filled the days and the cacophonous nights. It was hard in the beginning to see a friend cut down, to watch a slender silver shape go spinning down a river and know that with it went some of your brother, some of your mate, some of yourself. But as the hundreds became thousands and the thousands millions, witnessing death became about as significant as watching your friend get his hair cut. The basic ids each spread through the changing, mutating population like a stain, crossed and recrossed by the strains of the others, co-existing, eating each other and being eaten and all the while passing down through the generations.

There was a cloud over the savannah, high over the ruins of the compound. It was a thing of many colors and of no particular shape, and it was bigger than one might imagine, not knowing how far away it was.

From it dropped a golden spot that became a thread, and down came a golden mass. It spread and swung, exploded into a myriad of individuals. Some descended on the compound, erasing and changing, lifting, breaking—always careful to kill nothing. Others blanketed the planet, streaking silently through the green aisles, flashing unimpeded through the tangled thickets. They combed the riverbanks and the half-light of hill waves, and everywhere they went they found and touched the mushroom and stripped it of its spores, the compaction and multiplication of what had once been the representatives of a very high reptile culture.

Primates climbed and leaped, crawled and crept to the jungle margins to watch. Eater lay by eaten; the hunted stood on the hunter's shoulder, and a platypoid laid an egg in the open which nobody touched.

Simian forms hung from the trees in loops and ropes, in swarms and beards, and more came all the time, brought by some ineffable magnetism to watch at the hill. It was a fast and a waiting, with no movement but jostling for position, a crowding forward from behind and a pressing back from the slightest chance of interfering with the golden visitors.

Down from the polychrome cloud drifted a mass of the golden beings, carrying with them a huge sleek ship. They held it above the ground, sliced it, lifted it apart, set down this piece and that until a shape began to grow. Into it went bales and bundles, stocks and stores, and then the open tops were covered. It was a much bigger installation than the one before.

Quickly, it was done, and the golden cloud hung waiting.

The jungle was trembling with quiet.

In one curved panel of the new structure, something spun, fell outward, and out of the opening came a procession of stately creatures, long-headed, bright-eyed, three-toed, richly plumed and feathered. They tested their splendid wings, then stopped suddenly, crouched and looking upward.

They were given their obeisance by the golden ones, and after there appeared in the sky the exquisite symbol of a beauty that rides up and up, turns and spirals down again only to rise again; the symbol of that which has no beginning and no end, and the sign of those whose worship and whose work it is to bring to all the Universe that which has shown itself worthy in parts of it.

Then they were gone, and the jungle exploded into killing and flight, eating and screaming, so that the feathered ones dove back into their shelter and closed the door. . . .

And again to the green planet (when the time was right) came the cloud-ship, and found a world full of birds, and the birds watched in awe while they harvested their magic dust, and built a new shelter. In this they left four of their own for later harvesting, and this was to make of Viridis a most beautiful place.

From Viridis, the ship vaulted through the galaxies, searching for worlds worthy of what is human in humanity, whatever their manner of being alive. These they seeded, and of these, perhaps one would produce something new; something which could be reduced to the dust of Viridis, and from dust return.

MR. COSTELLO, HERO

"Come in, Purser. And shut the door."

"I beg your pardon, sir?" The Skipper never invited anyone in—not to his quarters. His office, yes, but not here.

He made an abrupt gesture, and I came in and closed the door. It was about as luxurious as a compartment on a spaceship can get. I tried not to goggle at it as if it was the first time I had ever seen it, just because it was the first time I had ever seen it.

I sat down.

He opened his mouth, closed it, forced the tip of his tongue through his thin lips. He licked them and glared at me. I'd never seen the Iron Man like this. I decided that the best thing to say would be nothing, which is what I said.

He pulled a deck of cards out of the top-middle drawer and slid them across the desk. "Deal."

I said, "I b—"

"And don't say you beg my pardon!" he exploded.

Well, all right. If the skipper wanted a cozy game of gin rummy to while away the parsecs, far be it from me to . . . I shuffled. Six years under this cold-blooded, fish-eyed automatic computer with eyebrows, and this was the first time that he—

"Deal," he said. I looked up at him. "Draw, five-card draw. You do play draw poker, don't you, Purser?"

"Yes, sir." I dealt and put down the pack. I had three threes and couple of court cards. The skipper scowled at his hand and threw down two. He glared at me again.

I said, "I got three of a kind, sir."

He let his cards go as if they no longer existed, slammed out of his chair and turned his back to me. He tilted his head back and stared up at the see-it-all, with its complex of speed, time, position, and distance-run coordinated. Borinquen, our destination planet, was at spitting distance—only a day or so off—and Earth was a long way behind. I heard a sound and dropped my eyes. The Skipper's hands were locked behind him, squeezed together so hard that they crackled.

"Why didn't you draw?" he grated.

"I beg your—"

"When *I* played poker—and I used to play a hell of a lot of poker—as I recall it, the dealer would find out how many cards each player wanted after the deal and give him as many as he discarded. Did you ever hear of that, Purser?"

"Yes, sir, I did."

"You *did*." He turned around. I imagine he had been scowling this same way at the see-it-all, and I wondered why it was he hadn't shattered the cover glass.

"Why, then, Purser," he demanded, "did you show your three of a kind without discarding, without drawing—without, mister, asking me how many cards I might want?"

I thought about it. "I—we—I mean, sir, we haven't been playing poker that way lately."

"You've been playing draw poker without drawing!" He sat down again and beamed that glare at me again. "And who changed the rules?"

"I don't know, sir. We just—that's the way we've been playing."

He nodded thoughtfully. "Now tell me something, Purser. How much time did you spend in the galley during the last watch?"

"About an hour, sir."

"About an hour."

"Well, sir," I explained hurriedly, "it was my turn."

He said nothing, and it suddenly occurred to me that these galley-watches weren't in the ship's orders.

I said quickly, "It isn't *against* your orders to stand such a watch, is it, sir?"

"No," he said, "it isn't." His voice was so gentle, it was ugly. "Tell me, Purser, doesn't Cooky mind these galley-watches?"

"Oh, no, sir! He's real pleased about it." I knew he was thinking about the size of the galley. It was true that two men made quite a crowd in a place like that. I said, "That way, he knows everybody can trust him."

"You mean that way you know he won't poison you."

"Well—yes, sir."

"And tell me," he said, his voice even gentler, "who suggested he might poison you?"

"I really couldn't say, Captain. It's just sort of something that came up. Cooky doesn't mind," I added. "If he's watched all the time, he knows nobody's going to suspect him. It's all right."

Again he repeated my words.

"It's all right." I wished he wouldn't. I wished he'd stop looking at me like that. "How long," he asked, "has it been customary for the deck officer to bring a witness with him when he takes over the watch?"

"I really couldn't say, sir. That's out of my department."

"You really couldn't say. Now think hard, Purser. Did you ever stand galley-watches, or see deck-officers bring witnesses with them when they relieve the bridge, or see draw poker played without drawing—before this trip?"

"Well, no, sir. I don't think I have. I suppose we just never thought of it before."

"We never had Mr. Costello as a passenger before, did we?"

"No, sir."

I thought for a moment he was going to say something else, but he didn't, just: "Very well, Purser. That will be all."

I went out and started back aft, feeling puzzled and sort of upset. The Skipper didn't have to hint things like that about Mr. Costello. Mr. Costello was a very nice man. Once, the Skipper had picked a fight with Mr. Costello. They'd shouted at each other in the day-room. That is, the Skipper had shouted—Mr. Costello never did. Mr. Costello was as good-natured as they come. A good-natured soft-spoken man, with the kind of a face they call open. Open and honest. He'd once been a Triumver back on Earth—the youngest ever appointed, they said.

You wouldn't think such an easygoing man was as smart as that. Triumvers are usually life-time appointees, but Mr. Costello wasn't satisfied. Had to keep moving, you know. Learning all the time, shaking hands all around, staying close to the people. He loved people.

I don't know why the Skipper couldn't get along with him. Everybody else did. And besides—Mr. Costello didn't play poker; why should he care one way or the other how *we* played it? He didn't eat the galley food—he had his own stock in his cabin—so what difference would it make to him if the cook poisoned anyone? Except, of course, that he cared about *us*. People—he *liked* people.

Anyway, it's better to play poker without the draw. Poker's a good game with a bad reputation. And where do you suppose it gets the bad reputation? From cheaters. And how do people cheat at poker? Almost never when they deal. It's when they pass out cards after the discard. That's when a shady dealer knows what he holds, and he knows what to give the others so he can win. All right, remove the discard and you remove nine-tenths of the cheaters. Remove the cheaters and the honest men can trust each other.

That's what Mr. Costello used to say, anyhow. Not that he cared one way or the other for himself. He wasn't a gambling man.

I went into the dayroom and there was Mr. Costello with the Third Officer. He gave me a big smile and a wave, so I went over. "Come on, sit down, Purser," he said. "I'm landing tomorrow. Won't have much more chance to talk to you."

I sat down. The Third snapped shut a book he'd been holding open on the table and sort of got it out of sight.

Mr. Costello laughed at him. "Go ahead, Third, show the Purser. You can trust him—he's a good man. I'd be proud to be shipmates with the Purser."

The Third hesitated and then raised the book from his lap. It was the *Space Code* and expanded *Rules of the Road*. Every licensed officer has to bone up on it a lot, to get his license. But it's not the kind of book you ordinarily kill time with.

"The Third here was showing me all about what a captain can and can't do," said Mr. Costello.

"Well, you asked me to," the Third said.

"Now just a minute," said Mr. Costello rapidly, "now just a minute." He had a way of doing that sometimes. It was a part of him, like the thinning hair on top of his head and the big smile and the way he had of cocking his head to one side and asking you what it was you just said, as if he didn't hear so well. "Now just a minute, you *wanted* to show me this material, didn't you?"

"Well, yes, Mr. Costello," the Third said.

"You're going over the limitations of a spacemaster's power of your own free will, aren't you?"

'Well," said the Third, "I guess so. Sure."

"Sure," Mr. Costello repeated happily. "Tell the Purser the part you just read me."

"The one you found in the book?"

"You know the one. You read it out your own self, didn't you?"

"Oh," said the Third. He looked at me—sort of uneasily, I thought—and reached for the book.

Mr. Costello put his hand on it. "Oh, don't bother looking it up," he said. "You can remember it."

"Yeah, I guess I do," the Third admitted. "It's a sort of safe-guard against letting the Skipper's power go to his head, in case it ever does. Suppose a time comes when a Captain begins to act up, and the crew gets the idea that a lunatic has taken over the bridge. Well, something has to be done about it. The crew has the power to appoint one officer and send him up to the Captain for an accounting. If the Skipper refuses, or if the crew doesn't' like his accounting, then they have the right to confine him to his quarters and take over the ship."

"I think I heard about that," I said. "But the Skipper has rights, too. I mean the crew has to report everything by space-radio the second it happens, and then the Captain has a full hear-ing along with the crew at the next port."

Mr. Costello looked at us and shook his big head, full of admiration. When Mr. Costello thought you were good, it made you feel good all over.

The Third looked at his watch and got up. "I got to relieve the bridge. Want to come along, Purser?"

"I'd like to talk to him for a while," Mr. Costello said. "Do you suppose you could get somebody else for a witness?"

"Oh, sure, if you say so," said the Third.

"But you're going to get someone."

"Absolutely," said the Third.

"Safest ship I was ever on," said Mr. Costello. "Gives a fellow a nice feeling to know that the watch is never going to get the orders wrong."

I thought so myself and wondered why we never used to do it before. I watched the Third leave and stayed where I was, feeling good, feeling safe, feeling glad that Mr. Costello wanted to talk to me. And me just a Purser, him an ex-Triumver.

Mr. Costello gave me the big smile. He nodded toward the door. "That young fellow's going far. A good man. You're all good men here." He stuck a sucker-cup in the heater and passed it over to me with his own hands. "Coffee," he said. "My own brand. All I ever use."

I tasted it and it was fine. He was a very generous man. He sat back and beamed at me while I drank it.

"What do you know about Borinquen?" he wanted to know.

I told him all I could. Borinquen's a pretty nice place, what they call "four-nines Earth Normal"—which means that the climate, gravity, atmosphere, and ecology come within .9999 of being the same as Earth's. There are only about six known planets like that. I told him about the one city it had and the trapping that used to be the main industry. Coats made of *glunker* fur last forever. They shine green in white light and real warm ember-red in blue light, and you can take a full-sized coat and scrunch it up and hide it in your two hands, it's that light and fine. Being so light, the fur made ideal space-cargo.

Of course, there was a lot more on Borinquen now—rare isotope ingots and foodstuffs and seeds for the drug business and all, and I suppose the *glunker* trade could dry right up and Borinquen could still carry its weight. But furs settled the planet, furs supported the city in the early days, and half the population still lived out in the bush and trapped.

Mr. Costello listened to everything I said in a way I can only call respectful.

I remember I finished up by saying, "I'm sorry you have to get off there, Mr. Costello. I'd like to see you some more. I'd like to come see you at Borinquen, whenever we put in, though I don't suppose a man like you would have much spare time."

He put his big hand on my arm. "Purser, if I don't have time when you're in port, I'll make time. Hear?" Oh, he had a wonderful way of making a fellow feel good.

Next thing you know, he invited me right into his cabin. He sat me down and handed me a sucker full of a mild red wine with a late flavor of cinnamon, which was a new one on me, and he showed me some of his things.

He was a great collector. He had one or two little bits of colored paper that he said were stamps they used before the Space Age, to prepay carrying charges on paper letters. He said no matter where he was, just one of those things could get him a fortune. Then he had some jewels, not rings or anything, just stones, and a fine story for every single one of them.

"What you're holding in your hand," he said, "cost the life of a king and the loss of an empire half again as big as United Earth." And: "This one was once so well guarded that most people didn't know whether it existed or not. There was a whole religion based on it—and now it's gone, and so is the religion."

It gave you a queer feeling, being next to this man who had so much, and him just as warm and friendly as your favorite uncle.

"If you can assure me these bulkheads are soundproof, I'll show you something else I collect," he said.

I assured him they were, and they were, too. "If ships' architects ever learned anything," I told him, "they learned that a man has just got to be by himself once in a while."

He cocked his head to one side in a way that he had. "How's that again?"

"A man's just got to be by himself once in a while," I said. "So, mass or no, cost or no, a ship's bulkheads are built to give a man his privacy."

"Good," he said. "Now let me show you." He unlocked a hand case and opened it, and from a little compartment inside he took out a thing about the size of the box a watch comes in. He handled it very gently as he put it down on his desk. It was square, and it had a fine grille on the top and two little silver studs on the side. He pressed one of them and turned to me, smiling. And let me tell you, I almost fell right off the bunk where I was sitting, because here was the Captain's voice as loud and clear and natural as if he was right there in the room with us. And do you know what he said?

He said, "My crew questions my sanity—yet you can be sure that if a single man aboard questions my authority, he will learn that I am master here, even if he must learn it at the point of a gun."

What surprised me so much wasn't only the voice but the words—and what surprised me especially about the words was that I had heard the Skipper say them myself. It was the time he had had the argument with Mr. Costello. I remembered it well because I had walked into the dayroom just as the Captain started to yell.

"Mr. Costello," he said in that big heavy voice of his, "in spite of your conviction that my crew questions my sanity . . ." and all the rest of it, just like on this recording Mr. Costello had. And I remember he said, too, "Even if he must learn it at the point of a gun. *That, sir, applies to passengers—the crew has legal means of their own.*"

I was going to mention this to Mr. Costello, but before I could open my mouth, he asked me, "Now tell me, Purser, is that the voice of the Captain of your ship?"

And I said, "Well, if it isn't, I'm not the Purser here. Why, I heard him speak those words my very own self."

Mr. Costello swatted me on the shoulder. "You have a good ear, Purser. And how do you like my little toy?"

Then he showed it to me, a little mechanism on the jeweled pin he wore on his tunic, a fine thread of wire to a pushbutton in his side pocket.

"One of my favorite collections," he told me. "Voices. Anybody, anytime, anywhere." He took off the pin and slipped a tiny bead out of the setting. He slipped this into a groove in the box and pressed the stud.

And I heard my own voice say, "I'm sorry you have to get off there, Mr. Costello. I'd like to see you some more." I laughed and laughed. That was one of the cleverest things I ever saw. And just think of my voice in his collection, along with the Captain and space only knows how many great and famous people!

He even had the voice of the Third Officer, from just a few minutes before, saying, "A lunatic has taken over the bridge. Well, something has to be done about it."

All in all, I had a wonderful visit with him, and then he asked me to do whatever I had to do about his clearance papers. So I went back to my office and got them out. They are kept in the Purser's safe during a voyage. And I went through them with the okays. There were a lot of them—he had more than most people.

I found one from Earth Central that sort of made me mad. I guess it was a mistake. It was a *Know All Ye* that warned consular officials to report every six months, Earth time, on the activities of Mr. Costello.

I took it to him, and it was a mistake, all right—he said so himself. I tore it out of his passport book and adhesed an official note, reporting the accidental destruction of a used page of fully stamped visas. He gave me a beautiful blue gemstone for doing it.

When I said, "I better not; I don't want you thinking I take bribes from passengers," he laughed and put one of those beads in his recorder, and it came out, in my voice, "I take bribes from passengers." He was a great joker.

We lay at Borinquen for four days. Nothing much happened except I was busy. That's what's tough about pursering. You got nothing to do for weeks in space, and then, when you're in spaceport, you have too much work to do even to go ashore much, unless it's a long layover.

I never really minded much. I'm one of those mathematical geniuses, you know, even if I don't have too much sense otherwise, and I take pride in my work. Everybody has something he's good at, I guess. I couldn't tell you how the gimmick works that makes the ship travel faster than light, but I'd hate to trust the Chief Engineer with one of my interplanetary cargo manifests, or a rate-of-exchange table, *glunker* pelts to U.E. dollars.

Some hard-jawed character with Space Navy Investigator credentials came inboard with a portable voice recorder and made me and the Third Officer recite a lot of nonsense for some sort of test, I don't know what. The SNI is always doing a lot of useless and mysterious things. I had an argument with the Port Agent, and I went ashore with Cooky for a fast drink. The usual thing.

Then I had to work overtime signing on a new Third—they transferred the old one to a corvette that was due in, they told me.

Oh, yes, that was the trip the Skipper resigned. I guess it was high time. He'd been acting very nervous. He gave me the damnedest look when he went ashore that last time, like he didn't know whether to kill me or burst into tears. There was a rumor around that he'd gone berserk and threatened the crew with a gun, but I don't listen to rumors. And anyway, the Port Captain signs on new skippers. It didn't mean any extra work for me, so it didn't matter much.

We upshipped again and made the rounds. Boötes Sigma and Nightingale and Caranho and Earth—chemical glassware, blackprints, *sho* seed and glitter crystals; perfume, music tape, *glizzard* skins and Aldebar—all the usual junk for all the usual months. And round we came again to Borinquen.

Well, you wouldn't believe a place could change so much in so short a time. Borinquen used to be a pretty free-and-easy planet. There was just the one good-sized city, see, and then trapper camps all through the unsettled area. If you liked people, you settled in the city, and you could go to work in the processing plants or maintenance or some such. If you didn't, you could trap *glunkers*. There was always something for everybody on Borinquen.

But things were way different this trip. First of all, a man with a Planetary Government badge came aboard, by God, to censor the music tapes consigned for the city, and he had the credentials for it, too. Next thing I find out, the municipal authorities have confiscated the warehouses—*my* warehouses—and they were being converted into barracks.

And where were the goods—the pelts and ingots for export? Where was the space for our cargo? Why, in houses—in hundreds of houses, all spread around every which way, all indexed up with a whole big new office full of conscripts and volunteers to mix up and keep mixed up! For the first time since I went to space, I had to request layover so I could get things unwound.

Anyway it gave me a chance to wander around the town, which I don't often get.

You should have seen the place! Everybody seemed to be moving out of the houses. All the big buildings were being made over into hollow shells, filled with rows and rows of mattresses.

There were banners strung across the streets: ARE YOU A MAN OR ARE YOU ALONE? A SINGLE SHINGLE IS A SORRY SHELTER! THE DEVIL HATES A CROWD!

All of which meant nothing to me. But it wasn't until I noticed a sign painted in whitewash on the glass front of a barroom, saying—TRAPPERS STAY OUT!—that I was aware of one of the biggest changes of all.

There were no trappers on the streets—none at all. They used to be one of the tourist attractions of Borinquen, dressed in *glunker* fur, with the long tailwings afloat in the wind of their walking, and a kind of distance in their eyes that not even spacemen had. As soon as I missed them, I began to see the TRAPPERS STAY OUT! signs just about everywhere—on the stores, the restaurants, the hotels and theaters.

I stood on a street corner, looking around me and wondering what in hell was going on here, when a Borinquen cop yelled something at me from a monowheel prowl car. I didn't understand him, so I just shrugged. He made a U-turn and coasted up to me.

"What's the matter, country boy? Lose your traps?"

I said, "What?"

He said, "If you want to go it alone, *glunker*, we got solitary cells over at the Hall that'll suit you fine."

I just gawked at him. And, to my surprise, another cop poked his head up out of the prowler. A one-man prowler, mind. They were really jammed in there.

This second one said, "Where's your trapline, jerker?"

I said, "I don't have a trapline." I pointed to the mighty tower of my ship, looming over the spaceport. "I'm the Purser off that ship."

"Oh, for God's sakes!" said the first cop. "I might have known. Look, Spacer, you'd better double up or you're liable to get yourself mobbed. This is no spot for a soloist."

"I don't get you, Officer. I was just—"

"I'll take him," said someone. I looked around and saw a tall Borinqueña standing just inside the open doorway of one of the hundreds of empty houses. She said, "I came back here to pick up some of my things. When I got done in here, there was nobody on the sidewalks. I've been here an hour, waiting for somebody to go with." She sounded a little hysterical.

"You know better than to go in there by yourself," said one of the cops.

"I know—I know. It was just to get my things. I wasn't going to stay." She hauled up a duffelbag and dangled it in front of her. "Just to get my things," she said again, frightened.

The cops looked at each other. "Well, all right. But watch yourself. You go along with the Purser here. Better straighten him out—he don't seem to know what's right."

"I will," she said thankfully.

But by then the prowler had moaned off, weaving a little under its double load.

I looked at her. She wasn't pretty. She was sort of heavy and stupid.

She said, "You'll be all right now. Let's go."

"Where?"

"Well, Central Barracks, I guess. That's where most everybody is."

"I have to get back to the ship."

"Oh, dear," she said, all distressed again. "Right away?"

"No, not right away. I'll go in town with you, if you want." She picked up her duffelbag, but I took it from her and heaved it up on my shoulder. "Is everybody here crazy?" I asked her, scowling.

"Crazy?" She began walking, and I went along. "I don't *think* so."

"All this," I persisted. I pointed to a banner that said, NO LADDER HAS A SINGLE RUNG. "What's that mean?"

"Just what it says."

"You have to put up a big thing like that just to tell me . . ."

"Oh," she said. "You mean what does it *mean!*" She looked at me strangely. "We've found out a new truth about humanity. Look, I'll try to tell it to you the way the Lucilles said it last night."

"Who's Lucille?"

"*The* Lucilles," she said, in a mildly shocked tone. "Actually, I suppose there's really only one—though, of course, there'll be someone else in the studio at the time," she added quickly. "But on trideo it looks like four Lucilles, all speaking at once, sort of in chorus."

"You just go on talking," I said when she paused. "I catch on slowly."

"Well, here's what they say. They say no one human being ever did *anything*. They say it takes a hundred pairs of hands to build a house, ten thousand pairs to build a ship. They say a single pair is not only useless—it's *evil*. All humanity is a thing made up of many parts. No part is good by itself. Any part that wants to go off by itself hurts the whole main thing—the thing that has become so great. So we're seeing to it that no part ever gets separated. What good would your hand be if a finger suddenly decided to go off by itself?"

I said, "And you believe this—what's your name?"

"Nola. *Believe* it? Well, it's true, isn't it? Can't you see it's true? Everybody *knows* it's true."

"Well, it *could* be true," I said reluctantly. "What do you do with people who want to be by themselves?"

"We help them."

"Suppose they don't want help?"

"Then they're trappers," she said immediately. "We push them back into the bush, where the evil soloists come from."

"Well, what about the fur?"

"*No*body uses furs any more!"

So that's what happened to our fur consignments! And I was thinking those amateur red-tapers had just lost 'em somewhere.

She said, as if to herself, "All sin starts in the lonesome dark," and when I looked up, I saw she'd read it approvingly off another banner.

We rounded a corner and I blinked at a blaze of light. It was one of the warehouses.

"There's the Central," she said. "Would you like to see it?"

"I guess so."

I followed her down the street to the entrance. There was a man sitting at a table in the doorway. Nola gave him a card. He checked it against a list and handed it back.

"A visitor," she said. "From the ship."

I showed him my Purser's card and he said, "Okay. But if you want to stay, you'll have to register."

"I won't want to stay," I told him. "I have to get back."

I followed Nola inside.

The place had been scraped out to the absolute maximum. Take away one splinter of vertical structure more and it wouldn't have held a roof. There wasn't a concealed corner, a shelf, a drape, an overhang. There must have been two thousand beds, cots and mattresses spread out, cheek by jowl, over the entire floor, in blocks of four, with only a hand's-breadth between them.

The light was blinding—huge floods and spots bathed every square inch in yellow-white fire.

Nola said, "You'll get used to the light. After a few nights you don't even notice it."

"The lights never get turned off?"

"Oh, dear, no!"

Then I saw the plumbing—showers, tubs, sinks and everything else. It was all lined up against one wall.

Nola followed my eyes. "You get used to that, too. Better to have everything out in the open than to let the devil in for one secret second. That's what the Lucilles say."

I dropped her duffelbag and sat down on it. The only thing I could think of was, "Whose idea was all this? Where did it start?"

"The Lucilles," she said vaguely. Then, "Before them, I don't know. People just started to realize. Somebody bought a warehouse—no, it was a hangar—I don't know," she said again, apparently trying hard to remember. She sat down next to me and said in a subdued voice, "Actually, some people didn't take to it so well at first." She looked around. "*I* didn't. I mean it, I really didn't. But you believed, or you had to act as if you believed, and one way or another everybody just came to this." She waved her hand.

"What happened to the ones who wouldn't come to Centrals?"

"People made fun of them. They lost their jobs, the schools wouldn't take their children, the stores wouldn't honor their ration cards. Then the police started to pick up soloists—like they did you." She looked around again, a sort of contented familiarity in her gaze. "It didn't take long."

I turned away from her, but found myself staring at all that plumbing again. I jumped up. "I have to go, Nola. Thanks for your help. Hey—how do I get back to the ship, if the cops are out to pick up any soloist they see?"

"Oh, just tell the man at the gate. There'll be people waiting to go your way. There's always somebody waiting to go everywhere."

She came along with me. I spoke to the man at the gate, and she shook hands with me. I stood by the little table and watched her hesitate, then step up to a woman who was entering. They went in together. The doorman nudged me over toward a group of what appeared to be loungers.

"*North!*" he bawled.

I drew a pudgy little man with bad teeth, who said not one single word. We escorted each other two-thirds of the way to the spaceport, and he disappeared into a factory. I scuttled the rest of the way alone, feeling like a criminal, which I suppose I was. I swore I would never go into that crazy city again.

And the next morning, who should come out for me, in an armored car with six two-man prowlers as escort, but Mr. Costello himself!

It was pretty grand seeing him again. He was just like always, big and handsome and good-natured. He was not alone. All spread out in the back corner of the car was the most beautiful blonde woman that ever struck me speechless. She didn't say very much. She would just look at me every once in a while and sort of smile, and then she would look out of the car window and bite on her lower lip a little, and then look at Mr. Costello and not smile at all.

Mr. Costello hadn't forgotten me. He had a bottle of that same red cinnamon wine, and he talked over old times the same as ever, like he was a special uncle. We got a sort of guided tour. I told him about last night, about the visit to the Central, and he was pleased as could be. He said he knew I'd like it. I didn't stop to think whether I liked it or not.

"Think of it!" he said, "All humankind, a single unit. You know the principle of cooperation, Purser?"

When I took too long to think it out, he said, "You know. Two men working together can produce more than two men working separately. Well, what happens when a thousand—a million—work, sleep, eat, think, breathe together?" The way he said it, it sounded fine.

He looked out past my shoulder and his eyes widened just a

little. He pressed a button and the chauffeur brought us to a sliding stop.

"Get that one," Mr. Costello said into a microphone beside him.

Two of the prowlers hurtled down the street and flanked a man. He dodged right, dodged left, and then a prowler hit him and knocked him down.

"Poor chap," said Mr. Costello, pushing the *Go* button. "Some of 'em just won't learn."

I think he regretted it very much. I don't know if the blonde woman did. She didn't even look.

"Are you the mayor?" I asked him.

"Oh, no," he said. "I'm a sort of broker. A little of this, a little of that. I'm able to help out a bit."

"Help out?"

"Purser," he said confidentially, "I'm a citizen of Borinquen now. This is my adopted land and I love it. I mean to do everything in my power to help it. I don't care about the cost. This is a people that has found the *truth*, Purser. It awes me. It makes me humble."

"I . . ."

"Speak up, man. I'm your *friend*."

"I appreciate that, Mr. Costello. Well, what I was going to say, I saw that Central and all. I just haven't made up my mind. I mean whether it's good or not."

"Take your time, take your time," he said in the big soft voice. "Nobody has to *make* a man see a truth, am I right? A real truth? A man just sees it all by himself."

"Yeah," I agreed. "Yeah, I guess so." Sometimes it was hard to find an answer to give Mr. Costello.

The car pulled up beside a building. The blonde woman pulled herself together. Mr. Costello opened the door for her with his own hands. She got out. Mr. Costello rapped the trideo screen in front of him.

He said, "Make it a real good one, Lucille, real good. I'll be watching."

She looked at him. She gave me a small smile. A man came down the steps and she went with him up into the building.

We moved off.

I said, "She's the prettiest woman I ever saw."

He said, "She likes you fine, Purser."

I thought about that. It was too much.

He asked, "How would you like to have her for your very own?"

"Oh," I said, "she wouldn't."

"Purser, I owe you a big favor. I'd like to pay it back."

"You don't owe me a thing, Mr. Costello!"

We drank some of the wine. The big car slid silently along. It went slowly now, headed back out to the spaceport.

"I need some help," he said after a time. "I know you, Purser. You're just the kind of man I can use. They say you're a mathematical genius."

"Not mathematics exactly, Mr. Costello. Just numbers—statistics—conversion tables and like that. I couldn't do astrogation or theoretical physics and such. I got the best job I could have right now."

"No, you haven't. I'll be frank with you. I don't want any more responsibility on Borinquen than I've got, you understand, but the people are forcing it on me. They want order, peace and order—tidiness. They want to be as nice and tidy as one of your multiple manifests. Now I could organize them, all right, but I need a tidy brain like yours to keep them organized. I want full birth- and death-rate statistics, and then I want them projected so we can get policy. I want calorie-counts and rationing, so we can use the food supply the best way. I want—well, you see what I mean. Once the devil is routed—"

"What devil?"

"The trappers," he said grayly.

"Are the trappers really harming the city people?"

He looked at me, shocked. "They go out and spend weeks alone by themselves, with their own evil thoughts. They are wandering cells, wild cells in the body of humanity. They must be destroyed."

I couldn't help but think of my consignments. "What about the fur trade, though?"

He looked at me as if I had made a pretty grubby little mistake. "My dear Purser," he said patiently, "would you set the price of a few pelts above the immortal soul of a race?"

I hadn't thought of it that way.

He said urgently, "This is just the beginning, Purser. Borinquen is only a start. The unity of that great being, Humanity, will become known throughout the Universe." He closed his eyes. When he opened them, the organ tone was gone. He said in his old, friendly voice, "And you and I, we'll show 'em how to do it, hey, boy?"

I leaned forward to look up to the top of the shining spire of the spaceship. "I sort of like the job I've got. But—my contract *is* up four months from now . . ."

The car turned into the spaceport and hummed across the slag area.

"I think I can count on you," he said vibrantly. He laughed. "Remember this little joke, Purser?"

He clicked a switch, and suddenly my own voice filled the tonneau. "*I take bribes from passengers.*"

"Oh that," I said, and let loose one *ha* of a *ha-ha* before I understood what he was driving at. "Mr. Costello, you wouldn't use that against me."

"What do you take me for?" he demanded, in wonderment.

Then we were at the ramp. He got out with me. He gave me his hand. It was warm and hearty.

"If you change your mind about the Purser's job when your contract's up, son, just buzz me through the field phone. They'll connect me. Think it over until you get back here. Take your time." His hand clamped down on my biceps so hard I winced. "But you're not going to take any longer than that, are you, my boy?"

"I guess not," I said.

He got into the front, by the chauffeur, and zoomed away.

I stood looking after him and, when the car was just a dark spot on the slag area, I sort of came to myself. I was standing alone on the foot of the ramp. I felt very exposed.

I turned and ran up to the airlock, hurrying, hurrying to get near people.

That was the trip we shipped the crazy man. His name was Hynes. He was United Earth Consul at Borinquen and he was going back to report. He was no trouble at first, because diplomatic passports are easy to process. He knocked on my door the fifth watch out from Borinquen. I was glad to see him. My room was making me uneasy and I appreciated his company.

Not that he was really company. He was crazy. That first time, he came busting in and said, "I hope you don't mind, Purser, but if I don't talk to somebody about this, I'll go out of my mind." Then he sat down on the end of my bunk and put his head in his hands and rocked back and forth for a long time, without saying anything. Next thing he said was, "Sorry," and out he went. Crazy, I tell you.

But he was back in again before long. And then you never heard such ravings.

"Do you know what's happened to Borinquen?" he'd demand. But he didn't want any answers. He had the answers. "I'll tell you what's wrong with Borinquen—Borinquen's gone mad!" he'd say.

I went on with my work, though there wasn't much of it in space, but that Hynes just couldn't get Borinquen out of his mind.

He said, "You wouldn't believe it if you hadn't seen it done. First the little wedge, driven in the one place it might exist—between the urbans and the trappers. There was never any conflict between them—never! All of a sudden, the trapper was a menace. How it happened, why, God only knows. First, these laughable attempts to show that they were an unhealthy influence. Yes, laughable—how could you take it seriously?

"And then the changes. You didn't have to prove that a trapper had done anything. You only had to prove he was a trapper. That was enough. And the next thing—how could you *anticipate* anything as mad as this?" —he almost screamed—"the next thing was to take anyone who wanted to be alone and lump him with the trappers. It all happened so fast—it happened in our sleep. And all of a sudden you were afraid to be alone in a room for a *second*. They left their homes. They built barracks. Everyone afraid of everyone else, afraid, afraid . . .

"Do you know what they *did*?" he roared. "They burned the paintings, every painting on Borinquen they could find that had been done by one artist. And the few artists who survived as artists—I've seen them. By twos and threes, they work together on the one canvas."

He cried. He actually sat there and cried.

He said, "There's food in the stores. The crops come in. Trucks run, planes fly, the schools are in session. Bellies get full, cars get washed, people get rich. I know a man called Costello, just in from Earth a few months, maybe a year or so, and already owns half the city."

"Oh, I know Mr. Costello," I said.

"Do you now! How's that?"

I told him about the trip out with Mr. Costello. He sort of backed off from me. "*You're* the one!"

"The one what?" I asked in puzzlement.

"*You're* the man who testified against your Captain, broke him, made him resign."

"I did no such a thing."

"I'm the Consul. It was my hearing, man! I was *there!* A recording of the Captain's voice, admitting to insanity, declaring he'd take a gun to his crew if they overrode him. Then your recorded testimony that it was his voice, that you were present when he made the statement. And the Third Officer's recorded statement that all was not well on the bridge. The man denied it, but it was his voice."

"Wait, wait," I said. "I don't believe it. That would need a trial. There was no trial. I wasn't called to any trial."

"There would have been a trial, you idiot! But the Captain started raving about draw poker without a draw, about the crew fearing poisoning from the cook, about the men wanting witnesses even to change the bridge-watch. Maddest thing I ever heard. He realized it suddenly, the Captain did. He was old, sick, tired, beaten. He blamed the whole thing on Costello, and Costello said he got the recordings from you."

"Mr. Costello wouldn't do such a thing!" I guess I got mad at Mr. Hynes then. I told him a whole lot about Mr. Costello, what a big man he was. He started to tell me how Mr. Costello was forced off the Triumverate for making trouble in the high court, but they were lies and I wouldn't listen. I told him about the poker, how Mr. Costello saved us from the cheaters, how he saved us from poisoning, how he made the ship safe for us all.

I remember how he looked at me then. He sort of whispered, "What has happened to human beings? What have we done to

ourselves with these centuries of peace, with confidence and cooperation and no conflict? Here's distrust by man for man, waiting
under a thin skin to be punctured by just the right vampire, waiting to hate itself and kill itself all over again . . .

"My *God!*" he suddenly screamed at me. "Do you know what
I've been hanging onto? The idea that, for all its error, for all its
stupidity, this One Humanity idea on Borinquen was a *principle*? I
hated it, but because it was a principle, I could respect it. It's
Costello—Costello, who doesn't gamble, but who uses fear to
change the poker rules—Costello, who doesn't eat your food, but
makes you fear poison—Costello, who can see three hundred
years of safe interstellar flight, but who through fear makes the
watch officers doubt themselves without a witness—Costello, who
runs things without being seen!

"My God, Costello doesn't *care!* It isn't a principle at all. It's
just Costello spreading fear anywhere, everywhere, to make himself strong!"

He rushed out, crying with rage and hate. I have to admit I
was sort of jolted. I guess I might even have thought about the
things he said, only he killed himself before we reached Earth. He
was crazy.

We made the rounds, same as ever, scheduled like an interurban
line: Load, discharge, blastoff, fly, and planetfall. Refuel, clearance, manifest. Eat, sleep, work. There was a hearing about
Hynes. Mr. Costello sent a spacegram with his regrets when he
heard the news. I didn't say anything at the hearing, just that Mr.
Hynes was upset, that's all, and it was about as true as anything
could be. We shipped a second engineer who played real good
accordion. One of the inboard men got left on Caránho. All the
usual things, except I wrote up my termination with no options,
ready to file.

So in its turn we made Borinquen again, and what do you
know, there was the space fleet of United Earth. I never guessed
they had that many ships. They sheered us off, real Navy: all
orders and no information. Borinquen was buttoned up tight;
there was some kind of fighting going on down there. We couldn't
get or give a word of news through the quarantine. It made the

skipper mad and he had to use part of the cargo for fuel, which messed up my records six ways from the middle. I stashed my termination papers away for the time being.

And in its turn, Sigma, where we lay over a couple of days to get back in the rut, and, same as always, Nightingale, right on schedule again.

And who should be waiting for me at Nightingale, but Barney Roteel, who was medic on my first ship, years back when I was fresh from the Academy. He had a pot belly now and looked real successful. We got the jollity out of the way and he settled down and looked me over, real sober. I said it's a small Universe—I'd known he had a big job on Nightingale, but imagine him showing up at the spaceport just when I blew in!

"I showed up *because* you blew in, Purser," he answered.

Then before I could take that apart, he started asking me questions. Like how was I doing, what did I plan to do.

I said, "I've been a purser for years and years. What makes you think I want to do anything different?"

"Just wondered."

I wondered, too. "Well," I said, "I haven't exactly made up my mind, you might say—and a couple of things have got in the way—but I did have a kind of offer." I told him just in a general way about how big a man Mr. Costello was on Borinquen now, and how he wanted me to come in with him. "It'll have to wait, though. The whole damn Space Navy has a cordon around Borinquen. They wouldn't say why. But whatever it is, Mr. Costello'll come out on top. You'll see."

Barney gave me a sort of puckered-up look. I never saw a man look so weird. Yes, I did, too. It was the old Iron Man, the day he got off the ship and resigned.

"Barney, what's the matter?" I asked.

He got up and pointed through the glass door-lights to a white monowheel that stood poised in front of the receiving station. "Come on," he said.

"Aw, I can't. I got to—"

"Come *on!*"

I shrugged. Job or no, this was Barney's bailiwick, not mine. He'd cover me.

He held the door open and said, like a mind reader, "I'll cover you."

We went down the ramp and climbed in and skimmed off.

"Where are we going?"

But he wouldn't say. He just drove.

Nightingale's a beautiful place. The most beautiful of them all, I think, even Sigma. It's run by the U. E. one hundred per cent; this is one planet with no local options, but *none*. It's a regular garden of a world and they keep it that way.

We topped a rise and went down a curving road lined with honest-to-God Lombardy poplars from Earth. There was a little lake down there and a sandy beach. No people.

The road curved and there was a yellow line across it and then a red one, and after it a shimmering curtain, almost transparent. It extended from side to side as far as I could see.

"Force-fence," Barney said and pressed a button on the dash.

The shimmer disappeared from the road ahead, though it stayed where it was at each side. We drove through it and it formed behind us, and we went down the hill to the lake.

Just this side of the beach was the coziest little Sigma cabana I've seen yet, built to hug the slope and open its arms to the sky. Maybe when I get old they'll turn me out to pasture in one half as good.

While I was goggling at it, Barney said, "Go on."

I looked at him and he was pointing. There was a man down near the water, big, very tanned, built like a spacetug. Barney waved me on and I walked down there.

The man got up and turned to me. He had the same wide-spaced, warm deep eyes, the same full, gentle voice. "Why, it's the Purser! Hi, old friend. So you came, after all!"

It was sort of rough for a moment. Then I got it out. "Hi, Mr. Costello."

He banged me on the shoulder. Then he wrapped one big hand around my left biceps and pulled me a little closer. He looked uphill to where Barney leaned against the monowheel, minding his own business. Then he looked across the lake, and up in the sky.

He dropped his voice. "Purser, you're just the man I need. But I told you that before, didn't I?" He looked around again. "We'll do it yet, Purser. You and me, we'll hit the top. Come with me. I want to show you something."

He walked ahead of me toward the beach margin. He was wearing only a breech-ribbon, but he moved and spoke as if he still had the armored car and the six prowlers. I stumbled after him.

He put a hand behind him and checked me, and then knelt. He said, "To look at them, you'd think they were all the same, wouldn't you? Well, son, you just let me show you something."

I looked down. He had an anthill. They weren't like Earth ants. These were bigger, slower, blue, and they had eight legs. They built nests of sand tied together with mucus, and tunneled under them so that the nests stood up an inch or two like on little pillars.

"They look the same, they act the same, but you'll see," said Mr. Costello.

He opened a synthine pouch that lay in the sand. He took out a dead bird and the thorax of what looked like a Caránho roach, the one that grows as long as your forearm. He put the bird down here and the roach down yonder.

"Now," he said, "watch."

The ants swarmed to the bird, pulling and crawling. Busy. But one or two went to the roach and tumbled it and burrowed around. Mr. Costello picked an ant off the roach and dropped it on the bird. It weaved around and shouldered through the others and scrabbled across the sand and went back to the roach.

"You see, you *see?*" he said, enthusiastic. "Look."

He picked an ant off the dead bird and dropped it by the roach. The ant wasted no time or even curiosity on the piece of roach. It turned around once to get its bearings, and then went straight back to the dead bird.

I looked at the bird with its clothing of crawling blue, and I looked at the roach with its two or three voracious scavengers. I looked at Mr. Costello.

He said raptly, "See what I mean? About one in thirty eats something different. And that's all we need. I tell you, Purser, wherever you look, if you look long enough, you can find a way to make most of a group turn on the rest."

I watched the ants. "They're not fighting."

"Now wait a minute," he said swiftly. "Wait a minute. All we have to do is let these bird-eaters know that the roach-eaters are dangerous."

"They're not dangerous," I said. "They're just different."

"What's the difference, when you come right down to it? So we'll get the bird-eaters scared and they'll kill all the roach-eaters."

"Yes, but why, Mr. Costello?"

He laughed. "I like you, boy. I do the thinking, you do the work. I'll explain it to you. They all look alike. So once we've made 'em drive out these—" he pointed to the minority around the roach—"they'll never know which among 'em might be a roach-eater. They'll get so worried, they'll do anything to keep from being suspected of roach-eating. When they get scared enough, we can make 'em do anything we want."

He hunkered down to watch the ants. He picked up a roach-eater and put it on the bird. I got up.

"Well, I only just dropped in, Mr. Costello," I said.

"I'm not an ant," said Mr. Costello. "As long as it makes no difference to me what they eat, I can make 'em do anything in the world I want."

"I'll see you around," I said.

He kept on talking quietly to himself as I walked away. He was watching the ants, figuring, and paid no attention to me.

I went back to Barney. I asked, sort of choked, "What is he doing, Barney?"

"He's doing what he has to do," Barney said.

We went back to the monowheel and up the hill and through the force-gate. After a while, I asked, "How long will he be here?"

"As long as he wants to be." Barney was kind of short about it.

"Nobody wants to be locked up."

He had that odd look on his face again. "Nightingale's not a jail."

"He can't get out."

"Look chum, we could start him over. We could even make a purser out of him. But we stopped doing that kind of thing a long time ago. We let a man do what he wants to do."

"He never wanted to be boss over an anthill."

"He didn't?"

I guess I looked as if I didn't understand that, so he said, "All his life he's pretended he's a man and the rest of us are ants. Now it's come true for him. He won't run human anthills any more because he will never again get near one."

I looked through the windshield at the shining finger that was my distant ship. "What happened on Borinquen, Barney?"

"Some of his converts got loose around the System. That Humanity One idea had to be stopped." He drove a while, seeing badly out of a thinking face. "You won't take this hard, Purser, but you're a thick-witted ape. I can say that if no one else can."

"All right," I said. "Why?"

"We had to *smash* into Borinquen, which used to be so free and easy. We got into Costello's place. It was a regular fort. We got him and his files. We didn't get his girl. He killed her, but the files were enough."

After a time I said, "He was always a good friend to me."

"Was he?"

I didn't say anything. He wheeled up to the receiving station and stopped the machine.

He said, "He was all ready for you if you came to work for him. He had a voice recording of you large as life, saying 'Sometimes a man's just *got* to be by himself.' Once you went to work for him, all he needed to do to keep you in line was to threaten to put that on the air."

I opened the door. "What did you have to show him to me for?"

"Because we believe in letting a man do what he wants to do, as long as he doesn't hurt the rest of us. If you want to go back to the lake and work for Costello, for instance, I'll take you there."

I closed the door carefully and went up the ramp to the ship.

I did my work and when the time came, we blasted off. I was mad. I don't think it was about anything Barney told me. I wasn't especially mad about Mr. Costello or what happened to him, because Barney's the best Navy psych doc there is and Nightingale's the most beautiful hospital planet in the Universe.

What made me mad was the thought that never again would a man as big as Mr. Costello give that big, warm, soft, strong friendship to a lunkhead like me.

BIANCA'S HANDS

Bianca's mother was leading her when Ran saw her first. Bianca was squat and small, with dank hair and rotten teeth. Her mouth was crooked and it drooled. Either she was blind or she just didn't care about bumping into things. It didn't really matter because Bianca was an imbecile. Her hands . . .

They were lovely hands, graceful hands, hands as soft and smooth and white as snowflakes, hands whose color was lightly tinged with pink like the glow of Mars on snow. They lay on the counter side by side, looking at Ran. They lay there half closed and crouching, each pulsing with a movement like the panting of a field creature, and they looked. Not watched. Later, they watched him. Now they looked. They did, because Ran felt their united gaze, and his heart beat strongly.

Bianca's mother demanded cheese stridently. Ran brought it to her in his own time while she berated him. She was a bitter woman, as any woman has a right to be who is wife of no man and mother to a monster. Ran gave her the cheese and took her money and never noticed that it was not enough, because of Bianca's hands. When Bianca's mother tried to take one of the hands, it scuttled away from the unwanted touch. It did not lift from the counter, but ran on its fingertips to the edge and leaped into a fold

109

of Bianca's dress. The mother took the unresisting elbow and led Bianca out.

Ran stayed there at the counter unmoving, thinking of Bianca's hands. Ran was strong and bronze and not very clever. He had never been taught about beauty and strangeness, but he did not need that teaching. His shoulders were wide and his arms were heavy and thick, but he had great soft eyes and thick lashes. They curtained his eyes now. He was seeing Bianca's hands again dreamily. He found it hard to breathe . . .

Harding came back. Harding owned the store. He was a large man whose features barely kept his cheeks apart. He said, "Sweep up, Ran. We're closing early today." Then he went behind the counter, squeezing past Ran.

Ran got the broom and swept slowly.

"A woman bought cheese," he said suddenly. "A poor woman, with very old clothes. She was leading a girl. I can't remember what the girl looked like, except—who was she?"

"I saw them go out," said Harding. "The woman is Bianca's mother, and the girl is Bianca. I don't know their other name. They don't talk to people much. I wish they wouldn't come in here. Hurry up, Ran."

Ran did what was necessary and put away his broom. Before he left he asked, "Where do they live, Bianca and her mother?"

"On the other side. A house on no road, away from people. Good night, Ran."

Ran went from the shop directly over to the other side, not waiting for his supper. He found the house easily, for it was indeed away from the road, and stood rudely by itself. The townspeople had cauterized the house by wrapping it in empty fields.

Harshly, "What do you want?" Bianca's mother asked as she opened the door.

"May I come in?"

"What do you want?"

"May I come in?" he asked again. She made as if to slam the door, and then stood aside. "Come."

Ran went in and stood still. Bianca's mother crossed the room and sat under an old lamp, in the shadow. Ran sat opposite her, on a three-legged stool. Bianca was not in the room.

The woman tried to speak, but embarrassment clutched at her voice. She withdrew into her bitterness, saying nothing. She kept peeping at Ran, who sat quietly with his arms folded and the uncertain light in his eyes. He knew she would speak soon, and he could wait.

"Ah, well . . ." She was silent after that, for a time, but now she had forgiven him his intrusion. Then, "It's a great while since anyone came to see me; a great while . . . it was different before. I was a pretty girl—"

She bit her words off and her face popped out of the shadows, shriveled and sagging as she leaned forward. Ran saw that she was beaten and cowed and did not want to be laughed at.

"Yes," he said gently. She sighed and leaned back so that her face disappeared again. She said nothing for a moment, sitting looking at Ran, liking him.

"We were happy, the two of us," she mused, "until Bianca came. He didn't like her, poor thing, he didn't, no more than I do now. He went away. I stayed by her because I was her mother. I'd go away myself, I would, but people know me, and I haven't a penny—not a penny . . . They'd bring me back to her, they would, to care for her. It doesn't matter much now, though, because people don't want me any more than they want her, they don't . . ."

Ran shifted his feet uneasily, because the woman was crying. "Have you room for me here?" he asked.

Her head crept out into the light. Ran said swiftly, "I'll give you money each week, and I'll bring my own bed and things." He was afraid she would refuse.

She merged with the shadows again. "If you like," she said, trembling at her good fortune. "Though why you'd want to . . . still, I guess if I had a little something to cook up nice, and a good reason for it, I could make someone real cozy here. But—*why?*" She rose. Ran crossed the room and pushed her back into the chair. He stood over her, tall.

"I never want you to ask me that," he said, speaking very slowly. "Hear?"

She swallowed and nodded. "I'll come back tomorrow with the bed and things," he said.

He left her there under the lamp, blinking out of the dimness, folded round and about with her misery and her wonder.

People talked about it. People said, "Ran has moved to the house of Bianca's mother." "It must be because—" "Ah," said some, "Ran was always a strange boy. It must be because—" "Oh, *no!*" cried others, appalled. "Ran is such a good boy. He wouldn't—"

Harding was told. He frightened the busy little woman who told him. He said, "Ran is very quiet, but he is honest and he does his work. As long as he comes here in the morning and earns his wage, he can do what he wants, where he wants, and it is not my business to stop him." He said this so very sharply that the little woman dared not say anything more.

Ran was very happy, living there. Saying little, he began to learn about Bianca's hands.

He watched Bianca being fed. Her hands would not feed her, the lovely aristocrats. Beautiful parasites they were, taking their animal life from the heavy squat body that carried them, and giving nothing in return. They would lie one on each side of her plate, pulsing while Bianca's mother put food into the disinterested drooling mouth. They were shy, those hands, of Ran's bewitched gaze. Caught out there naked in the light and open on the table-top, they would creep to the edge and drop out of sight—all but four rosy fingertips clutching the cloth.

They never lifted from a surface. When Bianca walked, her hands did not swing free, but twisted in the fabric of her dress. And when she approached a table or the mantelpiece and stood, her hands would run lightly up and leap, landing together, resting silently, watchfully, with that pulsing peculiar to them.

They cared for each other. They would not touch Bianca herself, but each hand groomed the other. It was the only labor to which they would bend themselves.

Three evenings after he came, Ran tried to take one of the hands in his. Bianca was alone in the room, and Ran went to her and sat beside her. She did not move, nor did her hands. They rested on a small table before her, preening themselves. This, then, was when they really began watching him. He felt it, right down to the depths of his enchanted heart. The hands kept stroking each other, and yet they knew he was there, they knew of his desire. They stretched themselves before him, archly, languorously, and his blood pounded hot. Before he could stay himself he reached and tried to grasp them. He was strong, and his move was sudden and clumsy. One of the hands seemed to disappear, so swiftly did it drop into Bianca's lap. But the other—

Ran's thick fingers closed on it and held it captive. It writhed, all but tore itself free. It took no power from the arm on which it lived, for Bianca's arms were flabby and weak. Its strength, like its beauty, was intrinsic, and it was only by shifting his grip to the puffy forearm that Ran succeeded in capturing it. So intent was he on touching it, holding it, that he did not see the other hand leap from the idiot girl's lap, land crouching at the table's edge. It reared back, fingers curling spiderlike, and sprang at him, fastening on his wrist. It clamped down agonizingly, and Ran felt bones give and crackle. With a cry he released the girl's arm. Her hands fell together and ran over each other, feeling for any small scratch, any tiny damage he might have done them in his passion. And as he sat there clutching his wrist, he saw the hands run to the far side of the little table, hook themselves over the edge and, contracting, draw her out of her place. She had no volition of her own—ah, but her hands had! Creeping over the walls, catching obscure and precarious holds in the wainscoting, they dragged the girl from the room.

And Ran sat there and sobbed, not so much from the pain in his swelling arm, but in shame for what he had done. They might have been won to him in another, gentler way . . .

His head was bowed, yet suddenly he felt the gaze of those hands. He looked up swiftly enough to see one of them whisk round the doorpost. It had come back, then, to see . . . Ran rose heavily and took himself and his shame away. Yet he was compelled to stop in the doorway, even as had Bianca's hands. He watched covertly and saw them come into the room dragging the unprotesting idiot girl. They brought her to the long bench where Ran had sat with her. They pushed her onto it, flung themselves to the table, and began rolling and flattening themselves most curiously about. Ran suddenly realized that there was something of his there, and he was comforted, a little. They were rejoicing, drinking thirstily, reveling in his tears.

Afterwards for nineteen days, the hands made Ran do penance. He knew them as inviolate and unforgiving; they would not show themselves to him, remaining always hidden in Bianca's dress or under the supper table. For those nineteen days Ran's passion and desire grew. More—his love became true love, for only true love knows reverence—and the possession of the hands became his reason for living, his goal in the life which that reason had given him.

Ultimately they forgave him. They kissed him coyly when he was not looking, touched him on the wrist, caught and held him for one sweet moment. It was at table . . . a great power surged through him, and he gazed down at the hands, now returned to Bianca's lap. A strong muscle in his jaw twitched and twitched, swelled and fell. Happiness like a golden light flooded him; passion spurred him, love imprisoned him, reverence was the gold of the golden light. The room wheeled and whirled about him and forces unimaginable flickered through him. Battling with himself, yet lax in the glory of it, Ran sat unmoving, beyond the world, enslaved and yet possessor of all. Bianca's hands flushed pink, and if ever hands smiled to each other, then they did.

He rose abruptly, flinging his chair from him, feeling the strength of his back and shoulders. Bianca's mother, by now beyond surprise, looked at him and away. There was that in his eyes which she did not like, for to fathom it would disturb her, and she wanted no trouble. Ran strode from the room and outdoors, to be by himself that he might learn more of this new thing that had possessed him.

It was evening. The crooked-bending skyline drank the buoyancy of the sun, dragged it down, sucking greedily. Ran stood on a knoll, his nostrils flaring, feeling the depth of his lungs. He sucked in the crisp air and it smelled new to him, as though the sunset shades were truly in it. He knotted the muscles of his thighs and stared at his smooth, solid fists. He raised his hands high over his head and, stretching, sent out such a great shout that the sun sank. He watched it, knowing how great and tall he was, how strong he was, knowing the meaning of longing and belonging. And then he lay down on the clean earth and he wept.

When the sky grew cold enough for the moon to follow the sun beyond the hills, and still an hour after that, Ran returned to the house. He struck a light in the room of Bianca's mother, where she slept on a pile of old cloths. Ran sat beside her and let the light wake her. She rolled over to him and moaned, opened her eyes and shrank from him. "Ran . . . what do you want?"

"Bianca. I want to marry Bianca."

Her breath hissed between her gums. "No!" It was not a refusal, but astonishment. Ran touched her arm impatiently. Then she laughed.

"To—marry—Bianca. It's late, boy. Go back to bed, and in the morning you'll have forgotten this thing, this dream."

"I've not been to bed," he said patiently, but growing angry. "Will you give me Bianca, or not?"

She sat up and rested her chin on her withered knees. "You're right to ask me, for I'm her mother. Still and all—Ran, you've been good to us, Bianca and me. You're—you are a good boy but—forgive me, lad, but you're something of a fool. Bianca's a monster. I say it though I am what I am to her. Do what you like, and never a word will I say. You should have known. I'm sorry you asked me, for you have given me the memory of speaking so to you. I don't understand you; but do what you like, boy."

It was to have been a glance, but it became a stare as she saw his face. He put his hands carefully behind his back, and she knew he would have killed her else.

"I'll—marry her, then?" he whispered.

She nodded, terrified. "As you like, boy."

He blew out the light and left her.

Ran worked hard and saved his wage, and made one room beautiful for Bianca and himself. He built a soft chair, and a table that was like an altar for Bianca's sacred hands. There was a great bed, and heavy cloth to hide and soften the walls, and a rug.

They were married, though marrying took time. Ran had to go far afield before he could find one who would do what was necessary. The man came far and went again afterwards, so that none knew of it, and Ran and his wife were left alone. The mother spoke for Bianca, and Bianca's hand trembled frighteningly at the touch of the ring, writhed and struggled and then lay passive, blushing and beautiful. But it was done. Bianca's mother did not protest, for she didn't dare. Ran was happy, and Bianca—well, nobody cared about Bianca.

After they were married Bianca followed Ran and his two

brides into the beautiful room. He washed Bianca and used rich lotions. He washed and combed her hair, and brushed it many times until it shone, to make her more fit to be with the hands he had married. He never touched the hands, though he gave them soaps and creams and tools with which they could groom themselves. They were pleased. Once one of them ran up his coat and touched his cheek and made him exultant.

He left them and returned to the shop with his heart full of music. He worked harder than ever, so that Harding was pleased and let him go home early. He wandered the hours away by the bank of a brook, watching the sun on the face of the chuckling water. A bird came to circle him, flew unafraid through the aura of gladness about him. The delicate tip of a wing brushed his wrist with the touch of the first secret kiss from the hands of Bianca. The singing that filled him was part of the nature of laughing, the running of water, the sound of the wind in the reeds by the edge of the stream. He yearned for the hands, and he knew he could go now and clasp them and own them; instead he stretched out on the bank and lay smiling, all lost in the sweetness and poignance of waiting, denying desire. He laughed for pure joy in a world without hatred, held in the stainless palms of Bianca's hands.

As it grew dark he went home. All during that nuptial meal Bianca's hands twisted about one of his while he ate with the other, and Bianca's mother fed the girl. The fingers twined about each other and about his own, so that three hands seemed to be wrought of one flesh, to become a thing of lovely weight at his arm's end. When it was quite dark they went to the beautiful room and lay where he and the hands could watch, through the window, the clean, bright stars swim up out of the forest. The house and the room were dark and silent. Ran was so happy that he hardly dared to breathe.

A hand fluttered up over his hair, down his cheek, and crawled into the hollow of his throat. Its pulsing matched the beat of his heart. He opened his own hands wide and clenched his fingers, as though to catch and hold this moment.

Soon the other hand crept up and joined the first. For perhaps an hour they lay there passive with their coolness against Ran's warm neck. He felt them with his throat, each smooth convolution, each firm small expanse. He concentrated, with his mind and his heart on his throat, on each part of the hands that touched him, feeling with all his being first one touch and then another, though the contact was there unmoving. And he knew it would be soon now, soon.

As if at a command, he turned on his back and dug his head into the pillow. Staring up at the vague dark hangings on the wall, he began to realize what it was for which he had been working and dreaming so long. He put his head back yet farther and smiled, waiting. This would be possession, completion. He breathed deeply, twice, and the hands began to move.

The thumbs crossed over his throat and the fingertips settled one by one under his ears. For a long moment they lay there, gathering strength. Together, then, in perfect harmony, each cooperating with the other, they became rigid, rock-hard. Their touch was still light upon him, still light . . . no, now they were passing their rigidity to him, turning it to a contraction. They settled to it slowly, their pressure measured and equal. Ran lay silent. He could not breathe now, and did not want to. His great arms were crossed on his chest, his knotted fists under his armpits, his mind knowing a great peace. Soon, now . . .

Wave after wave of engulfing, glorious pain spread and receded. He saw color impossible, without light. He arched his back, up, up . . . the hands bore down with all their hidden strength, and Ran's body bent like a bow, resting on feet and shoulders. Up, up . . .

Something burst within him—his lungs, his heart—no matter. It was complete.

There was blood on the hands of Bianca's mother when they found her in the morning in the beautiful room, trying to soothe Ran's neck. They took Bianca away, and they buried Ran, but they hanged Bianca's mother because she tried to make them believe Bianca had done it, Bianca whose hands were quite dead, drooping like brown leaves from her wrists.

THE SKILLS OF XANADU

And the Sun went nova and humanity fragmented and fled; and such is the self-knowledge of humankind that it knew it must guard its past as it guarded its being, or it would cease to be human; and such was its pride in itself that it made of its traditions a ritual and a standard.

The great dream was that wherever humanity settled, fragment by fragment by fragment, however it lived, it would continue rather than begin again, so that all through the universe and the years, humans would be humans, speaking as humans, thinking as humans, aspiring and progressing as humans; and whenever human met human, no matter how different, how distant, he would come in peace, meet his own kind, speak his own tongue.

Humans, however, being humans—

Bril emerged near the pink star, disliking its light, and found the fourth planet. It hung waiting for him like an exotic fruit. (And was it ripe, and could he ripen it? And what if it were poison?) He left his machine in orbit and descended in a bubble. A young savage watched him come and waited by a waterfall.

"Earth was my mother," said Bril from the bubble. It was the formal greeting of all humankind, spoken in the Old Tongue.

"And my father," said the savage, in an atrocious accent.

Watchfully, Bril emerged from the bubble, but stood very close by it. He completed his part of the ritual. "I respect the disparity of our wants, as individuals, and greet you."

"I respect the identity of our needs, as humans, and greet you. I am Wonyne," said the youth, "son of Tanyne, of the Senate, and Nina. This place is Xanadu, the district, on Xanadu, the fourth planet."

"I am Bril of Kit Carson, second planet of the Sumner System, and a member of the Sole Authority," said the newcomer, adding, "and I come in peace."

He waited then, to see if the savage would discard any weapons he might have, according to historic protocol. Wonyne did not; he apparently had none. He wore only a cobwebby tunic and a broad belt made of flat, black, brilliantly polished stones and could hardly have concealed so much as a dart. Bril waited yet another moment, watching the untroubled face of the savage, to see if Wonyne suspected anything of the arsenal hidden in the sleek black uniform, the gleaming jackboots, the metal gauntlets.

Wonyne said only, "Then in peace, welcome." He smiled. "Come with me to Tanyne's house and mine, and be refreshed."

"You say Tanyne, your father, is a Senator? Is he active now? Could he help me to reach your center of government?"

The youth paused, his lips moving slightly, as if he were translating the dead language into another tongue. Then, "Yes. Oh, yes."

Bril flicked his left gauntlet with his right fingertips and the bubble sprang away and up, where at length it would join the ship until it was needed. Wonyne was not amazed—probably, thought Bril, because it was beyond his understanding.

Bril followed the youth up a winding path past a wonderland of flowering plants, most of them purple, some white, a few scarlet, and all jeweled by the waterfall. The higher reaches of the path were flanked by thick soft grass, red as they approached, pale pink as they passed.

Bril's narrow black eyes flickered everywhere, saw and recorded everything: the easy-breathing boy's spring up the slope ahead, and the constant shifts of color in his gossamer garment as the wind touched it; the high trees, some of which might conceal a man or a weapon; the rock outcroppings and what oxides they told of; the birds he could see and the birdsongs he heard which might be something else.

He was a man who missed only the obvious, and there is so little that is obvious.

Yet he was not prepared for the house; he and the boy were halfway across the parklike land which surrounded it before he recognized it as such.

It seemed to have no margins. It was here high and there only a place between flower beds; yonder a room became a terrace, and elsewhere a lawn was a carpet because there was a roof over it. The house was divided into areas rather than rooms, by open grilles and by arrangements of color. Nowhere was there a wall. There was nothing to hide behind and nothing that could be locked. All the land, all the sky, looked into and through the house, and the house was one great window on the world.

Seeing it, Bril felt a slight shift in his opinion of the natives. His feeling was still one of contempt, but now he added suspicion. A cardinal dictum on humans as he knew them was. *Every man has something to hide.* Seeing a mode of living like this did not make him change his dictum: he simply increased his watchfulness, asking: *How do they hide it?*

"Tan! Tan!" the boy was shouting. "I've brought a friend!"

A man and a woman strolled toward them from a garden. The man was huge, but otherwise so like the youth Wonyne that there could be no question of their relationship. Both had long, narrow, clear gray eyes set very wide apart, and red—almost orange—hair. The noses were strong and delicate at the same time, their mouths thin-lipped but wide and good-natured.

But the woman—

It was a long time before Bril could let himself look, let himself believe that there was such a woman. After his first glance, he made of her only a presence and fed himself small nibbles of belief in his eyes, in the fact that there could be hair like that, face, voice, body. She was dressed, like her husband and the boy, in the smoky kaleidoscope which resolved itself, when the wind permitted, into a black-belted tunic.

"He is Bril of Kit Carson in the Sumner System," babbled the boy, "and he's a member of the Sole Authority and it's the second planet and he knew the greeting and got it right. So did I," he added, laughing. "This is Tanyne, of the Senate, and my mother Nina."

"You are welcome, Bril of Kit Carson," she said to him; and unbelieving in this way that had come upon him, he took away his gaze and inclined his head.

"You must come in," said Tanyne cordially, and led the way through an arbor which was not the separate arch it appeared to be, but an entrance.

The room was wide, wider at one end than the other, though it was hard to determine by how much. The floor was uneven, graded upward toward one corner, where it was a mossy bank. Scattered here and there were what the eye said were white and striated gray boulders; the hand would say they were flesh. Except for a few shelf- and tablelike niches on these and in the bank, they were the only furniture.

Water ran frothing and gurgling through the room, apparently as an open brook; but Bril saw Nina's bare foot tread on the invisible covering that followed it down to the pool at the other end. The pool was the one he had seen from outside, indeterminately in and out of the house. A large tree grew by the pool and leaned its heavy branches toward the bank, and evidently its wide-flung limbs were webbed and tented between by the same invisible substance which covered the brook, for they formed the only cover overhead yet, to the ear, felt like a ceiling.

The whole effect was, to Bril, intensely depressing, and he surprised himself with a flash of homesickness for the tall steel cities of his home planet.

Nina smiled and left them. Bril followed his host's example and sank down on the ground, or floor, where it became a bank, or wall. Inwardly, Bril rebelled at the lack of decisiveness, of discipline, of clear-cut limitation inherent in such haphazard design as this. But he was well trained and quite prepared, at first, to keep his feelings to himself among barbarians.

"Nina will join us in a moment," said Tanyne.

Bril, who had been watching the woman's swift movements across the courtyard through the transparent wall opposite, controlled a start. "I am unused to your ways and wondered what she was doing," he said.

"She is preparing a meal for you," explained Tanyne.

"Herself?"

Tanyne and his son gazed wonderingly. "Does that seem unusual to you?"

"I understood the lady was wife to a Senator," said Bril. It seemed adequate as an explanation, but only to him. He looked from the boy's face to the man's. "Perhaps I understand something different when I use the term 'Senator.'"

"Perhaps you do. Would you tell us what a Senator is on the planet Kit Carson?"

"He is a member of the Senate, subservient to the Sole Authority, and in turn leader of a free Nation."

"And his wife?"

"His wife shares his privileges. She might serve a member of the Sole Authority, but hardly anyone else—certainly not an unidentified stranger."

"Interesting," said Tanyne, while the boy murmured the astonishment he had not expressed at Bril's bubble, or Bril himself. "Tell me, have you not identified yourself, then?"

"He did, by the waterfall," the youth insisted.

"I gave you no proof," said Bril stiffly. He watched father and son exchange a glance. "Credentials, written authority." He touched the flat pouch hung on his power belt.

Wonyne asked ingenuously, "Do the credentials say you are *not* Bril of Kit Carson in the Sumner System?"

Bril frowned at him and Tanyne said gently, "Wonyne, take care." To Bril, he said, "Surely there are many differences between us, as there always are between different worlds. But I am certain of this one similarity: the young at times run straight where wisdom has built a winding path."

Bril sat silently and thought this out. It was probably some sort of apology, he decided, and gave a single sharp nod. Youth, he thought, was an attenuated defect here. A boy Wonyne's age would be a soldier on Carson, ready for a soldier's work, and no one would be apologizing for him. Nor would he be making blunders. *None!*

He said, "These credentials are for your officials when I meet with them. By the way, when can that be?"

Tanyne shrugged his wide shoulders. "Whenever you like."

"The sooner the better."

"Very well."

"Is it far?"

Tanyne seemed perplexed. "Is what far?"

"Your capital, or wherever it is your Senate meets."

"Oh, I see. It doesn't meet, in the sense you mean. It is always in session, though, as they used to say. We—"

He compressed his lips and made a liquid, bisyllabic sound, then he laughed. "I do beg your pardon," he said warmly. "The Old Tongue lacks certain words, certain concepts. What is your word for—er—the-presence-of-all-in-the-presence-of-one?"

"I think," said Bril carefully, "that we had better go back to the subject at hand. Are you saying that your Senate does not meet in some official place, at some appointed time?"

"I—" Tan hesitated, then nodded. "Yes, that is true as far as it—"

"And there is no possibility of my addressing your Senate in person?"

"I didn't say that." Tan tried twice to express the thought, while Bril's eyes slowly narrowed. Tan suddenly burst into laughter. "Using the Old Tongue to tell old tales and to speak with a friend are two different things," he said ruefully. "I wish you would learn our speech. Would you, do you suppose? It is rational and well based on what you know. Surely you have another language besides the Old Tongue on Kit Carson?"

"I honor the Old Tongue," said Bril stiffly, dodging the question. Speaking very slowly, as if to a retarded child, he said, "I should like to know when I may be taken to those in authority here, in order to discuss certain planetary and interplanetary matters with them."

"Discuss them with me."

"You are a Senator," Bril said, in a tone which meant clearly: *You are only a Senator.*

"True," said Tanyne.

With forceful patience, Bril asked, "And what is a Senator here?"

"A contact point between the people of his district and the people everywhere. One who knows the special problems of a small section of the planet and can relate them to planetary policy."

"And whom does the Senate serve?"

"The people," said Tanyne, as if he had been asked to repeat himself.

"Yes, yes, of course. And who, then, serves the Senate?"

"The Senators."

Bril closed his eyes and barely controlled the salty syllable which welled up inside him. "Who," he inquired steadily, "is your Government?"

The boy had been watching them eagerly, alternately, like a devotee at some favorite fast ball game. Now he asked, "What's a Government?"

Nina's interruption at that point was most welcome to Bril. She came across the terrace from the covered area where she had been doing mysterious things at a long work-surface in the garden. She carried an enormous tray—guided it, rather, as Bril saw when she came closer. She kept three fingers under the tray and one behind it, barely touching it with her palm. Either the transparent wall of the room disappeared as she approached, or she passed through a section where there was none.

"I do hope you find something to your taste among these," she said cheerfully, as she brought the tray down to a hummock near Bril. "This is the flesh of birds, this of small mammals, and, over here, fish. These cakes are made of four kinds of grain, and the white cakes here of just one, the one we call milk-wheat. Here is water, and these two are wines, and this one is a distilled spirit we call warm-ears."

Bril, keeping his eyes on the food, and trying to keep his universe from filling up with the sweet fresh scent of her as she bent over him, so near, said, "This is welcome."

She crossed to her husband and sank down at his feet, leaning back against his legs. He twisted her heavy hair gently in his fingers and she flashed a small smile up at him. Bril looked from the food, colorful as a corsage, here steaming, there gathering frost from the air, to the three smiling, expectant faces and did not know what to do.

"Yes, this is welcome," he said again, and still they sat there, watching him. He picked up the white cake and rose, looked out and around, into the house, through it and beyond. Where could one go in such a place?

Steam from the tray touched his nostrils and saliva filled his mouth. He was hungry, but . . .

He sighed, sat down, gently replaced the cake. He tried to smile and could not.

"Does none of it please you?" asked Nina, concerned.

"I can't eat here!" said Bril; then, sensing something in the natives that had not been there before, he added, "thank you." Again he looked at their controlled faces. He said to Nina, "It is very well prepared and good to look on."

"Then eat," she invited, smiling again.

This did something that their house, their garments, their appallingly easy ways—sprawling all over the place, letting their young speak up at will, the shameless admission that they had a patois of their own—that none of these things had been able to do. Without losing his implacable dignity by any slightest change of expression, he yet found himself blushing. Then he scowled and let the childish display turn to a flush of anger. He would be glad, he thought furiously, when he had the heart of this culture in the palm of his hand, to squeeze when he willed; then there would be an end to these hypocritical amenities and they would learn who could be humiliated.

But these three faces, the boy's so open and unconscious of wrong. Tanyne's so strong and anxious for him, Nina's—that face, that face of Nina's—they were all utterly guileless. He must not let them know of his embarrassment. If they had planned it, he must not let them suspect his vulnerability.

With an immense effort of will, he kept his voice low; still, it was harsh. "I think," he said slowly, "that we on Kit Carson regard the matter of privacy perhaps a little more highly than you do."

They exchanged an astonished look, and then comprehension dawned visibly on Tanyne's ruddy face. "You don't eat together!"

Bril did not shudder, but it was in his word: "No."

"Oh," said Nina. "I'm *so* sorry!"

Bril thought it wise not to discover exactly what she was sorry about. He said, "No matter. Customs differ. I shall eat when I am alone."

"Now that we understand," said Tanyne, "go ahead. Eat."

But they *sat* there!

"Oh," said Nina, "I wish you spoke our other language; it would be so easy to explain!" She leaned forward to him, put out her arms, as if she could draw meaning itself from the air and cast it over him. "Please try to understand, Bril. You are very mistaken about one thing—we honor privacy above almost anything else."

"We don't mean the same thing when we say it," said Bril.

"It means aloneness with oneself, doesn't it? It means to do things, think or make or just *be,* without intrusion."

"So?" replied Wonyne happily, throwing out both hands in a gesture that said *quod erat demonstrandum.* "Go on then—eat! We won't look!" and helped the situation not at all.

"Wonyne's right," chuckled the father, "but, as usual, a little too direct. He means we can't look, Bril. If you want privacy, *we can't see you.*"

Angry, reckless, Bril suddenly reached to the tray. He snatched up a goblet, the one she had indicated as water, thumbed a capsule out of his belt, popped it into his mouth, drank and swallowed. He banged the goblet back on the tray and shouted, "Now you've seen all you're going to see."

With an indescribable expression, Nina drifted upward to her feet, bent like a dancer and touched the tray. It lifted and she guided it away across the courtyard.

"All right," said Wonyne. It was precisely as if someone had spoken and he had acknowledged. He lunged out, following his mother.

What *had* been on her face?

Something she could not contain; something rising to that smooth surface, about to reveal outlines, break through ... anger? Bril hoped so. Insult? He could, he supposed, understand that. But—laughter? *Don't make it laugher,* something within him pleaded.

"Bril," said Tanyne.

For the second time, he was so lost in contemplation of the woman that Tanyne's voice made him start.

"What is it?"

"If you will tell me what arrangements you would like for eating, I'll see to it that you get them."

"You wouldn't know how," said Bril bluntly. He threw his

sharp, cold gaze across the room and back. "You people don't build walls you can't see through, doors you can close."

"Why, no, we don't." As always, the giant left the insult and took only the words.

I bet you don't, Bril said silently, *not even for*—and a horrible suspicion began to grow within him. "We of Carson feel that all human history and development are away from the animal, toward something higher. We are, of course, chained to the animal state, but we do what we can to eliminate every animal act as a public spectacle." Sternly, he waved a shining gauntlet at the great open house. "You have apparently not reached such an idealization. I have seen how you eat; doubtless you perform your other functions so openly."

"Oh, yes," said Tanyne. "But with this—" he pointed "—it's hardly the same thing."

"With what?"

Tanyne again indicated one of the boulderlike objects. He tore off a clump of moss—it was real moss—and tossed it to the soft surface of one of the boulders. He reached down and touched one of the gray streaks. The moss sank into the surface the way a pebble will in quicksand, but much faster.

"It will not accept living animal matter above a certain level of complexity," he explained, "but it instantly absorbs every molecule of anything else, not only on the surface but for a distance above."

"And that's a—a—where you—"

Tan nodded and said that that was exactly what it was.

"But—anyone can see you!"

Tan shrugged and smiled. "How? That's what I meant when I said it's hardly the same thing. Of eating, we make a social occasion. But this—" he threw another clump of moss and watched it vanish—"just isn't observed." His sudden laugh rang out and again he said, "I wish you'd learn the language. Such a thing is so easy to express."

But Bril was concentrating on something else. "I appreciate your hospitality," he said, using the phrase stiltedly, "but I'd like to be moving on." He eyed the boulder distastefully. "And very soon."

"As you wish. You have a message for Xanadu. Deliver it, then."

"To your Government."

"To our Government. I told you before, Bril—when you're ready, proceed."

"I cannot believe that you represent this planet!"

"Neither can I," said Tanyne pleasantly. "I don't. Through me, you can speak to forty-one others, all Senators."

"Is there no other way?"

Tanyne smiled. "Forty-one other ways. Speak to any of the others. It amounts to the same thing."

"And no higher government body?"

Tanyne reached out a long arm and plucked a goblet from a niche in the moss bank. It was chased crystal with a luminous metallic rim.

"Finding the highest point of the government of Xanadu is like finding the highest point on this," he said. He ran a finger around the inside of the rim and the goblet chimed beautifully.

"Pretty unstable," growled Bril.

Tanyne made it sing again and replaced it; whether that was an answer or not, Bril could not know.

He snorted, "No wonder the boy didn't know what Government was."

"We don't use the term," said Tanyne. "We don't need it. There are few things here that a citizen can't handle for himself; I wish I could show you how few. If you'll live with us a while, I will show you."

He caught Bril's eye squarely as it returned from another disgusted and apprehensive trip to the boulder, and laughed outright. But the kindness in his voice as he went on quenched Bril's upsurge of indignant fury, and a little question curled up: *Is he managing me?* But there wasn't time to look at it.

"Can your business wait until you know us, Bril? I tell you now, there is no centralized Government here, almost no government at all; we of the Senate are advisory. I tell you, too, that to speak to one Senator is to speak to all, and that you may do it now, this minute, or a year from now—whenever you like. I am telling you the truth and you may accept it or you may spend months, years, traveling this planet and checking up on me; you'll always come out with the same answer."

Noncommittally, Bril said, "How do I know that what I tell you is accurately relayed to the others?"

"It isn't relayed," said Tan frankly. "We all hear it simultaneously."

"Some sort of radio?"

Tan hesitated, then nodded. "Some sort of radio."

"I won't learn your language," Bril said abruptly. "I can't live as you do. If you can accept those conditions, I will stay a short while."

"Accept? We *insist!*" Tanyne bounded cheerfully to the niche where the goblet stood and held his palm up. A large, opaque sheet of shining white material rolled down and stopped. "Draw with your fingers," he said.

"Draw? Draw what?"

"A place of your own. How you would like to live, eat, sleep, everything."

"I require very little. None of us on Kit Carson do."

He pointed the finger of his gauntlet like a weapon, made a couple of dabs in the corner of the screen to test the line, and then dashed off a very creditable parallelepiped. "Taking my height as one unit, I'd want this one-and-a-half long, one-and-a-quarter high. Slit vents at eye level, one at each end, two on each side, screened against insects—"

"We have no preying insects," said Tanyne.

"Screened anyway, and with as near as unbreakable mesh as you have. Here a hook suitable for hanging a garment. Here a bed, flat, hard, with firm padding as thick as my hand, one-and-one-eighth units long, one-third wide. All sides under the bed enclosed and equipped as a locker, impregnable, and to which only I have the key or combination. Here a shelf one-third by one-quarter units, one-half unit off the floor, suitable for eating from a seated posture.

"One of—those, if it's self-contained and reliable," he said edgily, casting a thumb at the boulderlike convenience. "The whole structure to be separate from all others on high ground and overhung by nothing—no trees, no cliffs, with approaches clear and visible from all sides; as strong as speed permits; and equipped with a light I can turn off and a door that only I can unlock."

"Very well," said Tanyne easily. "Temperature?"

"The same as this spot now."

"Anything else? Music? Pictures? We have some fine moving—"

Bril, from the top of his dignity, snorted his most eloquent snort. "Water, if you can manage it. As to those other things, this is a dwelling, not a pleasure palace."

"I hope you will be comfortable in this—in it," said Tanyne, with barely a trace of sarcasm.

"It is precisely what I am used to," Bril answered loftily.

"Come, then."

"What?"

The big man waved him on and passed through the arbor. Bril, blinking in the late pink sunlight, followed him.

On the gentle slope above the house, halfway between it and the mountaintop beyond, was a meadow of the red grass Bril had noticed on his way from the waterfall. In the center of this meadow was a crowd of people, bustling like moths around a light, their flimsy, colorful clothes flashing and gleaming in a thousand shades. And in the middle of the crowd lay a coffin-shaped object.

Bril could not believe his eyes, then stubbornly would not, and at last, as they came near, yielded and admitted it to himself: this was the structure he had just sketched.

He walked more and more slowly as the wonder of it grew on him. He watched the people—children, even—swarming around and over the little building, sealing the edge between roof and wall with a humming device, laying screen on the slit-vents. A little girl, barely a toddler, came up to him fearlessly and in lisping Old Tongue asked for his hand, which she clapped to a tablet she carried.

"To make your keys," explained Tanyne, watching the child scurry off to a man waiting at the door.

He took the tablet and disappeared inside, and they could see him kneel by the bed. A young boy overtook them and ran past, carrying a sheet of the same material the roof and walls were made of. It seemed light, but its slightly rough, pale-tan surface gave an impression of great toughness. As they drew up at the door, they saw the boy take the material and set it in position between the end of the bed and the doorway. He aligned it carefully, pressing it against the wall, and struck it once with the heel of his hand, and there was Bril's required table, level, rigid, and that without braces and supports.

"You seemed to like the looks of some of this, anyway." It was Nina, with her tray. She floated it to the new table, waved cheerfully and left.

"With you in a moment," Tan called, adding three singing syllables in the Xanadu tongue which were, Bril concluded, an endearment of some kind; they certainly sounded like it. Tan turned back to him, smiling.

"Well, Bril, how is it?"

Bril could only ask, "Who gave the orders?"

"You did," said Tan, and there didn't seem to be any answer to that.

Already, through the open door, he could see the crowd drifting away, laughing, and singing their sweet language to each other. He saw a young man scoop up scarlet flowers from the pink sward and hand them to a smiling girl, and unaccountably the scene annoyed him. He turned away abruptly and went about the walls, thumping them and peering through the vents. Tanyne knelt by the bed, his big shoulders bulging as he tugged at the locker. It might as well have been solid rock.

"Put your hand there," he said, pointing, and Bril clapped his gauntlet to the plate he indicated.

Sliding panels parted. Bril got down and peered inside. It had its own light, and he could see the buff-colored wall of the structure at the back and the heavy filleted partition which formed the bed uprights. He touched the panel again and the doors slid silently shut, so tight that he could barely see their meeting.

"The door's the same," said Tanyne. "No one but you can open it. Here's water. You didn't say where to put it. If this is inconvenient . . ."

When Bril put his hand near the spigot, water flowed into a catch basin beneath. "No, that is satisfactory. They work like specialists."

"They are," said Tanyne.

"Then they have built such a strange structure before?"

"Never."

Bril looked at him sharply. This ingenuous barbarian surely could not be making a fool of him by design! No, this must be some slip of semantics, some shift in meaning over the years which separated each of them from the common ancestor. He would not forget it, but he set it aside for future thought.

"Tanyne," he asked suddenly, "how many are you in Xanadu?"

"In a district, three hundred. On the planet, twelve, almost thirteen thousand."

"We are one and a half billion," said Bril. "And what is your largest city?"

"City," said Tanyne, as if searching through the files of his memory. "Oh—city! We have none. There are forty-two districts like this one, some larger, some smaller."

"Your entire planetary population could be housed in one building within one city on Kit Carson. And how many generations have your people been here?"

"Thirty-two, thirty-five, something like that."

"We settled Kit Carson not quite six Earth centuries ago. In point of time, then, it would seem that yours is the older culture. Wouldn't you be interested in how we have been able to accomplish so much more?"

"Fascinated," said Tanyne.

"You have some clever little handicrafts here," Bril mused, "and a quite admirable cooperative ability. You could make a formidable thing of this world, if you wanted to, and if you had the proper guidance."

"Oh, could we really?" Tanyne seemed very pleased.

"I must think," said Bril somberly. "You are not what I—what I had supposed. Perhaps I shall stay a little longer than I had planned. Perhaps while I am learning about your people, you in turn could be learning about mine."

"Delighted," said Tanyne. "Now is there anything else you need?"

"Nothing. You may leave me."

His autocratic tone gained him only one of the big man's pleasant, open-faced smiles. Tanyne waved his hand and left. Bril heard him calling his wife in ringing baritone notes, and her glad answer. He set his mailed hand against the door plate and it slid shut silently.

Now what, he asked himself, *got me to do all that bragging?* Then the astonishment at the people of Xanadu rose up and answered the question for him. *What manner of people are specialists at something they have never done before?*

He got out of his stiff, polished, heavy uniform, his gauntlets, his boots. They were all wired together, power supply in the boots, controls and computers in the trousers and belt, sensory mechs in the tunic, projectors and field loci in the gloves.

He hung the clothes on the hook provided and set the alarm field for anything larger than a mouse any closer than thirty meters. He dialed a radiation dome to cover his structure and exclude all spy beams or radiation weapons. Then he swung his left gauntlet on its cable over to the table and went to work on one small corner.

In half an hour, he had found a combination of heat and pressure that would destroy the pale brown board, and he sat down on the edge of the bed, limp with amazement. You could build a spaceship with stuff like this.

Now he had to believe that they had it in stock sizes exactly to his specifications, which would mean warehouses and manufacturing facilities capable of making up those and innumerable other sizes; or he had to believe that they had machinery capable of making what his torches had just destroyed, in job lots, right now.

But they didn't have any industrial plant to speak of, and if they had warehouses, they had them where the Kit Carson robot scouts had been unable to detect them in their orbiting for the last fifty years.

Slowly he lay down to think.

To acquire a planet, you locate the central government. If it is an autocracy, organized tightly up to the peak, so much the better; the peak is small and you kill it or control it and use the organization. If there is no government at all, you recruit the people or you exterminate them. If there is a plant, you run it with overseers and make the natives work it until you can train your own people to it and eliminate the natives. If there are skills, you learn them or you control those who have them. All in the book; a rule for every eventuality, every possibility.

But what if, as the robots reported, there was high technology and no plant? Planetwide cultural stability and almost no communications?

Well, nobody ever heard of such a thing, so when the robots report it, you send an investigator. All he has to find out is how they do it. All he has to do is to parcel up what is to be kept and what eliminated when the time comes for an expeditionary force.

There's always one clean way out, thought Bril, putting his hands behind his head and looking up at the tough ceiling. Item, one Earth-normal planet, rich in natural resources, sparsely populated by innocents. You can always simply exterminate them.

But not before you find out how they communicate, how they cooperate, and how they specialize in skills they never tried before. How they manufacture superior materials out of thin air in no time.

He had a sudden heady vision of Kit Carson equipped as these people were, a billion and a half universal specialists with some heretofore unsuspected method of intercommunication, capable of building cities, fighting wars, with the measureless skill and split-second understanding and obedience with which this little house had been built.

No, these people must not be exterminated. They must be used. Kit Carson had to learn their tricks. If the tricks were—he hoped not!—inherent in Xanadu and beyond the Carson abilities, then what would be the next best thing?

Why, a cadre of the Xanadu, scattered through the cities and armies of Kit Carson, instantly obedient, instantly trainable. Instruct one and you teach them all; each could teach a group of Kit Carson's finest. Production, logistics, strategy, tactics—he saw it all in a flash.

Xanadu might be left almost exactly as is, except for its new export—aides de camp.

Dreams, these are only dreams, he told himself sternly. *Wait until you know more. Watch them make impregnable hardboard and anti-grav tea trays . . .*

The thought of the tea tray made his stomach growl. He got

up and went to it. The hot food steamed, the cold was still frosty and firm. He picked, he tasted. Then he bit. Then he gobbled.

Nina, that Nina . . .

No, they can't be exterminated, he thought drowsily, not when they can produce such a woman. In all of Kit Carson, there wasn't a cook like that.

He lay down again and dreamed, and dreamed until he fell asleep.

They were completely frank. They showed him everything, and it apparently never occurred to them to ask him why he wanted to know. Asking was strange because they seemed to lack that special pride of accomplishment one finds in the skilled potter, metal-worker, electronician, an attitude of: "Isn't it remarkable that I can do it!" They gave information accurately but impersonally, as if anyone could do it.

And on Xanadu, anyone could.

At first, it seemed to Bril totally disorganized. These attractive people in their indecent garments came and went, mingling play and work and loafing, without apparent plan. But their play would take them through a flower garden just where the weeds were, and they would take the weeds along. There seemed to be a group of girls playing jacks right outside the place where they would suddenly be needed to sort some seeds.

Tanyne tried to explain it: "Say we have a shortage of something—oh, strontium, for example. The shortage itself creates a sort of vacuum. People without anything special to do feel it; they think about strontium. They come, they gather it."

"But I have seen no mines," Bril said puzzledly. "And what about shipping? Suppose the shortage is here and the mines in another district?"

"That never happens any more. Where there are deposits, of course, there are no shortages. Where there are none, we find other ways, either to use something else or to produce it without mines."

"Transmute it?"

"Too much trouble. No, we breed a freshwater shellfish with a strontium carbonate shell instead of calcium carbonate. The children gather them for us when we need it."

He saw their clothing industry—part shed, part cave, part forest glen. There was a pool there where the young people swam, and a field where they sunned themselves. Between times, they went into the shadows and worked by a huge vessel where chemicals occasionally boiled, turned bright green, and then precipitated. The black precipitate was raised from the bottom of the vessel on screens, dumped into forms and pressed.

Just how the presses—little more than lids for the forms—operated, the Old Tongue couldn't tell him, but in four or five seconds the precipitate had turned into the black stones used in their belts, formed and polished, with a chemical formula in Old Tongue script cut into the back of the left buckle.

"One of our few superstitions," said Tanyne. "It's the formula for the belts—even a primitive chemistry could make them. We would like to see them copied, duplicated all over the Universe. They are what we are. Wear one, Bril. You would be one of us, then."

Bril snorted in embarrassed contempt and went to watch two children deftly making up the belts, as easily, and with the same idle pleasure, as they might be making flower necklaces in a minute or two. As each was assembled, the child would strike it against his own belt. All the colors there are would appear each time this happened, in a brief, brilliant, cool flare. Then the belt, now with a short trim of vague tongued light, was tossed in a bin.

Probably the only time Bril permitted himself open astonishment on Xanadu was the first time he saw one of the natives put on this garment. It was a young man, come dripping from the pool. He snatched up a belt from the bank and clasped it around his waist, and immediately the color and substance flowed up and down, a flickering changing collar for him, a moving coruscant kilt.

"It's alive, you see," said Tanyne. "Rather, it is not nonliving."

He put his fingers under the hem of his own kilt and forced his fingers up and outward. They penetrated the fabric, which fluttered away, untorn.

"It is not," he said gravely, "altogether material, if you will forgive an Old Tongue pun. The nearest Old Tongue term for it is 'aura.' Anyway, it lives, in its way. It maintains itself for—oh, a year or more. Then dip it in lactic acid and it is refreshed again. And just one of them could activate a million belts or a billion— how many sticks can a fire burn?"

"But why wear such a thing?"

Tanyne laughed. "Modesty." He laughed again. "A scholar of the very old times, on Earth before the Nova, passed on to me the words of one Rudofsky: 'Modesty is not so simple a virtue as honesty.' We wear these because they are warm when we need warmth, and because they conceal some defects some of the time—surely all one can ask of any human affectation."

"They are certainly not modest," said Bril stiffly.

"They express modesty just to the extent that they make us more pleasant to look at with than without them. What more public expression of humility could you want than that?"

Bril turned his back on Tanyne and the discussion. He understood Tanyne's words and ways imperfectly to begin with, and this kind of talk left him bewildered, or unreached, or both.

He found out about the hardboard. Hanging from the limb of a tree was a large vat of milky fluid—the paper, Tan explained, of a wasp they had developed, dissolved in one of the nucleic acids which they synthesized from a native weed. Under the vat was a flat metal plate and a set of movable fences. These were arranged in the desired shape and thickness of the finished panel, and then a cock was opened and the fluid ran in and filled the enclosure. Thereupon two small children pushed a roller by hand across the top of the fences. The white lake of fluid turned pale brown and solidified, and that was the hardboard.

Tanyne tried his best to explain to Bril about that roller, but the Old Tongue joined forces with Bril's technical ignorance and made the explanation incomprehensible. The coating of the roller was as simple in design, and as complex in theory, as a transistor, and Bril had to let it go at that, as he did with the selective analysis of the boulderlike "plumbing" and the anti-grav food trays (which, he discovered, had to be guided outbound, but which "homed" on the kitchen area when empty).

He had less luck, as the days went by, in discovering the nature of the skills of Xanadu. He had been quite ready to discard his own dream as a fantasy, an impossibility—the strange idea that what any could do, all could do. Tanyne tried to explain; at least, he answered every one of Bril's questions.

These wandering, indolent, joyful people could pick up anyone's work at any stage and carry it to any degree. One would pick up a flute and play a few notes, and others would stroll over, some with instruments and some without, and soon another instrument and another would join in, until there were fifty or sixty and the music was like a passion or a storm, or after-love or sleep when you think back on it.

And sometimes a bystander would step forward and take an instrument from the hands of someone who was tiring, and play on with all the rest, pure and harmonious; and, no, Tan would aver, he didn't think they'd ever played that particular piece of music before, those fifty or sixty people.

It always got down to *feeling,* in Tan's explanations.

"It's a *feeling* you get. The violin, now; I've heard one, we'll say, but never held one. I watch someone play and I understand how the notes are made. Then I take it and do the same, and as I concentrate on making the note, and the note that follows, it comes to me not only how it should sound, but how it should *feel*—to the fingers, the bowing arm, the chin and collarbone. Out of those feelings comes the feeling of how it feels to be making such music.

"Of course, there are limitations," he admitted, "and some might do better than others. If my fingertips are soft, I can't play as long as another might. If a child's hands are too small for the instrument, he'll have to drop an octave or skip a note. But the feeling's there, when we think in that certain way.

"It's the same with anything else we do," he summed up. "If I need something in my house, a machine, a device, I won't use iron where copper is better; it wouldn't *feel* right for me. I don't mean feeling the metal with my hands; I mean thinking about the device and its parts and what it's for. When I think of all the things I could make it of, there's only one set of things that feels right to me."

"So," said Bril then. "And that, plus this—this competition between the districts, to find all elements and raw materials in the neighborhood instead of sending for them—that's why you have no commerce. Yet you say you're standardized—at any rate, you all have the same kind of devices, ways of doing things."

"We all have whatever we want and we make it ourselves, yes." Tan agreed.

In the evenings, Bril would sit in Tanyne's house and listen to the drift and swirl of conversation or the floods of music, and wonder; and then he would guide his tray back to his cubicle and lock the door and eat and brood. He felt at times that he was under an attack with weapons he did not understand, on a field which was strange to him.

He remembered something Tanyne had said once, casually, about men and their devices: "Ever since there were human beings, there has been conflict between Man and his machines. They will run him or he them; it's hard to say which is the less disastrous way. But a culture which is composed primarily of men has to destroy one made mostly of machines, or be destroyed. It was always that way. We lost a culture once on Xanadu. Didn't you ever wonder, Bril, why there are so few of us here? And why almost all of us have red hair?"

Bril had, and had secretly blamed the small population on the shameless lack of privacy, without which no human race seems to be able to whip up enough interest in itself to breed readily.

"We were billions once," said Tan surprisingly. "We were wiped out. Know how many were left? *Three!*"

That was a black night for Bril, when he realized how pitiable were his efforts to learn their secret. For if a race were narrowed to a few, and a mutation took place, and it then increased again, the new strain could be present in all the new generations. He might as well, he thought, try to wrest from them the secret of having red hair. That was the night he concluded that these people would have to go; and it hurt him to think that, and he was angry at himself for thinking so. That, too, was the night of the ridiculous disaster.

He lay on his bed, grinding his teeth in helpless fury. It was past noon and he had been there since he awoke, trapped by his own stupidity, and ridiculous, ridiculous. His greatest single possession—his dignity—was stripped from him by his own carelessness, by a fiendish and unsportsmanlike gadget that—

His approach alarm hissed and he sprang to his feet in an agony of embarrassment, in spite of the strong opaque walls and the door which only he could open.

It was Tanyne: his friendly greeting bugled out and mingled with birdsong and the wind. "Bril! You there?"

Bril let him come a little closer and then barked through the vent, "I'm not coming out." Tanyne stopped dead, and even Bril himself was surprised by the harsh, squeezed sound of his voice.

"But Nina asked for you. She's going to weave today; she thought you'd like—"

"No," snapped Bril. "Today I leave. Tonight, that is. I've summoned my bubble. It will be here in two hours. After that, when it's dark, I'm going."

"Bril, you can't. Tomorrow I've set up a sintering for you; show you how we plate—"

"No!"

"Have we offended you, Bril? Have I?"

"No." Bril's voice was surly, but at least not a shout.

"What's happened?"

Bril didn't answer.

Tanyne came closer. Bril's eyes disappeared from the slit. He was cowering against the wall, sweating.

Tanyne said, "Something's happened, something's wrong. I . . . feel it. You know how I feel things, my friend, my good friend, Bril."

The very thought made Bril stiffen in terror. Did Tanyne know? Could he?

He might, at that. Bril damned these people and all their devices, their planet and its sun and the fates which had brought him here.

"There is nothing in my world or in my experience you can't tell me about. You know I'll understand," Tanyne pleaded. He came closer. "Are you ill? I have all the skills of the surgeons who have lived since the Three. Let me in."

"No!" It was hardly a word; it was an explosion.

Tanyne fell back a step. "I beg your pardon, Bril. I won't ask again. But—tell me. Please tell me. I must be able to help you!"

All right, thought Bril, half hysterically, *I'll tell you and you can laugh your fool red head off. It won't matter once we seed your planet with Big Plague.* "I can't come out. I've ruined my clothes."

"Bril! What can that matter? Here, throw them out; we can fix them, no matter what it is."

"No!" He could just see what would happen with these universal talents getting hold of the most compact and deadly armory this side of the Sumner system.

"Then wear mine." Tan put his hands to the belt of his black stones.

"I wouldn't be seen dead in a flimsy thing like that. Do you think I'm an exhibitionist?"

With more heat (it wasn't much) than Bril had ever seen in him, Tanyne said, "You've been a lot more conspicuous in those winding sheets you've been wearing than you ever would be in this."

Bril had never thought of that. He looked longingly at the bright nothing which flowed up and down from the belt, and then at his own black harness, humped up against the wall under its hook. He hadn't been able to bear the thought of putting them back on since the accident happened, and he had not been this long without clothes since he'd been too young to walk.

"What happened to your clothes, anyway?" Tan asked sympathetically.

Laugh, thought Bril, *and I'll kill you right now and you'll never have a chance to see your race die.* "I sat down on the—I've been using it as a chair; there's only room for one seat in here. I must have kicked the switch. I didn't even feel it until I got up. The whole back of my—" Angrily he blurted, "Why doesn't that ever happen to you people?"

"Didn't I tell you?" Tan said, passing the news item by as if it meant nothing. Well, to him it probably was nothing. "The unit only accepts nonliving matter."

"Leave that thing you call clothes in front of the door." Bril grunted after a strained silence. "Perhaps I'll try it."

Tanyne tossed the belt up against the door and strode away, singing softly. His voice was so big that even his singing seemed to go on forever.

But eventually Bril had the field to himself, the birdsong and the wind. He went to the door and away, lifted his seatless breeches sadly and folded them out of sight under the other things on the hook. He looked at the door again and actually whimpered once, very quietly. At last he put the gauntlet against the doorplate, and the door, never designed to open a little way, obediently slid wide. He squeaked, reached out, caught up the belt, scampered back and slapped at the plate.

"No one saw," he told himself urgently.

He pulled the belt around him. The buckle parts knew each other like a pair of hands.

The first thing he was aware of was the warmth. Nothing but the belt touched him anywhere and yet there was a warmth on him, soft, safe, like a bird's breast on eggs. A split second later, he gasped.

How could a mind fill so and not feel pressure? How could so much understanding flood into a brain and not break it?

He understood about the roller which treated the hardboard; it was a certain way and no other, and he could feel the rightness of that sole conjecture.

He understood the ions of the mold press that made the belts, and the life analog he wore as a garment. He understood how his finger might write on a screen, and the vacuum of demand he might send out to have this house built so, and so, and exactly so; and how the natives would hurry to fill it.

He remembered without effort Tanyne's description of the *feel* of playing an instrument, making, building, molding, holding, sharing, and how it must be to play in a milling crowd beside a task, moving randomly and only for pleasure, yet taking someone's place at vat or bench, furrow or fishnet, the very second another laid down a tool.

He stood in his own quiet flame, in his little coffin cubicle, looking at his hands and knowing without question that they would build him a model of a city on Kit Carson if he liked, or a statue of the soul of the Sole Authority.

He knew without question that he had the skills of this people, and that he could call on any of those skills just by concentrating on a task until it came to him how the right way (for him) would *feel*. He knew without surprise that these resources transcended even death; for a man could have a skill and then it was everyman's, and if the man should die, his skill still lived in everyman.

Just by concentrating—that was the key, the key way, the keystone to the nature of this device. A device, that was all—no mutations, nothing "extrasensory" (whatever that meant); only a machine like other machines. You have a skill, and a feeling about it; I have a task. Concentration on my task sets up a demand for your skill; through mine, I receive. Then I perform; and what bias I put upon that performance depends on my capabilities. Should I add something to that skill, then mine is the higher, the more complete; the *feeling* of it is better, and it is I who will transmit next time there is a demand.

And he understood the authority that lay in this new aura, and it came to him then how his home planet could be welded into a unit such as the universe had never seen. Xanadu had not done it, because Xanadu had grown randomly with its gift, without the preliminary pounding and shaping and milling of authority and discipline.

But Kit Carson! Carson with all skills and all talents shared among all its people, and overall and commanding, creating that vacuum of need and instant fulfillment, the Sole Authority and the State. It must be so (even though, far down, something in him wondered why the State kept so much understanding away from its people), for with this new depth came a solemn new dedication to his home and all it stood for.

Trembling, he unbuckled the belt and turned back its left buckle. Yes, there it was, the formula for the precipitate. And now he understood the pressing process and he had the flame to strike into new belts and make them live—by the millions. Tanyne had said, the billions.

Tanyne had said . . . why had he never said that the garments of Xanadu were the source of all their wonders and perplexities?

But had Bril ever asked?

Hadn't Tanyne begged him to take a garment so he could be one with Xanadu? The poor earnest idiot, to think he could be swayed away from Carson this way! Well, then, Tanyne and his people would have an offer, too, and it would all be even; soon they could, if they would join the shining armies of a new Kit Carson.

From his hanging black suit, a chime sounded. Bril laughed and gathered up his old harness and all the fire and shock and paralysis asleep in its mighty, compact weapons. He slapped open the door and sprang to the bubble which waited outside, and flung his old uniform in to lie crumpled on the floor, a broken chrysalis.

Shining and exultant, he leaped in after it and the bubble sprang away skyward.

Within a week after Bril's return to Kit Carson in the Sumner System, the garment had been duplicated, and duplicated again, and tested.

Within a month, nearly two hundred thousand had been distributed, and eighty factories were producing round the clock.

Within a year, the whole planet, all the millions, were shining and unified as never before, moving together under their Leader's will like the cells of a hand.

And then, in shocking unison, they all flickered and dimmed, every one, so it was time for the lactic acid dip which Bril had learned of. It was done in panic, without test or hesitation; a small taste of this luminous subjection had created a mighty appetite. All was well for a week—

And then, as the designers in Xanadu had planned, all the other segments of the black belts joined the first meager two in full operation.

A billion and a half human souls, who had been given the techniques of music and the graphic arts, and the theory of technology, now had the others: philosophy and logic and love; sympathy, empathy, forbearance, unity in the idea of their species rather than in their obedience; membership in harmony with all life everywhere.

A people with such feelings and their derived skills cannot be slaves. As the light burst upon them, there was only one concentration possible to each of them—to be free, and the accomplished feeling of being free. As each found it, he was an expert in freedom, and expert succeeded expert, transcended expert, until (in a moment) a billion and a half human souls had no greater skill than the talent of freedom.

So Kit Carson, as a culture, ceased to exist, and something new started there and spread through the stars nearby.

And because Bril knew what a Senator was and wanted to be one, he became one.

In each other's arms, Tanyne and Nina were singing softly, when the goblet in the mossy niche chimed.

"Here comes another one," said Wonyne, crouched at their feet. "I wonder what will make *him* beg, borrow, or steal a belt."

"Doesn't matter," said Tanyne, stretching luxuriously, "as long as he gets it. Which one is he, Wo—that noisy mechanism on the other side of the small moon?"

"No," said Wonyne. "That one's still sitting there squalling and thinking we don't know it's there. No, this is the force-field that's been hovering over Fleetwing District for the last two years."

Tanyne laughed. "That'll make conquest number eighteen for us."

"Nineteen," corrected Nina dreamily. "I remember because eighteen was the one that just left and seventeen was that funny little Bril from the Sumner System. Tan, for a time that little man loved me." But that was a small thing and did not matter.

KILLDOZER!

Before the race was the deluge, and before the deluge another race, whose nature it is not for mankind to understand. Not unearthly, not alien, for this was their earth and their home.

There was a war between this race, which was a great one, and another. The other was truly alien, a sentient cloudform, an intelligent grouping of tangible electrons. It was spawned in mighty machines by some accident of science beyond our aboriginal conception of technology. And then the machines, servants of the people, became the people's masters, and great were the battles that followed. The electron-beings had the power to warp the delicate balances of atom-structure, and their life-medium was metal, which they permeated and used to their own ends. Each weapon the people developed was possessed and turned against them, until a time when the remnants of that vast civilization found a defense—

An insulator. The terminal product or by-product of all energy research—neutronium.

In its shelter they developed a weapon. What it was we shall never know, and our race will live—or we shall know, and our race will perish as theirs perished. Sent to destroy the enemy, it got out of hand and its measureless power destroyed them with it, and their cities, and their possessed machines. The very earth dissolved in *flame, the crust writhed and shook and the oceans boiled. Nothing escaped it, nothing that we know as life, and nothing of the pseudo-life that had evolved within the mysterious force-fields of their incomprehensible machines, save one hardy mutant.*

Mutant it was, and ironically this one alone could have been killed by the first simple measures used against its kind—but it was past time for simple expediences. It was an organized electron-field possessing intelligence and mobility and a will to destroy, and little else. Stunned by the holocaust, it drifted over the grumbling globe, and in a lull in the violence of the forces gone wild on Earth, sank to the steaming ground in its half-conscious exhaustion. There it found shelter—shelter built by and for its dead enemies. An envelope of neutronium. It drifted in, and its consciousness at last fell to its lowest ebb. And there it lay while the neutronium, with its strange constant flex, its interminable striving for perfect balance, extended itself and closed the opening. And thereafter in the turbulent eons that followed, the envelope tossed like a gray bubble on the surface of the roiling sphere, for no substance on Earth would have it or combine with it.

The ages came and went, and chemical action and reaction did their mysterious work, and once again there was life and evolution. And a tribe found the mass of neutronium, which is not a substance but a static force, and were awed by its aura of indescribable chill, and they worshipped it and built a temple around it and made sacrifices to it. And ice and fire and the seas came and went, and the land rose and fell as the years went by, until the ruined temple was on a knoll, and the knoll was an island. Islanders came and went, lived and built and died, and races forgot. So now, somewhere in the Pacific to the west of the archipelago called Islas Revillagigeda, there was an uninhabited island. And one day—

Chub Horton and Tom Jaeger stood watching the *Sprite* and her squat tow of three cargo lighters dwindle over the glassy sea. The big ocean-going towboat and her charges seemed to be moving out of focus rather than traveling away. Chub spat cleanly around the cigar that grew out of the corner of his mouth.

"That's that for three weeks. How's it feel to be a guinea pig?"

"We'll get it done." Tom had little crinkles all around the outer ends of his eyes. He was a head taller than Chub and rangy, and not so tough, and he was a real operator. Choosing him as a foreman for the experiment had been wise, for he was competent and he commanded respect. The theory of airfield construction that they were testing appealed vastly to him, for here were no officers-in-charge, no government inspectors, no time-keeping or reports. The government had allowed the company a temporary land grant, and the idea was to put production-line techniques into the layout and grading of the project. There were six operators and two mechanics and more than a million dollars' worth of the best equipment that money could buy. Government acceptance was to be on a partially completed basis, and contingent on government standards. The theory obviated both goldbricking and graft, and neatly sidestepped the man-power problem. "When that black-topping crew gets here, I reckon we'll be ready for 'em," said Tom.

He turned and scanned the island with an operator's vision and saw it as it was, and in all the stages it would pass through, and as it would look when they had finished, with five thousand feet of clean-draining runway, hard-packed shoulders, four acres of plane-park, the access road and the short taxiway. He saw the lay of each lift that the power shovel would cut as it brought down the marl bluff, and the ruins on top of it that would give them stone to haul down the salt-flat to the little swamp at the other end, there to be walked in by the dozers.

"We got time to run the shovel up there to the bluff before dark."

They walked down the beach toward the outcropping where the equipment stood surrounded by crates and drums of supplies. The three tractors were ticking over quietly, the two-cycle Diesels chuckling through their mufflers and the big D-7 whacking away its metronomic compression knock on every easy revolution. The Dumptors were lined up and silent, for they would not be ready to work until the shovel was ready to load them. They looked like a mechanical interpretation of Dr. Dolittle's "Pushme-pullyou," the fantastic animal with two front ends. They had two large driving wheels and two small steerable wheels. The motor and the driver's seat were side by side over the front—or smaller—wheels; but the driver faced the dump body between the big rear wheels, exactly the opposite of the way he would sit in a dump truck. Hence, in traveling from shovel to dumping-ground, the operator drove backwards, looking over his shoulder, and in dumping he backed the machine up but he himself traveled forward—quite a trick for fourteen hours a day! The shovel squatted in the midst of all the others, its great hulk looming over them, humped there with its boom low and its iron chin on the ground, like some great tired dinosaur.

Rivera, the Puerto Rican mechanic, looked up grinning as Tom and Chub approached, and stuck a bleeder wrench into the top pocket of his coveralls.

"She says 'Sígalo,'" he said, his white teeth flashlighting out of the smear of grease across his mouth. "She says she wan' to get dirt on dis paint." He kicked the blade of the Seven with his heel.

Tom sent the grin back—always a surprising thing in his grave face.

"That Seven'll do that, and she'll take a good deal off her bitin' edge along with the paint before we're through. Get in the saddle, Goony. Build a ramp off the rocks down to the flat there, and blade us off some humps from here to the bluff yonder. We're walking the dipper up there."

The Puerto Rican was in the seat before Tom had finished, and with a roar the Seven spun in its length and moved back along the outcropping to the inland edge. Rivera dropped his blade and the sandy marl curled and piled up in front of the dozer, loading the blade and running off in two even rolls at the ends. He shoved the load toward the rocky edge, the Seven revving down as it took the load, *blat blat blatting* and pulling like a supercharged ox as it fired slowly enough for them to count the revolutions.

"She's a hunk of machine," said Tom.

"A hunk of operator, too," gruffed Chub, and added, "for a mechanic."

"The boy's all right," said Kelly. He was standing there with them, watching the Puerto Rican operate the dozer, as if he had been there all along, which was the way Kelly always arrived places. He was tall, slim, with green eyes too long and an easy stretch to the way he moved, like an attenuated cat. He said, "Never thought I'd see the day when equipment was shipped set up ready to run like this. Guess no one ever thought of it before."

"There's times when heavy equipment has to be unloaded in a

hurry these days," Tom said. "If they can do it with tanks, they can do it with construction equipment. We're doin' it to build something instead, is all. Kelly, crank up the shovel. It's oiled. We're walking it over to the bluff."

Kelly swung up into the cab of the big dipper-stick and, diddling the governor control, pulled up the starting handle. The Murphy Diesel snorted and settled down into a thudding idle. Kelly got into the saddle, set up the throttle a little, and began to boom up.

"I still can't get over it," said Chub. "Not more'n a year ago we'd a had two hundred men on a job like this."

Tom smiled. "Yeah, and the first thing we'd have done would be to build an office building, and then quarters. Me, I'll take this way. No timekeepers, no equipment-use reports, no progress and yardage summaries, no nothin' but eight men, a million bucks worth of equipment, an' three weeks. A shovel an' a mess of tool crates'll keep the rain off us, an' army field rations'll keep our bellies full. We'll get it done, we'll get out and we'll get paid."

Rivera finished the ramp, turned the Seven around and climbed it, walking the new fill down. At the top he dropped his blade, floated it, and backed down the ramp, smoothing out the rolls. At a wave from Tom he started out across the shore, angling up toward the bluff, beating out the humps and carrying fill into the hollows. As he worked, he sang, feeling the beat of the mighty motor, the micrometric obedience of that vast implacable machine.

"Why doesn't that monkey stick to his grease guns?"

Tom turned and took the chewed end of a match stick out of his mouth. He said nothing, because he had for some time been trying to make a habit of saying nothing to Joe Dennis. Dennis was an ex-accountant, drafted out of an office at the last gasp of a defunct project in the West Indies. He had become an operator because they needed operators badly. He had been released with alacrity from the office because of his propensity for small office politics. It was a game he still played, and completely aside from his boiled-looking red face and his slightly womanish walk, he was out of place in the field; for boot-licking and back-stabbing accomplish even less out on the field than they do in an office. Tom, trying so hard to keep his mind on his work, had to admit to himself that of all Dennis' annoying traits the worst was that he was as good a pan operator as could be found anywhere, and no one could deny it.

Dennis certainly didn't.

"I've seen the day when anyone catching one of those goonies so much as sitting on a machine during lunch would kick his fanny," Dennis groused. "Now they give 'em a man's work and a man's pay."

"*Doin'* a man's work, ain't he?" Tom said.

"He's a damn Puerto Rican!"

Tom turned and looked at him levelly. "Where was it you said you come from," he mused. "Oh yeah. Georgia."

"What do you mean by that?"

Tom was already striding away. "Tell you as soon as I have to," he flung back over his shoulder. Dennis went back to watching the Seven.

Tom glanced at the ramp and then waved Kelly on. Kelly set his housebrake so the shovel could not swing, put her into travel gear, and shoved the swing lever forward. With a crackling of drive chains and a massive scrunching of compacting coral sand, the shovel's great flat pads carried her over and down the ramp. As she tipped over the peak of the ramp the heavy manganese steel bucket-door gaped open and closed, like a hungry mouth, slamming up against the bucket until suddenly it latched shut and was quiet. The big Murphy Diesel crooned hollowly under compression as the machine ran downgrade and then the sensitive governor took hold and it took up its belly-beating thud.

Peebles was standing by one of the dozer-pan combines, sucking on his pipe and looking out to sea. He was grizzled and heavy, and from under the bushiest gray brows looked the calmest gray eyes Tom had ever seen. Peebles had never gotten angry at a machine—a rare trait in a born mechanic—and in fifty-odd years he had learned it was even less use getting angry at a man. Because no matter what, you could always fix what was wrong with a machine. He said around his pipestem:

"Hope you'll give me back my boy, there."

Tom's lips quirked in a little grin. There had been an understanding between old Peebles and himself ever since they had met. It was one of those things which exists unspoken—they knew little about each other because they had never found it necessary to make small talk to keep their friendship extant. It was enough to know that each could expect the best from the other, without persuasion.

"Rivera?" Tom asked. "I'll chase him back as soon as he finishes that service road for the dipper-stick. Why—got anything on?"

"Not much. Want to get that arc welder drained and flushed and set up a grounded table in case you guys tear anything up." He paused. "Besides, the kid's filling his head up with too many things at once. Mechanicking is one thing; operating is something else."

"Hasn't got in his way much so far, has it?"

"Nope. Don't aim t' let it, either. 'Less you need him."

Tom swung up on the pan tractor. "I don't need him that bad, Peeby. If you want some help in the meantime, get Dennis."

Peebles said nothing. He spat. He didn't say anything at all.

"What's the matter with Dennis?" Tom wanted to know.

"Look yonder," said Peebles, waving his pipestem. Out on the beach Dennis was talking to Chub, in Dennis' indefatigable style, standing beside Chub, one hand on Chub's shoulder. As they watched they saw Dennis call his side-kick, Al Knowles.

"Dennis talks too much," said Peebles. "That most generally don't amount to much, but that Dennis, he sometimes says too much. Ain't got what it takes to run a show, and knows it. Makes up for it by messin' in between folks."

"He's harmless," said Tom.

Still looking up the beach, Peebles said slowly:

"Is, so far."

Tom started to say something, then shrugged. "I'll send you Rivera," he said, and opened the throttle. Like a huge electric dynamo, the two-cycle motor whined to a crescendo. Tom lifted the dozer with a small lever by his right thigh and raised the pan with the long control sprouting out from behind his shoulder. He moved off, setting the rear gate of the scraper so that anything the blade bit would run off to the side instead of loading into the pan. He slapped the tractor into sixth gear and whined up to and around the crawling shovel, cutting neatly in under the boom and running on ahead with his scraper blade just touching the ground, dragging to a fine grade the service road Rivera had cut.

Dennis was saying, "It's that little Hitler stuff. Why should I take that kind of talk? 'You come from Georgia,' he says. What is he— a Yankee or something?"

"A crackah f'm Macon," chortled Al Knowles, who came from Georgia, too. He was tall and stringy and round-shouldered. All of his skill was in his hands and feet, brains being a commodity he had lived without all his life until he had met Dennis and used him as a reasonable facsimile thereof.

"Tom didn't mean nothing by it," said Chub.

"No, he didn't mean nothin'. Only that we do what he says the way he says it, specially if he finds a way we don't like it. *You* wouldn't do like that, Chub. Al, think Chub would carry on that-away?"

"Sure wouldn't," said Al, feeling it expected of him.

"Nuts," said Chub, pleased and uncomfortable, and thinking, what have I got against Tom?—not knowing, not liking Tom as well as he had. "Tom's the man here, Dennis. We got a job to do— let's skit and git. Man can take anything for a lousy six weeks."

"Oh, sho'," said Al.

"Man can take just so much," Dennis said. "What they put a man like that on top for, Chub? What's the matter with you? Don't you know grading and drainage as good as Tom? Can Tom stake out a side hill like you can?"

"Sure, sure, but what's the difference, long as we get a field built? An' anyhow, hell with bein' the boss-man. Who gets the blame if things don't run right, anyway?'

Dennis stepped back, taking his hand off Chub's shoulder, and stuck an elbow in Al's ribs.

"You see that, Al? Now there's a smart man. That's the thing Uncle Tom didn't bargain for. Chub, you can count on Al and me to do just that little thing."

"Do just what little thing?" asked Chub, genuinely puzzled.

"Like you said. If the job goes wrong, the boss gets blamed. So, if the boss don't behave, the job goes wrong."

"Uh-huh," agreed Al with the conviction of mental simplicity.

Chub double-took this extraordinary logical process and grasped wildly at anger as the conversation slid out from under him. "I didn't say any such thing! This job is goin' to get done, no matter what! There'll be no damn goldbrick badge on me or anybody else around here if I can help it."

"Tha's the ol' fight," feinted Dennis. "We'll show that guy what we think of his kind of slowdown."

"You talk too much," said Chub and escaped with the remnants of coherence. Every time he talked with Dennis he walked away feeling as if he had an unwanted membership card stuck in his pocket that he couldn't throw away with a clear conscience.

Rivera ran his road up under the bluff, swung the Seven around, punched out the master clutch and throttled down, idling. Tom was making his pass with the pan, and as he approached, Rivera slipped out of the seat and behind the tractor, laying a sensitive hand on the final drive casing and sprocket bushings, checking for overheating. Tom pulled alongside and beckoned him up on the pan tractor.

"*Qué pasa*, Goony? Anything wrong?"

Rivera shook his head and grinned. "Nothing wrong. She is perfect, that '*De Siete.*' She—"

"That what? 'Daisy Etta'?"

"*De siete.* In Spanish, D-7. It means something in English?"

"Got you wrong," smiled Tom. "But Daisy Etta is a girl's name in English, all the same."

He shifted the pan tractor into neutral and engaged the clutch, and jumped off the machine. Rivera followed. They climbed aboard the Seven, Tom at the controls.

Rivera said "Daisy Etta," and grinned so widely that a soft little clucking noise came from behind his back teeth. He reached out his hand, crooked his little finger around one of the tall steering clutch levers, and pulled it all the way back. Tom laughed outright.

"You got something there," he said. "The easiest runnin' cat ever built. Hydraulic steerin', clutches and brakes that'll bring you to a dead stop if you spit on 'em. Forward an' reverse lever so's you got all your speeds front and backwards. A little different from the old jobs. They had no booster springs, eight-ten years ago; took a sixty-pound pull to get a steerin' clutch back. Cuttin' a side-hill with an angle-dozer really was a job in them days. You try it sometime, dozin' with one hand, holdin' her nose out o' the bank with the other, ten hours a day. And what'd it get you? Eighty cents an hour an'"—Tom took his cigarette and butted the fiery end out against the horny palm of his hand—"these."

"*Santa María!*"

"Want to talk to you, Goony. Want to look over the bluff, too, at the stone up there. It'll take Kelly pret' near an hour to get this far and sumped in, anyhow."

They growled up the slope, Tom feeling the ground under the four-foot brush, taking her up in a zigzag course like a hairpin road on a mountainside. Though the Seven carried a muffler on the exhaust stack that stuck up out of the hood before them, the blat of the four big cylinders hauling fourteen tons of steel upgrade could outshout any man's conversation, so they sat without talking. Tom driving, Rivera watching his hands flick over the controls.

The bluff started in a low ridge running almost the length of the little island, like a lopsided backbone. Toward the center it rose abruptly, sent a wing out toward the rocky outcropping at the beach where their equipment had been unloaded, and then rose again to a small, almost square plateau area, half a mile across. It was humpy and rough until they could see all of it, when they realized how incredibly level it was, under the brush and ruins that covered it. In the center—and exactly in the center they realized suddenly—was a low, overgrown mound. Tom threw out the clutch and revved her down.

"Survey report said there was stone up here," Tom said, vaulting out of the seat. "Let's walk around some."

They walked toward the knoll, Tom's eyes casting about as he went. He stooped down into the heavy, short grass and scooped up a piece of stone, blue-gray, hard and brittle.

"Rivera—look at this. This is what the report was talking about. See—more of it. All in small pieces, though. We need big stuff for the bog if we can get it."

"Good stone?" asked Rivera.

"Yes, boy—but it don't belong here. Th' whole island's sand and marl and sandstone on the outcrop down yonder. This here's a bluestone, like a diamond clay. Harder'n blazes. I never saw this stuff on a marl hill before. Or near one. Anyhow, root around and see if there is any big stuff."

They walked on. Rivera suddenly dipped down and pulled grass aside.

"Tom—here's a beeg one."

Tom came over and looked down at the corner of stone sticking up out of the topsoil. "Yeh. Goony, get your girlfriend over here and we'll root it out."

Rivera sprinted back to the idling dozer and climbed aboard. He brought the machine over to where Tom waited, stopped, stood up and peered over the front of the machine to locate the stone, then sat down and shifted gears. Before he could move the machine Tom was on the fender beside him, checking him with a hand on his arm.

"No, boy—no. Not third. First. And half throttle. That's it. Don't try to bash a rock out of the ground. Go on up to it easy; set your blade against it, lift it out, don't boot it out. Take it with the middle of your blade, not the corner—get the load on both hydraulic cylinders. Who told you to do like that?"

"No one tol' me, Tom. I see a man do it, I do it."

"Yeah? Who was it?"

"Dennis, but—"

"Listen, Goony, if you want to learn anything from Dennis, watch him while he's on a pan. He dozes like he talks. That reminds me—what I wanted to talk to you about. You ever have any trouble with him?"

Rivera spread his hands. "How I have trouble when he never talk to me?"

"Well, that's all right then. You keep it that way. Dennis is O.K., I guess, but you better keep away from him."

He went on to tell the boy then about what Peebles had said concerning being an operator and a mechanic at the same time. Rivera's lean dark face fell, and his hand strayed to the blade control, touching it lightly, feeling the composition grip and the machined locknuts that held it. When Tom had quite finished he said:

"O.K., Tom—if you want, you break 'em, I feex 'em. But if you wan' help some time, I run *Daisy Etta* for you, no?"

"Sure, kid, sure. But don't forget, no man can do everything."

"You can do everything," said the boy.

Tom leaped off the machine and Rivera shifted into first and crept up to the stone, setting the blade gently against it. Taking the load, the mighty engine audibly bunched its muscles; Rivera opened the throttle a little and the machine set solidly against the stone, the tracks slipping, digging into the ground, piling loose earth up behind. Tom raised a fist, thumb up, and the boy began lifting his blade. The Seven lowered her snout like an ox pulling through mud; the front of the tracks buried themselves deeper and the blade slipped upward an inch on the rock, as if it were on a ratchet. The stone shifted, and suddenly heaved itself up out of the earth that covered it, bulging the sod aside like a ship's slow bow-wave. And the blade lost its grip and slipped over the stone. Rivera slapped out the master clutch within an ace of letting the mass of it poke through his radiator core. Reversing, he set the blade against it again and rolled it at last into daylight.

Tom stood staring at it, scratching the back of his neck. Rivera got off the machine and stood beside him. For a long time they said nothing.

The stone was roughly rectangular, shaped like a brick with one end cut at about a thirty-degree angle. And on the angled face was a square-cut ridge, like the tongue on a piece of milled lumber. The stone was 3 x 3 x 2 feet, and must have weighed six or seven hundred pounds.

"Now that," said Tom, bug-eyed, "didn't grow *here,* and if it did it never grew that way."

"Una piedra de una casa," said Rivera softly. "Tom, there was a building here, no?"

Tom turned suddenly to look at the knoll.

"There is a building here—or what's left of it. Lord on'y knows how old—"

They stood there in the slowly dwindling light, staring at the knoll; and there came upon them a feeling of oppression, as if there were no wind and no sound anywhere. And yet there was a wind, and behind them *Daisy Etta* whacked away with her muttering idle, and nothing had changed and—was that it? That nothing had changed? That nothing would change, or could, here?

Tom opened his mouth twice to speak, and couldn't, or didn't want to—he didn't know which. Rivera slumped down suddenly on his hunkers, back erect, and his eyes wide.

It grew very cold. "It's cold," Tom said, and his voice sounded harsh to him. And the wind blew warm on them, the earth was warm under Rivera's knees. The cold was not a lack of heat, but a lack of something else—warmth, but the specific warmth of life-force, perhaps. The feeling of oppression grew, as if their recognition of the strangeness of the place had started it, and their increasing sensitivity to it made it grow.

Rivera said something, quietly, in Spanish.

"What are you looking at?" asked Tom.

Rivera started violently, threw up an arm, as if to ward off the crash of Tom's voice.

"I . . . there is nothin' to see, Tom. I feel this way wance before. I dunno—" He shook his head, his eyes wide and blank. "An' after, there was being wan hell of a thunderstorm—" His voice petered out.

Tom took his shoulder and hauled him roughly to his feet. "Goony! You slap-happy?"

The boy smiled, almost gently. The down on his upper lip held little spheres of sweat. "I ain' nothin', Tom. I'm jus' scare like hell."

"You scare yourself right back up there on that cat and git to work," Tom roared. More quietly then, he said, "I know there's something—wrong—here, Goony, but that ain't goin' to get us a runway built. Anyway, I know what to do about a dawg 'at gits gun-shy. Ought to be able to do as much fer you. Git along to th' mound now and see if it ain't a cache o' big stone for us. We got a swamp down there to fill."

Rivera hesitated, started to speak, swallowed and then walked slowly over to Seven. Tom stood watching him, closing his mind to the impalpable pressure of something, somewhere near, making his guts cold.

The bulldozer nosed over to the mound, grunting, reminding Tom suddenly that the machine's Spanish slang name was *puerco*—pig, boar. Rivera angled into the edge of the mound with the cutting corner of the blade. Dirt and brush curled up, fell away from the mound and loaded from the bank side, out along the moldboard. The boy finished his pass along the mound, carried the load past it and wasted it out on the flat, turned around and started back again.

Ten minutes later Rivera struck stone, the manganese steel screaming along it, a puff of gray dust spouting from the cutting corner. Tom knelt and examined it after the machine had passed. It was the same kind of stone they had found out on the flat—and shaped the same way. But here it was a wall, the angled faces of the block ends obviously tongued and grooved together.

Cold, cold as—

Tom took one deep breath and wiped sweat out of his eyes.

"I don't care," he whispered, "I got to have that stone. I got to fill me a swamp." He stood back and motioned to Rivera to blade into a chipped crevice in the buried wall.

The Seven swung into the wall and stopped while Rivera shifted into first, throttled down and lowered his blade. Tom looked up into his face. The boy's lips were white. He eased in the master clutch, the blade dipped and the corner swung neatly into the crevice.

The dozer blatted protestingly and began to crab sideways, pivoting on the end of the blade. Tom jumped out of the way, ran around behind the machine, which was almost parallel with the wall now, and stood in the clear, one hand raised ready to signal, his eyes on the straining blade. And then everything happened at once.

With a toothy snap the block started and came free, pivoting outward from its square end, bringing with it its neighbor. The block above them dropped, and the whole mound seemed to settle. And *something* whooshed out of the black hole where the rocks had been. Something like a fog, but not a fog that could be seen, something huge that could not be measured. With it came a gust of that cold which was not cold, and the smell of ozone, and the prickling crackle of a mighty static discharge.

Tom was fifty feet from the wall before he knew he had moved. He stopped and saw the Seven suddenly buck like a wild stallion, once, and Rivera turning over twice in the air. Tom shouted some meaningless syllable and tore over to the boy, where he sprawled in the rough grass, lifted him in his arms, and ran. Only then did he realize that he was running from the machine.

It was like a mad thing. Its moldboard rose and fell. It curved away from the mound, howling governor gone wild, controls flailing. The blade dug repeatedly into the earth, gouging it up in great dips through which the tractor plunged, clanking and bellowing furiously. It raced away in a great irregular arc, turned and came snorting back to the mound, where it beat at the buried wall, slewed and scraped and roared.

Tom reached the edge of the plateau sobbing for breath, and kneeling, laid the boy gently down on the grass.

"Goony, boy . . . hey—"

The long silken eyelashes fluttered, lifted. Something wrenched in Tom as he saw the eyes, rolled right back so that only the whites showed. Rivera drew a long quivering breath which caught suddenly. He coughed twice, threw his head from side to side so violently that Tom took it between his hands and steadied it.

"*Ay . . . María madre . . . qué me ha pasado,* Tom—w'at has happen to me?"

"Fell off the Seven, stupid. You . . . how you feel?"

Rivera scrabbled at the ground, got his elbows half under him, then sank back weakly. "Feel O.K. Headache like hell. W-what happen to my feets?"

"Feet? They hurt?"

"No hurt—" The young face went gray, the lips tightened with effort. "No nothin', Tom."

"You can't move 'em?"

Rivera shook his head, still trying. Tom stood up. "You take it easy. I'll go get Kelly. Be right back."

He walked very quickly and when Rivera called to him he did not turn around. Tom had seen a man with a broken back before.

At the edge of the little plateau Tom stopped, listening. In the deepening twilight he could see the bulldozer standing by the mound. The motor was running; she had not stalled herself. But what stopped Tom was that she wasn't idling, but revving up and down as if an impatient hand were on the throttle—*hroom hrooom,* running up and up far faster than even a broken governor should permit, then coasting down to near silence, broken by the explosive punctuation of sharp and irregular firing. Then it would run up and up again, almost screaming, sustaining a r.p.m. that threatened every moving part, shaking the great machine like some deadly ague.

Tom walked swiftly toward the Seven, a puzzled and grim frown on his weather-beaten face. Governors break down occasionally, and once in a while you will have a motor tear itself to pieces, revving up out of control. But it will either do that or it will rev down and quit. If an operator is fool enough to leave his machine with the master clutch engaged, the machine will take off and run the way the Seven had—but it will not turn unless the blade corner catches in something unresisting, and then the chances are very strong that it will stall. But in any case, it was past reason for any machine to act this way, revving up and down, running, turning, lifting and dropping the blade.

The motor slowed as he approached, and at last settled down into something like a steady and regular idle. Tom had the sudden crazy impression that it was watching him. He shrugged off the feeling, walked up and laid a hand on the fender.

The Seven reacted like a wild stallion. The big Diesel roared, and Tom distinctly saw the master clutch lever snap back over center. He leaped clear, expecting the machine to jolt forward, but apparently it was a reverse gear, for it shot backwards, one track locked, and the near end of the blade swung in a swift vicious arc, breezing a bare fraction of an inch past his hip as he danced back out of the way.

And as if it had bounced off a wall, the tractor had shifted and was bearing down on him, the twelve-foot blade rising, the two big headlights looming over him on their bow-legged supports, looking like the protruding eyes of some mighty toad. Tom had no choice but to leap straight up and grasp the top of the blade in his two hands, leaning back hard to brace his feet against the curved moldboard. The blade dropped and sank into the soft topsoil, digging a deep little swale in the ground. The earth loading on the moldboard rose and churned around Tom's legs; he stepped wildly, keeping them clear of the rolling drag of it. Up came the blade then, leaving a four-foot pile at the edge of the pit; down and up the tractor raced as the tracks went into it; up and up as they climbed the pile of dirt. A quick balance and overbalance as the machine lurched up and over like a motorcycle taking a jump off a ramp, and then a spine-shaking crash as fourteen tons of metal smashed blade-first into the ground.

Part of the leather from Tom's tough palms stayed with the blade as he was flung off. He went head over heels backwards, but had his feet gathered and sprang as they touched the ground; for he knew that no machine could bury its blade like that and get out easily. He leaped to the top of the blade, got one hand on the radiator cap, vaulted. Perversely, the cap broke from its hinge and came away in his hand, in that split instant when only that hand rested on anything. Off balance, he landed on his shoulder with his legs flailing the air, his body sliding off the hood's smooth shoulder toward the track now churning the earth beneath. He made a wild grab at the air intake pipe, barely had it in his fingers when the dozer freed itself and shot backwards up and over the hump. Again that breathless fight pivoting over the top, and the clanking crash as the machine landed, this time almost flat on its tracks.

The jolt tore Tom's hand away, and as he slid back over the hood the crook of his elbow caught the exhaust stack, the dull red metal biting into his flesh. He grunted and clamped the arm around it. His momentum carried him around it, and his feet crashed into the steering clutch levers. Hooking one with his instep, he doubled his legs and whipped himself back, scrabbling at the smooth warm metal, crawling frantically backward until he finally fell heavily into the seat.

"Now," he gritted through the red wall of pain, "you're gonna git operated." And he kicked out the master clutch.

The motor wailed, with the load taken off so suddenly. Tom grasped the throttle, his thumb down on the ratchet release, and he shoved the lever forward to shut off the fuel.

It wouldn't shut off; it went down to a slow idle, but it wouldn't shut off.

"There's one thing you can't do without," he muttered, "compression."

He stood up and leaned around the dash, reaching for the compression-release lever. As he came up out of the seat, the engine revved up again. He turned to the throttle, which had snapped back into the "open" position. As his hand touched it the master clutch lever snapped in and the howling machine lurched forward with a jerk that snapped his head on his shoulders and threw him heavily back into the seat. He snatched at the hydraulic blade control and threw it to "float" position; and then as the falling moldboard touched the ground, into "power down." The cutting edge bit into the ground and the engine began to labor. Holding the blade control, he pushed the throttle forward with his other hand. One of the steering clutch levers whipped back and struck him agonizingly on the kneecap. He involuntarily let go of the blade control and the moldboard began to rise. The engine began to turn faster and he realized that it was not responding to the throttle. Cursing, he leaped to his feet; the suddenly flailing steering clutch levers struck him three times in the groin before he could get between them.

Blind with pain, Tom clung gasping to the dash. The oil-pressure gauge fell off the dash to his right, with a tinkling of broken glass, and from its broken quarter-inch line scalding oil drenched him. The shock of it snapped back his wavering consciousness. Ignoring the blows of the left steering clutch and the master clutch which had started the same mad punching, he bent over the left end of the dash and grasped the compression lever. The tractor rushed forward and spun sickeningly, and Tom knew he was thrown. But as he felt himself leave the decking his hand punched the compression lever down. The great valves at the cylinder heads opened and locked open; atomized fuel and super-heated air chattered out, and as Tom's head and shoulders struck the ground the great wild machine rolled to a stop, stood silently except for the grumble of water boiling in the cooling system.

Minutes later Tom raised his head and groaned. He rolled over and sat up, his chin on his knees, washed by wave after wave of pain. As they gradually subsided, he crawled to the machine and pulled himself to his feet, hand over hand on the track. And groggily he began to cripple the tractor, at least for the night.

He opened the cock under the fuel tank, left the warm yellow fluid gushing out on the ground. He opened the drain on the reservoir by the injection pump. He found a piece of wire in the crank box and with it tied down the compression release lever. He crawled up on the machine, wrenched the hood and ball jar off the air intake precleaner, pulled off his shirt and stuffed it down the pipe. He pushed the throttle all the way forward and locked it with the locking pin. And he shut off the fuel on the main line from the tank to the pump.

Then he climbed heavily to the ground and slogged back to the edge of the plateau where he had left Rivera.

They didn't know Tom was hurt until an hour and a half later—there had been too much to do—rigging a stretcher for the Puerto

Rican, building him a shelter, an engine crate with an Army pup tent for a roof. They brought out the first-aid-kit and the medical books and did what they could—tied and splinted and dosed with an opiate. Tom was a mass of bruises, and his right arm, where it had hooked the exhaust stack, was a flayed mass. They fixed him up then, old Peebles handling the sulfa powder and bandages like a trained nurse. And only then was there talk.

"I've seen a man thrown off a pan," said Dennis, as they sat around the coffee urn munching C rations. "Sittin' up on the arm rest on a cat, looking backwards. Cat hit a rock and bucked. Threw him off on the track. Stretched him out ten feet long." He in-whistled some coffee to dilute the mouthful of food he had been talking around, and masticated noisily. "Man's a fool to set up there on the side of his butt even on a pan. Can't see why th' goony was doin' it on a dozer."

"He wasn't," said Tom.

Kelly rubbed his pointed jaw. "He set flat on th' seat an' was th'owed?"

"That's right."

After an unbelieving silence Dennis said, "What was he doin'—drivin' over sixty?"

Tom looked around the circle of faces lit up by the over-artificial brilliance of a pressure lantern, and wondered what the reaction would be if he told it all just as it was. He had to say something, and it didn't look as if it could be the truth.

"He was workin'," he said finally. "Bucking stone out of the wall of an old building up on the mesa there. One turned loose an' as it did the governor must've gone haywire. She bucked like a loco hoss and run off."

"Run off?"

Tom opened his mouth and closed it again, and just nodded.

Dennis said, "Well, reckon that's what happens when you put a mechanic to operatin'."

"That had nothin' to do with it," Tom snapped.

Peebles spoke up quickly. "Tom—what about the Seven? Broke up any?"

"Some," said Tom. "Better look at the steering clutches. An' she was hot."

"Head's cracked," said Harris, a burly young man with shoulders like a buffalo and a famous thirst.

"How do you know?"

"Saw it when Al and me went up with the stretcher to get the kid while you all were building the shelter. Hot water runnin' down the side of the block."

"You mean you walked all the way out to the mound to look at that tractor while the kid was lyin' there? I told you where he was!"

"Out to the mound!" Al Knowles' pop eyes teetered out of their sockets. "We found that cat stalled twenty feet away from where the kid was!"

"What!"

"That's right, Tom," said Harris. "What's eatin' you? Where'd you leave it?"

"I told you . . . by the mound . . . the ol' building we cut into."

"Leave the startin' motor runnin'?"

"Starting motor?" Tom's mind caught the picture of the small, two-cylinder gasoline engine bolted to the side of the big Diesel's crankcase, coupled through the Bendix gear and clutch to the flywheel of the Diesel to crank it. He remembered his last glance at the still machine, silent but for the sound of water boiling. "Hell no!"

Al and Harris exchanged a glance. "I guess you were sort of slaphappy at the time, Tom," Harris said, not unkindly. "When we were halfway up the hill we heard it, and you know you can't mistake that racket. Sounded like it was under a load."

Tom beat softly at his temples with his clenched fists. "I left that machine dead," he said quietly. "I got compression off her and tied down the lever. I even stuffed my shirt in the intake. I drained the tank. But—I didn't touch the starting motor."

Peebles wanted to know why he had gone to all that trouble. Tom just looked vaguely at him and shook his head. "I shoulda pulled the wires. I never thought about the starting motor," he whispered. Then, "Harris—you say you found the starting motor running when you got to the top?"

"No—she was stalled. And hot—awmighty hot. I'd say the startin' motor was seized up tight. That must be it, Tom. You left the startin' motor runnin' and somehow engaged the clutch an' Bendix." His voice lost conviction as he said it—it takes seventeen separate motions to start a tractor of this type. "Anyhow, she was in gear an' crawled along on the little motor."

"I done that once," said Chub. "Broke a con rod on a Eight, on a highway job. Walked her about three-quarters of a mile on the startin' motor that way. Only I had to stop every hundred yards and let her cool down some."

Not without sarcasm, Dennis said, "Seems to me like the Seven was out to get th' goony. Made one pass at him and then went back to finish the job."

Al Knowles haw-hawed extravagantly.

Tom stood up, shaking his head, and went off among the crates to the hospital they had jury-rigged for the kid.

A dim light was burning inside, and Rivera lay very still, with his eyes closed. Tom leaned in the doorway—the open end of the engine crate—and watched him for a moment. Behind him he could hear the murmur of the crew's voices; the night was otherwise windless and still. Rivera's face was the peculiar color that olive skin takes when drained of blood. Tom looked at his chest and for a panicky moment thought he could discern no movement there. He entered and put a hand over the boy's heart. Rivera shivered, his eyes flew open, and he drew a sudden breath which caught raggedly at the back of his throat. "Tom . . . Tom!" he cried weakly.

"O.K., Goony . . . *qué pasa?*"

"She comeen back . . . Tom!"

"Who?"

"El de siete."

Daisy Etta—"She ain't comin' back, kiddo. You're off the mesa now. Keep your chin up, fella."

Rivera's dark, doped eyes stared up at him without expression. Tom moved back and the eyes continued to stare. They weren't seeing anything. "Go to sleep," he whispered. The eyes closed instantly.

Kelly was saying that nobody ever got hurt on a construction job unless somebody was dumb. "An' most times you don't realize how dumb what you're doin' is until somebody does get hurt."

"The dumb part was getting' a kid, an' not even an operator at that, up on a machine," said Dennis in his smuggest voice.

"I heard you try to sing that song before," said old Peebles quietly. "I hate to have to point out anything like this to a man because it don't do any good to make comparisons. But I've worked with that fella Rivera for a long time now, an I've seen 'em as good but doggone few better. As far as you're concerned, you're O.K. on a pan, but the kid could give you cards and spades and still make you look like a cost accountant on a dozer."

Dennis half rose and mouthed something filthy. He looked at Al Knowles for backing and got it. He looked around the circle and got none. Peebles lounged back, sucking on his pipe, watching from under those bristling brows. Dennis subsided, running now on another tack.

"So what does that prove? The better you say he is, the less reason he had to fall off a cat and get himself hurt."

"I haven't got the thing straight yet," said Chub, in a voice whose tone indicated "I hate to admit it, but—"

About this time Tom returned, like a sleepwalker, standing with the brilliant pressure lantern between him and Dennis. Dennis rambled right on, not knowing he was anywhere near: "That's something you never will find out. That Puerto Rican is a pretty husky kid. Could be Tom said something he didn't like an' he tried to put a knife in Tom's back. They all do, y'know. Tom didn't get all that bashin' around just stoppin' a machine. They must of went round an' round for a while an' the goony wound up with a busted back. Tom sets the dozer to walk him down while he lies there and comes on down here and tries to tell us—" His voice fluttered to a stop as Tom loomed over him.

Tom grabbed the pan operator up by the slack of his shirt front with his uninjured arm and shook him like an empty burlap bag.

"Skunk," he growled. "I oughta lower th' boom on you." He set Dennis on his feet and backhanded his face with the edge of his forearm. Dennis went down—cowered down, rather than fell. "Aw, Tom, I was just talkin'. Just a joke, Tom, I was just—"

"Yellow, too," snarled Tom, stepping forward, raising a solid Texan boot. Peebles barked "Tom!" and the foot came back to the ground.

"Out o' my sight," rumbled the foreman. "Git!"

Dennis got. Al Knowles said vaguely, "Naow, Tom, y'all cain't—"

"You, y'wall-eyed string-bean!" Tom raved, his voice harsh and strained. "Go 'long with your Siamese twin!"

"O.K., O.K.," said Al, white-faced, and disappeared into the dark with Dennis.

"Nuts to this," said Chub. "I'm turnin' in." He went to a crate and hauled out a mosquito-hooded sleeping bag and went off without another word. Harris and Kelly, who were both on their feet, sat down again. Old Peebles hadn't moved.

Tom stood staring out into the dark, his arms straight at his sides, his fists knotted.

"Sit down," said Peebles gently, Tom turned and stared at him.

"Sit down. I can't change that dressing 'less you do." He pointed at the bandage around Tom's elbow. It was red, a widening stain, the tattered tissues having parted as the big Georgian bunched his infuriated muscles. He sat down.

"Talkin' about dumbness," said Harris calmly, as Peebles went to work, "I was about to say that I got the record. I done the dumbest thing anybody ever did on a machine. You can't top it."

"I could," said Kelly. "Runnin' a crane dragline once. Put her in boom gear and started to boom her up. Had an eighty-five-foot stick on her. Machine was standing on wooden mats in the middle of a swamp. Heard the motor miss and got out of the saddle to look at the filter-glass. Messed around back there longer than I figured, and the boom went straight up in the air and fell backwards over the cab. Th' jolt tilted my mats an' she slid backwards slow and stately as you please, butt-first into the mud. Buried up to the eyeballs, she was." He laughed quietly. "Looked like a ditching machine!"

"I still say I done the dumbest thing ever, bar none," said Harris. "It was on a river job, widening a channel. I come back to work from a three-day binge, still rum-dumb. Got up on a dozer an' was workin' around on the edge of a twenty-foot cliff. Down at the foot of the cliff was a big hickory tree, an' growin' right along the edge was a great big limb. I got the dopey idea I should break it off. I put one track on the limb and the other on the cliff edge and run out away from the trunk. I was about halfway out, an' the branch saggin' some, before I thought what would happen if it broke. Just about then it did break. You know hickory—if it breaks at all it breaks altogether. So down we go into thirty feet of water—me an' the cat. I got out from under somehow. When all them bubbles stopped comin' up I swum around lookin' down at it. I was still paddlin' around when the superintendent came rushin' up. He wants to know what's up. I yell at him, 'Look down there, the way that water is movin' an' shiftin', looks like the cat is workin' down there.'" He pursed his lips and *tsk tsked.* "My, that man said some nasty things to me."

"Where'd you get your next job?" Kelly exploded.

"Oh, he didn't fire me," said Harris soberly. "Said he couldn't afford to fire a man as dumb as that. Said he wanted me around to look at whenever he felt bad."

Tom said, "Thanks, you guys. That's as good a way as any of sayin' that everybody makes mistakes." He stood up, examining the new dressing, turning his arm in front of his lantern. "You all can think what you please, but I don't recollect there was any dumbness went on on that mesa this evenin'. That's finished with, anyway. Do I have to say that Dennis' idea about it is all wet?"

Harris said one foul word that completely disposed of Dennis and anything he might say.

Peebles said, "It'll be all right. Dennis an' his popeyed friend'll hang together, but they don't amount to anything. Chub'll do whatever he's argued into."

"So you get 'em all lined up, hey?" Tom shrugged. "In the meantime, are we going to get an airfield built?"

"We'll get it built," Peebles said. "Only—Tom, I got no right to give you any advice, but go easy on the rough stuff after this. It does a lot of harm."

"I will if I can," said Tom gruffly. They broke up and turned in.

Peebles was right. It did do harm. It made Dennis use the word "murder" when they found, in the morning, that Rivera had died during the night.

The work progressed in spite of everything that had happened. With equipment like that, it's hard to slow things down. Kelly bit two cubic yards out of the bluff with every swing of the big shovel, and Dumptors are the fastest short haul earth movers yet devised. Dennis kept the service road clean for them with his pan, and Tom and Chub spelled each other on the bulldozer they had detached from its pan to make up for the lack of the Seven, spending their alternate periods with transit and stakes. Peebles was rod-man for the surveys, and in between times worked on setting up his field shop, keeping the water cooler and battery chargers running, and lining up his forge and welding tables. The operators fueled and serviced their own equipment, and there was little delay. The rocks and marl that came out of the growing cavity in the side of the central mesa—a whole third of it had to come out—were spun down to the edge of the swamp, which lay across the lower end of the projected runway, in the hornet-howling dump-tractors, their big driving wheels churning up vast clouds of dust, and were dumped and spread and walked in by the whining two-cycle dozer. When muck began to pile up in front of the fill, it was blasted out of the way with carefully placed charges of sixty percent dynamite and the craters filled with rocks and stone from the ruins, and surfaced with easily compacting marl, run out of a clean deposit by the pan.

And when he had his shop set up, Peebles went up the hill to get the Seven. When he got it he just stood there for a moment scratching his head, and then, shaking his head, he ambled back down the hill and went for Tom.

"Been looking at the Seven," he said, when he had flagged the moaning two-cycle and Tom had climbed off.

"What'd you find?"

Peebles held out an arm. "A list as long as that." He shook his head. "Tom, what really happened up there?"

"Governor went haywire and she run away," Tom said promptly, deadpan.

"Yeah, but—" For a long moment he held Tom's eyes. Then he sighed. "O.K., Tom. Anyway, I can't do a thing up there. We'll have to bring her back and I'll have to have this tractor to tow her down. And first I have to have some help—the track idler adjustment bolt's busted and the right track is off the track rollers."

"Oh-h-h. So that's why she couldn't get to the kid, running on the starting motor. Track would hardly turn, hey?"

"It's a miracle she ran as far as she did. That track is really jammed up. Riding right up on the roller flanges. And that ain't the half of it. The head's gone, like Harris said, and Lord only knows what I'll find when I open her up."

"Why bother?"

"What?"

"We can get along without that dozer," said Tom suddenly. "Leave her where she is. There's lots more for you to do."

"But what for?"

"Well, there's no call to go to all that trouble."

Peebles scratched the side of his nose and said, "I got a new head, track master pins—even a spare starting motor. I got tools to make what I don't stock." He pointed at the long row of dumps left by the hurtling dump-tractors while they had been talking. "You got a pan tied up because you're using this machine to doze with, and you can't tell me you can't use another one. You're gonna have to shut down one or two o' those Dumptors if you go on like this."

"I had all that figured out as soon as I opened my mouth," Tom said sullenly. "Let's go."

They climbed on the tractor and took off, stopping for a moment at the beach outcropping to pick up a cable and some tools.

Daisy Etta sat at the edge of the mesa, glowering out of her stilted headlights at the soft sward which still bore the impression of a young body and the tramplings of the stretcher-bearers. Her general aspect was woebegone—there were scratches on her olive-drab paint and the bright metal of the scratches was already dulled red by the earliest powder-rust. And though the ground was level, she was not, for her right track was off its lower rollers, and she stood slightly canted, like a man who has had a broken hip. And whatever passed for consciousness within her mulled over that paradox of the bulldozer that every operator must go through while he is learning his own machine.

It is the most difficult thing of all for the beginner to understand, that paradox. A bulldozer is a crawling powerhouse, a behemoth of noise and toughness, the nearest thing to the famous irresistible force. The beginner, awed and with the pictures of unconquerable Army tanks printed on his mind from the newsreels, takes all in his stride and with a sense of limitless power treats all obstacles alike, not knowing the fragility of a cast-iron radiator core, the mortality of tempered manganese, the friability of over-heated babbitt, and most of all, the ease with which a tractor can bury itself in mud. Climbing off to stare at a machine which he has reduced in twenty seconds to a useless hulk, or which was running a half-minute before on ground where it now has its tracks out of sight, he has that sense of guilty disappointment which overcomes any man on having made an error in judgment.

So, as she stood, *Daisy Etta* was broken and useless. These soft persistent bipeds had built her, and if they were like any other race that built machines, they could care for them. The ability to reverse the tension of a spring, or twist a control rod, or reduce to zero the friction in a nut and lock-washer, was not enough to repair the crack in a cylinder head nor bearings welded to a crankshaft in an overheated starting motor. There had been a lesson to learn. It had been learned. *Daisy Etta* would be repaired, and the next time—well, at least she would know her own weaknesses.

Tom swung the two-cycle machine and edged in next to the Seven, with the edge of his blade all but touching *Daisy Etta*'s push-beam. They got off and Peebles bent over the drum-tight right track.

"Watch yourself," said Tom.

"Watch what?"

"Oh—nothin', I guess." He circled the machine, trained eyes probing over frame and fittings. He stepped forward suddenly and grasped the fuel-tank drain cock. It was closed. He opened it; golden oil gushed out. He shut it off, climbed up on the machine and opened the fuel cap on top of the tank. He pulled out the bayonet gauge, wiped it in the crook of his knee, dipped and withdrew it.

The tank was more than three quarters full.

"What's the matter?" asked Peebles, staring curiously at Tom's drawn face.

"Peeby, I opened the cock to drain this tank. I left it with oil runnin' out on the ground. She shut herself off."

"Now, Tom, you're lettin' this thing get you down. You just thought you did. I've seen a main-line valve shut itself off when it's worn bad, but only 'cause the fuel pump pulls it shut when the motor's runnin'. But not a gravity drain."

"Main-line valve?" Tom pulled the seat up and looked. One glance was enough to show him this one was open.

"She opened this one, too."

"O.K.—O.K. Don't look at me like that!" Peebles was as near to exasperation as he could possibly get. "What difference does it make?"

Tom did not answer. He was not the type of man who, when faced with something beyond his understanding, would begin to doubt his own sanity. His was a dogged insistence that what he saw and sensed was what had actually happened. In him was none of the fainting fear of madness that another, more sensitive, man might feel. He doubted neither himself nor his evidence, and so could free his mind for searching out the consuming "why" of a problem. He knew instinctively that to share "unbelievable" happenings with anyone else, even if they had really occurred, was to put even further obstacles in his way. So he kept his clamlike silence and stubbornly, watchfully, investigated.

The slipped track was so tightly drawn up on the roller flanges that there could be no question of pulling the master pin and opening the track up. It would have to be worked back in place—a very delicate operation, for a little force applied in the wrong direction would be enough to run the track off altogether. To complicate things, the blade of the Seven was down on the ground and would have to be lifted before the machine could be maneuvered, and its hydraulic hoist was useless without the motor.

Peebles unhooked twenty feet of half-inch cable from the rear of the smaller dozer, scratched a hole in the ground under the Seven's blade, and pushed the eye of the cable through. Climbing over the moldboard, he slipped the eye on the big towing hook bolted to the underside of the belly-guard. The other end of the cable he threw out on the ground in front of the machine. Tom mounted the other dozer and swung into place, ready to tow. Peebles hooked the cable onto Tom's drawbar, hopped up on the Seven. He put her in neutral, disengaged the master clutch, and put the blade control over into "float" position, then raised an arm.

Tom perched upon the arm rest of his machine, looking backwards, moved slowly, taking up the slack in the cable. It straightened and grew taut, and as it did it forced the Seven's blade upward. Peebles waved for slack and put the blade control into "hold." The cable bellied downward away from the blade.

"Hydraulic system's O.K., anyhow," called Peebles, as Tom throttled down. "Move over and take a strain to the right, sharp as you can without fouling the cable on the track. We'll see if we can walk this track back on."

Tom backed up, cut sharply right, and drew the cable out almost at right angles to the other machine. Peebles held the right track of the Seven with the brake and released both steering clutches. The left track now could turn free, the right not at all. Tom was running at a quarter throttle in his lowest gear, so that his machine barely crept along, taking the strain. The Seven shook gently and began to pivot on the taut right track, unbelievable foot-pounds of energy coming to bear on the front of the track where it rode high up on the idler wheel. Peebles released the right brake with his foot and applied it again in a series of skilled, deft jerks. The track would move a few inches and stop again, force being applied forward and sideward alternately, urging the track persuasively back in place. Then, a little jolt and she was in, riding true on the five truck rollers, the two track carrier rollers, the driving sprocket and the idler.

Peebles got off and stuck his head in between the sprocket and the rear carrier, squinting down and sideways to see if there were any broken flanges or roller bushes. Tom came over and pulled him out by the seat of his trousers. "Time enough for that when you get her in the shop," he said, masking his nervousness. "Reckon she'll roll?"

"She'll roll. I never saw a track in that condition come back that easy. By gosh, it's as if she was tryin' to help!"

"They'll do it sometimes," said Tom, stiffly. "You better take the two-tractor, Peeby. I'll stay with this'n."

"Anything you say."

And cautiously they took the steep slope down, Tom barely holding the brakes, giving the other machine a straight pull all the way. And so they brought *Daisy Etta* down to Peebles' outdoor shop, where they pulled her cylinder head off, took off her starting motor, pulled out a burned clutch facing, had her quite helpless—

And put her together again.

"I tell you it was outright, cold-blooded murder," said Dennis hotly. "An' here we are takin' orders from a guy like that. What are we goin' to do about it?" They were standing by the cooler—Dennis had run his machine there to waylay Chub.

Chub Horton's cigar went down and up like a semaphore with a short circuit. "We'll skip it. The blacktopping crew will be here in another two weeks or so, an' we can make a report. Besides, I don't know what happened up there any more than you do. In the meantime we got a runway to build."

"You don't know what happened up there? Chub, you're a smart man. Smart enough to run this job better than Tom Jaeger even if he wasn't crazy. And you're surely smart enough not to believe all that cock and bull about the tractor runnin' out from under that grease-monkey. Listen—" He leaned forward and tapped Chub's chest. "He said it was the governor. I saw that governor myself an' heard ol' Peebles say there wasn't a thing wrong with it. Th' throttle control rod had slipped off its yoke, yeah—but you know what a tractor will do when the throttle control goes out. It'll idle or stall. It won't run away, whatever."

"Well, maybe so, but—"

"But nothin'! A guy that'll commit murder ain't sane. If he did it once, he can do it again and I ain't fixin' to let that happen to me."

Two things crossed Chub's steady but not too bright mind at this. One was that Dennis, whom he did not like but could not shake, was trying to force him into something that he did not want to do. The other was that under all of his swift talk Dennis was scared spitless.

"What do you want to do—call up the sheriff?"

Dennis ha-ha-ed appreciatively—one of the reasons he was so hard to shake. "I'll tell you what we can do. As long as we have you here, he isn't the only man who knows the work. If we stop takin' orders from him, you can give 'em as good or better. An' there won't be anything he can do about it."

"Doggone it, Dennis," said Chub, with sudden exasperation. "What do you think you're doin'—handin' me over the keys to the kingdom or something? What do you want to see me bossin' around here for?" He stood up. "Suppose we did what you said? Would it get the field built any quicker? Would it get me any more money in my pay envelope? What do you think I want—glory? I passed up a chance to run for councilman once. You think I'd raise a finger to get a bunch of mugs to do what I say—when they do it anyway?"

"Aw, Chub—I wouldn't cause trouble just for the fun of it. That's not what I mean at all. But unless we do something about that guy we ain't safe. Can't you get that through your head?"

"Listen, windy. If a man keeps busy enough he can't get into trouble. That goes for Tom—you might keep that in mind. But it goes for you, too. Get back up on that rig an' get back to the marl pit." Dennis, completely taken by surprise, turned to his machine.

"It's a pity you can't move earth with your mouth," said Chub as he walked off. "They could have left you do this job single-handed."

Chub walked slowly toward the outcropping, switching at beach pebbles with a grade stake and swearing to himself. He was essentially a simple man and believed in the simplest possible approach to everything. He liked a job where he could do everything required and where nothing turned up to complicate things. He had been in the grading business for a long time as an operator and survey party boss, and he was remarkable for one thing—he had always held aloof from the cliques and internecine politics that are the breath of life to most construction men. He was disturbed and troubled at the back-stabbing that went on around him on various jobs. If it was blunt, he was disgusted, and subtlety simply left him floundering and bewildered. He was stupid enough so that his basic honesty manifested itself in his speech and actions, and he had learned that complete honesty in dealing with men above and below him was almost invariably painful to all concerned, but he had not the wit to act otherwise, and did not try to. If he had a bad tooth, he had it pulled out as soon as he could. If he got a raw deal from a superintendent over him, that superintendent would get told exactly what the trouble was, and if he didn't like it, there were other jobs. And if the pulling and hauling of cliques got in his hair, he had always said so and left. Or he had sounded off and stayed; his completely selfish reaction to things that got in the way of his work had earned him a lot of regard from men he had worked under. And so, in this instance, he had no hesitation about choosing a course of action. Only—how did you go about asking a man if he was a murderer?

He found the foreman with an enormous wrench in his hand, tightening up the new track adjustment bolt they had installed in the Seven.

"Hey, Chub! Glad you turned up. Let's get a piece of pipe over the end of this thing and really bear down." Chub went for the pipe, and they fitted it over the handle of the four-foot wrench and hauled until the sweat ran down their backs, Tom checking the track clearance occasionally with a crowbar. He finally called it good enough and they stood there in the sun gasping for breath.

"Tom," panted Chub, "did you kill that Puerto Rican?"

Tom's head came up as if someone had burned the back of his neck with a cigarette.

"Because," said Chub, "if you did you can't go on runnin' this job."

Tom said, "That's a lousy thing to kid about."

"You know I ain't kiddin'. Well, did you?"

"No!" Tom sat down on a keg, wiped his face with a bandanna. "What's got into you?"

"I just wanted to know. Some of the boys are worried about it."

Tom's eyes narrowed. "Some of the boys, huh? I think I get it. Listen to me, Chub. Rivera was killed by that thing there." He thumbed over his shoulder at the Seven, which was standing ready now, awaiting only the building of a broken cutting corner on the blade. Peebles was winding up the welding machine as he spoke. "If you mean, did I put him up on the machine before he was thrown, the answer is yes. That much I killed him, and don't think I don't feel it. I had a hunch something was wrong up there, but I couldn't put my finger on it and I certainly didn't think anybody was going to get hurt."

"Well, what was wrong?"

"I still don't know." Tom stood up. "I'm tired of beatin' around the bush, Chub, and I don't much care any more what anybody thinks. There's somethin' wrong with that Seven, something that wasn't built into her. They don't make tractors better'n that one, but whatever it was happened up there on the mesa has queered this one. Now go ahead and think what you like, and dream up any story you want to tell the boys. In the meantime you can pass the word—nobody runs that machine but me, understand? Nobody!"

"Tom—"

Tom's patience broke. "That's all I'm going to say about it! If anybody else gets hurt, it's going to be me, understand? What more do you want?"

He strode off, boiling. Chub stared after him, and after a long moment reached up and took the cigar from his lips. Only then did he realize that he had bitten it in two; half the butt was still inside his mouth. He spat and stood there shaking his head.

"How's she going, Peeby?"

Peebles looked up from the welding machine. "Hi, Chub, have her ready for you in twenty minutes." He gauged the distance between the welding machine and the big tractor. "I should have forty feet of cable," he said, looking at the festoons of arc and ground cables that hung from the storage hooks in the back of the welder. "Don't want to get a tractor over here to move the thing, and don't feel like cranking up the Seven just to get it close enough." He separated the arc cable and threw it aside, walked to the tractor, paying the ground cable off his arms. He threw out the last of his slack and grasped the ground clamp when he was eight feet from the machine. Taking it in his left hand, he pulled hard, reaching out with his right to grasp the moldboard of the Seven, trying to get it far enough to clamp on to the machine.

Chub stood there watching him, chewing on the cigar, absent-mindedly diddling with the controls on the arc-welder. He pressed the starter-button, and the six-cylinder motor responded with a purr. He spun the work-selector dials idly, threw the arc generator switch—

A bolt of incredible energy, thin, searing, blue-white, left the rod holder at his feet, stretched itself *fifty feet* across to Peebles, whose fingers had just touched the moldboard of the tractor. Peebles' head and shoulders were surrounded for a second by a violet nimbus, and then he folded over and dropped. A circuit breaker clacked behind the control board of the welder, but too late. The Seven rolled slowly backward, without firing, on level ground, until it brought up against the road-roller.

Chub's cigar was gone, and he didn't notice it. He had the knuckles of his right hand in his mouth, and his teeth sunk into the pudgy flesh. His eyes protruded; he crouched there and quivered, literally frightened out of his mind. For old Peebles was burned almost in two.

They buried him next to Rivera. There wasn't much talk afterwards; the old man had been a lot closer to all of them than they had realized until now. Harris, for once in his rum-dumb, light-headed life, was quiet and serious, and Kelly's walk seemed to lose some of its litheness. Hour after hour Dennis' flabby mouth worked, and he bit at his lower lip until it was swollen and tender. Al Knowles seemed more or less unaffected, as was to be expected from a man who had something less than the brains of a chicken. Chub Horton had snapped out of it after a couple of hours and was very nearly himself again. And in Tom Jaeger swirled a black, furious anger at this unknowable curse that had struck the camp.

And they kept working. There was nothing else to do. The shovel kept up its rhythmic swing and dig, swing and dump, and the Dumptors screamed back and forth between it and the little that was left of the swamp. The upper end of the runway was grassed off; Chub and Tom set grade stakes and Dennis began the long job of cutting and filling the humpy surface with his pan. Harris manned the other and followed him, a cut behind. The shape of the runway emerged from the land, and then that of the paralleling taxiway; and three days went by. The horror of Peebles' death wore off enough so that they could talk about it, and very little of the talk helped anybody. Tom took his spells at everything, changing over with Kelly to give him a rest from the shovel, making a few rounds with a pan, putting in hours on a Dumptor. His arm was healing slowly but clean, and he worked grimly in spite of it, taking a perverse sort of pleasure from the pain of it. Every man on the job watched his machine with the solicitude of a mother with her first-born; a serious break-down would have been disastrous without a highly skilled mechanic.

The only concession that Tom allowed himself in regard to Peebles' death was to corner Kelly one afternoon and ask him about the welding machine. Part of Kelly's rather patchy past had been spent in a technical college, where he had studied electrical engineering and women. He had learned a little of the former and enough of the latter to get him thrown out on his ear. So, on the off-chance that he might know something about the freak arc, Tom put it to him.

Kelly pulled off his high-gauntlet gloves and batted sandflies with them. "What sort of an arc was that? Boy, you got me there. Did you ever hear of a welding machine doing like that before?"

"I did not. A welding machine just don't have that sort o' push. I saw a man get a full jolt from a 400-amp welder once, an' although it sat him down it didn't hurt him any."

"It's not amperage that kills people," said Kelly, "it's voltage. Voltage is the pressure behind a current, you know. Take an amount of water, call it amperage. If I throw it in your face, it won't hurt you. If I put it through a small hose you'll feel it. But if I pump it through them tiny holes on a Diesel injector nozzle at about twelve hundred pounds, it'll draw blood. But a welding arc generator just is not wound to build up that kind of voltage. I can't see where any short circuit anywhere through the armature or field windings could do such a thing."

"From what Chub said, he had been foolin' around with the work selector. I don't think anyone touched the dials after it happened. The selector dial was run all the way over to the low current application segment, and the current control was around the halfway mark. That's not enough juice to get you a good bead with a quarter-inch rod, let alone kill somebody—or roll a tractor back thirty feet on level ground."

"Or jump fifty feet," said Kelly. "It would take thousands of volts to generate an arc like that."

"Is it possible that something in the Seven could have pulled that arc? I mean, suppose the arc wasn't driven over, but was drawn over? I tell you, she was hot for four hours after that."

Kelly shook his head. "Never heard of any such thing. Look, just to have something to call them, we call direct current terminals positive and negative, and just because it works in theory we say that current flows from negative to positive. There couldn't be any more positive attraction in one electrode than there is negative drive in the other; see what I mean?"

"There couldn't be some freak condition that would cause a sort of oversize positive field? I mean one that would suck out the negative flow all in a heap, make it smash through under a lot of pressure like the water you were talking about through an injector nozzle?"

"No, Tom. It just don't work that way, far as anyone knows. I dunno, though—there are some things about static electricity that nobody understands. All I can say is that what happened couldn't happen and if it did it couldn't have killed Peebles. And you know the answer to that."

Tom glanced away at the upper end of the runway, where the two graves were. There was bitterness and turbulent anger naked there for a moment, and he turned and walked away without another word. And when he went back to have another look at the welding machine, *Daisy Etta* was gone.

Al Knowles and Harris squatted together near the water cooler.

"Bad," said Harris.

"Nevah saw anythin' like it," said Al. "Ol' Tom come back f'm the shop theah just raisin' Cain. 'Weah's 'at Seven gone? Weah's 'at Seven?' I never heered sech cah'ins on."

"Dennis did take it, huh?"

"Sho' did."

Harris said. "He came spoutin' around to me a while back, Dennis did. Chub'd told him Tom said for everybody to stay off that machine. Dennis was mad as a wet hen. Said Tom was carryin' that kind o' business too far. Said there was probably somethin' about the Seven Tom didn't want us to find out. Might incriminate him. Dennis is ready to say Tom killed the kid."

"Reckon he did, Harris?"

Harris shook his head. "I've known Tom too long to think that. If he won't tell us what really happened up on the mesa, he has a reason for it. How'd Dennis come to take the dozer?"

"Blew a front tire on his pan. Came back heah to git anothah rig—maybe a Dumptor. Saw th' Seven standin' theah ready to go. Stood theah lookin' at it and cussin' Tom. Said he was tired of bashin' his kidneys t'pieces on them othah rigs an' bedamned if he wouldn't take suthin' that rode good fo' a change. I tol' him ol' Tom'd raise th' roof when he found him on it. He had a couple mo' things t'say 'bout Tom then."

"I didn't think he had the guts to take the rig."

"Aw, he talked hisself blind mad."

They looked up as Chub Horton trotted up, panting. "Hey, you guys, come on. We better get up there to Dennis."

"What's wrong?" asked Harris, climbing to his feet.

"Tom passed me a minute ago lookin' like the wrath o' God and hightailin' it for the swamp fill. I asked him what was the matter and he hollered that Dennis had taken the Seven. Said he was always talkin' about murder and he'd get his fill of it foolin' around that machine." Chub went wall-eyed, licked his lips beside his cigar.

"Oh-oh," said Harris quietly. "That's the wrong kind o' talk for just now."

"You don't suppose he—"

"*Come on!*"

They saw Tom before they were halfway there. He was walking slowly, with his head down. Harris shouted. Tom raised his face, stopped, stood there waiting with a peculiarly slumped stance.

"Where's Dennis?" barked Chub.

Tom waited until they were almost up to him and then weakly raised an arm and thumbed over his shoulder. His face was green.

"Tom—is he—"

Tom nodded, and swayed a little. His granite jaw was slack.

"Al, stay with him. He's sick. Harris, let's go."

Tom was sick, then and there. Very. Al stood gaping at him, fascinated.

Chub and Harris found Dennis. All of twelve square feet of him, ground and churned and rolled out into a torn-up patch of earth. *Daisy Etta* was gone.

Back at the outcropping, they sat with Tom while Al Knowles took a Dumptor and roared away to get Kelly.

"You saw him?" he said dully after a time.

Harris said, "Yeh."

The screaming Dumptor and a mountainous cloud of dust arrived, Kelly driving, Al holding on with a death-grip to the dump-bed guards. Kelly flung himself off, ran to Tom. "Tom—what is all this? Dennis dead? And you . . . you—"

Tom's had came up slowly, the slackness going out of his long face, a light suddenly coming into his eyes. Until this moment it had not crossed his mind what these men might think.

"I—what?"

"Al says you killed him."

Tom's eyes flicked at Al Knowles, and Al winced as if the glance had been a quirt.

Harris said, "What about it, Tom?"

"Nothing about it. He was killed by that Seven. You saw that for yourself."

"I stuck with you all along," said Harris slowly. "I took everything you said and believed it."

"This is too strong for you?" Tom asked.

Harris nodded. "Too strong, Tom."

Tom looked at the grim circle of faces and laughed suddenly. He stood up, put his back against a tall crate. "What do you plan to do about it?"

There was a silence. "You think I went up there and knocked that windbag off the machine and ran over him?" More silence. "Listen. I went up there and saw what you saw. He was dead before I got there. That's not good enough either?" He paused and licked his lips. "So after I killed him I got up on the tractor and drove it far enough away so you couldn't see or hear it when you got there. And then I sprouted wings and flew back so's I was halfway here when you met me—*ten minutes* after I spoke to Chub on my way up!"

Kelly said vaguely, "Tractor?"

"Well," said Tom harshly to Harris, "was the tractor there when you and Chub went up and saw Dennis?"

"No—"

Chub smacked his thigh suddenly. "You could of drove it into the swamp, Tom."

Tom said angrily, "I'm wastin' my time. You guys got it all figured out. Why ask me anything at all?"

"Aw, take it easy," said Kelly. "We just want the facts. Just what did happen? You met Chub and told him that Dennis would get all the murderin' he could take if he messed around that machine. That right?"

"That's right."

"Then what?"

"Then the machine murdered him."

Chub, with remarkable patience, asked, "What did you mean

the day Peebles was killed when you said that something had queered the Seven up there on the mesa?"

Tom said furiously, "I meant what I said. You guys are set to crucify me for this and I can't stop you. Well, listen. Something's got into that Seven. I don't know what it is and I don't think I ever will know. I thought that after she smashed herself up that it was finished with. I had an idea that when we had her torn down and helpless we should have left her that way. I was dead right but it's too late now. She's killed Rivera and she's killed Dennis and she sure had something to do with killing Peebles. And my idea is that she won't stop as long as there's a human being alive on this island."

"Whaddaya know!" said Chub.

"Sure, Tom, sure," said Kelly quietly. "That tractor is out to get us. But don't worry; we'll catch it and tear it down. Just don't you worry about it any more; it'll be all right."

"That's right, Tom," said Harris. "You just take it easy around camp for a couple of days till you feel better. Chub and the rest of us will handle things for you. You had too much sun."

"You're a swell bunch of fellows," gritted Tom, with the deepest sarcasm. "You want to live," he shouted, "git out there and throw that maverick bulldozer!"

"That maverick bulldozer is at the bottom of the swamp where you put it," growled Chub. His head lowered and he started to move in. "Sure we want to live. The best way to do that is to put you where you can't kill anybody else. Get him!"

He leaped. Tom straightened him with his left and crossed with his right. Chub went down, tripping Harris. Al Knowles scuttled to a toolbox and dipped out a fourteen-inch crescent wrench. He circled around, keeping out of trouble, trying to look useful. Tom loosed a haymaker at Kelly, whose head seemed to withdraw like a turtle's; it whistled over, throwing Tom badly off balance. Harris, still on his knees, tackled Tom's legs; Chub hit him in the small of the back with a meaty shoulder, and Tom went flat in his face. Al Knowles, holding the wrench in both hands, swept it up and back like a baseball bat; at the top of its swing Kelly reached over, snatched it out of his hands and tapped Tom delicately behind the ear with it. Tom went limp.

It was late, but nobody seemed to feel like sleeping. They sat around the pressure lantern, talking idly. Chub and Kelly played an inconsequential game of casino, forgetting to pick up their points; Harris paced up and down like a man in a cell, and Al Knowles was squinched up close to the light, his eyes wide and watching, watching—

"I need a drink," said Harris.

"Tens," said one of the casino players.

Al Knowles said, "We shoulda killed him. We oughta kill him now."

"There's been too much killin' already," said Chub. "Shut up, you." And to Kelly, "With big casino," sweeping up cards.

Kelly caught his wrist and grinned. "Big casino's ten of diamonds, not the ten of hearts. Remember?"

"Oh."

"How long before the blacktopping crew will be here?" quavered Al Knowles.

"Twelve days," said Harris. "And they better bring some likker."

"Hey, you guys."

They fell silent.

"Hey!"

"It's Tom," said Kelly. "Building sixes, Chub."

"I'm gonna go kick his ribs in," said Knowles, not moving.

"I heard that," said the voice from the darkness. "If I wasn't hogtied—"

"We know what you'd do," said Chub. "How much proof do you think we need?"

"Chub, you don't have to do any more to him!" It was Kelly, flinging his cards down and getting up. "Tom, you want water?"

"Yes."

"Siddown, siddown," said Chub.

"Let him lay there and bleed," Al Knowles said.

"Nuts!" Kelly went and filled a cup and brought it to Tom. The big Georgian was tied thoroughly, wrists together, taut rope between elbow and elbow behind his back, so that his hands were immovable over his solar plexus. His knees and ankles were bound as well, although Knowles' little idea of a short rope between ankles and throat hadn't been used.

"Thanks, Kelly." Tom drank greedily, Kelly holding his head. "Goes good." He drank more. "What hit me?"

"One of the boys. 'Bout the time you said the cat was haunted."

"Oh, yeah." Tom rolled his head and blinked with pain.

"Any sense asking you if you blame us?"

"Kelly, does somebody else have to get killed before you guys wake up?"

"None of us figure there will be any more killin'—now."

The rest of the men drifted up. "He willing to talk sense?" Chub wanted to know.

Al Knowles laughed, "Hyuk! hyuk! Don't he look dangerous now."

Harris said suddenly, "Al, I'm gonna hafta tape your mouth with the skin off your neck."

"Am I the kind of guy that makes up ghost stories?"

"Never have that I know of, Tom." Harris kneeled down beside him. "Never killed anyone before, either."

"Oh, get away from me. Get away," said Tom tiredly.

"Get up and make us," jeered Al.

Harris got up and backhanded him across the mouth. Al squeaked, took three steps backward and tripped over a drum of grease. "I told you," said Harris almost plaintively. "I *told* you, Al."

Tom stopped the bumble of comment. "Shut up!" he hissed. "SHUT UP!" he roared.

They shut.

"Chub," said Tom, rapidly, evenly. "What did you say I did with that Seven?"

"Buried it in the swamp."

"Yeh. Listen."

"Listen at what?"

"Be quiet and listen!"

So they listened. It was another still, windless night, with a thin crescent of moon showing nothing true in the black and muffled silver landscape. The smallest whisper of surf drifted up from the beach, and from far off to the right, where the swamp was, a scandalized frog croaked protest at the manhandling of his mud-hole. But the sound that crept down, freezing their bones, came from the bluff behind their camp.

It was the unmistakable staccato of a starting engine.

"The Seven!"

"'At's right, Chub," said Tom.

"Wh-who's crankin' her up?"

"Are we all here?"

"All but Peebles and Dennis and Rivera," said Tom.

"It's Dennis' ghost," moaned Al.

Chub snapped, "Shut up, lamebrain."

"She's shifted to Diesel," said Kelly, listening.

"She'll be here in a minute," said Tom. "Y'know, fellas, we can't all be crazy, but you're about to have a time convincin' yourself of it."

"You like this, doncha?"

"Some ways. Rivera used to call that machine *Daisy Etta,* 'cause she's *de siete* in Spig. *Daisy Etta,* she wants her a man."

"Tom," said Harris. "I wish you'd stop that chatterin'. You make me nervous."

"I got to do somethin'. I can't run," Tom drawled.

"We're going to have a look," said Chub. "If there's nobody on that cat, we'll turn you loose."

"Mighty white of you. Reckon you'll get back before she does?"

"We'll get back. Harris, come with me. We'll get one of the pan tractors. They can outrun a Seven. Kelly, take Al and get the other one."

"Dennis' machine has a flat tire on the pan," said Al's quivering voice.

"Pull the pin and cut the cables, then! Git!" Kelly and Al Knowles ran off.

"Good huntin', Chub."

Chub went to him, bent over. "I think I'm goin' to have to apologize to you, Tom."

"No you ain't. I'd a done the same. Get along now, if you think you got to. But hurry back."

"I got to. An' I'll hurry back."

Harris said, "Don't go 'way, boy." Tom returned the grin, and they were gone. But they didn't hurry back. They didn't come back at all.

It was Kelly who came pounding back, with Al Knowles on his heels, a half hour later. "Al—gimme your knife."

He went to work on the ropes. His face was drawn.

"I could see some of it," whispered Tom. "Chub and Harris?"

Kelly nodded. "There wasn't nobody on the Seven like you said." He said it as if there was nothing else in his mind, as if the most rigid self-control was keeping him from saying it over and over.

"I could see the lights," said Tom. "A tractor angling up the hill. Pretty soon another, crossing it, lighting up the whole slope."

"We heard it idling up there somewhere," Kelly said. "Olive-drab paint—couldn't see it."

"I saw the pan tractor turn over—oh, four, five times down the hill. It stopped, lights still burning. Then something hit it and rolled it again. That sure blacked it out. What turned it over first?"

"The Seven. Hanging up there just at the brow of the bluff. Waited until Chub and Harris were about to pass, sixty, seventy feet below. Tipped over the edge and rolled down on them with her clutches on. Must've been going thirty miles an hour when she hit. Broadside. They never had a chance. Followed the pan as it rolled down the hill and when it stopped booted it again."

"Want me to rub yo' ankles?" asked Al.

"You! Get outa my sight!"

"Aw, Tom—" whimpered Al.

"Skip it, Tom," said Kelly. "There ain't enough of us left to carry on that way. Al, you mind your manners from here on out, hear?"

"Ah jes' wanted to tell y'all. I knew you weren't lyin' 'bout Dennis, Tom, if only I'd stopped to think. I recollect when Dennis said he'd take that tractuh out . . . 'membah, Kelly? . . . He went an' got the crank and walked around to th' side of th' machine and stuck it in th' hole. It was barely in theah befo' the startin' engine kicked off. 'Whadda ya know!' he says t'me. 'She started by herse'f! I nevah pulled that handle!' And I said, 'She sho' rarin' to go!'"

"You pick a fine time to 'recollec'' something," gritted Tom. "C'mon—let's get out of here."

"Where to?"

"What do you know that a Seven can't move or get up on?"

"That's a large order. A big rock, maybe."

"Ain't nothing that big around here," said Tom.

Kelly thought a minute, then snapped his fingers. "Up on the top of my last cut with the shovel," he said. "It's fourteen feet if it's an inch. I was pullin' out small rock an' topsoil, and Chub told me to drop back and dip out marl from a pocket there. I sumped in back of the original cut and took out a whole mess o' marl. That left a big neck of earth sticking thirty feet or so out of the cliff. The narrowest part is only about four feet wide. If *Daisy Etta* tries to get us from the top, she'll straddle the neck and hang herself. If she tries to get us from below, she can't get traction to climb; it's too loose and too steep."

"And what happens if she builds herself a ramp?"

"We'll be gone from there."

"Let's go."

Al agitated for the choice of a Dumptor because of its speed, but was howled down. Tom wanted something that could not get a flat tire and that would need something really powerful to turn it over. They took the two-cycle pan tractor with the bulldozer blade that had been Dennis' machine and crept out into the darkness.

It was nearly six hours later that *Daisy Etta* came and woke them up. Night was receding before a paleness in the east, and a fresh ocean breeze had sprung up. Kelly had taken the first lookout and Al the second, letting Tom rest the night out. And Tom was far too tired to argue the arrangement. Al had immediately fallen asleep on his watch, but fear had such a sure, cold hold on his vitals that the first faint growl of the big Diesel engine snapped him erect. He tottered on the edge of the tall neck of earth that they slept on and squeaked as he scrabbled to get his balance.

"What's giving?" asked Kelly, instantly wide awake.

"It's coming," blubbered Al. "Oh my, oh my—"

Kelly stood up and stared into the fresh, dark dawn. The motor boomed hollowly, in a peculiar way heard twice at the same time as it was thrown to them and echoed back by the bluffs under and around them.

"It's coming and what are we goin' to do?" chanted Al. "What is going to happen?"

"My head is going to fall off," said Tom sleepily. He rolled to a sitting position, holding the brutalized member between his hands. "If that egg behind my ears hatches, it'll come out a full-sized jack-hammer." He looked at Kelly. "Where is she?"

"Don't rightly know," said Kelly. "Somewhere down around the camp."

"Probably pickin' up our scent."

"Figure it can do that?"

"I figure it can do anything," said Tom. "Al, stop your moanin'."

The sun slipped its scarlet edge into the thin slot between sea and sky, and rosy light gave each rock and tree a shape and a shadow. Kelly's gaze swept back and forth, back and forth, until, minutes later, he saw movement.

"There she is!"

"Where?"

"Down by the grease rack."

Tom rose and stared. "What's she doin'?"

After an interval Kelly said, "She's working'. Diggin' a swale in front of the fuel drums."

"You don't say. Don't tell me she's goin' to give herself a grease job."

"She don't need it. She was completely greased and new oil put in the crankcase after we set her up. But she might need fuel."

"Not more'n half a tank."

"Well, maybe she figures she's got a lot of work to do today." As Kelly said this Al began to blubber. They ignored him.

The fuel drums were piled in a pyramid at the edge of the camp, in forty-four-gallon drums piled on their sides. The Seven was moving back and forth in front of them, close up, making pass after pass, gouging earth up and wasting it out past the pile. She soon had a huge pit scooped out, about fourteen feet wide, six feet deep and thirty feet long, right at the very edge of the pile of drums.

"What you reckon she's playin' at?"

"Search me. She seems to want fuel, but I don't . . . look at that! She stopped in the hole; . . . turnin' . . . smashing the top corner of the moldboard into one of the drums on the bottom!"

Tom scraped the stubble on his jaw with his nails. "An' you

wonder how much that critter can do! Why, she's got the whole
thing figured out. She knows if she tried to punch a hole in a fuel
drum that she'd only kick it around. If she did knock a hole in it,
how's she going to lift it? She's not equipped to handle hose, so . . .
see? Look at her now! She just get herself lower than the bottom
drum on the pile, and punches a hole. She can do that then, with
the whole weight of the pile holding it down. Then she backs her
tank under the stream of fuel runnin' out!"

"How'd she get the cap off?"

Tom snorted and told them how the radiator cap had come
off its hinges as he vaulted over the hood the day Rivera was hurt.

"You know," he said after a moment's thought, "if she knew
as much then as she does now, I'd be snoozin' beside Rivera and
Peebles. She just didn't know her way around then. She run herself
like she'd never run before. She's learned plenty since."

"She has," said Kelly, "and here's where she uses it on us. She's
headed this way."

She was. Straight out across the roughed-out runway she
came, grinding along over the dew-sprinkled earth, yesterday's
dust swirling up from under her tracks. Crossing the shoulder line,
she took the tougher ground skillfully, angling up over the occasional swags in the earth, by-passing stones, riding free and fast
and easily. It was the first time Tom had actually seen her clearly
running without an operator, and his flesh crept as he watched.
The machine was unnatural, her outline somehow unreal and
dreamlike purely through the lack of the small silhouette of a man
in the saddle. She looked hulked, compact, dangerous.

"What are we gonna do?" wailed Al Knowles.

"We're gonna sit and wait," said Kelly, "and you're gonna
shut your trap. We won't know for five minutes yet whether she's
going to go after us from down below or from up here."

"If you want to leave," said Tom gently, "go right ahead." Al
sat down.

Kelly looked ruminatively down at his beloved power shovel,
sitting squat and unlovely in the cut below them and away to their
right. "How do you reckon she'd stand up against the dipper
stick?"

"If it ever came to a rough-and-tumble," said Tom, "I'd say it
would be just too bad for *Daisy Etta*. But she wouldn't fight.

There's no way you could get the shovel within punchin' range; *Daisy*'d just stand there and laugh at you."

"I can't see her now," whined Al.

Tom looked. "She's taken the bluff. She's going to try it from up here. I move we sit tight and see if she's foolish enough to try to walk out here over that narrow neck. If she does, she'll drop on her belly with one track on each side. Probably turn herself over trying to dig out."

The wait then was interminable. Back over the hill they could hear the laboring motor; twice they heard the machine stop momentarily to shift gears. Once they looked at each other hopefully as the sound rose to a series of bellowing roars, as if she were backing and filling; then they realized that she was trying to take some particularly steep part of the bank and having trouble getting traction. But she made it; the motor revved up as she made the brow of the hill, and she shifted into fourth gear and came lumbering out into the open. She lurched up to the edge of the cut, stopped, throttled down, dropped her blade on the ground and stood there idling. Al Knowles backed away to the very edge of the tongue of earth they stood on, his eyes practically on stalks.

"O.K.—put up or shut up," Kelly called across harshly.

"She's looking the situation over," said Tom. "That narrow pathway don't fool her a bit."

Daisy Etta's blade began to rise, and stopped just clear of the ground. She shifted without clashing her gears, began to back slowly, still at little more than an idle.

"She's gonna jump!" screamed Al. "I'm getting' out of here!"

"Stay here, you fool," shouted Kelly. "She can't get us as long as we're up here! If you go down, she'll hunt you down like a rabbit."

The blast of the Seven's motor was the last straw for Al. He squeaked and hopped over the edge, scrambling and sliding down the almost sheer face of the cut. He hit the bottom running.

Daisy Etta lowered her blade and raised her snout and growled forward, the blade loading. Six, seven, seven and a half cubic yards of dirt piled up in front of her as she neared the edge. The loaded blade bit into the narrow pathway that led out to their perch. It was almost all soft, white, crumbly marl, and the great machine sank nose down into it, the monstrous overload of topsoil spilling down on each side.

"She's going to bury herself!" shouted Kelly.

"No—wait." Tom caught his arm. "She's trying to turn—she made it! She made it! She's ramping herself down to the flat!"

"She is—and she's cut us off from the bluff!"

The bulldozer, blade raised as high as it could possibly go, the hydraulic rod gleaming clean in the early light, freed herself of her tremendous load, spun around and headed back upward, sinking her blade again. She made one more pass between them and the bluff, making a cut now far too wide for them to jump, particularly to the crumbly footing at the bluff's edge. Once down again, she turned to face their haven, now an isolated pillar of marl, and revved down, waiting.

"I never thought of this," said Kelly guiltily. "I knew we'd be safe from her ramping up, and I never thought she'd try it the other way!"

"Skip it. In the meantime, here we sit. What happens—do we wait up here until she idles out of fuel, or do we starve to death?"

"Oh, this won't be a siege, Tom. That thing's too much of a killer. Where's Al? I wonder if he's got guts enough to make a pass near here with our tractor and draw her off?"

"He had just guts enough to take our tractor and head out," said Tom. "Didn't you know?"

"He took our—*what?*" Kelly looked out toward where they had left their machine the night before. It was gone. "Why the dirty little yellow rat!"

"No sense cussin'," said Tom steadily, interrupting what he knew was the beginning of some really flowery language. "What else could you expect?"

Daisy Etta decided, apparently, how to go about removing their splendid isolation. She uttered the snort of too-quick throttle, and moved into their peak with a corner of her blade, cutting out a huge swipe, undercutting the material over it so that it fell on her side and track as she passed. Eight inches disappeared from that side of their little plateau.

"Oh-oh. That won't do a-tall," said Tom.

"Fixin' to dig us down," said Kelly grimly. "Take her about twenty minutes. Tom, I say leave."

"It won't be healthy. You just got no idea how fast that thing can move now. Don't forget, she's a good deal more than she was

when she had a man runnin' her. She can shift from high to reverse
to fifth speed forward like that"—he snapped his fingers—"and
she can pivot faster'n you can blink and throw that blade just
where she wants it."

The tractor passed under them, bellowing, and their little
table was suddenly a foot shorter.

"Awright," said Kelly. "So what do you want to do? Stay here
and let her dig the ground out from under our feet?"

"I'm just warning you," said Tom. "Now listen. We'll wait
until she's taking a load. It'll take her a second to get rid of it when
she knows we're gone. We'll split—she can't get both of us. You
head out in the open, try to circle the curve of the bluff and get
where you can climb it. Then come back over here to the cut. A
man can scramble off a fourteen-foot cut faster'n any tractor ever
built. I'll cut in close to the cut, down at the bottom. If she takes
after you, I'll get clear all right. If she takes after me, I'll try to
make the shovel and at least give her a run for her money. I can
play hide an' seek in an' around and under that dipper-stick all day
if she wants to play."

"Why me out in the open?"

"Don't you think those long laigs o' yours can outrun her in
that distance?"

"Reckon they got to," grinned Kelly. "O.K., Tom."

They waited tensely. *Daisy Etta* backed close by, started
another pass. As the motor blatted under the load, Tom said,
"Now!" and they jumped. Kelly, catlike as always, landed on his
feet. Tom, whose knees and ankles were black and blue with rope
bruises, took two staggering steps and fell. Kelly scooped him to
his feet as the dozer's steel prow came around the bank. Instantly
she was in fifth gear and howling down at them. Kelly flung himself to the left and Tom to the right, and they pounded away, Kelly
out toward the runway, Tom straight for the shovel. *Daisy Etta* let
them diverge for a moment, keeping her course, trying to pursue
both; then she evidently sized Tom up as the slower, for she swung
toward him. The instant's hesitation was all Tom needed to get the
little lead necessary. He tore up to the shovel, his legs going like
pistons, and dived down between the shovel's tracks.

As he hit the ground, the big manganese-steel moldboard hit
the right track of the shovel, and the impact set all forty-seven

tons of the great machine quivering. But Tom did not stop. He scrabbled his way under the rig, stood up behind it, leaped and caught the sill of the rear window, clapped his other hand on it, drew himself up and tumbled inside. Here he was safe for the moment; the huge tracks themselves were higher than the Seven's blade could rise, and the floor of the cab was a good sixteen inches higher than the top of the track. Tom went to the cab door and peeped outside. The tractor had drawn off and was idling.

"Study away," gritted Tom, and went to the big Murphy Diesel. He unhurriedly checked the oil with the bayonet gauge, replaced it, took the governor cut-out rod from its rack and inserted it in the governor casing. He set the master throttle at the halfway mark, pulled up the starter-handle, twitched the cut-out. The motor spat a wad of blue smoke out of its hooded exhaust and caught. Tom put the rod back, studied the fuel-flow glass and pressure gauges, and then went to the door and looked out again. The Seven had not moved, but it was revving up and down in the uneven fashion it had shown up on the mesa. Tom had the extra-ordinary idea that it was gathering itself to spring. He slipped into the saddle, threw the master clutch. The big gears that half-filled the cab obediently began to turn. He kicked the brake-locks loose with his heels, let his feet rest lightly on the pedals as they rose.

Then he reached over his head and snapped back the throttle. As the Murphy picked up he grasped both hoist and swing levers and pulled them back. The engine howled; the two-yard bucket came up off the ground with a sudden jolt as the cold friction grabbed it. The big machine swung hard to the right; Tom snapped his hoist lever forward and checked the bucket's rise with his foot on the brake. He shoved the crowd lever forward; the bucket ran out to the end of its reach, and the heel of the bucket wiped across the Seven's hood, taking with it the exhaust stack, muffler and all, and the pre-cleaner on the air intake. Tom cursed. He had figured on the machine's leaping backward. If it had, he would have smashed the cast-iron radiator core. But she had stood still, making a split-second decision.

Now she moved, though, and quickly. With that incredibly fast shifting, she leaped backwards and pivoted out of range before Tom could check the shovel's mad swing. The heavy swing-friction blocks smoked acridly as the machine slowed, stopped, and swung back. Tom checked her as he was facing the Seven, hoisted his bucket a few feet, and rehauled, bringing it about halfway back, ready for anything. The four great dipper-teeth gleamed in the sun. Tom ran a practiced eye over cables, boom and dipper-stick, liking the black polish of crater compound on the sliding parts, the easy tension of well-greased cables and links. The huge machine stood strong, ready and profoundly subservient for all its brute power.

Tom looked searchingly at the Seven's ruined engine hood. The gaping end of the broken air-intake pipe stared back at him. "Aha!" he said. "A few cupfuls of nice dry marl down there'll give you something to chew on."

Keeping a wary eye on the tractor, he swung into the bank, dropped his bucket and plunged it into the marl. He crowded it deep, and the Murphy yelled for help but kept on pushing. At the peak of the load a terrific jar rocked him in the saddle. He looked back over his shoulder through the door and saw the Seven backing off again. She had run up and delivered a terrific punch to the counterweight at the back of the cab. Tom grinned tightly. She'd have to do better than that. There was nothing back there but eight or ten tons of solid steel. And he didn't much care at the moment whether or not she scratched his paint.

He swung back again, white marl running away on both sides of the heaped bucket. The shovel rode perfectly now, for a shovel is counterweighted to balance true when standing level with the bucket loaded. The hoist and swing frictions and the brake linings had heated and dried themselves of the night's condensation moisture, and she answered the controls in a way that delighted the operator in him. He handled the swing lever lightly, back to swing to the right, forward to swing to the left, following the slow dance the Seven had started to do, stepping warily back and forth like a fighter looking for an opening. Tom kept the bucket between himself and the tractor, knowing that she could not hurt a tool that was built to smash hard rock for twenty hours a day and like it.

Daisy Etta bellowed and rushed in. Tom snapped the hoist lever back hard, and the bucket rose, letting the tractor run underneath. Tom punched the bucket trip, and the great steel jaw opened, cascading marl down on the broken hood. The tractor's fan blew it back in a huge billowing cloud. The instant that it took Tom to check and dump was enough, however, for the tractor to dance back out of the way, for when he tried to drop it on the machine to smash the coiled injector tubes on top of the engine block, she was gone.

The dust cleared away, and tractor moved in again, feinted to the left, then swung her blade at the bucket, which was just clear of the ground. Tom swung to meet her, her feint having gotten her in a little closer than he liked, and bucket met blade with a shower of sparks and a clank that could be heard for half a mile. She had come in with her blade high, and Tom let out a wordless shout as he saw that the A-frame brace behind the blade had caught between two of his dipper-teeth. He snatched at his hoist lever and the bucket came up, lifting with it the whole front end of the bull-dozer.

Daisy Etta plunged up and down and her tracks dug violently into the earth as she raised and lowered her blade, trying to shake herself free. Tom rehauled, trying to bring the tractor in closer, for the boom was set too low to attempt to lift such a dead weight. As it was, the shovel's off track was trying its best to get off the ground. But the crowd and rehaul frictions could not handle her alone; they began to heat and slip.

Tom hoisted a little; the shovel's off track came up a foot off the ground. Tom cursed and let the bucket drop, and in an instant the dozer was free and running clear. Tom swung wildly at her, missed. The dozer came in on a long curve; Tom swung to meet her again, took a vicious swipe at her which she took on her blade. But this time she did not withdraw after being hit, but bored right in, carrying the bucket before her. Before Tom realized what she was doing his bucket was around in front of the tracks and between them, on the ground. It was as swift and skillful a maneu-ver as could be imagined, and it left the shovel without the ability to swing as long as *Daisy Etta* could hold the bucket trapped between the tracks.

Tom crowded furiously, but that succeeded only in lifting the boom higher in the air since there is nothing to hold a boom down but its own weight. Hoisting did nothing but make his frictions smoke and rev the engine down dangerously close to the stalling point.

Tom swore again and reached down to the cluster of small levers at his left. These were the gears. On this type of shovel, the swing lever controls everything except crowd and hoist. With the swing lever, the operator, having selected his gear, controls the travel—that is, power to the tracks—in forward and reverse; booming up and booming down; and swinging. The machine can do only one of these things at a time. If she is in travel gear, she cannot swing. If she is in swing gear, she cannot boom up or down. Not once in years of operating would this inability bother an operator; now, however, nothing was normal.

Tom pushed the swing gear control down and pulled up on the travel. The clutches involved were jaw clutches, not frictions, so that he had to throttle down to an idle before he could make the castellations mesh. As the Murphy revved down, *Daisy Etta* took it as a signal that something could be done about it, and she shoved furiously into the bucket. But Tom had all controls in neutral and all she succeeded in doing was to dig herself in, her sharp new cleats spinning deep into the dirt.

Tom set his throttle up again and shoved the swing lever forward. There was a vast crackling of drive chains; and the big tracks started to turn.

Daisy Etta had sharp cleats; her pads were twenty inches wide and her tracks were fourteen feet long, and there were fourteen tons of steel on them. The shovel's big flat pads were three feet wide and twenty feet long, and forty-seven tons aboard. There was simply no comparison. The Murphy bellowed the fact that the work was hard, but gave no indications of stalling. *Daisy Etta* performed the incredible feat of shifting into forward gear while she was moving backwards, but it did her no good. Round and round her tracks went, trying to drive for forward, gouging deep; and slowly and surely she was forced backward toward the cut wall by the shovel.

Tom heard a sound that was not part of a straining machine; he looked out and saw Kelly on top of the cut, smoking, swinging his feet over the edge, making punching motions with his hands as if he had a ringside seat at a big fight—which he certainly had.

Tom now offered the dozer little choice. If she did not turn aside before him, she would be borne back against the bank and her fuel tank crushed. There was every possibility that, having her pinned there, Tom would have time to raise his bucket over her and smash her to pieces. And if she turned before she was forced against the bank, she would have to free Tom's bucket. This she had to do.

The Murphy gave him warning, but not enough. It crooned as the load came off, and Tom knew that the dozer was shifting into a reverse gear. He whipped the hoist lever back, and the bucket rose as the dozer backed away from him. He crowded it out and let it come smashing down—and missed. For the tractor danced aside—and while he was in travel gear he could not swing to follow it. *Daisy Etta* charged then, put one track on the bank and went over almost on her beam-ends, throwing one end of her blade high in the air. So totally unexpected was it that Tom was quite unprepared. The tractor flung itself on the bucket, and the cutting edge of the blade dropped between the dipper teeth. This time there was the whole weight of the tractor to hold it there. There would be no way for her to free herself—but at the same time she had trapped the bucket so far out from the center pin of the shovel that Tom couldn't hoist without overbalancing and turning the monster over.

Daisy Etta ground away in reverse, dragging the bucket out until it was checked by the bumper-blocks. Then she began to crab sideways, up against the bank, and when Tom tried tentatively to rehaul, she shifted and came right with him, burying one whole end of her blade deep into the bank.

Stalemate. She had hung herself up on the bucket, and she had immobilized it. Tom tried to rehaul, but the tractor's anchorage in the bank was too solid. He tried to swing, to hoist. All the overworked frictions could possibly give out was smoke. Tom grunted and throttled to an idle, leaned out the window. *Daisy Etta* was idling too, loudly without her muffler, the stackless exhaust giving out an ugly flat sound. But after the roar of the two great motors the partial silence was deafening.

Kelly called down, "Double knockout, hey?"

"Looks like it. What say we see if we can't get close enough to her to quiet her down some?"

Kelly shrugged. "I dunno. If she's really stopped herself, it's the first time. I respect that rig, Tom. She wouldn't have got herself into that spot if she didn't have an ace up her sleeve."

"Look at her, man! Suppose she was a civilized bulldozer and you had to get her out of there. She can't raise her blade high enough to free it from those dipper-teeth, y'know. Think you'd be able to do it?"

"It might take several seconds," Kelly drawled. "She's sure high and dry."

"O.K., let's spike her guns."

"Like what?"

"Like taking a bar and prying out her tubing." He referred to the coiled brass tubing that carried the fuel, under pressure, from the pump to the injectors. There were many feet of it, running from the pump reservoir, stacked in expansion coils over the cylinder head.

As he spoke *Daisy Etta*'s idle burst into that maniac revving up and down characteristic of her.

"What do you know!" Tom called above the racket. "Eavesdropping!"

Kelly slid down the cut, stood up on the track of the shovel and poked his head in the window. "Well, you want to get a bar and try?"

"Let's go!"

Tom went to the toolbox and pulled out a pinch bar that Kelly used to replace cables on his machine, and swung to the ground. They approached the tractor warily. She revved up as they came near, began to shudder. The front end rose and dropped and the tracks began to turn as she tried to twist out of the vise her blade had dropped into.

"Take it easy, sister," said Tom. "You'll just bury yourself. Set still and take it, now, like a good girl. You got it comin'."

"Be careful," said Kelly. Tom hefted the bar and laid a hand on the fender.

The tractor literally shivered, and from the rubber hose connection at the top of the radiator, a blinding stream of hot water shot out. It fanned and caught them both full in the face. They staggered back, cursing.

"You O.K., Tom?" Kelly gasped a moment later. He had got most of it across the mouth and cheek. Tom was on his knees, his shirt tail out, blotting his face.

"My eyes . . . oh, my eyes—"

"Let's see!" Kelly dropped down beside him and took him by the wrists, gently removing Tom's hands from his face. He whistled. "Come on," he gritted. He helped Tom up and led him away a few feet. "Stay here," he said hoarsely. He turned, walked back toward the dozer, picking up the pinch-bar. "You dirty—!" he yelled, and flung it like a javelin at the tube coils. It was a little high. It struck the ruined hood, made a deep dent in the metal. The dent promptly inverted with a loud *thung-g-g!* and flung the bar back at him. He ducked; it whistled over his head and caught Tom in the calves of his legs. He went down like a poled ox, but staggered to his feet again.

"Come on!" Kelly snarled, and taking Tom's arm, hustled him around the turn of the cut. "Sit down! I'll be right back."

"Where are you going? Kelly—be careful!"

"Careful and how!"

Kelly's long legs ate up the distance back to the shovel. He swung into the cab, reached back over the motor and set up the master throttle all the way. Stepping up behind the saddle, he opened the running throttle and the Murphy howled. Then he hauled back on the hoist lever until it knuckled in, turned and leaped off the machine in one supple motion.

The hoist drum turned and took up slack; the cable straightened as it took the strain. The bucket stirred under the dead weight of the bulldozer that rested on it; and slowly, then, the great flat tracks began to lift their rear ends off the ground. The great obedient mass of machinery teetered forward on the tips on her tracks, the Murphy revved down and under the incredible load, but it kept the strain. A strand of the two-part hoist cable broke and whipped around, singing; and then she was balanced— over-balanced—

And the shovel had hauled herself right over and had fallen with an earth-shaking crash. The boom, eight tons of solid steel, clanged down onto the blade of the bulldozer, and lay there, crushing it down tightly onto the imprisoning row of dipper-teeth.

Daisy Etta sat there, not trying to move now, racing her motor impotently. Kelly strutted past her, thumbing his nose, and went back to Tom.

"Kelly! I thought you were never coming back! What happened?"

"Shovel pulled herself over on her nose."

"Good boy! Fall on the tractor?"

"Nup. But the boom's laying across the top of her blade. Caught like a rat in a trap."

"Better watch out the rat don't chew its leg off to get out," said Tom, dryly. "Still runnin', is she?"

"Yep. But we'll fix that in a hurry."

"Sure. Sure. How?"

"How? I dunno. Dynamite, maybe. How's the optics?"

Tom opened one a trifle and grunted. "Rough. I can see a little, though. My eyelids are parboiled, mostly. Dynamite, you say? Well, let's think first. Think."

Tom sat back against the bank and stretched out his legs. "I tell you, Kelly, I been too blessed busy these last few hours to think much, but there's one thing that keeps comin' back to me— somethin' I was mullin' over long before the rest of you guys knew anything was up at all, except that Rivera had got hurt in some way I wouldn't tell you all about. But I don't reckon you'll call me crazy if I open my mouth now and let it all run out?"

"From now on," Kelly said fervently, "nobody's crazy. After this I'll believe anything." He sat down.

"O.K. Well, about that tractor. What do you suppose has got into her?"

"Search me. I dunno."

"No—don't say that. I just got an idea we can't stop at 'I dunno.' We got to figure all the angles on this thing before we know just what to do about it. Let's just get this thing lined up. When did it start? On the mesa. How? Rivera was opening an old building with the Seven. This thing came out of there. Now here's what I'm getting at. We can dope these things out about it: It's intelligent. It can only get into a machine and not into a man. It—"

"What about that? How do you know it can't?"

"Because it had the chance to and didn't. I was standing right by the opening when it kited out. Rivera was up on the machine at the time. It didn't directly harm either of us. It got into the tractor, and the tractor did. By the same token, it can't hurt a man when it's out of a machine, but that's all it wants to do when it's in one. O.K.?

"To get on: once it's in the machine it can't get out again. We know that because it had plenty of chances and didn't take them. That scuffle with the dipper-stick, f'r instance. My face woulda been plenty red if it had taken over the shovel—and you can bet it would have if it could."

"I got you so far. But what are we going to do about it?"

"That's the thing. You see, I don't think it's enough to wreck the tractor. We might burn it, blast it, and still not hurt whatever it was that got into it up on the mesa."

"That makes sense. But I don't see what else we can do than just break up the dozer. We haven't got a line on actually what the thing is."

"I think we have. Remember I asked you all those screwy questions about the arc that killed Peebles. Well, when that happened, I recollected a flock of other things. One—when it got out of that hole up there, I smelled that smell that you notice when you're welding; sometimes when lightning strikes real close."

"Ozone," said Kelly.

"Yeah—ozone. Then, it likes metal, not flesh. But most of all, there was that arc. Now, that was absolutely screwy. You know as well as I do—better—that an arc generator simply don't have the push to do a thing like that. It can't kill a man, and it can't throw an arc no fifty feet. But it did. An' that's why I asked you if there could be something—a field, or some such—that could *suck* current out of a generator, all at once, faster than it could flow. Because this thing's electrical; it fits all around."

"Electronic," said Kelly doubtfully, thoughtfully.

"I wouldn't know. Now then. When Peebles was killed, a funny thing happened. Remember what Chub said? The Seven moved back—straight back, about thirty feet, until it bumped into a road-roller that was standing behind it. It did that with no fuel in the starting engine—without even using the starting engine, for that matter—and with the compression valves locked open!

"Kelly, that thing in the dozer can't do much, when you come right down to it. It couldn't fix itself up after that joyride on the mesa. It can't make the machine do too much more than the machine can do ordinarily. What it actually can do, seems to me, is to make a spring push instead of pull, like the control levers, and make a fitting slip when it's supposed to hold, like the ratchet on the throttle lever. It can turn a shaft, like the way it cranks its own starting motor. But if it was so all-fired high-powered, it wouldn't have to use the starting motor! The absolute biggest job it's done so far, seems to me, was when it walked back from that welding machine when Peebles got his. Now, why did it do that just then?"

"Reckon it didn't like the brimstone smell, like it says in the Good Book," said Kelly sourly.

"That's pretty close, seems to me. Look, Kelly—this thing *feels* things. I mean, it can get sore. If it couldn't it never woulda kept driving in at the shovel like that. It can think. But if it can do all those things, then it can be *scared!*"

"Scared? Why should it be scared?"

"Listen. Something went on in that thing when the arc hit it. What's that I read in a magazine once about heat—something about molecules runnin' around with their heads cut off when they got hot?"

"Molecules do. They go into rapid motion when heat is applied. But—"

"But nothin'. That machine was hot for four hours after that. But she was hot in a funny way. Not just around the place where the arc hit, like as if it was a welding arc. But hot all over—from the moldboard to the fuel-tank cap. Hot everywhere. And just as hot behind the final drive housings as she was at the top of the blade where the poor guy put his hand.

"And look at this." Tom was getting excited, as his words crystallized his ideas. "She was scared—scared enough to back off from that welder, putting everything she could into it, to get back from that welding machine. And after that, she was sick. I say that because in the whole time she's had that what-ever-ya-call-it in her, she's never been near men without trying to kill them, except for those two days after the arc hit her. She had juice enough to start herself when Dennis came around with the crank, but she still needed someone to run her till she got her strength back."

"But why didn't she turn and smash up the welder when Dennis took her?"

"One of two things. She didn't have the strength, or she didn't have the guts. She was scared, maybe, and wanted out of there, away from that thing."

"But she had all night to go back for it!"

"Still scared. Or . . . oh, *that's* it! She had other things to do first. Her main idea is to kill men—there's no other way you can figure it. It's what she was built to do. Not the tractor—they don't build 'em sweeter'n that machine; but the thing that's runnin' it."

"What *is* that thing?" Kelly mused. "Coming out of that old building—temple—what have you—how old is it? How long was it there? What kept it in there?"

"What kept it in there was some funny gray stuff that lined the inside of the buildin'," said Tom. "It was like rock, an' it was like smoke.

"It was a color that scared you to look at it, and it gave Rivera and me the creeps when we got near it. Don't ask me what it was. I went up there to look at it, and it's gone. Gone from the building, anyhow. There was a little lump of it on the ground. I don't know whether that was a hunk of it, or all of it rolled up into a ball. I get the creeps again thinkin' about it."

Kelly stood up. "Well, the heck with it. We been beatin' our gums up here too long anyhow. There's just enough sense in what you say to make me want to try something nonsensical, if you see what I mean. If that welder can sweat the Ol' Nick out of that tractor, I'm on. Especially from fifty feet away. There should be a Dumptor around here somewhere; let's move from here. Can you navigate now?"

"Reckon so, a little." Tom rose and together they followed the cut until they came on the Dumptor. They climbed on, cranked it up and headed toward camp.

About halfway there Kelly looked back, gasped, and putting his mouth close to Tom's ear, bellowed against the scream of the motor. "Tom! 'Member what you said about the rat in the trap biting off a leg?

"Well, *Daisy* did too! She's left her blade an' pushbeams an' she's followin' us in!"

They howled into the camp, gasping against the dust that followed when they pulled up by the welder.

Kelly, said, "You cast around and see if you can find a drawpin to hook that rig up to the Dumptor with. I'm goin' after some water an' chow!"

Tom grinned. Imagine old Kelly forgetting that a Dumptor

had no drawbar! He groped around to a toolbox, peering out of the narrow slit beneath swollen lids, felt behind it and located a shackle. He climbed up on the Dumptor, turned it around and backed up to the welding machine. He passed the shackle through the ring at the end of the steering tongue of the welder, screwed in the pin and dropped the shackle over the front towing hook of the Dumptor. A Dumptor being what it is, having no real front and no real rear, and direct reversing gears in all speeds, it was no trouble to drive it "backwards" for a change.

Kelly came pounding back, out of breath. "Fix it? Good. Shackle? No drawbar! *Daisy*'s closin' up fast; I say let's take the beach. We'll be concealed until we have a good lead out o' this pocket, and the going's pretty fair, long as we don't bury this jalopy in the sand."

"Good," said Tom as they climbed on and he accepted an open tin of K. "Only go easy; bump around too much and the welder'll slip off the hook. An' I somehow don't want to lose it just now."

They took off, zooming up the beach. A quarter of a mile up, they sighted the Seven across the flat. It immediately turned and took a course that would intercept them.

"Here she comes," shouted Kelly, and stepped down hard on the accelerator. Tom leaned over the back of the seat, keeping his eye on their tow. "Hey! Take it easy! Watch it!

"Hey!"

But it was too late. The tongue of the welding machine responded to that one bump too many. The shackle jumped up off the hook, the welder lurched wildly, slewed hard to the left. The tongue dropped to the sand and dug in; the machine rolled up on it and snapped it off, finally stopped, leaning crazily askew. By a miracle it did not quite turn over.

Kelly tramped on the brakes and both their heads did their utmost to snap off their shoulders. They leaped off and ran back to the welder. It was intact, but towing it was now out of the question. "If there's going to be a showdown, it's gotta be here."

The beach here was about thirty yards wide, the sand almost level, and undercut banks of sawgrass forming the landward edge in a series of little hummocks and headlands. While Tom stayed with the machine, testing starter and generator contacts, Kelly walked up one of the little mounds, stood up on it and scanned the beach back the way he had come. Suddenly he began to shout and wave his arms.

"What's got into you?"

"It's Al!" Kelly called back. "With the pan tractor!"

Tom dropped what he was doing, and came to stand beside Kelly. "Where's the Seven? I can't see."

"Turned on the beach and followin' our track. Al! Al! You little skunk, c'mere!"

Tom could now dimly make out the pan tractor cutting across directly toward them and the beach.

"He don't see *Daisy Etta*," remarked Kelly disgustedly, "or he'd sure be headin' the other way."

Fifty yards away Al pulled up and throttled down. Kelly shouted and waved to him. Al stood up on the machine, cupped his hand around his mouth. "Where's the Seven?"

"Never mind that! Come here with that tractor!"

Al stayed where he was. Kelly cursed and started out after him. "You stay away from me," he said when Kelly was closer.

"I ain't got time for you now," said Kelly. "Bring that tractor down to the beach."

"Where's that *Daisy Etta*?" Al's voice was oddly strained.

"Right behind us." Kelly tossed a thumb over his shoulder. "On the beach."

Al's pop eyes clicked wide almost audibly. He turned on his heel and jumped off the machine and started to run. Kelly uttered a wordless syllable that was somehow more obscene than anything else he had ever uttered, and vaulted into the seat of the machine. "Hey!" he bellowed after Al's rapidly diminishing figure. "You're runnin' right into her." Al appeared not to hear, but went pelting down the beach.

Kelly put her into fifth gear and poured on the throttle. As the tractor began to move he whacked out the master clutch, snatched the overdrive lever back to put her into sixth, rammed the clutch in again, all so fast that she did not have time to stop rolling. Bucking and jumping over the rough ground the fast machine whined for the beach.

Tom was fumbling back to the welder, his ears telling him better than his eyes how close the Seven was—for she was certainly no nightingale, particularly without her exhaust stack. Kelly reached the machine as he did.

"Get behind it," snapped Tom. "I'll jam the tierod with the shackle, and you see if you can't bunt her up into that pocket between those two hummocks. Only take it easy—you don't want to tear up that generator. Where's Al?"

"Don't ask me. He run down the beach to meet *Daisy.*"

"He *what?*"

The whine of the two-cycle drowned out Kelly's answer, if any. He got behind the welder and set his blade against it. Then in a low gear, slipping his clutch in a little, he slowly nudged the machine toward the place Tom indicated. It was a little hollow in between two projecting banks. The surf and the high-tide mark dipped inland here to match it; the water was only a few feet away.

Tom raised his arm and Kelly stopped. From the other side of the projecting shelf, out of their sight now, came the flat roar of the Seven's exhaust. Kelly sprang off the tractor and went to help Tom, who was furiously throwing out coils of cable from the rack of the welder. "What's the game?"

"We got to ground that Seven some way," panted Tom. He threw the last bit of cable out to clear it of kinks and turned to the panel.

"How was it—about sixty volts and the amperage on 'special application'?" He spun the dials, pressed the started button. The motor responded instantly. Kelly scooped up ground clamp and rod holder and tapped them together. The solenoid governor picked up the load and the motor hummed as a good live spark took the jump.

"Good," said Tom, switching off the generator. "Come on, Lieutenant General Electric, figure me out a way to ground that maverick."

Kelly tightened his lips, shook his head. "I dunno—unless somebody actually claps this thing on her."

"No, boy, can't do that. If one of us gets killed—"

Kelly tossed the ground clamp idly, his lithe body taut. "Don't give me that, Tom. You know I'm elected because you can't see good enough yet to handle it. You know you'd do it if you could. You—"

He stopped short, for the steadily increasing roar of the

approaching Seven had stopped, was blatting away now in that extraordinary irregular throttling that *Daisy Etta* affected.

"Now, what's got into her?"

Kelly broke away and scrambled up the bank. "Tom!" he gasped. "Tom—come up here!"

Tom followed, and they lay side by side, peering out over the top of the escarpment at the remarkable tableau.

Daisy Etta was standing on the beach, near the water, not moving. Before her, twenty or thirty feet away, stood Al Knowles, his arms out in front of him, talking a blue streak. *Daisy* made far too much racket for them to hear what he was saying.

"Do you reckon he's got guts enough to stall her off for us?" said Tom.

"If he has, it's the queerest thing that's happened yet on this old island," Kelly breathed, "an' that's saying something."

The Seven revved up till she shook, and then throttled back. She ran down so low then that they thought she had shut herself down, but she caught on the last two revolutions and began to idle quietly. And then they could hear.

Al's voice was high, hysterical. "—I come t' he'p you, I come t' he'p you, don' kill me, I'll he'p you—" He took a step forward; the dozer snorted and he fell to his knees. "I'll wash you an' grease you and change yo' ile," he said in a high singsong.

"The guy's not human," said Kelly wonderingly.

"He ain't housebroke either," Tom chuckled.

"—lemme he'p you. I'll fix you when you break down. I'll he'p you kill those other guys—"

"She don't need any help!" said Tom.

"The louse," growled Kelly. "The rotten little double-crossing polecat!" He stood up. "Hey, you Al! Come out o' that. I mean now! If she don't get you I will, if you don't move."

Al was crying now. "Shut up!" he screamed. "I know who's bawss hereabouts, an' so do you!" He pinned at the tractor. "She'll kill us all iff'n we don't do what she wants!" He turned back to the machine. "I'll k-kill 'em fo' you. I'll wash you and shine you up and f-fix yo' hood. I'll put yo' blade back on. . . ."

Tom reached out and caught Kelly's legs as the tall man started out, blind mad. "Git back here," he barked. "What you want to do—get killed for the privilege of pinnin' his ears back?"

Kelly subsided and came back, threw himself down beside Tom, put his face in his hands. He was quivering with rage.

"Don't take on so," Tom said. "The man's plumb loco. You can't argue with him any more'n you can with *Daisy,* there. If he's got to get his, *Daisy*'ll give it to him."

"Aw, Tom, it ain't that. I know he ain't worth it, but I can't sit up here and watch him get himself killed. I can't, Tom."

Tom thumped him on the shoulder, because there were simply no words to be said. Suddenly he stiffened, snapped his fingers.

"There's our ground," he said urgently, pointing seaward. "The water—the wet beach where the surf runs. If we can get our ground clamp out there and her somewhere near it—"

"Ground the pan tractor. Run it out into the water. It ought to reach—partway, anyhow."

"That's it—c'mon."

They slid down the bank, snatched up the ground clamp, attached it to the frame on the pan tractor.

"I'll take it," said Tom, and as Kelly opened his mouth, Tom shoved him back against the welding machine. "No time to argue," he snapped, swung on to the machine, slapped her in gear and was off. Kelly took a step toward the tractor, and then his quick eyes saw a bight of the ground cable about to foul a wheel of the welder. He stopped and threw it off, spread out the rest of it so it would pay off clear. Tom, with the incredible single-mindedness of the trained operator, watched only the black line of the trailing cable on the sand behind him. When it straightened he stopped. The front of the tracks were sloshing in the gentle surf. He climbed off the side away from the Seven and tried to see. There was movement, and the growl of her motor now running at a bit more than idle, but he could not distinguish much.

Kelly picked up the rod holder and went to peer around the head of the protruding bank. Al was on his feet, still crooning hysterically, sidling over toward *Daisy Etta.* Kelly ducked back, threw the switch on the arc generator, climbed the bank and crawled along through the sawgrass paralleling the beach until the holder in his hand tugged and he knew he had reached the end of the cable. He looked out at the beach; measured carefully with his eye the arc he would travel if he left his position and, keeping the cable taut, went out on the beach. At no point would he come within seventy feet of the possessed machine, let alone fifty. She had to be drawn in closer. And she had to be maneuvered out to the wet sand, or in the water—

Al Knowles, encouraged by the machine's apparent decision not to move, approached, though warily, and still running off at the mouth. "—we'll kill 'em off an' then we'll keep it a secret and th' bahges'll come an' take us offen th' island and we'll go to anothah job an' kill lots mo' . . . an' when yo' tracks git dry an' squeak we'll wet 'em with blood, and you'll be rightly king o' the hill . . . look yondah, look yondah, *Daisy Etta,* see them theah, by the otheh tractuh, theah they are, kill 'em, *Daisy,* kill 'em, *Daisy,* an' lemme he'p . . . heah me. *Daisy,* heah me, say you heah me—" and the motor roared in response. Al laid a timid hand on the radiator guard, leaning far over to do it, and the tractor still stood there grumbling but not moving. Al stepped back, motioned with his arm, began to walk off slowly toward the pan tractor, looking backwards as he did so like a man training a dog. "C'mon, c'mon, theah's one theah, le's *kill'm, kill'm, kill'm . . .*"

And with a snort the tractor revved up and followed.

Kelly licked his lips without effect because his tongue was dry, too. The madman passed him, walking straight up the center of the beach, and the tractor, now no longer a bulldozer, followed him; and there the sand was bone dry, sun-dried, dried to powder. As the tractor passed him, Kelly got up on all fours, went over the edge of the bank onto the beach, crouched there.

Al crooned, "I love ya, honey, I love ya, 'deed I do—"

Kelly ran crouching, like a man under machine-gun fire, making himself as small as possible and feeling as big as a barn door. The torn-up sand where the tractor had passed was under his feet now; he stopped, afraid to get too much closer, afraid that a weakened, badly grounded arc might leap from the holder in his hand and serve only to alarm and infuriate the thing in the tractor. And just then Al saw him.

"There!" he screamed; and the tractor pulled up short. "Behind you! Get'm, *Daisy! Kill'm, kill'm, kill'm.*"

Kelly stood up almost wearily, fury and frustration too much to be borne. "In the water," he yelled, because it was what his whole being wanted. "Get'er in the water! Wet her tracks, Al!"

"Kill'm, kill'm—"

As the tractor started to turn, there was a commotion over by the pan tractor. It was Tom, jumping, shouting, waving his arms, swearing. He ran out from behind his machine, straight at the Seven. *Daisy Etta*'s motor roared and she swung to meet him, Al barely dancing back out of the way. Tom cut sharply, sand spouting under his pumping feet, and ran straight into the water. He went out to about waist deep, suddenly disappeared. He surfaced, spluttering, still trying to shout. Kelly took a better grip on his rod holder and rushed.

Daisy Etta, in following Tom's crazy rush, had swung in beside the pan tractor, not fifteen feet away; and she, too, was now in the surf. Kelly closed up the distance as fast as his long legs would let him; and as he approached to within that crucial fifty feet, Al Knowles hit him.

Al was frothing at the mouth, gibbering. The two men hit full tilt; Al's head caught Kelly in the midriff as he missed a straightarm, and the breath went out of him in one great *whoosh!* Kelly went down like tall timber, the whole world to one swirling red-gray haze. Al flung himself on the bigger man, clawing, smacking, too berserk to ball his fists.

"Ah'm go' to kill you," he gurgled. "She'll git one, I'll git t'other, an' then she'll know—"

Kelly covered his face with his arms, and as some wind was sucked at last into his laboring lungs, he flung them upward and sat up in one mighty surge. Al was hurled upward and to one side, and as he hit the ground Kelly reached out a long arm, and twisted his fingers into the man's coarse hair, raised him up, and came across with his other fist in a punch that would have killed him had it landed square. But Al managed to jerk to one side enough so that it only amputated a cheek. He fell and lay still. Kelly scrambled madly around in the sand for his welding-rod holder, found it and began to run again. He couldn't see Tom at all now, and the Seven was standing in the surf, moving slowly from side to side, backing out, ravening. Kelly held the rod-clamp and its trailing cable blindly before him and ran straight at the machine. And then it came—that thin, soundless bolt of energy. But this time it had its full force, for poor old Peebles' body had not been the ground that this swirling water offered. *Daisy Etta* literally leaped backwards toward him, and the water around her tracks spouted upward in hot steam. The sound of her engine ran up, broke, took on the rhythmic, uneven beat of a swing drummer. She threw herself from side to side like a cat with a bag over its head. Kelly stepped a little closer, hoping for another bolt to come from the clamp in his hand, but there was none, for—

"The circuit breaker!" cried Kelly.

He threw the holder up on the deck plate of the Seven in front of the seat, and ran across the little beach to the welder. He reached behind the switchboard, got his thumb on the contact hinge and jammed it down.

Daisy Etta leaped again, and then again, and suddenly her motor stopped. Heat in turbulent waves blurred the air over her. The little gas tank for the starting motor went out with a cannon's roar, and the big fuel tank, still holding thirty-odd gallons of Diesel oil, followed. It puffed itself open rather than exploded, and threw a great curtain of flame over the ground behind the machine. Motor or no motor, then, Kelly distinctly saw the tractor shudder convulsively. There was a crawling movement of the whole frame, a slight wave of motion away from the fuel tank, approaching the front of the machine, and moving upward from the tracks. It culminated in the crown of the radiator core, just in front of the radiator cap; and suddenly an area of six or seven square inches literally *blurred* around the edges. For a second, then, it was normal, and finally it slumped molten, and liquid metal ran down the sides, throwing out little sparks as it encountered what was left of the charred paint. And only then was Kelly conscious of agony in his left hand. He looked down. The welding machine's generator had stopped, though the motor was still turning, having smashed the friable coupling on its drive shaft. Smoke poured from the generator, which had become little more than a heap of slag. Kelly did not scream, though, until he looked and saw what had happened to his hand—

When he could see straight again, he called for Tom, and there was no answer. At last he saw something out in the water, and plunged in after it. The splash of cold salt water on his left hand he hardly felt, for the numbness of shock had set in. He grabbed at Tom's shirt with his good hand, and then the ground seemed to pull itself out from under his feet. That was it, then—a deep hole right off the beach. The Seven had run right to the edge of it, had kept Tom there out of his depth and—

He flailed wildly, struck out for the beach, so near and so hard to get to. He gulped a stinging lungful of brine, and only the lovely shock of his knee striking solid beach kept him from giving up to the luxury of choking to death. Sobbing with effort, he dragged Tom's dead weight inshore and clear of the surf. It was then that he became conscious of a child's shrill weeping; for a mad moment he thought it was he himself, and then he looked and saw that it was Al Knowles. He left Tom and went over to the broken creature.

"Get up, you," he snarled. The weeping only got louder. Kelly rolled him over on his back—he was quite unresisting—and belted him back and forth across the mouth until Al began to choke. Then he hauled him to his feet and led him over to Tom.

"Kneel down, scum. Put one of your knees between his knees." Al stood still. Kelly hit him again and he did as he was told.

"Put your hands on his lower ribs. There. O.K. Lean, you rat. Now sit back." He sat down, holding his left wrist in his right hand, letting the blood drop from the ruined hand. "Lean. Hold it—sit back. Lean. Sit. Lean. Sit."

Soon Tom sighed and began to vomit weakly, and after that he was all right.

This is the story of *Daisy Etta,* the bulldozer that went mad and had a life of its own, and not the story of the missile test that they don't talk about except to refer to it as the missile test that they don't talk about. But you may have heard about it for all that—rumors, anyway. The rumor has it that an early IRBM tested out a radically new controls system by proving conclusively that it did not work. It was a big bird and contained much juice, and flew far, far afield. Rumor goes on to assert that a) it alighted somewhere in the unmapped rain forests of South America and that b) there were no casualties. What they *really* don't talk about is the closely guarded report asserting that both a) and b) are false. There are only two people (aside from yourself, now) who know for sure that though a) is certainly false, b) is strangely true, and there were indeed no casualties.

Al Knowles may well know too, but he doesn't count.

It happened two days after the death of *Daisy Etta,* as Tom and Kelly sat in (of all places) the coolth of the ruined temple. They were poring over paper and pencil, trying to complete the impossible task of making a written statement of what had happened on the island, and why they and their company had failed to complete their contract. They had found Chub and Harris, and had buried them next to the other three. Al Knowles was back in the shadows, tied up, because they had heard him raving in his sleep, and it seemed he could not believe *Daisy* was dead and he still wanted to go around killing operators for her. They knew that there must be an investigation, and they knew just how far their story would go; and having escaped a monster like *Daisy Etta,* they found life too sweet to want any part of it spent under observation or in jail.

The warhead of the missile struck near the edge of their camp, just between the pyramid of fuel drums and the dynamite stores. The second stage alighted a moment later two miles away, in the vicinity of the five graves. Kelly and Tom stumbled out to the rim of the mesa, and for a long while watched the jetsam fall and the flotsam rise. It was Kelly who guessed what must have happened, and "Bless their clumsy little hearts," he said happily. And he took the scribbled papers from Tom and tore them across.

But Tom shook his head, and thumbed back at the mound. "He'll talk."

"Him?" said Kelly, with such profound eloquence in his tone that he clearly evoked the image of Al Knowles, with his mumbling voice and his drooling mouth and his wide glazed eyes. "Let him," Kelly said, and tore the papers again.

So they let him.

BRIGHT SEGMENT

He had never held a girl before. He was not terrified; he had used that up earlier when he had carried her in and kicked the door shut behind him and had heard the steady drip of blood from her soaked skirt, and before that, when he had thought her dead there on the curb, and again when she made that sound, that sigh or whispered moan. He had brought her in and when he saw all that blood he had turned left, turned right, put her down on the floor, his brains all clabbered and churned and his temples athump with the unaccustomed exercise. All he could act on was *Don't get blood on the bedspread.* He turned on the overhead light and stood for a moment blinking and breathing hard; suddenly he leaped for the window to lower the blind against the street light staring in and all other eyes. He saw his hands reach for the blind and checked himself; they were red and ready to paint anything he touched. He made a sound, a detached part of his mind recognizing it as the exact duplicate of that agonized whisper she had uttered out there on the dark, wet street, and leaped to the light switch, seeing the one red smudge already there, knowing as he swept his hand over it he was leaving another. He stumbled to the sink in the corner and washed his hands, washed them again, every few seconds looking over his shoulder at the girl's body and the thick flat finger of blood which crept curling toward him over the linoleum.

He had his breath now, and moved more carefully to the window. He drew down the blind and pulled the curtains and looked at the sides and the bottom to see that there were no crevices. In pitch blackness he felt his way to the opposite wall, going around the edges of the linoleum, and turned on the light again. The finger of blood was a tentacle now, fumbling toward the soft, stain-starved floorboards. From the enamel table beside the stove he snatched a plastic sponge and dropped it on the tentacle's seeking tip and was pleased, it was a reaching thing no more, it was only something that could be mopped up.

He took off the bedspread and hung it over the brass head-rail. From the drawer of the china closet and from the gate leg table he took his two plastic table cloths. He covered the bed with them, leaving plenty of overlap, then stood a moment rocking with worry and pulling out his lower lip with a thumb and forefinger. *Fix it right,* he told himself firmly. So she'll die before you fix it, never mind, fix it, right.

He expelled air from his nostrils and got books from the shelf in the china closet—a six-year-old World Almanac, a half-dozen paperbacked novels, a heavy catalog of jewelry findings. He pulled the bed away from the wall and put books one by one under two of the legs so that the bed was tilted slightly down to the foot and slightly to one side. He got a blanket and rolled it and slipped it under the plastic so that it formed a sort of fence down the high side. He got a six-quart aluminum pot from under the sink and set it on the floor by the lowest corner of the bed and pushed the trailing end of plastic down into it. *So bleed now*, he told the girl silently, with satisfaction.

He bent over her and grunted, lifting her by the armpits. Her head fell back as if she had no bones in her neck and he almost dropped her. He dragged her to the bed, leaving a wide red swath as her skirt trailed through the scarlet puddle she had lain in. He lifted her clear of the floor, settled his feet, and leaned over the bed with her in his arms. It took an unexpected effort to do it. He realized only then how drained, how tired he was, and how old. He put her down clumsily, almost dropping her in an effort to leave the carefully arranged tablecloths undisturbed, and he very nearly fell into the bed with her. He levered himself away with rubbery arms and stood panting. Around the soggy hem of her skirt blood began to gather, and as he watched, began to find its way lazily to the low corner. *So much, so much blood in a person,* he marveled, and *stop it, how to make it stop if it won't stop?*

He glanced at the locked door, the blinded window, the clock. He listened. It was raining harder now, drumming and hissing in the darkest hours. Otherwise nothing; the house was asleep and the street, dead. He was alone with his problem.

He pulled at his lip, then snatched his hand away as he tasted her blood. He coughed and ran to the sink and spat, and washed his mouth and then his hands.

So all right, go call up. . . .

Call up? Call what, the hospital they should call the cops? Might as well call the cops altogether. *Stupid.* What could I tell them, she's my sister, she's hit by a car, they going to believe me? Tell them the truth, a block away I see somebody push her out of a car, drive off, no lights, I bring her in out of the rain, only inside I find she is bleeding like this, they believe me? *Stupid.* What's the matter with you, mind your own business why don't you.

He thought he would pick her up now and put her back in the rain. Yes and somebody sees you, *stupid.*

He saw that the wide, streaked patch of blood on the linoleum was losing gloss where it lay thin, drying and soaking in. He picked up the sponge, two-thirds red now and the rest its original baby-blue except at one end where it looked like bread drawn with a sharp red pencil. He turned it over so it wouldn't drip while he carried it and took it to the sink and rinsed it, wringing it over and over in the running water. *Stupid,* call up somebody and get help.

Call who?

He thought of the department store where for eighteen years, he had waxed floors and vacuumed rugs at night. The neighborhood, where he knew the grocery and the butcher. Closed up, asleep, everybody gone; names, numbers he didn't know and anyway, who to trust? *My God in fifty-three years you haven't got a friend?*

He took the clean sponge and sank to his knees on the linoleum, and just then the bank of blood creeping down the bed reached the corner and turned to a sharp streak; *ponk* it went into the pan, and *pitti-pittipitti* in a rush, then drip-drip-drip-drip, three to the second and not stopping. He knew then with absolute and belated certainty that this bleeding was not going to stop by itself. He whimpered softly and then got up and went to the bed. *"Don't be dead,"* he said aloud, and the way his voice sounded, it frightened him. He put out his hand to her chest, but drew it back when he saw her blouse was torn and blood came from there too.

He swallowed hard and then began fumbling with her clothes. Flat ballet slippers, worn, soggy, thin like paper and little silken things he had never seen before, like just the foot of a stocking. More blood on—but no, that was peeled and chipped enamel on her cold white toes. The skirt had a button at the side and a zipper which baffled him for a moment, but he got it down and tugged the skirt off in an interminable series of jerks from the hem, one side and the other, while she rolled slightly and limply to the motion. Small silken pants, completely soaked and so badly cut on the left side that he snapped them apart easily between his fingers; but the other side was surprisingly strong and he had to get his scissors to cut them away. The blouse buttoned up the front and was no problem; under it was a brassiere which was cut right in two near the front. He lifted it away but had to cut one of the straps with his scissors to free it altogether.

He ran to the sink with his sponge, washed it and wrung it out, filled a saucepan with warm water and ran back. He sponged the body down; it looked firm but too thin, with its shadow-ladder of ribs down each side and the sharp protrusion of the hip-bones. Under the left breast was a long cut, starting on the ribs in front and curving upward almost to the nipple. It seemed deep but the blood merely welled out. The other cut, though, in her groin, released blood brightly in regular gouts, one after the other, eager but weakly. He had seen the like before, the time Garber pinched his arm off in the elevator cable-room, but then the blood squirted a foot away. Maybe this did, too, he thought suddenly, but now it's slowing up, now it's going to stop, yes, and you, stupid, you have a dead body, you can tell stories to the police.

He wrung out the sponge in the water and mopped the wound. Before it could fill up again he spread the sides of the cut and looked down into it. He could clearly see the femoral artery, looking like an end of spaghetti and cut almost through; and there was nothing but blood again.

He squatted back on his heels, pulling heedlessly at his lip with his bloody hand trying to think. *Pinch, shut, squeeze. Squeezers. Tweezers!.* He ran to his toolbox and clawed it open. Years ago he had learned to make fine chains out of square silver wire, and he used to pass the time away by making link after tiny link, soldering each one closed with an alcohol torch and a needle-tipped iron. He picked up the tweezers and dropped them in favor of the small spring clamp which he used for holding the link while he worked on it. He ran to the sink and washed the clamp and came back to the bed. Again he sponged away the little lake of blood, and quickly reached down and got the fine jaws of the clamp on the artery near its cut. Immediately there was another gush of blood. Again he sponged it away, and in a blaze of inspiration, released the clamp, moved it to the other side of the cut, and clamped it again.

Blood still oozed from the inside of the wound, but that terrible pulsing gush was gone. He sat back on his heels and painfully released a breath he must have held for two minutes. His eyes ached from the strain, and his brain was still whirling, but with these was a feeling, a new feeling almost like an ache or a pain, but it was nowhere and everywhere inside him; it wanted him to laugh but at the same time his eyes stung and hot salt squeezed out through holes too small for it.

After a time he recovered, blinking away his exhaustion and sprang up, overwhelmed by urgency. *Got to fix everything.* He went to the medicine cabinet over the sink. Adhesive tape, pack of gauze pads. Maybe not big enough; okay tape together, fix right. New tube this sulfa-thia-dia-what-chamacall-um, fix anything, time I got vacuum-cleaner grit in cut hand, infection. Fixed boils too.

He filled a kettle and his saucepan with clean water and put them on a stove. Sew up, yes. He found needles, white thread, dumped them into the water. He went back to the bed and stood musing for a long time, looking at the oozing gash under the girl's breast. He sponged out the femoral wound again and stared pensively into it until the blood slowly covered the clamped artery. He could not be positive, but he had a vague recollection of something about tourniquets, they should be opened up every once in a while or there is trouble; same for an artery, maybe? Better he should sew up the artery; it was only opened, not cut through. If he could find out how to do it and still let it be like a pipe, not like a darned sock.

So into the pot went the tweezers, a small pair of needlenose pliers, and, after some more thought, a dozen silver brooch-pins out of his jewelry kit. Waiting for the water to boil, he inspected the wounds again. He pulled on his lip, frowning, then got another fine needle, held it with pliers in the gas flame until it was red, and with another of his set of pliers bent it around in a small semicircle and dropped it into the water. From the sponge he cut a number of small flat slabs and dropped them in too.

He glanced at the clock, and then for ten minutes he scrubbed the white enamel table-top with cleanser. He tipped it into the sink, rinsed it at the faucet, and then slowly poured the contents of the kettle over it. He took it to the stove, held it with one hand while he fished in the boiling saucepan with a silver knife until he had the pliers resting with their handles out of the water. He grasped them gingerly with a clean washcloth and carefully, one by one, transferred everything from saucepan to table. By the time he had found the last of the needles and the elusive silver pins, sweat was running into his eyes and the arm that held the table-top threatened to drop right off. But he set his stumpy yellow teeth and kept at it.

Carrying the table-top, he kicked a wooden chair bit by bit across the room until it rested by the bed, and set his burden down on its seat. *This no hospital,* he thought, *but I fix everything.*

Hospital! Yes, in the movies—

He went to a drawer and got a clean white handkerchief and tried to tie it over his mouth and nose like in the movies. His knobby face and square head were too much for one handkerchief; it took three before he got it right, with a great white tassel hanging down the back like in an airplane picture.

He looked helplessly at his hands, then shrugged; so no rubber gloves, what the hell. I wash good. His hands were already pink and wrinkled from his labors, but he went back to the sink and scratched a bar of soap until his horny nails were packed with it, then cleaned them with a file until they hurt, and washed and cleaned them again. And at last he knelt by the bed, holding his shriven hands up in a careful salaam. Almost, he reached for his lip to pull it, but not quite.

He squeezed out two globs of the sulfa ointment onto the table-top and, with the pliers, squashed two slabs of sponge until the creamy stuff was through and through them. He mopped out the femoral wound and placed a medicated sponge on each side of the wound, leaving the artery exposed at the bottom. Using tweezers and pliers, he laboriously threaded the curved needle while quelling the urge to stick the end of the thread into his mouth.

He managed to get four tiny stitches into the artery below the break, out of it above the break. Each one he knotted with exquisite care so that the thread would not cut the tissue but still would draw the severed edges together. Then he squatted back on his heels to rest, his shoulders afire with tension, his eyes misted. Then, taking a deep breath, he removed the clamp.

Blood filled the wound and soaked the sponges. But it came slowly, without spurting. He shrugged grimly. So what's to do, use a tire patch? He mopped the blood out once more, and quickly filled the incision with ointment, slapping a piece of gauze over it more to hide it than to help it.

He wiped his eyebrows first with one shoulder, then the other, and fixed his eyes on the opposite wall the way he used to do when he worked on his little silver chains. When the mist went away he turned his attention to the long cut on the underside of the breast. He didn't know how to stitch one this size, but he could cook and he knew how to skewer up a chicken. Biting his tongue, he stuck the first of his silver pins into the flesh at right angles to the cut, pressing it across the wound and out the other side. He started the next pin not quite an inch away, and the same with the third. The fourth grated on something in the wound; it startled him like a door slamming and he bit his tongue painfully. He backed the pin out and probed carefully with his tweezers. Yes, something hard in there. He probed deeper with both points of the tweezers, feeling them enter uncut tissue with a soft crunching that only a fearful fingertip could hear. He conquered a shudder and glanced up at the girl's face. He resolved not to look up there again. It was a very dead face.

Stupid! but the self-insult was lost in concentration even as it was born. The tweezers closed on something hard, slippery and stubborn. He worked it gently back and forth, feeling a puzzled annoyance at this unfamiliar flesh that yielded as he moved. Gradually, very gradually, a sharp angular corner of *something* appeared. He kept at it until there was enough to grasp with his fingers; then he set his tweezers aside and gently worked it loose. Blood began to flow freely before it was half out, but he did not stop until he could draw it free. The light glinted on the strip of hollow-ground steel and its shattered margins; he turned it over twice before it came to him that it was a piece of straight razor. He set it down on his enamel table, thinking of what the police might have said to him if he had turned her over to them with that story about a car accident.

He stanched the blood, pulled the wound as wide apart as he could. The nipple writhed under his fingers, its pink halo shrunken and wrinkled; he grunted, thinking that a bug had crawled under his hand, and then aware that whatever the thing meant, it couldn't mean death, not yet anyway. He had to go back and start over, stanching the cut and spreading it, and quickly squeezing in as much ointment as it would hold. Then he went on with his insertion of the silver pins, until there was a little ladder of twelve of them from one end of the wound to the other. He took his thread, doubled it, put the loop around the topmost pin and drew the two parts of the thread underneath. Holding them both in one hand, he gently pinched the edges of the wound together at the pin. Then he drew the loop tight without cutting, crossed the threads and put them under the next pin, and again closed the wound. He continued this all the way down, lacing the cut closed around the ladder of pins. At the bottom he tied the thread off and cut it. There was blood and ointment all over his handiwork, but when he mopped up it looked good to him.

He stood up and let sensation flow agonizingly into his numb feet. He was sopping wet; he could feel perspiration searching its way down through the hairs of his legs; like a migration of bed-bugs. He looked down at himself; wrinkles and water and blood. He looked across at the wavery mirror, and saw a bandaged goblin with brow-ridges like a shelf and sunken eyes with a cast to them, with grizzled hair which could be scrubbed only to the color of grime, and with a great gout of blood where the mouth hid behind

the bandage. He snatched it down and looked again. *More better
you cover your face, no matter what.* He turned away, not from his
face, but with it, in the pained patience of a burro with saddle
sores.

Wearily he carried his enameled table-top to the sink. He
washed his hands and forearms and took off the handkerchiefs
from around his neck and washed his face. Then he got what was
left of his sponge and a pan of warm soapy water and came back
to the bed.

It took him hours. He sponged the tablecloths on which she
lay, shifted her gently so as to put no strain on the wounds, and
washed and dried where she had lain. He washed her from head to
toe, going back for clean water, and then had to dry the bed again
afterward. When he lifted her head he found her hair matted and
tacky with rain and drying blood, and fresh blood with it, so he
propped up her shoulders with a big pillow under the plastic and
tipped her head back and washed and dried her hair, and found an
ugly lump and a bleeding contusion on the back of her head. He
combed her hair away from it on each side and put cold water on
it, and it stopped bleeding, but there was a lump the size of a
plum. He separated half a dozen of the gauze pads and packed
them around the lump so that it need not take the pressure off her
head; he dared not turn her over.

When her hair was wet and fouled it was only a dark mat, but
cleaned and combed, it was the darkest of auburns, perfectly
straight. There was a broad lustrous band of it on the bed on each
side of her face, which was radiant with pallor, cold as a moon. He
covered her with the bedspread, and for a long while stood over
her, full of that strange nowhere-everywhere almost-pain, not liking it but afraid to turn away from it . . . maybe he would never
have it again.

He sighed, a thing that came from his marrow and his years,
and doggedly set to work scrubbing the floor. When he had finished, and the needles and thread were put away, the bit of tape
which he had not used, the wrappers of the gauze pads and the
pan of blood from the end of the bed disposed of, and all the tools
cleaned and back in their box, the night was over and daylight
pressed weakly against the drawn blind. He turned out the light
and stood without breathing, listening with all his mind, wanting

to know from where he stood if she still lived. To bend close and find out she was gone—oh no. He wanted to know from here.

But a truck went by, and a woman called a child, and someone laughed; so he went and knelt by the bed and closed his eyes and slowly put his hand on her throat. It was cool—please, not cold!—and quiet as a lost glove.

Then the hairs on the back of his hand stirred to her breath, and again, the faintest of motions. The stinging came to his eyes and through and through him came the fiery urge to *do:* make some soup, buy some medicine, maybe, for her, a ribbon or a watch; clean the house, run to the store . . . and while doing all these things, all at once, to shout and shout great shaking wordless bellows to tell himself over and over again, so he could hear for sure, that she was alive. At the very peak of this explosion of urges, there was a funny little side-slip and he was fast asleep.

He dreamed someone was sewing his legs together with a big curved sail needle, and at the same time drawing the thread from his belly; he could feel the spool inside spinning and emptying. He groaned and opened his eyes, and knew instantly where he was and what had happened, and hated himself for the noise he made. He lifted his hand and churned his fingers to be sure they could feel, and lowered them gently to her throat. It was warm—no, hot, too hot. He pushed back from the bed and scrabbled half-across the floor on his knuckles and his numb, rubbery legs. Cursing silently he made a long lunge and caught the wooden chair to him, and used it to climb to his feet. He dared not let it go, so clumped softly with it over to the corner, where he twisted and hung gasping to the edge of the sink, while boiling acid ate downward through his legs. When he could, he splashed cold water on his face and neck and, still drying himself on a towel, stumbled across to the bed. He flung the bedspread off and *stupid!* he almost screamed as it plucked at his fingers on the way; it had adhered to the wound in her groin and he was sure he had ripped it to shreds, torn a whole section out of the clumsily patched artery. And he couldn't see; it must be getting dark outside; how long had he crouched there? He ran to the light switch, leaped back. Yes, bleeding, it was bleeding again——

But a little, only a very little. The gauze was turned up perhaps halfway, and though the exposed wound was wet with blood, blood was not running. It had, while he was asleep, but hardly enough to find its way to the mattress. He lifted the loose corner of the gauze very gently, and found it stuck fast. But the sponges, the little sponges to put on the sulfa-whatchama, they were still in the wound. He'd meant to take them out after a couple of hours, not let the whole clot form around them!

He ran for warm water, his big sponge. Soap in it, yes. He squatted beside the bed, though his legs still protested noisily, and began to bathe the gauze with tiny, gentle touches.

Something made him look up. She had her eyes open, and was looking down at him. Her face and her eyes were utterly without expression. He watched them close slowly and slowly open again, lackluster and uninterested. "All right, all right," he said harshly, "I fix everything." She just kept on looking. He nodded violently, it was all that soothes, all that encourages, hope for her and a total promise for her, but it was only a rapid bobbing of his big ugly head. Annoyed as he always was at his own speechlessness, he went back to work. He got the gauze off and began soaking the edge of the sponges. When he thought it was ready to come, he tugged gently at it.

In a high, whispery soprano, "Ho-o-o-o . . . ?" she said; it was like a question and a sob. Slowly she turned her head to the left. "Ho-o-o-o?" She turned her head again and slipped back to unconsciousness.

"I," he said loudly, excitedly, and "I——" and that was all; she wouldn't hear him anyway. He held still until his hands stopped trembling, and went on with the job.

The wound looked wonderfully clean, though the skin all around it was dry and hot.

Down inside the cut he could see the artery in a nest of wet jelly; that was probably right—he didn't know, but it looked all right, he wouldn't disturb it. He packed the opening full of ointment, pressed the edges gently together, and put on a piece of tape. It promptly came unstuck, so he discarded it and dried the flesh all around the wound, put on gauze first, then the tape, and this time it held.

The other cut was quite closed, though more so where the

pins were than between them. It too was surrounded by hot, dry, red flesh.

The scrape on the back of her head had not bled, but the lump was bigger than ever. Her face and neck were dry and very warm, though the rest of her body seemed cool. He went for a cold cloth and put it across her eyes and pressed it down on her cheeks, and she sighed. When he took it away she was looking at him again.

"You all right?" he asked her, and inanely, "You all right," he told her. A small frown flickered for a moment and then her eyes closed. He knew somehow that she was asleep. He touched her cheeks with the back of his fingers. "Very hot," he muttered.

He turned out the light and in the dimness changed his clothes. From the bottom of a drawer he took a child's exercise book, and from it a piece of paper with a telephone number in large black penciled script. "I come back," he said to the darkness. She didn't say anything. He went out, locking the door behind him.

Laboriously he called the office from the big drugstore, referring to his paper for each digit and for each, holding the dial against the stop for a full three or four seconds as if to be sure the number would stick. He got the big boss Mr. Laddie first of all, which was acutely embarrassing; he had not spoken to him in a dozen years. At the top of his bull voice he collided with Laddie's third impatient "Hello?" with "Sick! I—uh, *sick!*" He heard the phone say "—in God's name . . .?" and Mr. Wismer's laughter, and "Gimme the phone, that's got to be that orangutan of mine," and right in his ear, "Hello?"

"Sick tonight," he shouted.

"What's the matter with you?"

He swallowed. "I can't," he yelled.

"That's just old age," said Mr. Wismer. He heard Mr. Laddie laughing too. Mr. Wismer said, "How many nights you had off in the last fifteen years?"

He thought about it. "No!" he roared. Anyway, it was eighteen years.

"You know, that's right," said Mr. Wismer, speaking to Mr.

Laddie without trying to cover his phone, "fifteen years and never asked for a night off before."

"So who needs him? Give him all his nights off."

"Not at those prices," said Mr. Wismer, and to his phone, "Sure, dummy, take off. Don't work no con games." The phone clicked off on laughter, and he waited there in the booth until he was sure nothing else would be said. Then he hung up his receiver and emerged into the big drugstore where everyone all over was looking at him. Well, they always did. That didn't bother him. Only one thing bothered him, and that was Mr. Laddie's voice saying over and over in his head, "So who needs him?" He knew he would have to stop and face those words and let them and all that went with them go through his mind. But not now, please not now.

He kept them away by being busy; he bought tape and gauze and ointment and a canvas cot and three icebags and, after some thought, aspirin, because someone had told him once ... and then to the supermarket where he bought enough to feed a family of nine for nine days. And for all his bundles, he still had a thick arm and a wide shoulder for a twenty-five-pound cake of ice.

He got the door open and the ice in the box, and went out in the hall and picked up the bundles and brought those in, and then went to her. She was burning up, and her breathing was like the way seabirds fly into the wind, a small beat, a small beat, and a long wait, balancing. He cracked a corner off the ice-cake, wrapped it in a dishtowel and whacked it angrily against the sink. He crowded the crushed ice into one of the bags and put it on her head. She sighed but did not open her eyes. He filled the other bags and put one on her breast and one on her groin. He wrung his hands uselessly over her until it came to him *she has to eat, losing blood like that.*

So he cooked, tremendously, watching her every second minute. He made minestrone and baked cabbage and mashed potatoes and veal cutlets. He cut a pie and warmed cinnamon buns, and he had hot coffee with ice cream ready to spoon into her. She didn't eat it, any of it, nor did she drink a drop. She lay there and occasionally let her head fall to the side, so he had to run and pick up the icebag and replace it. Once again she sighed, and once he thought she opened her eyes, but couldn't be sure.

On the second day she ate nothing and drank nothing, and

her fever was unbelievable. During the night, crouched on the floor beside her, he awoke once with the echoes of weeping still in the room, but he may have dreamed it.

Once he cut the tenderest, juiciest piece of veal he could find on a cutlet, and put it between her lips. Three hours later he pressed them apart to put in another piece, but the first one was still there. The same thing happened with aspirin, little white crumbs on a dry tongue.

And the time soon came when he had busied himself out of things to do, and fretted himself into a worry-reflex that operated by itself, and the very act of thinking new thoughts trapped him into facing the old ones, and then of course there was nothing to do but let them run on through, with all the ache and humiliation they carried with them. He was trying to think a new thing about what would happen if he called a doctor, and the doctor would want to take her to a hospital; he would say, "She needs treatment, old man, she doesn't need you," and there it was in his mind, ready to run, so:

Be eleven years old, bulky and strong and shy, standing in the kitchen doorway, holding your wooden box by its string and trying to shape your mouth so that the reluctant words can press out properly; and there's Mama hunched over a gin bottle like a cat over a half-eaten bird, peering; watch her lipless wide mouth twitch and say, "Don't stand there clackin' and slurpin'! Speak up, boy! What are you tryin' to say, you're leaving?"

So nod, it's easier, and she'll say "Leave, then, leave, who needs you?" and you go:

And be a squat, powerful sixteen and go to the recruiting station and watch the sergeant with the presses and creases asking "Whadda *you* want?" and you try, you try and you can't say it so you nod your head at the poster with the pointing finger, UNCLE SAM NEEDS YOU; and the sergeant glances at it and at you, and suddenly his pointing finger is half an inch away from your nose; crosseyed you watch it while he barks, "Well, Uncle don't need *you!*" and you wait, watching the finger that way, not moving until you understand; you understand things real good, it's just that you hear slowly. So there you hang crosseyed and they all laugh.

Or 'way back, you're eight years old and in school, that Phyllis with the row of springy brown sausage-curls flying when she tosses her head, pink and clean and so pretty; you have the chocolates wrapped in gold paper tied in goldstring mesh; you go up the aisle to her desk and put the chocolates down and run back; she comes down the aisle and throws them so hard the mesh breaks on your desk and she says, loud, "I don't need these and I don't need you, and you know what, you got snot on your face," and you put up your hand and sure enough you have.

That's all. Only every time anyone says "Who needs him?" or the like, you have to go through all of them, every one. Sooner or later, however much you put it off, you've got to do it all.

I get doctor, you don't need me.

You die, you don't need me.

Please . . .

Far back in her throat, a scraping hiss, and her lips moved. She held his eyes with hers, and her lips moved silently, and a little late for the lips, the hiss came again. He didn't know how he guessed right, but he did and brought water, dribbling it slowly on her mouth. She licked at it greedily, lifting her head up. He put a hand under it, being careful of the lump, and helped her. After a while she slumped back and smiled weakly at the cup. Then she looked up into his face and though the smile disappeared, he felt much better. He ran to the icebox and the stove, and got glasses and straws—one each of orange juice, chocolate milk, plain milk, consommé from a can, and ice water. He lined them up on the chair-seat by the bed and watched them and her eagerly, like a circus seal waiting to play "America" on the bulb-horns. She did smile this time, faintly, briefly, but right at him, and he tried the consommé. She drank almost half of it through the straw without stopping and fell asleep.

Later, when he checked to see if there was any bleeding, the plastic sheet was wet, but not with blood. *Stupid!* he raged at himself, and stamped out and bought a bedpan.

She slept a lot now, and ate often but lightly. She began to watch him as he moved about; sometimes when he thought she was asleep, he would turn and meet her eyes. Mostly, it was his hands she watched, those next two days. He washed and ironed her clothes, and sat and mended them with straight small stitches;

he hung by his elbows to the edge of the enameled table and worked his silver wire, making her a brooch like a flower on a fan, and a pendant on a silver chain, and a bracelet to match them. She watched his hands while he cooked; he made his own spaghetti— tagliatelli, really,—rolling and rolling the dough until it was a huge tough sheet, winding it up like a jelly-roll only tight, slicing it in quick, accurate flickers of a paring-knife so it came out like yellow-white flat shoelaces. He had hands which had never learned their limitations, because he had never thought to limit them. Nothing else in life cared for this man but his hands, and since they did everything, they could do anything.

But when he changed her dressings or washed her, or helped with the bedpan, she never looked at his hands. She would lie perfectly still and watch his face.

She was very weak at first and could move nothing but her head. He was glad because her stitches were healing nicely. When he withdrew the pins it must have hurt, but she made not a sound; twelve flickers of her smooth brow, one for each pin as it came out.

"Hurts," he rumbled.

Faintly, she nodded. It was the first communication between them, except for those mute, crowded eyes following him about. She smiled too, as she nodded, and he turned his back and ground his knuckles into his eyes and felt wonderful.

He went back to work on the sixth night, having puttered and fussed over her all day to keep her from sleeping until he was ready to leave, then not leaving until he was sure she was fast asleep. He would lock her in and hurry to work, warm inside and ready to do three men's work; and home again in the dark early hours as fast as his bandy legs would carry him, bringing her a present—a little radio, a scarf, something special to eat, every single day. He would lock the door firmly and then hurry to her, touching her forehead and cheek to see what her temperature was, straightening the bed gently so she wouldn't wake. Then he would go out of her sight, away back by the sink, and undress and change to the long drawers he slept in, and come back and curl up on the camp cot. For perhaps an hour and a half he would sleep like a stone, but after that the slightest rustle of her sheet, the smallest catch of breath, would bring him to her in a bound, croaking, "You all right?" and hanging over her tensely, frantically trying to divine what she might need, what he might do or get for her.

And when the daylight came he would give her warm milk with an egg beaten in it, and then he would bathe her and change her dressings and comb her hair, and when there was nothing left to do for her he would clean the room, scrub the floor, wash clothes and dishes and, interminably, cook. In the afternoon he shopped, moving everywhere at a half trot, running home again as soon as he could to show her what he had bought, what he had planned for her dinner. All these days, and then these weeks, he glowed inwardly, hugging the glow while he was away from her, fanning it with her presence when they were together.

He found her crying one afternoon late in the second week, staring at the little radio with the tears streaking her face. He made a harsh cooing syllable and wiped her cheeks with a dry washcloth and stood back with torture on his animal face. She patted his hand weakly, and made a series of faint gestures which utterly baffled him He sat on the bedside chair and put his face close to hers as if he could tear the meaning out of her with his eyes. There was something different about her; she had watched him, up to now, with the fascinated, uncomprehending attention of a kitten watching a tankful of tropical fish; but now there was something more in her gaze, in the way she moved and in what she did.

"You hurt?" he rasped.

She shook her head. Her mouth moved, and she pointed to it and began to cry again.

"Oh, you hungry. I fix, fix good." He rose, but she caught his wrist, shaking her head and crying, but smiling too. He sat down, torn apart by his perplexity. Again she moved her mouth, pointing to it, shaking her head.

"No talk," he said. She was breathing so hard it frightened him, but when he said that she gasped and half sat up; he caught her shoulders and put her down, but she was nodding urgently. "You can't talk!" he said.

Yes, yes! she nodded.

He looked at her for a long time. The music on the radio stopped and someone began to sell used cars in a crackling baritone. She glanced at it and her eyes filled with tears again. He leaned across her and shut the set off. After a profound effort he formed his mouth in the right shape and released a disdainful snort: "Ha! What you want talk? Don't talk. I fix everything, no talk. I——" He ran out of words, so instead slapped himself powerfully on the chest and nodded at her, the stove, the bedpan, the tray of bandages. He said again, "What you want talk?"

She looked up at him, overwhelmed by his violence, and shrank down. He tenderly wiped her cheeks again, mumbling, "I fix everything."

He came home in the dark one morning, and after seeing that she was comfortable according to his iron standards, went to bed. The smell of bacon and fresh coffee was, of course, part of a dream; what else could it be? And the faint sounds of movement around the room had to be his weary imagination.

He opened his eyes on the dream and closed them again, laughing at himself for a crazy stupid. Then he went still inside, and slowly opened his eyes again.

Beside his cot was the bedside chair, and on it was a plate of fried eggs and crisp bacon, a cup of strong black coffee, toast with the gold of butter disappearing into its older gold. He stared at these things in total disbelief, and then looked up.

She was sitting on the edge of the bed, where it formed an eight-inch corridor between itself and the cot. She wore her pressed and mended blouse and her skirt. Her shoulders sagged with weariness and she seemed to have some difficulty in holding her head up; her hands hung limply between her knees. But her face was suffused with delight and anticipation as she watched him waking up to his breakfast.

His mouth writhed and he bared his blunt yellow teeth, and ground them together while he uttered a howl of fury. It was a strangled, rasping sound and she scuttled away from it as if it had burned her, and crouched in the middle of the bed with her eyes huge and her mouth slack. He advanced on her with his arms raised and his big fists clenched; she dropped her face on the bed and covered the back of her neck with both hands and lay there trembling. For a long moment he hung over her, then slowly dropped his arms. He tugged at the skirt. "Take off," he grated. He tugged it again, harder.

She peeped up at him and then slowly turned over. She fumbled weakly at the button. He helped her. He pulled the skirt away and tossed it on the cot, and gestured sternly at the blouse. She unbuttoned it and he lifted it from her shoulders. He pulled down the sheet, taking it right out from under her. He took her ankles gently in his powerful hands and pulled them down until she was straightened out on the bed, and then covered her carefully. He was breathing hard. She watched him in terror.

In a frightening quiet he turned back to his cot and the laden chair beside it. Slowly he picked up the cup of coffee and smashed it on the floor. Steadily as the beat of a woodsman's axe the saucer followed, the plate of toast, the plate of eggs. China and yolk squirted and sprayed over the floor and on the walls. When he had finished he turned back to her. "I fix everything," he said hoarsely. He emphasized each syllable with a thick forefinger as he said again, "*I* fix everything."

She whipped over on her stomach and buried her face in the pillow, and began to sob so hard he could feel the bed shaking the floor through the soles of his feet. He turned angrily away from her and got a pan and a scrub-brush and a broom and dustpan, and laboriously, methodically, cleaned up the mess.

Two hours later he approached her where she lay, still on her stomach, stiff and motionless. He had had a long time to think of what to say: "Look, you see, you *sick* . . . you see?" He said it, as gently as he could. He put his hands on her shoulder but she twitched violently, flinging it away. Hurt and baffled, he backed away and sat down on the couch, watching her miserably.

She wouldn't eat any lunch.

She wouldn't eat any dinner.

As the time approached for him to go to work, she turned over. He still sat on the cot in his long johns, utter misery on his face and in every line of his ugly body. She looked at him and her eyes filled with tears. He met her gaze but did not move. She sighed suddenly and held out her hand. He leaped to it and pulled it to his forehead, knelt, bowed over it and began to cry. She patted his wiry hair until the storm passed, which it did abruptly, at its height. He sprang away from her and clattered pans on the stove, and in a few minutes brought her some bread and gravy and a parboiled artichoke, rich with olive oil and basil. She smiled wanly and took the plate, and slowly ate while he watched each mouthful and radiated what could only be gratitude. Then he changed his clothes and went to work.

He brought her a red housecoat when she began to sit up, though he would not let her out of bed. He brought her a glass globe in which a flower would keep, submerged in water, for a week, and two live turtles in a plastic bowl and a pale-blue toy rabbit with a music box in it that played "Rock-a-bye Baby" and blinding vermilion lipstick. She remained obedient and more watchful than ever; when his fussing and puttering were over and he took up his crouch on the cot, waiting for whatever need in her he could divine next, their eyes would meet, and, increasingly, his would drop. She would hold the blue rabbit tight to her and watch him unblinkingly, or smile suddenly, parting her lips as if something vitally important and deeply happy was about to escape them. Sometimes she seemed inexpressibly sad, and sometimes she was so restless that he would go to her and stroke her hair until she fell asleep, or seemed to. It occurred to him that he had not seen her wounds for almost two days, and that perhaps they were bothering her during one of these restless spells, and so he pressed her gently down and uncovered her. He touched the scar carefully and she suddenly thrust his hand away and grasped her own flesh firmly, kneading it, slapping it stingingly. Shocked, he looked at her face and saw she was smiling, nodding. "Hurt?" She shook her head. He said, proudly, as he covered her, "I fix. I fix good." She nodded and caught his hand briefly between her chin and her shoulder.

It was that night, after he had fallen into that heavy first sleep on his return from the store, that he felt the warm firm length of her tight up against him on the cot. He lay still for a moment, somnolent, uncomprehending, while quick fingers plucked at the buttons of his long johns. He brought his hands up and trapped her wrists. She was immediately still, though her breath came swift and her heart pounded his chest like an angry little knuckle. He made a labored, inquisitive syllable, "Wh-wha . . . ?" and she moved against him and then stopped, trembling. He held her wrists for more than a minute, trying to think this out, and at last sat up. He put one arm around her shoulders and the other under her knees. He stood up. She clung to him and the breath hissed in her nostrils. He moved to the side of her bed and bent slowly and put her down. He had to reach back and detach her arms from around his neck before he could straighten up. "You sleep," he said. He fumbled for the sheet and pulled it over her and tucked it around her. She lay absolutely motionless, and he touched her hair and went back to his cot. He lay down and after a long time fell into a troubled sleep. But something woke him; he lay and listened, hearing nothing. He remembered suddenly and vividly the night she had balanced between life and death, and he had awakened to the echo of a sob which was not repeated; in sudden fright he jumped up and went to her, bent down and touched her head. She was lying face down. "You cry?" he whispered, and she shook her head rapidly. He grunted and went back to bed.

It was the ninth week and it was raining; he plodded homeward through the black, shining streets, and when he turned into his own block and saw the dead, slick river stretching between him and the streetlight in front of his house, he experienced a moment of fantasy, of dreamlike disorientation; it seemed to him for a second that none of this had happened, that in a moment the car would flash by him and dip toward the curb momentarily while a limp body tumbled out, and he must run to it and take it indoors, and it would bleed, it would bleed, it might die. . . . He shook himself like a big dog and put his head down against the rain, saying *Stupid!* to his inner self. Nothing could be wrong, now. He had found a way to live, and live that way he would, and he would abide no change in it.

But there was a change, and he knew it before he entered the house; his window, facing the street, had a dull orange glow which could not have been given it by the street light alone. But maybe she was reading one of those paperback novels he had inherited with the apartment; maybe she had to use the bedpan or was just looking at the clock . . . but the thoughts did not comfort him; he was sick with an unaccountable fear as he unlocked the hall door. His own entrance showed light through the crack at the bottom; he dropped his keys as he fumbled with them, and at last opened the door.

He gasped as if he had been struck in the solar plexus. The

bed was made, flat, neat, and she was not in it. He spun around; his frantic gaze saw her and passed her before he could believe his eyes. Tall, queenly in her red housecoat, she stood at the other end of the room, by the sink.

He stared at her in amazement. She came to him, and as he filled his lungs for one of his grating yells, she put a finger on her lips and, lightly, her other hand across his mouth. Neither of these gestures, both even, would have been enough to quiet him ordinarily, but there was something else about her, something which did not wait for what he might do and would not quail before him if he did it. He was instantly confused, and silent. He stared after her as, without breaking stride, she passed him and gently closed the door. She took his hand, but the keys were in the way; she drew them from his fingers and tossed them on the table and then took his hand again, firmly. She was sure, decisive; she was one who had thought things out and weighed and discarded, and now knew what to do. But she was triumphant in some way, too; she had the poise of a victor and the radiance of the witness to a miracle. He could cope with her helplessness, of any kind, to any degree, but this—he had to think, and she gave him no time to think.

She led him to the bed and put her hands on his shoulders, turning him and making him sit down. She sat close to him, her face alight, and when again he filled his lungs, "Shh!" she hissed, sharply, and smiling covered his mouth with her hand. She took his shoulders again and looked straight into his eyes, and said clearly, "I can talk now, I can talk!"

Numbly, he gaped at her.

"Three days already, it was a secret, it was a surprise." Her voice was husky, hoarse even, but very clear and deeper than her slight body indicated. "I been practicing, to be sure. I'm all right again, I'm all right. You fix everything!" she said, and laughed.

Hearing that laugh, seeing the pride and joy in her face, he could take nothing away from her. "Ahh . . ." he said, wonderingly.

She laughed again. "I can go, I can go!" she sang. She leaped up suddenly and pirouetted, and leaned over him laughing. He gazed up at her and her flying hair, and squinted his eyes as he would looking into the sun. "Go?" he blared, the pressure of his confusion forcing the syllable out as an explosive shout.

She sobered immediately, and sat down again close to him. "Oh, honey, don't, *don't* look as if you was knifed or something. You know I can't camp on you, live off you, just for*ever!*"

"No, no you stay," he blurted, anguish in his face.

"Now look," she said, speaking simply and slowly as to a child. "I'm all well again, I can talk now. It wouldn't be right, me staying, locked up here, that bedpan and all. Now wait, wait," she said quickly before he could form a word, "I don't mean I'm not grateful, you been . . . you been, well I just can't tell you. Look, nobody in my life ever did anything like this, I mean, I had to run away when I was thirteen, I done all sorts of bad things. And I got treated . . . I mean, nobody else . . . look, here's what I mean, up to now I'd steal, I'd rob anybody, what the hell. What I mean, why not, you see?" She shook him gently to make him see; then, recognizing the blankness and misery of his expression, she wet her lips and started over. "What I'm trying to say is, you been so kind, all this——" She waved her hand at the blue rabbit, the turtle tank, everything in the room—"I can't take any more. I mean, not a thing, not a breakfast. If I could pay you back some way, no matter what, I would, you know I would." There was a tinge of bitterness in her husky voice. "Nobody can pay you anything. You don't need anything or anybody. I can't give you anything you need, or do anything for you that needs doing, you do it all yourself. If there was something you wanted from me——" She curled her hands inward and placed her fingertips between her breasts, inclining her head with a strange submissiveness that made him ache. "But no, you fix everything," she mimicked. There was no mockery in it.

"No, no, you don't go," he whispered harshly.

She patted his cheek, and her eyes loved him. "I do go," she said, smiling. Then the smile disappeared. "I got to explain to you, those hoods who cut me, I asked for that. I goofed. I was doing something real bad—well, I'll tell you. I was a runner, know what I mean? I mean dope, I was selling it."

He looked at her blankly. He was not catching one word in ten; he was biting and biting only on emptiness and uselessness, aloneness, and the terrible truth of this room without her or the blue rabbit or anything else but what it had contained all these years—linoleum with the design scrubbed off, six novels he couldn't read, a stove waiting for someone to cook for, grime and regularity and who needs you?

She misunderstood his expression. "Honey, honey, don't look at me like that, I'll never do it again. I only did it because I didn't care, I used to get glad when people hurt themselves; yeah, I mean that. I never knew someone could be kind, like you; I always thought that was sort of a lie, like the movies. Nice but not real, not for me.

"But I have to tell you, I swiped a cache, my God, twenty, twenty-two G's worth. I had it all of forty minutes, they caught up with me." Her eyes widened and saw things not in the room. "With a razor, he went to hit me with it so hard he broke it on top of the car door. He hit me here *down* and here *up*, I guess he was going to gut me but the razor was busted." She expelled air from her nostrils, and her gaze came back into the room. "I guess I got the lump on the head when they threw me out of the car. I guess that's why I couldn't talk, I heard of that. Oh *honey!* Don't look like that, you're tearing me apart!"

He looked at her dolefully and wagged his big head helplessly from side to side. She knelt before him suddenly and took both his hands. "Listen, you *got* to understand. I was going to slide out while you were working but I stayed just so I could make you understand. After all you done. . . . See, I'm well, I can't stay cooped up in one room forever. If I could, I'd get work some place near here and see you all the time, honest I would. But my life isn't worth a rubber dime in this town. I got to leave here and that means I got to leave town. I'll be all right, honey. I'll write to you; I'll never forget you, how could I?"

She was far ahead of him. He had grasped that she wanted to leave him; the next thing he understood was that she wanted to leave town too.

"You don't go," he choked. "You need me."

"You don't need me," she said fondly, "and I don't need you. It comes to that, honey; it's the way you fixed it. It's the right way; can't you see that?"

Right in there was the third thing he understood.

He stood up slowly, feeling her hands slide from his, from his knees to the floor as he stepped away from her. "Oh God!" she cried from the floor where she knelt, "you're killing me, taking it this way! Can't you be happy for me?"

He stumbled across the room and caught himself on the lower shelf of the china closet. He looked back and forward along the dark, echoing corridor of his years, stretching so far and drearily, and he looked at this short bright segment slipping away from him. . . . He heard her quick footsteps behind him and when he turned he had the flatiron in his hand. She never saw it. She came to him bright-faced, pleading, and he put out his arms and she ran inside, and the iron curved around and crashed into the back of her head.

He lowered her gently down on the linoleum and stood for a long time over her, crying quietly.

Then he put the iron away and filled the kettle and a saucepan with water, and in the saucepan he put needles and a clamp and thread and little slabs of sponge and a knife and pliers. From the gateleg table and from a drawer he got his two plastic tablecloths and began arranging them on the bed. "I fix everything," he murmured as he worked. "Fix it right."

THE SEX OPPOSITE

Budgie slid into the laboratory without knocking, as usual.

She was flushed and breathless, her eyes bright with speed and eagerness. "Whatcha got, Muley?"

Muhlenberg kicked the morgue door shut before Budgie could get in line with it. "Nothing," he said flatly, "and of all the people I don't want to see—and at the moment that means all the people there are—you head the list. Go away."

Budgie pulled off her gloves and stuffed them into an over-sized shoulder-bag, which she hurled across the laboratory onto a work-surface. "Come on, Muley. I saw the meat-wagon outside. I know what it brought, too. That double murder in the park. Al told me."

"Al's jaw is one that needs more tying up than any of the stiffs he taxis around," said Muhlenberg bitterly. "Well, you're not getting near this pair."

She came over to him, stood very close. In spite of his annoyance, he couldn't help noticing how soft and full her lips were just then. *Just then*—and the sudden realization added to the annoyance. He had known for a long time that Budgie could turn on mechanisms that made every one of a man's ductless glands purse up its lips and blow like a trumpet. Every time he felt it he hated himself. "Get away from me," he growled. "It won't work."

"What won't, Muley?" she murmured.

Muhlenberg looked her straight in the eye and said something about his preference for raw liver over Budgie-times-twelve.

The softness went out of her lips, to be replaced by no particular hardness. She simply laughed good-naturedly. "All right, you're immune. I'll try logic."

"Nothing will work," he said. "You will not get in there to see those two, and you'll get no details from me for any of that *couche-con-carne* stew you call a newspaper story."

"Okay," she said surprisingly. She crossed the lab and picked up her handbag. She found a glove and began to pull it on. "Sorry I interrupted you, Muley. I do get the idea. You want to be alone."

His jaw was too slack to enunciate an answer. He watched her go out, watched the door close, watched it open again, heard her say in a very hurt tone, "But I do think you could tell me *why* you won't say anything about this murder."

He scratched his head. "As long as you behave yourself, I guess I do owe you that." He thought for a moment. "It's not your kind of a story. That's about the best way to put it."

"Not my kind of a story? A double murder in Lover's Lane? The maudlin mystery of the mugger, or mayhem in Maytime? No kidding, Muley—you're not serious!"

"Budgie, this one isn't for fun. It's ugly. Very *damn* ugly. And it's serious. It's mysterious for a number of other reasons than the ones you want to siphon into your readers."

"What other reasons?"

"Medically. Biologically. Sociologically."

"My stories got biology. Sociology they got likewise; stodgy truisms about social trends is the way I dish up sex in the public prints, or didn't you know? So—that leaves medical. What's so strange medically about this case?"

"Good night, Budgie."

"Come on, Muley. You can't horrify *me*."

"That I know. You've trod more primrose pathology in your research than Krafft-Ebing plus eleven comic books. No, Budgie. No more."

———

"Dr. F. L. Muhlenberg, brilliant young biologist and special medical consultant to the City and State Police, intimated that these aspects of the case—the brutal murder and disfigurement of the embarrassed couple—were superficial compared with the unspeakable facts behind them. 'Medically mysterious,' he was quoted as saying." She twinkled at him. "How's that sound?" She looked at her watch. "And I can make the early edition, too, with a head. Something like DOC SHOCKED SPEECHLESS—and a subhead: Lab Sleuth Suppresses Medical Details of Double Park Killing. Yeah, and your picture."

"If you dare to print anything of the sort," he raged, "I'll—"

"All right, all right," she said conciliatingly. "I won't. I really won't."

"Promise me?"

"I promise, Muley . . . *if—*"

"Why should I bargain?" he demanded suddenly. "Get out of here."

He began to close the door. "And something for the editorial page," she said. "Is a doctor within his rights in suppressing information concerning a murderous maniac and his methods?" She closed the door.

Muhlenberg bit his lower lip so hard he all but yelped. He ran to the door and snatched it open. "Wait!"

Budgie was leaning against the doorpost lighting a cigarette. "I *was* waiting," she said reasonably.

"Come in here," he grated. He snatched her arm and whirled her inside, slamming the door.

"You're a brute," she said rubbing her arm and smiling dazzlingly.

"The only way to muzzle you is to tell you the whole story. Right?"

"Right. If I get an exclusive when you're ready to break the story."

"There's probably a kicker in that, too," he said morosely. He glared at her. Then, "Sit down," he said.

She did. "I'm all yours."

"Don't change the subject," he said with a ghost of his natural humor. He lit a thoughtful cigarette. "What do you know about this case so far?"

"Too little," she said. "This couple were having a conversation without words in the park when some muggers jumped them and killed them, a little more gruesomely than usual. But instead of being delivered to the city morgue, they were brought straight to you on the orders of the ambulance intern after one quick look."

"How did you know about it?"

"Well, if you must know, I was in the park. There's a shortcut over by the museum, and I was about a hundred yards down the path when I . . ."

Muhlenberg waited as long as tact demanded, and a little longer. Her face was still, her gaze detached. "Go on."

". . . when I heard a scream," she said in the precise tone of voice which she had been using. Then she began to cry.

"Hey," he said. He knelt beside her, put a hand on her shoulder. She shoved it away angrily, and covered her face with a damp towel. When she took it down again she seemed to be laughing. She was doing it so badly that he turned away in very real embarrassment.

"Sorry," she said in a very shaken whisper. "It . . . was that kind of a scream. I've never heard anything like it. It did something to me. It had more agony in it than a single sound should be able to have." She closed her eyes.

"Man or woman?"

She shook her head.

"So," he said matter-of-factly, "what did you do then?"

"Nothing. Nothing at all, for I don't know how long." She slammed a small fist down on the table. "I'm supposed to be a reporter!" she flared. "And there I stand like a dummy, like a wharf rat in concussion-shock!" She wet her lips. "When I came around I was standing by a rock wall with one hand on it." She showed him. "Broke two perfectly good fingernails, I was holding on so tight. I ran toward where I'd heard the sound. Just trampled brush, nothing else. I heard a crowd milling around on the avenue. I went up there. The meat-wagon was there, Al and that young sawbones Regal—Ruggles—"

"Regalio."

"Yeah, him. They'd just put those two bodies into the ambulance. They were covered with blankets. I asked what was up. Regalio waved a finger and said 'Not for school-girls' and gave me a real death-mask grin. He climbed aboard. I grabbed Al and asked him what was what. He said muggers had killed this couple, and it was pretty rugged. Said Regalio had told him to bring them here, even before he made a police report. They were both about as upset as they could get."

"I don't wonder," said Muhlenberg.

"Then I asked if I could ride and they said no and took off. I grabbed a cab when I found one to grab, which was all of fifteen minutes later, and here I am. Here I am," she repeated, "getting a story out of you in the damndest way yet. You're asking, I'm answering." She got up. "You write the feature, Muley. I'll go on into your icebox and do your work."

He caught her arm. "Nah! No you don't! Like the man said— it's not for school-girls."

"Anything you have in there *can't* be worse than my imagination!" she snapped.

"Sorry. It's what you get for barging in on me before I've had a chance to think something through. You see, this wasn't exactly two people."

"I know!" she said sarcastically. "Siamese twins."

He looked at her distantly. "Yes. 'Taint funny, kiddo."

For once she had nothing to say. She put one hand slowly up to her mouth and apparently forgot it, for there it stayed. "That's what so ugly about this. Those two were . . . torn apart." He closed his eyes. "I can just see it. I wish I couldn't. Those thugs drifting through the park at night, out for anything they could get. They hear something . . . fall right over them . . . I don't know. Then—"

"All right, all right," she whispered hoarsely. "I can hear you."

"But, damn it," he said angrily, "I've been kicking around this field long enough to know every documented case of such a creature. And I just can't believe that one like this could exist without having been written up in some medical journal somewhere. Even if they were born in Soviet Russia, some translation of a report would've appeared somewhere."

"I know Siamese twins are rare. But surely such a birth wouldn't make international headlines!"

"This one would," he said positively. "For one thing, Siamese twins usually bear more anomalies than just the fact that they are attached. They're frequently fraternal rather than identical twins. More often than not one's born more fully developed than the other. Usually when they're born at all they don't live. But these—"

"What's so special?"

Muhlenberg spread his hands. "They're perfect. They're costally joined by a surprisingly small tissue-organ complex—"

"Wait, professor, 'Costally'—you mean at the chest?"

"That's right. And the link is—was—not major. I can't understand why they were never surgically separated. There may be a reason, of course, but that'll have to wait on the autopsy."

"Why wait?"

"It's all I can do to wait." He grinned suddenly. "You see, you're more of a help than you realize, Budge. I'm dying to get to work on them, but under the circumstances I have to wait until morning. Regalio reported to the police, and I know the coroner isn't going to come around this time of night, not if I could show him quintuplets in a chain like sausages. In addition, I don't have identities, I don't have relatives' releases—you know. So—a superficial examination, a lot of wild guesses, and a chance to sound off to you to keep myself from going nuts."

"You're *using* me!"

"That's bad?"

"Yes—when I don't get any fun out of it."

He laughed. "I love those incendiary statements of yours. I'm just not flammable."

She looked up at him, up and a little sidewise. "Not at all?"

"Not now."

She considered that. She looked down at her hands as if they were the problems of Muhlenberg's susceptibility. She turned the hands over. "Sometimes," she said, "I really enjoy it when we share something else besides twitches and moans. Maybe we should be more inhibited."

"Do tell."

She said, "We have nothing in common. I mean, but *nothing*. We're different to the core, to the bone. You hunt out facts and so do I, but we could never share that because we don't use facts for the same things. You use facts only to find more facts."

"What do you use them for?"

She smiled. "All sorts of things. A good reporter doesn't

report just what happens. He reports what he *sees*—in many cases a very different thing. Any way . . ."

"Wonder how these biological pressures affected our friends here," he mused, thumbing over his shoulder at the morgue.

"About the same, I'd judge, with certain important difficulties. But wait—were they men or women, or one of each?"

"I didn't tell you, did I?" he said with real startlement.

"No," she said.

He opened his mouth to answer, but could not. The reason came.

It came from downstairs, or outside, or perhaps from nowhere or everywhere, or from a place without a name. It was all around them, inside, behind them in time as well as space. It was the echo of their own first cry when they lost the first warmth and found loneliness, early, as everyone must. It was hurt: some the pain of impact, some of fever and delirium, and some the great pressure of beauty too beautiful to bear. And like pain, it could not be remembered. It lasted as long as it was a sound, and perhaps a little longer, and the frozen time after it died was immeasurable.

Muhlenberg became increasingly conscious of an ache in his calves and in the trapezoid muscles of his back. They sent him a gradual and completely intellectualized message of strain, and very consciously he relieved it and sat down. His movement carried Budgie's arm forward, and he looked down at her hand, which was clamped around his forearm. She moved it away, opening it slowly, and he saw the angry marks of her fingers, and knew they would be bruises in the morning.

She said, "That was the scream. The one I heard. Wasn't once enough?"

It was only then that he could look far enough out of himself to see her face. It was pasty with shock, and wet, and her lips were pale. He leapt to his feet. "Another one! *Come on!*"

He pulled her up and through the door. "Don't you understand?" he blazed. "Another one! It can't be, but somewhere out there it's happened again—"

She pulled back. "Are you sure it wasn't . . ." She nodded at the closed door of the morgue.

"Don't be ridiculous," he snorted. "*They* couldn't be alive."
He hurried her to the stairs.

It was very dark. Muhlenberg's office was in an aging business building which boasted twenty-five-watt bulbs on every other
floor. They hurtled through the murk, past the deepest door-
ways of the law firm, the doll factory, the import-export firm
which imported and exported nothing but phone calls, and all
the other dim mosaics of enterprise. The building seemed quite
deserted, and but for the yellow-orange glow of the landings
and the pathetic little bulbs, there were no lights anywhere. And it
was as quiet as it was almost dark; quiet as late night; quiet as
death.

They burst out onto the old brownstone steps and stopped, afraid
to look, wanting to look. There was nothing. Nothing but the
street, a lonesome light, a distant horn and, far up at the corner,
the distinct clicking of the relays in a traffic-light standard as they
changed an ignored string of emeralds to an unnoticed ruby rope.

"Go up to the corner," he said, pointing. "I'll go down the
other way. That noise wasn't far away—"

"No," she said. "I'm coming with you."

"Good," he said, so glad he was amazed at himself. They ran
north to the corner. There was no one on the street within two
blocks in any direction. There were cars, mostly parked, one coming, but none leaving.

"Now what?" she asked.

For a moment he did not answer. She waited patiently while
he listened to the small distant noises which made the night so
quiet. Then, "Good night, Budge."

"Good—*what!*"

He waved a hand. "You can go home now."

"But what about the—"

"I'm tired," he said. "I'm bewildered. That scream wrung me
like a floor-mop and pulled me down too many stairs too fast.
There's too much I don't know about this and not enough I can do
about it. So go home."

"Aw, Muley . . ."

He sighed. "I know. Your story. Budgie, I faithfully promise
you I'll give you an exclusive as soon as I have facts I can trust."

She looked carefully at his face in the dim light and nodded at what she saw there. "All right, Muley. The pressure's off. Call me?"

"I'll call you."

He stood watching her walk away. Quite a gal, he thought. He wondered what had moved her to make that odd remark about inhibitions. They'd certainly never bothered her before. But—perhaps she had something there. Sometimes when you take what is loosely called "everything," you have an odd feeling that you haven't gotten much. He shrugged and ambled back toward the laboratory, pondering morphology, teratology, and a case where *monstra per defectum* could coexist with *monstra per fabricam alienam.*

Then he saw the light.

It flickered out over the street, soft and warm. He stopped and looked up. The light showed in a third-story window. It was orange and yellow, but with it was a flaring blue-white. It was pretty. It was also in his laboratory. No—not the laboratory. The morgue.

Muhlenberg groaned. After that he saved his breath. He needed it badly by the time he got back to the laboratory.

Muhlenberg dove for the heavy morgue door and snatched it open. A great pressure of heat punted a gout of smoke into the lab. He slammed the door, ran to a closet, snatched out a full-length lab smock, spun the faucets in the sink and soaked the smock. From another cabinet he snatched up two glass-globe fire extinguishers. He wrapped the wet cloth twice around his face and let the rest drop over his chest and back. Cradling the extinguishers in one bent forearm, he reached for the side of the door and grabbed the pump-type extinguisher racked there.

Now, suddenly not hurrying, he stepped up on the sill and stood on tiptoe, peering through a fold of the wet cloth. Then he crouched low and peered again. Satisfied, he stood up and, carefully pegged the two glass extinguishers, one straight ahead, one to the right and down. Then he disappeared into the smoke, holding the third extinguisher at the ready.

There was a rising moan, and the smoke shook like a solid entity and rushed into the room and away. As it cleared, Muhlenberg, head and shoulders wrapped in sooty linen, found himself leaning against the wall, gasping, with one hand on a knife-switch on the wall. A three-foot exhaust fan in the top sash of one window was making quick work of the smoke.

Racks of chemicals, sterilizers, and glass cabinets full of glittering surgeon's tools lined the left wall. Out on the floor were four massive tables, on each of which was a heavy marble top. The rest of the room was taken up by a chemist's bench, sinks, a partitioned-off darkroom with lightproof curtains, and a massive centrifuge.

On one of the tables was a mass of what looked like burned meat and melted animal fat. It smelled bad—not rotten bad, but acrid and—and *wet*, if a smell can be described that way. Through it was the sharp, stinging odor of corrosive chemicals.

He unwound the ruined smock from his face and threw it into a corner. He walked to the table with the mess on it and stood looking bleakly at it for a time. Suddenly he put out a hand, and with thumb and forefinger pulled out a length of bone.

"What a job," he breathed at length.

He walked around the table, poked at something slumped there and snatched his hand away. He went to the bench and got a pair of forceps, which he used to pick up the lump. It looked like a piece of lava or slag. He turned on a hooded lamp and studied it closely.

"Thermite, by God," he breathed.

He stood quite still for a moment, clenching and unclenching his square jaw. He took a long slow turn around the seared horror on the morgue slab, then carefully picked up the forceps and hurled them furiously into a corner. Then he went out to the lab and picked up the phone. He dialed.

"Emergency," he said. "Hello, Sue. Regalio there? Muhlenberg. Thanks. . . . Hello, Doc. Are you sitting down? All right. Now get this. I'm fresh out of symmetrical teratomorphs. They're gone. . . . Shut up and I'll tell you! I was out in the lab talking to a reporter when I heard the damndest scream. We ran out and found nothing. I left the reporter outside and came back. I couldn't've been out more'n ten-twelve minutes. But somebody got in here, moved both stiffs onto one slab, incised them from the thorax to the pubis, crammed them full of iron oxide and granulated aluminum—I have lots of that sort of stuff around here—

fused 'em with a couple of rolls of magnesium foil and touched 'em off. Made a great big messy thermite bomb out of them. . . . No, dammit, of *course* there's nothing left of them! What would you think eight minutes at seven thousand degrees would do? . . . Oh, dry up, Regalio! I don't know who did it or why, and I'm too tired to think about it. I'll see you tomorrow morning. No—what would be the use of sending anyone down here? This wasn't done to fire the building; whoever did it just wanted to get rid of those bodies, and sure did a job. . . . The coroner? I don't know what I'll tell him. I'm going to get a drink and then I'm going to bed. I just wanted you to know. Don't tell the press. I'll head off that reporter who was here before. We can do without this kind of story. 'Mystery arsonist cremates evidence of double killing in lab of medical consultant.' A block from headquarters, yet. . . . Yeah, and get your driver to keep his trap shut, too. Okay, Regalio. Just wanted to let you know. . . . Well, you're no sorrier'n I am. We'll just have to wait another couple hundred years while something like that gets born again, I guess."

Muhlenberg hung up, sighed, went into the morgue. He turned off the fan and lights, locked the morgue door, washed up at the laboratory sink, and shut the place up for the night.

It was eleven blocks to his apartment—an awkward distance most of the time, for Muhlenberg was not of the fresh-air and deep-breathing fraternity. Eleven blocks was not far enough to justify a cab and not near enough to make walking a negligible detail. At the seventh block he was aware of an overwhelming thirst and a general sensation that somebody had pulled the plug out of his energy barrel. He was drawn as if by a vacuum into Rudy's, a Mexican bar with Yma Sumac and Villa-Lobos on the juke box.

"*Hola, amigo,*" said Rudy. "Tonight you don' smile."

Muhlenberg crawled wearily onto a stool. "*Deme una tequila* sour, and skip the cherry," he said in his bastard Spanish. "I don't know what I got to smile about." He froze, and his eyes bulged. "Come back here, Rudy."

Rudy put down the lemon he was slicing and came close. "I don't want to point, but who *is* that?"

Rudy glanced at the girl. "*Ay,*" he said rapturously. "*Qué chuchín.*"

Muhlenberg remembered vaguely that *chuchín* was untranslatable, but that the closest English could manage with it was "cute." He shook his head. "That won't do." He held up his hand. "Don't try to find me a Spanish word for it. There isn't any word for it. Who is she?"

Rudy spread his hands. "*No sé.*"

"She by herself?"

"*Sí.*"

Muhlenberg put his chin on his hand. "Make my drink. I want to think."

Rudy went, his mahogany cheeks drawn in and still in his version of a smile.

Muhlenberg looked at the girl in the booth again just as her gaze swept past his face to the bartender. "Rudy!" she called softly, "are you making a tequila sour?"

"*Sí, señorita.*"

"Make me one too?"

Rudy beamed. He did not turn his head toward Muhlenberg, but his dark eyes slid over toward him, and Muhlenberg knew that he was intensely amused. Muhlenberg's face grew hot, and he felt like an idiot. He had a wild fantasy that his ears had turned forward and snapped shut, and that the cello-and-velvet sound of her voice, captured, was nestling down inside his head like a warm little animal.

He got off the bar stool, fumbled in his pocket for change and went to the juke-box. She was there before him, slipping a coin in, selecting a strange and wonderful recording called *Ven a Mi Casa*, which was a *borracho* version of "C'mon-a-My House."

"I was just going to play that!" he said. He glanced at the juke-box. "Do you like Yma Sumac?"

"Oh, yes!"

"Do you like *lots* of Yma Sumac?" She smiled and, seeing it, he bit his tongue. He dropped in a quarter and punched out six sides of Sumac. When he looked up Rudy was standing by the booth with a little tray on which were two tequila sours. His face was utterly impassive and his head was tilted at the precise angle of inquiry as to where he should put Muhlenberg's drink. Muhlenberg met the girl's eyes, and whether she nodded ever so slightly or whether she did it with a single movement of her eyelids, he did not know, but it meant "yes." He slid into the booth opposite her.

Music came. Only some of it was from the records. He sat and listened to it all. Rudy came with a second drink before he said anything, and only then did he realize how much time had passed while he rested there, taking in her face as if it were quite a new painting by a favorite artist. She did nothing to draw his attention or to reject it. She did not stare rapturously into his eyes or avoid them. She did not even appear to be waiting, or expecting anything of him. She was neither remote nor intimate. She was close, and it was good.

He thought, in your most secret dreams you cut a niche in yourself, and it is finished early, and then you wait for someone to come along to fill it—but to fill it exactly, every cut, curve, hollow and plane of it. And people do come along, and one covers up the niche, and another rattles around inside it, and another is so surrounded by fog that for the longest time you don't know if she fits or not; but each of them hits you with a tremendous impact. And then one comes along and slips in so quietly that you don't know when it happened, and fits so well you almost can't feel anything at all. And that is it.

"What are you thinking about?" she asked him.

He told her, immediately and fully. She nodded as if he had been talking about cats or cathedrals or cam-shafts, or anything else beautiful and complex. She said, "That's right. It isn't all there, of course. It isn't even enough. But everything else isn't enough without it."

"What is 'everything else'?"

"You know," she said.

He thought he did. He wasn't sure. He put it aside for later. "Will you come home with me?"

"Oh, yes."

They got up. She stood by the door, her eyes full of him, while he went to the bar with his wallet.

"Cuánto le debo?"

Rudy's eyes had a depth he had never noticed before. Perhaps it hadn't been there before. *"Nada,"* said Rudy.

"On the house? *Muchisimas gracias, amigo.*" He knew, profoundly, that he shouldn't protest.

They went to his apartment. While he was pouring brandy—brandy because, if it's good brandy, it marries well with tequila—she asked him if he knew of a place called Shank's, down in the warehouse district. He thought he did; he knew he could find it. "I want to meet you there tomorrow night at eight," she said. "I'll be there," he smiled. He turned to put the brandy carafe back, full of wordless pleasure in the knowledge that all day tomorrow he could look forward to being with her again.

He played records. He was part sheer technician, part delighted child when he could demonstrate his sound system. He had a copy of the Confucian "Analects" in a sandalwood box. It was printed on rice-paper and hand-illuminated. He had a Finnish dagger with intricate scrollwork which, piece by piece and as a whole, made many pictures. He had a clock made of four glass discs, the inner two each carrying one hand, and each being rim-driven from the base so it seemed to have no works at all.

She loved all these things. She sat in his biggest chair while he stared out at the blue dark hours and she read aloud to him from "The Crock of Gold" and from Thurber and Shakespeare for laughter, and from Shakespeare and William Morris for a good sadness.

She sang, once.

Finally she said, "It's bedtime. Go and get ready."

He got up and went into the bedroom and undressed. He showered and rubbed himself pink. Back in the bedroom, he could hear the music she had put on the phonograph. It was the second movement of Prokofiev's "Classical" Symphony, where the orchestra is asleep and the high strings tiptoe in. It was the third time she had played it. He sat down to wait until the record was over, and when it was, and she didn't come or speak to him, he went to the living-room door and looked in.

She was gone.

He stood absolutely still and looked around the room. The whole time she had been there she had unostentatiously put everything back after they had looked at it. The amplifier was still on. The phonograph was off, because it shut itself off. The record album of the Prokofiev, standing edge-up on the floor by the amplifier, was waiting to receive the record that was still on the turntable.

He stepped into the room and switched off the amplifer. He was suddenly conscious that in doing so he had removed half of what she had left there. He looked down at the record album; then, without touching it, he turned out the lights and went to bed.

You'll see her tomorrow, he thought.

He thought, you didn't so much as touch her hand. If it weren't for your eyes and ears, you'd have no way of knowing her.

A little later something deep within him turned over and sighed luxuriously. Muhlenberg, it said to him, do you realize that not once during that entire evening did you stop and think: this is an Occasion, this is a Great Day? Not once. The whole thing was easy as breathing.

As he fell asleep he remembered he hadn't even asked her her name.

He awoke profoundly rested, and looked with amazement at his alarm clock. It was only eight, and after what he had been through at the lab last night, plus what he had drunk, plus staying up so late, this feeling was a bonus indeed. He dressed quickly and got down to the lab early. The phone was already ringing. He told the coroner to bring Regalio and to come right down.

It was all very easy to explain in terms of effects; the burned morgue room took care of that. They beat causes around for an hour or so without any conclusion. Since Muhlenberg was so close to the Police Department, though not a member of it, they agreed to kill the story for the time being. If relatives or a carnival owner or somebody came along, that would be different. Meantime, they'd let it ride. It really wasn't so bad.

They went away, and Muhlenberg called the paper.

Budgie had not come to work or called. Perhaps she was out on a story, the switchboard suggested.

The day went fast. He got the morgue cleaned up and a lot done on his research project. He didn't begin to worry until the fourth time he called the paper—that was about five P.M.—and Budgie still hadn't come or called. He got her home phone number and called it. No; she wasn't there. She'd gone out early to work. Try her at the paper.

He went home and bathed and changed, looked up the

address of Shank's and took a cab there. He was much too early. It was barely seven-fifteen.

Shank's was a corner bar of the old-fashioned type with plate-glass windows on its corner fronts and flyblown wainscoting behind them. The booths gave a view of the street corner which did the same for the booths. Except for the corner blaze of light, the rest of the place was in darkness, punctuated here and there by the unreal blues and greens of beer signs in neon script.

Muhlenberg glanced at his watch when he entered, and was appalled. He knew now that he had been artificially busier and busier as the day wore on, and that it was only a weak effort to push aside the thoughts of Budgie and what might have happened to her. His busyness had succeeded in getting him into a spot where he would have nothing to do but sit and wait, and think his worries through.

He chose a booth on the mutual margins of the cave-like darkness and the pallid light, and ordered a beer.

Somebody—let's be conventional and call him Mr. X—had gone 'way out of his way to destroy two bodies in his morgue. A very thorough operator. Of course, if Mr. X was really interested in suppressing information about the two pathetic halves of the murdered monster in the park, he'd only done part of the job. Regalio, Al, Budgie, and Muhlenberg knew about it. Regalio and Al had been all right when he had seen them this morning, and certainly no attempts had been made on him. On the other hand, he had been in and around the precinct station and its immediate neighborhood all day, and about the same thing applied to the ambulance staff.

But Budgie . . .

Not only was she vulnerable, she wasn't even likely to be missed for hours by anyone since she was so frequently out on stories. Stories! Why—as a reporter she presented the greatest menace of all to anyone who wanted to hide information!

With that thought came its corollary: Budgie was missing, and if she had been taken care of he, Muhlenberg, was next on the list. Had to be. He was the only one who had been able to take a good long look at the bodies. He was the one who had given the information to the reporter and the one who still had it to give. In other words, if Budgie had been taken care of, he could expect some sort of attack too, and quickly.

He looked around the place with narrowing eyes. This was a rugged section of town. Why was he here?

He had a lurching sense of shock and pain. The girl he'd met last night—that couldn't be a part of this thing. It mustn't be. And yet because of her he found himself here, like a sitting duck.

He suddenly understood his unwillingness to think about the significance of Budgie's disappearance.

"Oh, no," he said aloud.

Should he run?

Should he—and perhaps be wrong? He visualized the girl coming there, waiting for him, perhaps getting in some trouble in this dingy place, just because he'd gotten the wind up over his own fantasies.

He couldn't leave. Not until after eight anyway. What else then? If they got him, who would be next? Regalio, certainly. Then Al. Then the coroner himself.

Warn Regalio. That at least he might do, before it was too late. He jumped up.

There was, of course, someone in the phone booth. A woman. He swore and pulled the door open.

"Budgie!"

He reached in almost hysterically, pulled her out. She spun limply into his arms, and for an awful split second his thoughts were indescribable. Then she moved. She squeezed him, looked up incredulously, squeezed him again. "Muley! Oh, Muley, I'm so glad it's you!"

"Budgie, you lunkhead—where've you been?"

"Oh, I've had the most awful—the most wonderful—"

"Hey, yesterday you cried. Isn't that your quota for the year?"

"Oh, shut up. Muley, Muley, no one could get mixed up more than I've been!"

"Oh," he said reflectively, "I dunno. Come on over here. Sit down. Bartender! Two double whiskey sodas!" Inwardly, he smiled at the difference in a man's attitude toward the world when he has something to protect. "Tell me." He cupped her chin. "First of all, where have you been? You had me scared half to death."

She looked up at him, at each of his eyes in turn. There was a beseeching expression in her whole pose. "You won't laugh at me, Muley?"

"Some of this business is real un-funny."

"Can I *really* talk to you? I never tried." She said, as if there were no change of subject, "You don't know who I am."

"Talk then, so I'll know."

"Well," she began, "it was this morning. When I woke up. It was such a beautiful day! I went down to the corner to get the bus. I said to the man at the newstand, '*Post?*' and dropped my nickel in his cup, and right in chorus with me was this man . . ."

"This man," he prompted.

"Yes. Well, he was a young man, about—oh, I don't know how old. Just right, anyway. And the newsdealer didn't know who to give the paper to because he had only one left. We looked at each other, this fellow and I, and laughed out loud. The newsy heard my voice loudest, I guess, or was being chivalrous, and he handed the paper to me. The bus came along then and we got in, and the fellow, the young one, I mean, he was going to take a seat by himself but I said come on—help me read the paper—you helped me buy it."

She paused while the one-eyed bartender brought the drinks.

"We never did look at the paper. We sort of . . . talked. I never met anyone I could talk to like that. Not even you, Muley, even now when I'm trying so. The things that came out . . . as if I'd known him all my—no," she said, shaking her head violently, "not even like that. I don't know. I can't say. It was fine.

"We crossed the bridge and the bus ran alongside the meadow, out there between the park and the fairgrounds. The grass was too green and the sky was too blue and there was something in me that just wanted to explode. But good, I mean, good. I said I was going to play hookey. I didn't say I'd like to, or I felt like it. I said I was going to. And he said let's, as if I'd asked him, and I didn't question that, not one bit. I don't know where he was going or what he was giving up, but we pulled the cord and the bus stopped and we got out and headed cross country."

"What did you do all day?" Muhlenberg asked as she sipped.

"Chased rabbits. Ran. Lay in the sun. Fed ducks. Laughed a

lot. Talked. Talked a *whole* lot." Her eyes came back to the present, back to Muhlenberg. "Gosh, I don't know, Muley. I tried to tell myself all about it after he left me. I couldn't. Not so I'd believe it if I listened."

"And all this wound up in a crummy telephone booth?"

She sobered instantly. "I was supposed to meet him here. I couldn't just wait around home. I couldn't stomach the first faint thought of the office. So I just came here.

"I sat down to wait. I don't know why he asked me to meet him in a place like—what on earth is the matter with you?"

"Nothing," choked Muhlenberg. "I was having an original thought called 'It's a small world.'" He waved her forthcoming questions away. "Don't let me interrupt. You first, then me. There's something weird and wonderful going on here."

"Where was I? Oh. Well, I sat here waiting and feeling happy, and graduallly the feeling went away and the gloom began to seep in. Then I thought about you, and the murder in the park, and that fantastic business at your lab last night, and I began to get scared. I didn't know what to do. I was going to run from here, and then I had a reaction, and wondered if I was just scaring myself. Suppose he came and I wasn't here? I couldn't bear that. Then I got scared again and—wondered if he was part of the whole thing, the Siamese-twin murder and all. And I hated myself for even thinking such a thing. I went into a real hassle. At last I squared myself away and figured the only thing to do was to call you up. And you weren't at the lab. And the coroner didn't know where you'd gone and—oh-h-h, *Muley!*"

"It meant that much?"

She nodded.

"Fickle bitch! Minutes after having your lover-boy—"

She put her hand over his mouth. "Watch what you say," she said fiercely. "This was no gay escapade, Muley. This was like—like nothing I've ever heard of. He didn't touch me, or act as if he wanted to. He didn't have to; it wasn't called for. The whole thing *was* the whole thing, and not a preliminary to anything else. It was—it was—oh, *damn* this language!"

Muhlenberg thought about the Prokofiev album standing upright by his amplifier. Damn it indeed, he thought. "What was his name?" he asked gently.

"His—" She snapped her head up, turned slowly to him. She whispered, "I never asked him. . . ." and her eyes went quite round.

"I thought not." Why did I say that? he asked himself. I almost know. . . .

He said, suddenly, "Budgie, do you love him?"

Her face showed surprise. "I hadn't thought about it. Maybe I don't know what love is. I thought I knew. But it was less than this." She frowned. "It was more than this, though, some ways."

"Tell me something. When he left you, even after a day like that, did you feel . . . that you'd lost something?"

She thought about it. "Why . . . no. No, I didn't. I was full up to here, and what he gave me he left with me. That's the big difference. No love's like that. Can you beat that? I didn't *lose* anything!"

He nodded. "Neither did I," he said.

"You *what?*"

But he wasn't listening. He was rising slowly, his eyes on the door.

The girl was there. She was dressed differently, she looked trim and balanced. Her face was the same, though, and her incredible eyes. She wore blue jeans, loafers, a heavy, rather loose sweater, and two soft-collar points gleamed against her neck and chin. Her hair hardly longer than his own, but beautiful, beautiful. . . .

He looked down, as he would have looked away from a great light. He saw his watch. It was eight o'clock. And he became aware of Budgie looking fixedly at the figure in the door, her face radiant. "Muley, come on. Come on, Muley. There he is!"

The girl in the doorway saw him then and smiled. She waved and pointed at the corner booth, the one with windows on two streets. Muhlenberg and Budgie went to her.

She sat down as they came to her. "Hello. Sit there. Both of you."

Side by side they sat opposite her. Budgie stared in open admiration. Muhlenberg stared too, and something in the back of his mind began to grow, and grow, and— "No," he said, incredulously.

"Yes," she said, directly to him. "It's true." She looked at Budgie. "She doesn't know yet, does she?"

Muhlenberg shook his head. "I hadn't time to tell her."

"Perhaps you shouldn't," said the girl.

Budgie turned excitedly to Muhlenberg. "You know him!"

Muhlenberg said, with difficulty, "I know . . . know—"

The girl laughed aloud. "You're looking for a pronoun."

Budgie said, "Muley, what's he mean? Let me in on it."

"An autopsy would have shown it, wouldn't it?" he demanded.

The girl nodded. "Very readily. That was a close call."

Budgie looked from one to the other. "Will somebody tell me what in blazes this is all about?"

Muhlenberg met the girl's gaze. She nodded. He put an arm around Budgie. "Listen, girl reporter. Our—our friend here's something . . . something new and different."

"Not new," said the girl. "We've been around for thousands of years."

"Have you now!" He paused to digest that, while Budgie squirmed and protested, "But—but—but—"

"Shush, you," said Muhlenberg, and squeezed her shoulders gently. "What you spent the afternoon with isn't a man, Budgie, any more than what I spent most of the night with was a woman. Right?"

"Right," the girl said.

"And the Siamese twins weren't Siamese twins, but two of our friend's kind who—who—"

"They were in syzygy." An inexpressible sadness was in the smooth, almost contralto, all but tenor voice.

"In what?" asked Budgie.

Muhlenberg spelled it for her. "In some forms of life," he started to explain, "well, the microscopic animal called paramecium's a good example—reproduction is accomplished by fission. The creature elongates, and so does its nucleus. Then the nucleus breaks in two, and one half goes to each end of the animal. Then the rest of the animal breaks, and presto—two paramecia."

"But you—he—"

"Shaddup," he said. "I'm lecturing. The only trouble with

reproduction by fission is that it affords no variation of strains. A single line of paramecium would continue to reproduce that way until, by the law of averages, its dominant traits would all be non-survival ones, and bang—no more paramecia. So they have another process to take care of that difficulty. One paramecium rests beside another, and gradually their contacting side walls begin to fuse. The nuclei gravitate toward that point. The side walls then break down, so that the nuclei then have access to one another. The nuclei flow together, mix and mingle, and after a time they separate and half goes into each animal. Then the side walls close the opening, break away from one another, and each animal goes its way.

"That is syzygy. It is in no sense a sexual process, because paramecia have no sex. It has no direct bearing on reproduction either—that can happen with or without syzygy." He turned to their companion. "But I'd never heard of syzygy in the higher forms."

The faintest of smiles. "It's unique with us, on this planet anyway."

"What's the rest of it?" he demanded.

"Our reproduction? We're parthenogenetic females."

"Y-you're a female?" breathed Budgie.

"A term of convenience," said Muhlenberg. "Each individual has both kinds of sex organs. They're self-fertilizing."

"That's a—a what do you call it?—a hermaphrodite," said Budgie. "Excuse me," she added in a small voice.

Muhlenberg and the girl laughed uproariously; and the magic of that creature was that the laughter couldn't hurt. "It's a very different thing," said Muhlenberg. "Hermaphrodites are human. She—our friend there—isn't."

"You're the humanest thing I ever met in my whole life," said Budgie ardently.

The girl reached across the table and touched Budgie's arm. Muhlenberg suspected that that was the very first physical contact either he or Budgie had yet received from the creature, and that it was a rare thing and a great compliment.

"Thank you," the girl said softly. "Thank you very much for saying that." She nodded to Muhlenberg. "Go on."

"Technically—though I know of no case where it has actually been possible—hermaphrodites can have contact with either sex. But parthenogenetic females won't, can't, and wouldn't. They don't need to. Humans cross strains along with the reproductive process. Parthenogenesis separates the two acts completely." He turned to the girl. "Tell me, how often do you reproduce?"

"As often as we wish to."

"And syzygy?"

"As often as we must. Then—we must."

"And that is—"

"It's difficult. It's like the paramecia's, essentially, but it's infinitely more complex. There's cell meeting and interflow, but in tens and then dozens, hundreds, then thousands of millions of cells. The join begins here—" she put her hand at the approximate location of the human heart—"and extends. But you saw it in those whom I burned. You are one of the few human beings who ever have."

"That isn't what I saw," he reminded her gently.

She nodded, and again there was that deep sadness. "That murder was such a stupid, incredible, unexpected thing!"

"Why were they in the park?" he asked, his voice thick with pity. "Why, out there, in the open, where some such human slugs could find them?"

"They took a chance, because it was important to them," she said wearily. She looked up, and her eyes were luminous. "We love the outdoors. We love the earth, the feel and smell of it, what lives from it and in it. Especially then. It was such a deep thicket, such an isolated pocket. It was the merest accident that those—those men found them there. They couldn't move. They were—well, medically you could call it unconscious. Actually, there—there never was a consciousness like the one which comes with syzygy."

"Can you describe it?"

She shook her head slowly, and it was no violation of her complete frankness. "Do you know, you couldn't describe sexuality to me so that I could understand it? I have no—no comparison, no analogies. It—" she looked from one to the other—"it amazes me. In some ways I envy it. I know it is a strife, which we avoid, for we are very gentle. But you have a capacity for enjoying strife, and all the pain, all the misery and poverty and cruelty which you suffer, is the cornerstone of everything you build. And you build more than anyone or anything in the known universe."

Budgie was wide-eyed. "You envy *us. You?*"

She smiled. "Don't you think the things you admire me for are rather commonplace among my own kind? It's just that they're rare in humans."

Muhlenberg said slowly, "Just what is your relationship to humanity?"

"It's symbiotic, of course."

"Symbiotic? You live with us, and us with you, like the cellulose-digesting microbes in a termite? Like the yucca moth, which can eat only nectar from the yucca cactus, which can spread its pollen only through the yucca moth?"

She nodded. "It's purely symbiotic. But it isn't easy to explain. We live on that part of humans which makes them different from animals."

"And in turn—"

"We cultivate it in humans."

"I don't understand that," said Budgie flatly.

"Look into your legends. We're mentioned often enough there. Who were the sexless angels? Who is the streamlined fat boy on your Valentine's Day cards? Where does inspiration come from? Who knows three notes of a composer's new symphony, and whistles the next phrase as he walks by the composer's house? And—most important to you two—who really understands that part of love between humans which is not sexual—because we can understand no other kind? Read your history, and you'll see where we've been. And in exchange we get the building—bridges, yes, and aircraft and soon, now, space-ships. But other kinds of building too. Songs and poetry and this new thing, this increasing sense of the oneness of all your species. And now it is fumbling toward a United Nations, and later it will grope for the stars; and where it builds, we thrive."

"Can you name this thing you get from us—this thing that is the difference between men and the rest of the animals?"

"No. But call it a sense of achievement. Where you feel that most, you feed us most. And you feel it most when others of your kind enjoy what you build."

"Why do you keep yourselves hidden?" Budgie suddenly asked. "Why?" She wrung her hands on the edge of the table. "You're so beautiful!"

"We have to hide," the other said gently. "You still kill anything that's . . . different."

Muhlenberg looked at that open, lovely face and felt a sickness, and he could have cried. He said, "Don't you ever kill anything?" and then hung his head, because it sounded like a defense for the murdering part of humanity. Because it was.

"Yes," she said very softly, "we do."

"You can *hate* something?"

"It isn't hate. Anyone who hates, hates himself as well as the object of his hate. There's another emotion called righteous anger. That makes us kill."

"I can't conceive of such a thing."

"What time is it?"

"Almost eight-forty."

She raised herself from her booth and looked out to the corner. It was dark now, and the usual crowd of youths had gathered under the street-lights.

"I made appointments with three more people this evening," she said. "They are murderers. Just watch." Her eyes seemed to blaze.

Under the light, two of the youths were arguing. The crowd, but for a prodding yelp or two, had fallen silent and was beginning to form a ring. Inside the ring, but apart from the two who were arguing, was a third—smaller, heavier and, compared with the sharp-creased, bright-tied arguers, much more poorly dressed, in an Eisenhower jacket with one sleeve tattered up to the elbow.

What happened then happened with frightening speed. One of the arguers smashed the other across the mouth. Spitting blood, the other staggered back, made a lightning move into his coat pocket. The blade looked for all the world like a golden fan as it moved in the cyclic pulsations of the street-lamp. There was a bubbling scream, a deep animal grunt, and two bodies lay tangled and twitching on the sidewalk while blood gouted and seeped and defied the sharpness of creases and the colors of ties.

Far up the block a man shouted and a whistle shrilled. Then the street corner seemed to become a great repulsing pole for humans. People ran outward, rayed outward, until, from above, they must have looked like a great splash in mud, reaching out and out until the growing ring broke and the particles scattered and were gone. And then there were only the bleeding bodies and the third one, the one with the tattered jacket, who hovered and stepped and waited and did not know which way to go. There was the sound of a single pair of running feet, after the others had all run off to silence, and these feet belonged to a man who ran fast and ran closer and breathed heavily through a shrieking police whistle.

The youth in the jacket finally turned and ran away, and the policeman shouted once around his whistle, and then there were two sharp reports and the youth, running hard, threw up his hands and fell without trying to turn his face away, and skidded on it and lay still with one foot turned in and the other turned out.

The girl in the dark sweater and blue jeans turned away from the windows and sank back into her seat, looking levelly into the drawn faces across the table. "Those were the men who killed those two in the park," she said in a low voice, "and that is how we kill."

"A little like us," said Muhlenberg weakly. He found his hand-kerchief and wiped off his upper lip. "Three of them for two of you."

"Oh, you don't understand," she said, and there was pity in her voice. "It wasn't because they killed those two. It was because they pulled them apart."

Gradually, the meaning of this crept into Muhlenberg's awed mind, and the awe grew with it. For here was a race which separated insemination from the mixing of strains, and apart from them, in clean-lined definition, was a third component, a psychic interflow. Just a touch of it had given him a magic night and Budgie an enchanted day; hours without strife, without mixed motives or misinterpretations.

If a human, with all his grossly efficient combination of functions, could be led to appreciate one light touch to that degree, what must it mean to have that third component, pure and in essence, torn apart in its fullest flow? This was worse than any crime could be to a human; and yet, where humans can claim clear consciences while jailing a man for a year for stealing a pair of shoes, these people repay the cruelest sacrilege of all with a quick clean blow. It was removal, not punishment. Punishment was alien and inconceivable to them.

He slowly raised his face to the calm, candid eyes of the girl. "Why have you shown us all this?"

"You needed me," she said simply.

"But you came up to destroy those bodies so no one would know—"

"And I found you two, each needing what the other had, and blind to it. No, not blind. I remember you said that if you ever could really share something, you could be very close." She laughed. "Remember your niche, the one that's finished early and never exactly filled? I told you at the time that it wouldn't be enough by itself if it *were* filled, and anyone completely without it wouldn't have enough either. And you—" She smiled at Budgie. "You never made any secret about what you wanted. And there the two of you were, each taking what you already had, and ignoring what you needed."

"Headline!" said Budgie, "Common Share Takes Stock."

"Subhead!" grinned Muhlenberg, "Man With A Niche Meets Girl With An Itch."

The girl slid out of the booth. "You'll do," she said.

"Wait! You're not going to leave us! Aren't we ever going to see you again?"

"Not knowingly. You won't remember me, or any of this."

"How can you take away—"

"Shush, Muley. You know she can."

"Yes, I guess she—wait though—wait! You give us all this knowledge just so we'll understand—and then you take it all away again. What good will that do us?"

She turned toward them. It may have been because they were still seated and she was standing, but she seemed to tower over them. In a split second of fugue, he had the feeling that he was looking at a great light on a mountain.

"Why, you poor things—didn't you know? Knowledge and understanding aren't props for one another. Knowledge is a pile of bricks, and understanding is a way of building. Build for me!"

———

They were in a joint called Shank's. After the triple killing, and the wild scramble to get the story phoned in, they started home.

"Muley," she asked suddenly, "what's syzygy?"

"What on earth made you ask me that?"

"It just popped into my head. What is it?"

"A non-sexual interflow between the nuclei of two animals."

"I never tried that," she said thoughtfully.

"Well, don't until we're married," he said. They began to hold hands while they walked.

THE [WIDGET], THE [WADGET], AND BOFF

PART ONE

Throughout the continuum as we know it (and a good deal more, as we don't know it) there are cultures that fly and cultures that swim; there are boron folk and fluorine fellowships, cuprocoprophages and (roughly speaking) immaterial life-forms which swim and swirl around each other in space like so many pelagic shards of metaphysics. And some organize into superentities like a beehive or a slime-mold so that they live plurally to become singular, and some have even more singular ideas of plurality.

Now, no matter how an organized culture of intelligent beings is put together or where, regardless of what it's made of or how it lives, there is one thing all cultures have in common, and it is the most obvious of traits. There are as many names for it as there are cultures, of course, but in all it works the same way—the same way the inner ear functions (with its contributory synapses) in a human being when he steps on Junior's roller skate. He doesn't think about how far away the wall is, some wires or your wife, or in which direction: he *grabs,* and, more often than not, he *gets*—accurately and without analysis. Just so does an individual reflexively adjust when imbalanced in his socio-cultural matrix: he experiences the reflex of reflexes, a thing as large as the legendary view afforded a drowning man of his entire past, in a single illuminated instant wherein the mind moves, as it were, at right angles to time and travels high and far for its survey.

And this is true of every culture everywhere, the cosmos over. So obvious and necessary a thing is seldom examined: but it was once, by a culture which called this super-reflex "Synapse Beta sub Sixteen."

What came out of the calculator surprised them. They were, after all, expecting an answer.

Human eyes would never have recognized the device for what it was. Its memory bank was an atomic cloud, each particle of which was sealed away from the others by a self-sustaining envelope of force. Subtle differences in nuclei, in probability shells, and in internal tensions were the coding, and fields of almost infinite variability were used to call up the particles in the desired combinations. These were channeled in a way beyond description in earthly mathematics, detected by a principle as yet unknown to us, and translated into language (or, more accurately, an analog of what we understand as language). Since this happened so far away, temporally, spatially, and culturally, proper nouns are hardly proper; it suffices to say that it yielded results, in this particular setting, which were surprising. These were correlated into a report, the gist of which was this:

Prognosis positive, or prognosis negative, depending upon presence or absence of Synapse Beta sub Sixteen.

The pertinent catalog listed the synapse in question as "indetectible except by field survey." Therefore an expedition was sent.

All of which may seem fairly remote until one realizes that the prognosis was being drawn for that youthful and dangerous aggregate of bubbling yeasts called "human culture," and that when the term "prognosis negative" was used it meant *finis,* the end, zero, *ne plus ultra* altogether.

It must be understood that the possessors of the calculator, the personnel of the expedition to Earth, were not Watchers in the Sky and Arbiters of Our Fate. Living in our midst, here and now, is a man who occupies himself with the weight-gain of amoebæ from their natal instant to the moment they fission. There is a man who, having produced neurosis in cats, turns them into alcoholics for study. Someone has at long last settled the matter of the camel's capacity for, and retention of, water. People like these are innocent of designs on the destinies of *all* amoebæ, cats, camels and cultures; there are simply certain things they want to *know*. This is the case no matter how unusual, elaborate, or ingenious their methods might be. So—an expedition came here for information.

EXCERPT FROM FIELD EXPEDITION [NOTEBOOK]
[VOLUME] ONE:

CONCLUSION. . . . to restate the obvious, [we] have been on Earth long enough and more than long enough to have discovered anything and everything [we] [wished] about any [sensible-predictable-readable] culture anywhere. This one, however, is quite beyond [understanding-accounting-for]. At first sight, [one] was tempted to conclude immediately that it possesses the Synapse, because no previously known culture has advanced to this degree without it, ergo . . . And then [we] checked it with [our] [instruments] [! ! !] [Our] [gimmick] and our [kickshaw] gave [us] absolutely negative readings, so [we] activated a high-sensitivity [snivvy] and got results which approximate nonsense: the Synapse is scattered through the population randomly, here non-existent or dormant, there in brief full activity at [unheard-of] high levels. [I] thought [Smith] would go [out of (his) mind] and as for [myself], [I] had a crippling attack of the [   ]s at the very concept. More for [our] own protection than for the furtherance of the Expedition, [we] submitted all our data to [our] [ship]'s [computer] and got what appeared to be even further nonsense: the conclusion that this species possesses the Synapse but to all intents and purposes does not use it.

How can a species possess Synapse Beta sub Sixteen and not use it? Nonsense, nonsense, nonsense!

So complex and contradictory are [our] data that [we] can only fall back on a microcosmic analysis and proceed by its guidance. [We] shall therefore isolate a group of specimens under [laboratory] control, even though it means using a [miserable] [primitive] [battery]-

powered [wadget]. [We]'ll put our new-model [widget]
on the job, too. [We]'ve had enough of this [uncanny,
uncomfortable] feeling of standing in the presence of
[apology-for-obscenity] paradox.

[1]*TRANSLATOR'S NOTE: Despite the acknowledged fact that the translator is an expert on extraterrestrial language, culture, philosophy, and the
theory and design of xenological devices, the reader's indulgence is
requested in this instance. To go into detail about these machines and the
nature and modes of communication of the beings that operate them would
be like writing the story of a young lover on the way to his reward, springing
up his beloved's front steps, ringing the bell—and then stopping to present
explicit detail about circuitous wiring and dry, dry cells. It is deemed more
direct and more economical to use loose and convenient translations and to
indicate them by brackets, in order to confine the narrative to the subject at
hand. Besides, it pleases the translator's modesty to be so sparing with his
[omniscience].*

I

The town was old enough to have slums, large enough to have no
specific "tracks" with a right and a wrong side. Its nature was such
that a boarding house could, without being unusual, contain such
varied rungs on the social ladder as a young, widowed night-club
hostess and her three-year-old son; a very good vocational guidance expert; a young law clerk; the librarian from the high school;
and a stage-struck maiden from a very small small town. They
said Sam Bittelman, who nominally owned and operated the
boarding house, could have been an engineer, and if he had been,
a marine architect as well, but instead he had never risen higher
than shop foreman. Whether this constituted failure or success is
speculative; apply to a chief petty officer or top sergeant who
won't accept a commission, and to the president of your local
bank, and take your pick of their arguments. It probably never
occurred to Sam to examine the matter. He had other things to
amuse him. Tolerant, curious, intensely alive, old Sam had apparently never retired from anything but his job at the shipyards back
east.

He in turn was owned and operated by his wife, whom everyone called "Bitty" and who possessed the harshest countenance and the most acid idiom ever found in a charter member of the Suckers for Sick Kittens and Sob Stories Society. Between them they took care of their roomers in that special way possible only in boarding houses which feature a big dining table and a place set for everyone. Such places are less than a family, or more if you value your freedom. They are more than a hotel, or less if you like formality. To Mary Haunt, who claimed to be twenty-two and lied, the place was the most forgettable and soon-to-be-forgotten of stepping stones; to Robin it was home and more; it was the world and the universe, an environment as ubiquitous, unnoticed, and unquestioned as the water around a fish; but Robin would, of course, feel differently later. He was only three. The only other one of the Bittelmans' boarders who breathed what was uniquely the Bittelman quality as if it were air was Phil Halvorsen, a thoughtful young man in the vocational guidance field, whose mind was on food and housing only when they annoyed him, and since the Bittelmans made him quite comfortable, in effect they were invisible. Reta Schmidt appreciated the Bittelmans for a number of things, prime among which was the lengths to which her dollar went with them, for Miss Schmidt's employers were a Board of Education. Mr. Anthony O'Banion permitted himself a genuine admiration of almost nothing in these parts. So it remained for Sue Martin to be the only one in the place who respected and admired them, right from the start, with something approaching their due. Sue was Robin's widowed mother and worked in a night club as hostess and sometime entertainer. She had done, in the past, both better and worse. She still might do better for herself, but only that which would be worse for Robin. The Bittelmans were her godsend. Robin adored them, and the only thing they would not do for him was to spoil him. The Bittelmans were there to give him breakfast in the mornings, to dress him when he went out to play, to watch over him and keep him amused and content until Sue rose at 11. The rest of the day was for Sue and Robin together, right up to his bedtime, when she tucked him in and storied him to sleep. And when she left for work at 9 P.M., the Bittelmans were there, safe and certain, ready and willing to cope with anything from a bladder to a blaze. They were like insurance and fire extinguishers, hardly ever used but comforting by their presence. So she valued them . . . but then, Sue Martin was different from most people. So was Robin; however, this is a truism when speaking of three-year-olds.

Such was the population of Bittelman's boarding house, and if they seem too many and too varied to sort out all at once, have patience and remember that each of them felt the same way on meeting all the others.

II

A pawnshop is a dismal place.

A pawnshop in the rain. A closed pawnshop in the rain, on a Sunday.

Philip Halvorsen did not object. He had a liking for harmony, and the atmosphere suited him well just now, his thoughts, his feelings. A sunbeam would have been an intrusion. A flower shop could not have contributed so much. People, just now, would have been intolerable.

He leaned his forehead against the wet black steel of the burglar-proof gate and idly inventoried the contents of the window and his thoughts about them. Like the window and its contents, and the dark recesses inside, his thoughts were miscellaneous, cluttered, captured in that purgatory of uselessness wherein things are not dead, only finished with what they have been and uncaring of what will happen to them and when. His thoughts were binoculars without eyes, cameras without film, silent guitars and unwound watches.

He found himself approving more of the guitars than the two dirty violins hanging in the window. He almost wondered why this should be, almost let the question disappear into lethargy, and at last sighed and ran the matter down because he knew it would bother him otherwise and he was in no mood to be bothered. He looked at the instruments lazily, one, the other, analyzing and comparing. They had a great deal in common, and some significant differences. Having a somewhat sticky mind, to which wind-blown oddments of fact had been adhering for nearly thirty years now, he knew of the trial-and-error evolution of those resonance-chambers and of the high degree of perfection they had come to. Given that design followed function in both the violin and the guitar, and aside from any preference in the sounds they made (actually Halvorsen was completely indifferent to music anyway), then why should he intuitively prefer the guitars he saw over the violins? Size, proportion, number of strings, design of bridge, frets or lack of them, finish, peg and tailpiece mechanics—all these had their differences and all were perfect for the work they did.

Suddenly, then, he saw it, and his mind swiftly thumbed through the mental pictures of all the violins he had ever seen. They all checked out. One flickering glance at the guitars in the window settled the matter.

All violins have a scroll carved at the end of the neck—*all* of them. There is scrollwork on some guitars, none on others; it's obviously optional. The back-bending spiral at the end of a violin's neck is not optional, but traditional, and it has no function. Halvorsen nodded slightly and permitted his mind to wander away from the matter. It wasn't important—not in itself; only settling it was important. His original, intuitive approval of guitars over violins was not a matter of moment either; his preference for the functional over the purely traditional was just that—a preference.

None of this required much of Halvorsen's conscious effort or attention. The survey, the sequence, was virtually reflexive, and his thoughts moved as fish in some deep clear pool might move, hanging and hanging, fanning, then suddenly darting about with a swirl and a splash, to hang again fanning, alive and waiting.

He stood motionless, the fine rain soaking into the back of his collar and his eyes unseeking but receptive. Binoculars with mother-of-pearl; binoculars without. A watch with glass rubies in the face. Display cards: cheap combs, cheap wallets, cheap pens. An electric steam iron with a frayed cord. A rack of second-hand clothing.

Guns.

He felt again that vague dissatisfaction, set up a certain amount of lethargic resistance to it, and when it came through anyway he patiently gave it its head. He looked at the guns. What bothered him about the guns?

One had a pearl handle and rococo etching along the barrel,

but that wasn't it. He glanced down the row and settled on a .38 automatic, about as functional an artifact as could be imagined—small, square, here knurled and there polished, with the palm safety and lock-safety just where they should be. And still he felt that faint disapproval, that dissatisfaction that spelled criticism. He widened his scan to all the guns, and felt it just as much. Just as little.

It was categorical then. It had to do with all these guns, or with all guns. He looked again, and again, and within this scope found no crevice for the prying of his reason, so he turned the problem on its back and looked again: what would a gun be like if it satisfied this fastidious intuition of his?

It came in a flash, and he hardly believed it: a flimsy structure of rolled sheet metal with a simple firing pin on a piece hinged and sprung like the business part of a rattrap. There was no butt, there were no sights. No trigger either; just a simple catch and—what was that?—and a piece of string. He visualized it sitting on a polished surface on a wire stand, its thin barrel angled upwards about 45°, like a toy cannon. Its caliber was about .38. The feature which struck him most was the feeling of fragility, lightness, in the whole design. Design! What would an object like that be designed *for*?

He looked again at the pawned guns. Among the things they had in common was massiveness. Breeches were cast steel, muzzles thick-walled, probably all rifled; parts were tempered, hardened, milled, designed and built to contain and direct repeated explosions, repeated internal assaults by hot hurtling metal.

It was as if a little red signal-light flickered on the concept *repeated*. Was that it, that all these guns were designed for repeated use? Was he dissatisfied with that? Why?

He conjured up the image of a single-shot dueling pistol he had once handled: long-barreled, muzzle-loading, with a powder-pan for priming and a chip of flint fixed to the hammer. To his surprise he found the little metal red light still aflicker; this was a design that displeased him too, somewhere in the area labeled *repeated*.

Even a single-shot pistol was designed to be used over again; that must be it. Then to him, a gun satisfied its true function only if it was designed to be used only once. *Enough* is the criterion of optimum design, and in this case once was enough.

Halvorsen snorted angrily. He disliked being led by rational means to a patently irrational conclusion. He cast back over his reasoning, looking for the particular crossroads where he must have taken a wrong turning.

There was none.

At this point his leisurely, almost self-powered curiosity was replaced by an incandescent ferocity of examination. Logic burned in Halvorsen as fury did in other men, and he had no tolerance for the irrational. He attacked it as a personal indignity, and would not let up until he had wrapped it up, tied it down, in the fabric of his understanding.

He let himself visualize the "gun" of his satisfied imagination, with its mousetrap firing mechanism, its piece of string, its almost useless flimsiness, and for a moment pictured police, cattlemen, Army officers handling such a ridiculous object. But the vision dissolved and he shook his head; the guns ordinarily used by such people satisfied his sense of function perfectly. He slipped (hypothetically) into the consciousness of such a man and regarded his gun—*a* gun—any gun with satisfaction. No, this seemed a personal matter, unlike the dissatisfaction everyone should feel (if they cared) about the extraordinary fact that automobiles are streamlined only where they show, and are powered by a heat-engine which is inoperable without a cooling system.

What's so special about my mousetrap gun? he demanded of himself, and turned his eye inward to look at it again. There it sat, on a polished surface—table-top, was it?—with its silly piece of string leading forward toward him and its muzzle tilted upward, unabashedly showing off its sleazy construction.

Why could he see how thin the metal of that muzzle was?

Because it was aimed right at the bridge of his nose.

Make a statement, Halvorsen, and test it. Statement: Other guns satisfy other men because they can be used over and over again. This gun satisfies me because it goes off once, and once is enough.

Test: A dueling pistol goes off only once; yet it can be reloaded and used again. Why not this? Answer: Because whoever uses a dueling pistol expects to be able to use it again. Whoever sees it used expects it will be used again, because the world goes on.

After Halvorsen's mousetrap gun went off, the world wouldn't go on. Not for Halvorsen—which of course is the same thing. "I am the core and the center of the universe" is a fair statement for anyone.

So restate, and conclude: The optimum gun design is that which, having shot Halvorsen between the eyes, need no longer exist. Since *optimum* carried with it the flavor of *preferred performance,* it is fair to state that within himself Halvorsen found a preference for being shot to death. More specifically, for dying. Correction: for being dead—gladly.

Momentarily, Halvorsen felt such pleasure at having solved his problem that he neglected to look at the solution, and when he did, it chilled him far more than the fine rain could.

Why should he want to be dead?

He glanced at the racked guns in the pawnshop and saw them as if for the first time, each one very real and genuinely menacing. He shuddered, clung for a moment to the wet black steel of the gate, then abruptly turned away.

In all his thoughtful—thought-*filled*—life he had never consciously entertained such a concept. Perhaps this was because he was a receptive person rather than a transmissive one. What he collected he used on his external world—his job—rather than on himself. He had no need for the explanations and apologies, the interpretations and demands-to-be-heard of the outgoing person, so he had no need to indulge in self-seeking and the complicated semantics of ego-translation. He was rather a clearing-house for the facts he found, taking knowledge and experience from *here* and storing them virtually untouched until they could be applied *there.*

He walked slowly homeward, in a state that would be numbness except for the whirling, wondering core which turned and poked and worried at this revelation. Why should he want to be dead?

Philip Halvorsen loved being alive. Correction: He enjoyed being alive. (Question: Why the correction? File for later.) He was a vocational guidance worker employed by a national social service organization. He was paid what he should be, according to his sense of values, and thanks to the Bittelmans he lived a little better on it than he might otherwise. He did not work for money, anyway; his work was a way of thinking, a way of life. He found it intriguing, engrossing, deeply satisfying. Each applicant was a

challenge, each placement a victory over one or more of the enemies that plague mankind—insecurity, inferiority, blindness, and
ignorance. Each time he looked up from his desk and saw a new
applicant entering his cubicle, he experienced a strange silent
excitement. It was a pressure, a power, like flicking on the master
switch of a computing machine; he sat there with all relays open
and all circuits blank, waiting for the answers to those first two
questions: "What are you doing now?" and "What do you want to
do?" Just that; it was enough for that indefinable sense of satisfaction or dissatisfaction to make itself known to him. And just as he
had analyzed its source in the matter of guns, so he analyzed his
clients. That flickering light signaling wrongness, misapplication,
malfunction, misevaluation—all the flaws in design, the false
goals, the frustrations and hurts of those who wonder if they have
chosen the right vocation—that light burned on while he worked
on each case, and would not go out until he found the answer.
Once or twice he had wished, whimsically, that his imagined signal
light would illuminate a sign for the client which said *Steeplejack*
and for that one which said *Frog Farmer,* but it refused to be so
obliging. It only told him when he was wrong. Being right
involved laborious and meticulous work, but he did it gladly. And
when at last he was satisfied, he frequently found that his work
had just begun: to tell an eighty-dollar-a-week bank clerk that his
proper niche is in freight-handling with a two-year apprenticeship
at fifty is initially a thankless task. But Halvorsen knew how to be
quiet and wait, and had become a past master at the art of letting
a client fight himself, defeat himself, reconstruct himself, and at
last persuade himself that the vocational counselor was right. And
all of it, Halvorsen liked, from the challenge to the accomplishment. Why, why should there be a wish in him to have this cease, to
end the world in which all these intriguing problems existed? And
to be glad of its ending?

What would he advise a client, a stranger, if that stranger
blurted out such a desire?

Well, he wouldn't. It would depend. He would simply throw
that in with everything else about the client—age, education, tem-
perament, marital status, I.Q., and all the rest of it, and let the
death-wish throw its weight along with all the other factors. It
would, however, predispose him to conclude that the man was

intolerably misplaced in some area: in a marriage, a family situation, a social beartrap of some kind . . . or his job. His job. Was
he, Halvorsen, judge and arbiter of occupations—was he in the
wrong job?

He slouched along in the rain, huddled down into himself to
escape a far more penetrating chill than this drenching mist. So
uncharacteristically wrapped in his inward thought was he that he
had taken three steps on dry pavement before he became aware of
it. He stopped and took his bearings.

He stood under the marquee of the smallest and cheapest of
the town's four theaters. It was closed and dark, this being Sunday
in a "blue-law" district, but dead bulbs and locked doors did not
modify the shrillness of its decorations. Over the main entrance
were two groups of huge letters, one for each of the two features
on the bill. SIN FOR SALE, one shrieked, and the other blared
back SLAVES OF THE HELL-FLOWER. Under these was a
third sign, offering as a special added attraction *Love Rites of a
South Sea Eden.* From the sidewalk on the far left, up to the marquee, across and down the other side was an arch of cardboard
cut-outs of women, wilting and wet, unnaturally proportioned
and inhumanly posed, with scraps of ribbon and drape, locks of
hair and induced shadows performing a sort of indicative conceal-
ment on their unbelievable bodies. Over the box-office was the
stern advice: *Adults only!!!* and papering the supporting pillars just
inside the mirrored cavern of a lobby were still photographs of
highlights of the pictures: A bare-backed female with her hands
trussed to a high tree-branch, being whipped; a man standing, gun
in hand, over a delectable corpse whose head hung back and down
over the edge of the bed so that her carefully arranged hair swept
the floor, and some flyblown samples of the South Sea Eden with
the portraits of its inhabitants smeared strategically with rubber-
stamp ink in angry and careless obedience to some local by-law.

At the best of times this sort of display left Phil Halvorsen
cold. At the worst of times (up to now) he would have felt a mild
disgust leavened by enough amusement at the outhouse crudity of
it to make it supportable—and forgettable. But at the moment
things were a little worse than the worst had ever been before. It
was as if his earlier unpleasant revelation had in some obscure
way softened him up, opened a seam in a totally unexpected place

in his armor. The display smote him like a blast of heat. He blinked and stepped back a pace, half-raising his hands and screwing his eyes shut. Behind the lids, the picture of his ridiculous one-shot cannon rose up roaring. He thought he could see a bullet emerging from its smoking muzzle like the tip of a hot black tongue. He shuddered away from the millisecond nightmare and opened his eyes, only to get a second and even more overwhelming reaction from the theater-front.

My God, what's happening to me? he silently screamed to himself. He pounded his forehead with his fists twice, then put his head down and ran up the street, up the hill. His photographic eye had picked up the banner inside the lobby, and as he ran, part of him coldly read it:

SEE (in flaming scarlet) the big-city orgies.

SEE the temptation of a teen-ager.

SEE lust run riot.

SEE the uncensored rites of an island cult.

SEE. . . . SEE. . . . There was more. As he ran, he moaned.

And then he thought, at the Bittelmans there are people, it is light, it is warm, it is almost home.

He began to run to something instead of away.

III

The Bittelmans' kitchen was a vague "backstairs" area to O'Banion and a functional adjunct of the boarding house to Halvorsen; to Miss Schmidt it was forbidden ground which excited no special interest for that—almost all the world was forbidden ground to Miss Schmidt. In it Sue Martin was as content as she was anywhere, and among the torments of Mary Haunt, the kitchen was a special hell. But in Robin's world it was central, more so than the bedroom he shared with his mother, more so than his crib. He ate in the kitchen, played there when it was raining or especially cold. When he went outdoors it was through the kitchen door, and it was a place to come back to with a bruised knee, with a hollow stomach, with a sudden flood of loneliness or of a three-year-old's wild manic passion. It was big and warm and full of friends.

The most resourceful of these friends was, of course, Bitty, who without ever losing her gruffness knew the right time to apply a cookie or a story (usually about a little boy with a beautiful mother) or a swat on the bottom. Sam was a friend, too, mostly as something safe to climb on. Of late, O'Banion had carved a rather special niche for himself, and Robin had always liked a limited amount of Miss Schmidt's self-conscious passiveness; she was a wonderful listener. He treated Halvorsen with cheerful respect, and Mary Haunt as if she did not exist. There were other people, too, every bit as much so as anyone who ate and had a job and occupied rooms elsewhere in the house. There was the electric mixer and the washing machine—in Robin's economical language "Washeen"—the blendor and the coffeepot; in short, everything which had a motor in it. (The presence or absence of motors in percolators is arguable only by those with preconceptions.) To him they were all alive, responsive and articulate, and he held converse with them all. He showed them his toys and he told them the news, he bade them goodbye and good morning, hello, what's the matter, and happy birthday.

And besides all these people, there were Boff and Googie, who, though by no means limited to the kitchen, were often there.

They were not there on that dark Sunday while the sky grieved and Halvorsen fought his personal devils outdoors. "Mitster, Boff an' Googie gone for ride," Robin informed the electric mixer. Its name, Mits-ter, was identical in his vocabulary with "Mister" and was a clear link between the machine and the males he heard spoken of, and just another proof of the living personality he assigned to it. He got a kitchen chair and carried it effortfully over to the work-table, where he put it down and climbed on it. He tilted the mixer up and back and turned its control-cowling, and it began to hum softly. Bitty kept the beaters in a high drawer well out of his reach and let him play with the therefore harmless machine to his heart's content. "*Ats* right, Mitster," he crooned. "Eat your yunch. Hey, Washeen!" he called to the washing-machine, "Mitster's eatin' his yunch all up, I go' give him a cookie, he's a *good* boy." He revved the control up and down, the machine whining obediently. He spun the turntable, turned the motor off, listened to the ball-bearings clicking away in the turntable, stopped it and turned on the motor again. He turned suddenly at the nudge of some sixth sense and saw O'Banion in the doorway. "Goo' morning Tonio," he called, beaming. "Go picnic now?"

"Not today, it's raining," said O'Banion, "and it's 'good afternoon' now." He crossed to the table. "What you up to, fellow?"

"Mitster eatin' his yunch."

"Your mother asleep?"

"Yis."

O'Banion stood watching the child's complete preoccupation with the machine. Little son of a gun, he thought, how did you do it?

The question was all he could express about the strangely rewarding friendship which flowered between him and Robin. He had never liked (nor, for that matter, disliked) a child in his life. He had never been exposed to one before; his only sibling was an older sister and he had never associated with anyone but contemporaries since he was a child himself.

Robin had caught him alone one day and had demanded to know his name. "Tony O'Banion," he had growled reluctantly. "Tonio?" "Tony O'Banion," he had corrected distinctly. "Tonio," Robin had said positively, and from then on that was inalterably that. And surprisingly, O'Banion had come to like it. And when, on the outskirts of town, someone had set up something called a Kiddie Karnival, a sort of miniature amusement park, and he had been assigned to handle land rentals there for his firm, he found himself thinking of Robin every time he saw the place, and of the Karnival every time he saw Robin, until one warm Sunday he startled himself and everyone else concerned by asking Sue Martin if he could take the boy there. She had looked at him gravely for a moment and said, "Why?"

"I think he might like it."

"Well, thanks," she had said warmly, "I think that's wonderful." And so he and Robin had gone.

And they'd gone again, several times, mostly on Sundays when Sue Martin was taking her one luxurious afternoon nap of the week, but a couple of times during the week too, when O'Banion had business out there and could conveniently pick the child up on the way out from the office and drop him again on the way back. And then, just for a change, a picnic, Robin's very first, by

the bank of a brook where they had watched jewel-eyed baby
frogs and darting minnows and a terrifying miniature monster
that he later identified as a dragonfly nymph; and Robin had asked
so many questions that he had gone to a bookstore the next day
and bought a bird book and a wildflower guide.

Occasionally he asked himself *why?* What was he getting out
of it? and found the answers either uncomfortable or elusive. Perhaps it was the relaxation: for the first time he could have commu-
nion with another human being without the cautious and watchful
attention he usually paid to "Where did you go to school?" and
"Who are your people?" Perhaps it was the warmth of friendship
radiating from a face so disturbingly like the one which still
intruded itself between his eyes and his work once in a while, and
which was so masked and controlled when he encountered it in the
flesh.

And there had been the Sunday when Sue Martin, after having given her permission for one of these outings, had suddenly
said, "I haven't much to do this afternoon. Are these excursions of
yours strictly stag?" "Yes," he had said immediately, "they are."
He'd told *her.* But—it didn't feel like a victory, and she had not
seemed defeated when she shrugged and smiled and said, "Let me
know when you go coeducational." After that she didn't put a stop
to the picnics, either, which would have pleased him by permitting
him to resent her. He found himself wishing she would ask again,
but he knew she would not, not ever. And if he should ask her to
come, and she should refuse . . . he could not bear the thought.
Sometimes he thought the whole business of amusing the child
was done to impress the mother; he had overheard Mary Haunt
make a remark to Miss Schmidt once that intimated as much, and
had furiously sworn off for all of six hours, which was when Robin
asked him where they would go next. As long as it was simple, a
matter between him and the child, it required no excuses or explanations. As soon as he placed the matter in any matrix, he became
confused and uncertain. He therefore avoided analyses, and asked
himself admiringly and academically, little son of a gun, how did
you do it? while he watched Robin's animated conversation with
the electric mixer.

He rumpled Robin's hair and went to the stove, where he

picked up the coffeepot and swirled it. It was almost full, and he lit the gas under it.

"Wha' you do, Tonio? Make coffee?"

"Yea bo."

"Okay," said Robin, as if granting permission. "Boff doesn't drink coffee, Tonio," he confided. "Oh no."

"He doesn't, hm?" O'Banion looked around and up. "Is Boff here?"

"No," said Robin. "He not here."

"Where'd he go? Out with the Bittelmans?"

"Yis." The coffeepot grumbled and Robin said, "*Hello,* Coffeepot."

Halvorsen came in and stood blindly in the doorway. O'Banion looked up and greeted him, then said under his breath, "My God!" and crossed the room. "You all right, Halvorsen?"

Halvorsen directed blind eyes at the sound of his voice, and O'Banion could watch seeing enter them slowly, like the fade-in on a movie screen. "What?" His face was wet with the rain, fish-belly pale, and he stood slumping like a man with a weight on his back, raising his face to look up rather than lifting his head.

"You'd better sit down," said O'Banion. He told himself that this unwonted concern for the tribulations of a fellow-human was purely a selfish matter of not wanting to shovel the stunned creature up off the floor. Yet as Halvorsen turned toward the ell with its wooden chairs, O'Banion caught at the open front of Halvorsen's coat. "Let me take this, it's sopping."

"No," said Halvorsen. "No." But he let O'Banion take the coat; rather, he walked out of it, leaving O'Banion with it foolishly in his hands. O'Banion cast about him, then hung it up on the broom-hook and turned again to Halvorsen, who had just fallen heavily back into a chair.

Again Halvorsen went through that slow transition from blindness to sight, from isolation to awareness. He made some difficult, internal effort and then said, "Supper ready?"

"We roll our own," said O'Banion. "Bitty and Sam are taking their once-a-month trip to the fleshpots."

"Fleshpots," said Robin, without turning his head.

Carefully controlling his face and his voice, O'Banion continued, "They said to raid the refrigerator, only hands off the leg o' lamb, that's for tomorrow." Motioning toward Robin with his head, he added, "He doesn't miss a trick," and at last released a broad grin."

Halvorsen said, "I'm not hungry."

"I've got some coffee going."

"Good."

O'Banion dropped a round asbestos mat on the table and went for the coffeepot. On the way back he got a cup and saucer. He put them on the table and sat down. Sugar was already there; spoons were in a tumbler, handles down, country-style. He poured and added sugar and stirred. He looked across at Halvorsen, and saw something on that reserved face that he had read about but had never seen before; the man's lips were blue. Only then did it occur to him to get a cup for Halvorsen. He went for it, and remembered milk, too, just in case. He brought them back, hesitated, and then poured the second cup. He put a spoon in the saucer, and with sudden shyness pushed it and the milk toward the other man. "Hey!"

"What?" Halvorsen said in the same dead, flat tone, and "Oh. Oh! Thanks, O'Banion, thanks very I'm sorry." Suddenly he laughed forcefully and without mirth. He covered his eyes and said plaintively, "What's the *matter* with me?"

It was a question neither could answer, and they sat sipping coffee uncomfortably, a man who didn't know how to unburden himself and a man who had never taken up another's burden. Into this tableau walked Mary Haunt. She had on a startling yellow hostess gown and had a magazine tucked under her arm. She threw one swift gaze around the room and curled her lip.

"Grand Central Station," she growled and walked out.

O'Banion's anger came as a great relief to him at just that moment; he was almost grateful to the girl. "One of these days someone's going to grab that kid by the scruff of the neck and housebreak her," he snorted.

Halvorsen found a voice, too, and probably was as grateful for the change in focus. "It won't last," he said.

"What do you mean?"

"I mean she can't go on that way much longer," said Halvorsen thoughtfully. He paused and closed his eyes; O'Banion could see him pulling himself hand over hand out of his personal swamp, moving to dry ground, high ground, where he could look with familiarity at a real world again. When he opened his eyes he gave O'Banion a strange little smile and said, as if in parenthesis, "Thanks for the coffee, O'Banion," and went on: "She's waiting for the Big Break. She thinks she deserves it and that it will come to her if she only waits. She really believes that. You've heard of high-school kids who perch on drugstore stools hoping for a movie scout to come along and discover them. That's harmless as long as they do it an hour or two a day. But Mary Haunt does it every minute she's out of this house. None of us here could help her, so she treats us the way anyone treats useless things. But you ought to see her down at the station."

"What station?"

"She types continuities at the radio station," said Halvorsen. "From what I hear, she's not very good, but on the other hand they don't pay her much money, so nobody kicks. But to her a radio station is the edge of the world she wants to crash—it starts there and goes to TV and to the movies. I'll bet you anything you like she has a scene all rehearsed in her mind, where a big producer or director stops here and drops in at the radio station to see someone, and *bang!* our Mary's a starlet being groomed for the top."

"She'd better learn some manners," grumbled O'Banion.

"Oh, she's got manners when she thinks they'll do her some good."

"Why doesn't she use them on you, for example?"

"Me?"

"Yes. Don't you get people better jobs, that sort of thing?"

"I see a lot of people, a lot of different kinds of people," said Halvorsen, "but they have one thing in common: they aren't sure what they want to do, to be." He pointed his spoon at the doorway. "She is. She may be wrong, but she's certain."

"Well, what about Sue Martin?" said O'Banion. He pursued the subject quickly, almost thoughtlessly, because of a vague feeling that if he didn't, Halvorsen would slip back into that uncomfortable introspective silence. "Surely there's a lot about show business Mary Haunt could learn from her."

Halvorsen gave the nearest thing yet to a grin and reached for the coffeepot. "Mrs. Martin's a nightclub entertainer," he said, "and as far as Mary Haunt's concerned, night clubs are slums."

O'Banion blushed violently and cursed himself for it. "Why that little—no background, no—no—how could *she* look down on . . . I mean, she's a little *nobody!*" Conscious that he was spluttering under the direct and passionless gaze of Halvorsen's dark eyes, he reached for the first thing he could think of that was not an absolute non sequitur: "One night a couple of months ago Mrs. Martin and I saw her throw a fit of hysterics over something . . . oh, Miss Schmidt had a magazine she wanted . . . anyway, after it was all over, Mrs. Martin said something about Mary Haunt that could have been a compliment. I mean, to some people. I can't think of Mary Haunt ever doing as much for her."

"What did she say?"

"Mrs. Martin? Oh, she said anybody who gets between Mary Haunt and what she wants is going to have a Mary-sized hole through them."

"It wasn't a compliment," said Halvorsen immediately. "Mrs. Martin knows as well as you or I do what's between that girl and her Big Break."

"What is?"

"Mary Haunt."

O'Banion thought about that for a moment and then chuckled. "A Mary-sized hole wouldn't leave much." He looked up. "You're quite a psychologist."

"Me?" said Halvorsen in genuine surprise. At that moment Robin, who had all this while been murmuring confidences to the mixer, switched off the machine and looked up. "Boff!" he cried joyously. "Hello, *Boff!*" He watched something move toward him, turning slightly to follow it with his eyes until it settled on the spice shelf over his table. "Wash you doin', Boff? Come for dinner?" Then he laughed, as if he had thought of something pleasant and very funny.

"I thought Boff was out with the Bittelmans, Robin," O'Banion called.

"No, he hide," said Robin, and laughed uproariously. "Boff right here. He come back."

Halvorsen watched this with a dazed smile. "Who on earth is Boff?" he asked O'Banion.

"Imaginary playmate," said O'Banion knowledgeably. "I'm used to it now but I don't mind telling you it gave me the creeps at first. Lots of kids have them. My sister did, or so Mother says—Sister doesn't remember it now. A little girl called Ginny who used to live in the butler's pantry. You laugh off this 'Boff' and the other one—her name's Googie—until you see Robin holding the door open to let them in, or refusing to go out to play until they get downstairs. And he isn't kidding. That's a nice little kid most of the time, Halvorsen, but some things will make him blow up like a little bottle of nitro, and one of 'em is to deny that Boff and Googie are real. I know. I tried to once and it took half a day and six rides on a merry-go-round to calm him down." He emphasized with a forefinger: "Six rides for Boff and Googie too."

Halvorsen watched the child: "I'll be darned." He shook his head slightly. "Is that—unhealthy?"

"I bought a book," said O'Banion, and, unaccountably, found himself blushing again, "and it says no, long as the child has good contact with reality, and believe me, he has. They grow out of it. Nothing to worry about."

Just then Robin cocked his head up to the spice shelf, as if he had heard a sound. Then he said, "Okay, Boff," climbed down from his chair, carried the chair across the kitchen to its place against the wall, and said cheerfully, "Tonio, Boff wan see cars. Okay. Shall we?"

O'Banion rose, laughing. "My master's voice. I got the *Popular Electrics* special issue on this year's automobiles and Boff and Robin can't get enough of it."

"Oh?" Halvorsen smiled. "What do they like this year?"

"Red ones. Come on, Robin. See you, Halvorsen."

"See you."

Robin trotted after O'Banion, paused near the door. "Come *on*, Boff!"

He waved violently at Halvorsen. "See you, Have-sum-gum."

Halvorsen waved back, and they were gone.

Halvorsen sat numbly for a while, his hand still raised. The presence of the other man and the child had been a diversion from his strange inner explosion and its shock-waves. Now they were gone, but he would not permit himself to sink into that welter of approaching bullet, rain-damped torsos, *why do I want to be dead?* So he hung motionless for a moment between disturbance and diversion. He thought of following O'Banion into the parlor. He thought of sinking back into his panic, facing it, fighting it. But he wasn't ready to fight, not yet, and he didn't want to run . . . and he couldn't stay like this. It was like not breathing. Anyone can stop breathing, but not for long.

"Mr. Halvorsen?"

Soft-footed, soft-voiced, timidly peering about her to be sure she was not intruding, Miss Schmidt came in. Halvorsen could have hugged her. "Come in, come in!" he cried warmly.

The half-alive smile brightened like fanned embers at his tone. "Good afternoon, Mr. Halvorsen. I was looking, that is, wondering, you know, if Mr. Bittelman was back yet, and I thought perhaps that . . ." She wet her lips and apparently thought it was worth another try. "I wanted to see him about—I mean to say, ask him if he—about something." She exhaled, took a breath, and would surely have come out with more of the same, but Halvorsen broke in.

"No, not yet. Sure picked a miserable day for a joy-ride."

"It doesn't seem to matter to the Bittelmans. Every fourth week, like clockwork." She suddenly uttered a soft little bleat of a laugh. "I'm sure I don't mean clockwork, Mr. Halvorsen, I mean, four weeks."

He laughed politely, for her sake. "I know what you mean." He saw her drop her eyes to her kneading hands, divined that her next movement would be toward the door. He felt he couldn't bear that, not just now. "How about—uh—a cup of tea or something. Sandwich. I was just going to—" He rose.

She went pink and smiled again. "Why, I—"

There was a short, sibilant sound in the doorway, a sniff, a small snort of anger. Mary Haunt stood there glowering. Miss Schmidt said, faintly, "No, no thank you, I'd better, I mean, just go and . . . I only wanted to see if Mr. Bittelman was—" She faded out altogether and tiptoed apologetically to the door. Mary Haunt swung her shoulders but did not move her feet. Miss Schmidt slid out and escaped past her.

Halvorsen found himself standing, half angry, half foolish. His own last words echoed in his mind: "Sandwich. I was just going to—" and he let them push him to the other end of the kitchen. He was furious, but why? Nothing had happened; a lot had happened. He would have liked to rear back on his hind legs and blast her for persecuting a little defenseless rabbit like Miss Schmidt; yet what had she actually done? Couldn't she say with absolute truth, "Why, I never said a word to her!"? He felt ineffectual, unmanned; and the picture of the flimsy gun flickered inside his eyelids and shocked him. He trembled, pulled himself together, painfully aware of the bright angry eyes watching his back from the doorway. He fumbled into the breadbox and took out half a loaf of Bitty's magnificent home-baked bread. He took down the breadboard and got a knife from the drawer, and began to saw. Behind him he heard a sharp slap as Mary Haunt tossed her magazine on the table beside the coffeepot, and then he was conscious of her at his elbow. If she had said one word, she would have faced a blaze of anger out of all proportion to anything that had happened. But she didn't, and didn't: she simply stood there and watched him. He finished cutting the first slice, started on the second. He almost swung to face her but checked the motion, whereupon the knife bit into the first joint of his thumb. He closed his eyes, finished cutting the bread, and turned away to the refrigerator. He opened it and then bent over the shelves, holding his cut thumb in his other hand.

"What do you think you're doing?" asked the girl.

"What's it look like?" he growled. His cut suddenly began to hurt.

"I couldn't say," said Mary Haunt. She stepped to the breadboard, picked up the knife and with it whisked the bread he had cut into the sink.

"Hey!"

"You better push that cut up against the freezer coils for a second," she said with composure. She put a hand on the loaf and with one sweep straightened its hacked end. "Sit down," she said as he filled his lungs to roar at her. "If there's anything I hate it's to see someone clumsy paddling around in food." One, two, three, four even slices fell to the board as she spoke. And again she interrupted him just as he was forming a wounded-bear bellow, "You

want a sandwich or not? Just sit down over there and stay out
from underfoot."

Slackjawed, he watched her. Was she doing him a kindness?
Mary Haunt doing someone a *kindness*?

He found himself obeying her, pressing his cut against the
freezer coils. It felt good. He withdrew his hand just as she came
toward the refrigerator, and dodged out of her way. He backed to
the table, sat down, and watched her.

She was something to watch. The pale, over-manicured hands
flew. She set out mayonnaise, cream cheese, a platter of cold-cuts,
parsley, radishes. With almost a single motion she put a small frying pan and a butter-melter on the stove and lit the fire under
them. Into the frying pan went a couple of strips of bacon; into
the other, two tablespoons of water and half the fluid from a jar of
capers. She added spices, "by ear"—a shake, a pinch: poultry sea-
soning, oregano, garlic salt. The tiny pan began to hiss, and suddenly the kitchen smelt like the delivery entrance to paradise. She
snatched it off, scraped the contents into a bowl, added cream
cheese and mayonnaise, and thrust it under the electric mixer. She
turned the bacon, shoved two of the bread slices into the toaster,
and busied herself with a paring knife and the radishes.

Halvorsen shook his head unbelievingly and muttered an
exclamation. The girl threw him a look of such intense scorn that
he dropped his eyes. He found them resting on her magazine. It
was called *Family Day* and was a home-making publication from
a chain supermarket—in no way a movie magazine.

Out of the frying pan came the bacon, crackling. She drained
it on a paper towel and crumbled it into the bowl where the mixer
was working. As if some kitchen choreographer was directing the
work, the toast popped up as she reached her hand for it. She
dropped in the other two slices and went back to her alchemy with
the radishes. In a moment she turned off the mixer and spread the
contents of the bowl on the toast. On this she laid cold-cuts, narrow strips of various kinds, deftly weaving them so they formed a
beautiful basket pattern. As she finished the first two, the second
pair popped out of the toaster; it was a continuous thing, the way
she did all the different things she did; it was like music or a landscape flowing by a train window.

She did something swift with the knife, and set the results out on two plates: bite-sized sandwiches arranged like a star, and in the center what looked like a tiny bouquet of rosebuds—the radishes, prepared with curled petals and nested in a neat bed of parsley, its stems all drawn together by one clever half-hitch in one of them. The whole amazing performance had taken perhaps six minutes. "You can make your own coffee," she snapped.

He came over and picked up one of the plates. "Why, this is—is—well, *thanks!*" He looked at her and smiled. "Come on, let's sit down."

"With *you*?" She stalked to the table, carrying the other plate, and scooped up the magazine as if it were a guilty secret. She went to the door. "You can clean up," she said, "and if you ever tell anyone about this I'll snatch you baldheaded."

Staring after her, stunned, he absently picked up one of the sandwiches and bit into it, and for a moment forgot even his amazement, it was so delicious. He sat down slowly, and for the first time since he had started comparing violins with guitars in the pawn-shop, he gave himself up completely to his senses and forgot his troubles. He ate the sandwiches slowly and appreciatively and let them own him.

EXCERPT FROM FIELD EXPEDITION [NOTEBOOK]:

So [weary-irritated] [I] can barely [write]. As if this kind of research wasn't arduous enough at the best of times, which this is not, with the best of equipment, which [we] lack, [I] am plagued by a [partner-teammate] with insuperable enthusiasm and a quality [I] can only describe as headlong stubbornness. [Smith] means well, of course, but the universe is full of well-meaning [individuals] [who] have succeeded only in making [   ]s of themselves.

All during the tedious and infuriating process of re[charging] the [wadget] [Smith] argued that purely objective observation would get [us] nowhere and would take [forever]; that [we] have sufficient data now to apply stimuli to these specimens and determine once and for all if a reliable, functional condition of Synapse Beta sub Sixteen is possible to them. [I] of course objected that it is against [our] highest [ethic] to apply [force] to

alien species; [Smith] then argued that it would not really
be [force], but only the [magnification-amplification-
increased efficiency] of that which they already possessed. [I] then pointed out that even if [we] succeed,
[we] can only test the final result by means which may
readily kill some or all of the specimens. This [Smith] is
willing to worry about only when the time comes. [I]
pointed out further that in order to supply the necessary
stimuli [we] shall have to re[wire] not only the [widget],
but that [   ]ed, inefficient, [stone] age excuse for a
[mechanism], the [wadget]. [Smith] readily agreed, and
while [I] went on arguing [he] began re[wiring], and [I]
argued, and [he] [wired], and by the time [I]'d [made my
point] [he] was practically finished and [I] found [myself]
holding the [light] as well.

    [I] forgot to ask [Smith] what [he] planned to do if
one of the specimens finds out what [we]'re up to. Kill it?
Kill them all? It wouldn't [surprise] [me]. In the name of
[research] [Smith] would happily [watch] [his] [elderly
forebear]'s [knuckles] being [knurled].

IV

Miss Schmidt, muffled up to the pharynx in a quilted robe, bed-
socked, slippered and shawled, half-dozed in her easy chair. When
she heard the sounds she had waited for, she jumped up, went to
her door, which was ajar, and stood a moment to listen and be
sure. Then she tightened her sash, checked the hooks-and-eyes
under her chin, tugged her voluminous robe downward at the
hips, and pulled the shawl a little higher on her shoulders. She
crossed her arms at the wrists and pressed her hands modestly
against her collarbones, and scurried silently past the bathroom,
down the long hall to the foyer. Bitty was in the kitchen and Sam
Bittelman was hanging up a damp trench coat on the hall tree.
    "Mr. Bittelman—"
    "Sam," he corrected jovially. "Top of the morning to you,
Miss Schmidt. It turned morning, y'know, ten minutes ago."
    "Oh dear yes, I know it's late," she whispered. "And I'm terri-

bly sorry, really I am, I wouldn't for the world trouble you. I mean, I *am* sorry, I don't want to be a nuisance. Oh *dear!*" Her perennially frightened face crinkled with her small explosion of distress.

"Now you just tell me what's troubling you, lady, and we'll get it fixed," he said warmly.

"You're very kind. Very kind. It happens there is something. I mean, something to fix. In . . . in my *room."* She bent forward with this, as with a deep confidence.

"Well, let's go have a look. Bitty!" Miss Schmidt put a shocked hand over her lips as he raised his voice. "I'm going to fix something for the lady. Be right with you." He turned back to Miss Schmidt and made a jocular bow. "Lead on."

"We mustn't wake the . . . anybody," she reproved him, then blushed because she had. He only grinned, and followed her back to her room. She entered, opened the door as wide as it would go, and self-consciously picked up the wastepaper basket and set it to hold the door open. She looked up from this task right into Sam's twinkling eyes, and sent up a prayer that he wouldn't tease her about it. One never knew what Sam was going to say; sometimes he was beyond understanding and sometimes he was just—awful. "The window," she said. "The blind."

He looked at it. "Oh, that again. Durn things are always getting the cords frayed." The venetian blind hung askew, the bottom slats almost vertical, leaving a lower corner of the window exposed. Sam tugged at the raising-cord. It was double; one part was jammed tight and the other ran free. He pulled it all the way out and ruefully exhibited the broken end. "See? That's it, all right. Have to see if I can't put in a new cord for you in the morning, if I can find one."

"In the morning? But—I mean, well, Mr. uh—Sam, what about now? That is, what am I going to *do?*"

"Why, just don't worry your pretty little head about it! Get your beauty-sleep, little lady, and by the time you're back from school tomorrow I'll have it—"

"You don't understand," she wailed softly, "I can't go to bed with it like that. That's why I waited up for you. I've tried everything. The drapes won't go across it and there's nothing to hang a towel to and the chair-back isn't high enough to cover it and—and—oh, *dear!*"

"Oh-h-h."

Struck by something in his single, slow syllable, she looked sharply at him. There was something—what was it? like a hum in the room. But it wasn't a sound. He hadn't changed . . . and yet there was something in his eyes she had never seen before. She had never seen it in anyone's eyes. About Sam Bittelman there had always been a leisurely strength, and it was there now but easier, stronger, more comforting than ever. To her, with her multiple indecisions, unsurenesses, his friendly certitude was more wondrous than a halo might have been. He said, "Just what bothers you about the window?"

Her usual self moved quite clearly to indicate, indignantly, that part of the window was uncovered and surely that spoke for itself; yet her usual self was unaccountably silent, and she gave him his answer: "Somebody might look *in*!"

"You know what's outside that window?"

"Wh—Oh. Oh, the back of the garage."

"So nobody's going to see in. Well now, suppose there was no garage, and you turned out your lights. Could anybody see in?"

"N-no . . ."

"But it still bothers you."

"Yes, of course it does." She looked at the triangle of exposed glass, black with night outside, and shuddered. He leaned against the doorpost and scratched his head. "Let me ask you something," he said, as if her permission might make a difference. "S'pose we took away the garage, and you forgot and left your light on, *and* somebody saw you?"

She squeaked.

"Really bothers you, don't it?" He laughed easily. And instead of infuriating her, the sound flooded her with comfort. "What exactly is bothersome about that, aside from the fact that it's bothersome?"

"Why . . . why," she said breathlessly, "I know what *I'd* think of a hussy that would parade around that way with the lights on and—"

"I didn't say parade. Nor 'prance,' either, which is the other word people use, I don't know why. So what really bothers you is what some peepin' Tom might think, hm? Now, Miss Schmidt, is that really anything to worry about? What do you care what he thinks you are? Don't you know what you are?" He paused, but she had nothing to say. "You ever sleep naked?"

She gasped, and, round-eyed, shook her head.

"Why not?" he demanded.

"Why I—I—" She had to answer him; she had to. Fear rose like a thin column of smoke within her, and then a swift glance at his open, friendly face dispelled it completely. It was extraordinary, uncomfortable, exhilarating, disturbing, exciting all at once. He compelled her and comforted her at the same time.

She found her voice and answered him. "I just couldn't sleep . . . like that. Suppose there was a fire?"

"Who said that?" he snapped.

"I beg your—"

"Who said 'suppose there's a fire?' Who told you that?"

"Why, I suppose it—yes, it was my mother."

"Not your idea then. Figured as much. 'Thou shalt not kill.' Do you believe that?"

"Of course!"

"You do. How old were you when you learned that?"

"I don't—know. All children—"

"Children seven, eight, nine? All right. How old were you when you were taught not to unpin your diapers? Not to let anyone *see* you?"

She did not answer but the answer was there.

"Wouldn't you say you'd learned 'thou shalt not expose thy body' earlier, better, more down-deep than 'thou shalt not kill'?"

"I—yes."

"Do you realize it's a deeper commandment with you than any of the Ten? And aside from right-'n-wrong, isn't it deeper than the deepest, strongest one of all—save thyself? Can't you see yourself dying under a bush rather than walk naked out on the road and flag a car? 'Suppose there's a fire?' Can't you see yourself burn to death rather'n jump out a window without your bathrobe?"

She didn't answer except from her round eyes and her whole heart.

"Does that make any *sense,* to believe a thing like that?"

"I don't know," she whispered. "I—have to think."

Surprisingly, he said, "Retroactive." He pointed to the window. "What can we do about that?" he asked.

Absently she glanced at it. "Never mind it tonight, Mr. Bittelman."

"Sam. Okay. Goodnight, little lady."

She felt herself, abruptly, tottering on the edge of a bottomless pit. He had walked in here and disoriented her, ripped into shreds a whole idea-matrix which had rested undisturbed in the foundations of her thinking, like a cornerstone. Just at this startled second she had not made the admission, but she would have to admit to herself soon that she must think "retroactive," as he had put it, and that when she did she would find that the clothes convention was not the only one she would have to reappraise. The inescapable, horizonless, unfamiliar task loomed over her like a black cloud—her only comfort, her only handhold was Sam Bittelman, and he was leaving. "No!" she cried. "No! No! No!"

He turned back, smiling, and that magic happened again, his sureness and ease. She stood gasping as if she had run up a hill.

"It's all right, little lady."

"Why did you tell me all this? Why?" she asked pathetically.

"You know something? I didn't tell you a thing," he said. "I just asked questions. They were all questions you could've asked yourself. And what's got you scared is answers—answers that came from here—" He put a gentle knuckle against her damp forehead. "—and not from me. You've lived with it all quite a while; you got nothing to fear from it now." And before she could answer he had waved one capable hand, winked, and was gone.

For a long time she stood there, trembling and afraid to think. At last she let her open eyes see again, and although they saw nothing but the open door, it was as if some of Sam's comfort slipped in with vision. She turned around, and around again, taking in the whole room and reaping comfort and more comfort from the walls, as if Sam had hung it for her to gather like ripe berries. She put it all in the new empty place within her, not to fill, but at least to be there and to live with until she could get more. Suddenly her gaze met the silly little wastebasket sitting against the door, holding it open, and to her utter astonishment she laughed at it. She picked it up, shook her head at it as if it had been a ridiculous puppy which had been eating her talcum powder; she even spanked it lightly, once, and put it down, and closed the door. She got into bed and put out the light without even looking at the window.

V

"Aw, you shouldn't!" cried Bitty with a joyous sort of chagrin as she pushed open Sue Martin's door. "Here I've got all your fresh linen and you've went and made the bed!"

Sue Martin, sleep-tousled and lovely in a dark negligee, rose from the writing desk. "I'm sorry, Bitty. I forgot it was Thursday."

"Well, Thursday it is," the older woman scolded, "and now I'll have to do it up all over again. Young lady, I've told and *told* you I'll take care of the room."

"You have plenty to do," Sue smiled. "Here, I'll help. What's Robin up to?"

Together they took down the spread, the light blanket, then the sheets from the big double bed. "Kidnaped by that young idiot O'Banion again. He's driving out to the new project over Huttonville way and thought Robin might want to see the bulldozers."

"Robin loves bulldozers. He's not an idiot."

"He's an idiot," said Bitty gruffly, apparently needing no translation of the two parts of Sue's statement. "Time this was turned, since we're both here," she said, swatting the mattress.

"All right," Sue Martin loosely folded the spread and blanket and carried them to the chest. "Robin just loves him."

"So do you."

Sue's eyes widened. She shot a look at the other woman, but Bitty's back was turned as she bent over the bed. When she spoke, her voice was perfectly controlled. "Yes, for some time." She went to stand beside Bitty and they laid hold of the mattress straps. "Ready?" Together they heaved and the mattress rose up, teetered for a moment on edge, and fell back the other way. They pulled it straight.

"Well, what are you doing about it?" Bitty demanded.

Sue found her eyes captured by Bitty's for a strange moment.

She saw herself, in a flash of analog, walking purposefully away from some tired, dark place toward something she wanted; and as she walked there appeared humming softly behind her, around her, something like a moving wall. She had a deep certainty that she could not stop nor turn aside; but that as long as she kept moving at the same speed, in the same direction, the moving wall could not affect her. She—and it—were moving toward what she wanted, just as fast as she cared to go. While this was the case, she was not being restrained or compelled, helped nor hindered. So she would not fear this thing, fight it or even question it. It could not possibly change anything. In effect, irresistible as it might be, it need not and therefore did not exist for her. Here and now, some inexplicable something had happened to make it impossible not to answer Bitty's questions—and this compulsion was of no moment at all for her as long as Bitty asked questions she wanted to answer. "What are you doing about it?" was such a question.

"Everything I should do," said Sue Martin. "Nothing at all."

Bitty grunted noncommittally. She took a folded sheet from the top of the highboy and shook it out across the bed. Sue Martin went round to the other side and caught it. She said, "He has to know why, that's all, and he can't do anything or say anything until he does know."

"Why what?" Bitty asked bluntly.

"Why he loves me."

"Oh—you know that, do you?"

This was one question, compulsion or no, that Sue Martin did not bother to answer. It was on the order of "Is this really a bed?" or "Is it Thursday?" So Bitty asked another: "And you're just waiting, like a little edelweiss on an Alp, for him to climb the mountain and pick you?"

"Waiting?" Sue repeated, puzzled.

"You're not doing anything about it, are you?"

"I'm being myself," said Sue Martin. "I'm living my life. What I have to give him—anyone who's *right* for me—is all I am, all I do for the rest of my life. As long as he wants something more, or something different, nothing can happen." She closed her eyes for a moment. "No, I'm not waiting, exactly. Put it this way: I know how to be content with what I am and what I'm doing. Either

Tony will knock down that barrier he's built, or he won't. Either way I know what's going to happen, and it's good."

"That wall—why don't you take a pickax and beat it down?"

She flashed the older woman a smile, "He'd defend it. Men get very fond of the things they defend, especially when they find themselves defending something stupid."

Bitty shook out the second sheet. "And don't you have any of his kind of trouble—wondering *why* you love him?"

Sue Martin laughed. "Wouldn't we live in a funny world if we had to understand everything that was real, or it wouldn't exist? It's always good to know *why*. It isn't always necessary. Tony'll find that out one day." She sobered. "Or he won't. Hand me a pillowslip."

They finished their task in silence. Bitty bundled up the old linen and trudged out. Sue Martin stood looking after her. "I hope she wasn't disappointed," she murmured, and, "I don't think so . . . and what did I mean by that?"

VI

One morning Mary Haunt opened her eyes and refused to believe them. For a moment she lay still looking at the window numbly; there was something wrong with it, and a wrong feeling about the whole room. Then she identified it: there was sunlight streaming in and down through the venetian blind where no sunlight should be at her rising time. She snatched her watch off the night table and squinted at it, and moaned. She reared up in bed and peered at the alarm clock, then turned and punched furiously at the pillow. She bounded out of bed, struggled into her yellow robe, and flew out of the room with her bare feet slapping angrily down the long corridor. Sam Bittelman was sitting at the kitchen table peering at the morning paper over the tops of his black rimmed reading-glasses. Bitty was at the sink. "What 'm I, the forgotten man or something?" Mary Haunt demanded harshly.

Sam put down his paper and only then began to remove his gaze from it. "M-m-m? Oh, good morning, gal." Bitty went on with her business.

"Good *nothing*! Don't you know what time it is?"

"Sure do."

"What's the big fat idea leaving me to sleep like this? You know I got to get to work in the morning."

"Who called you four times?" said Bitty without turning around or raising her voice. "Who went in and shook you, and got told *get out of my room* for it?"

Mary Haunt poised between pace and pace, between syllables. Now that Bitty mentioned it, she *did* half-remember a vague hammering somewhere, a hand on her shoulder . . . but that was a dream, or the middle of the night or—or had she really chased the old lady out? *"Arrgh,"* she growled disgustedly. She stamped out into the foyer and snatched up the phone. She dialed. "Get me Muller," she snapped at the voice that answered.

"Muller," said the phone.

"Mary Haunt here. I'm sick today. I'm not coming in."

"So with this phone call," said the telephone, "I'll notice."

"Why you lousy Heine, without me you couldn't run a yo-yo, let alone a radio station!" she shouted, but she had hung up before she started to shout.

She padded back into the kitchen and sat down at the table. "Got coffee?"

Bitty, still with her back turned, nodded in the appropriate direction and said, "On the stove," but Sam folded his paper and got up. He went to the stove, touched the pot briefly with the back of his hand, picking up a cup and saucer on the way. "You'll want milk."

"You know better than that," she said, arching her lean body. While she poured herself a cup, Sam sat down at the other end of the table. He leaned his weight on his elbows, his forearms and worn hands flat on the table. Something like the almost-silent whisper from a high-speed fan made her look up. "What are you looking at?"

He didn't answer her question. "Why do you claim to be twenty-two?" he asked instead, and quick as the rebound of billiard ball from cue ball, propelled by hostility, inclusive as buckshot, her reply jetted up: *"What's it to you?"* But it never reached her lips; instead she said, "I have to," and then sat there astounded. Once she had worn out a favored phonograph record, knew every note, every beat of it, and she had replaced it; and for once the record company had made a mistake and the record was not what the label said it was. The first half-second of that new record was like this, a moment of expectation and stunned disbelief. This was even more immediate and personal, however; it was like mounting ten steps in the dark and finding, shockingly, that there were only nine in the flight. From this moment until she left the kitchen, she was internally numb and frightened, yet fascinated, as her mind formed one set of words and others came out.

"You have to," asked Sam mildly, "the way you have to be in the movies? You just *have* to?"

The snarl, *have I kept it a secret?* came out, "It's what I want."

"Is it?"

There didn't seem to be any answer to that, on any level. She waited, tense.

"What you're doing—the job at the radio station—living here in this town instead of someplace else—all of it; is what you're doing the best way to get what you want?"

Why else would I put up with it all—the town, the people—you? But she said, "I think so." Then she said, "I've thought so."

"Why don't you talk to young Halvorsen? He might be able to find something you'd do even better'n going to Hollywood."

"I don't *want* to find anything better!" This time there was no confusion.

From the other end of the room, Bitty asked, "Were you always so all-fired pretty, Mary Haunt? Even when you were a little girl?"

"Everyone always said so."

"Ever wish you weren't?"

Are you out of your mind? "I . . . don't think so," she whispered.

Gently, Sam asked her, "Did they throw you out, gal? Make you leave home?"

Defiantly, defensively, *They treated me like a little princess at home, like a piece of fine glassware. They carried my books and felt good all day if I smiled. They did what I wanted, what they thought I wanted, at home or in town. They acted as if I was too good to walk that ground, breathe that air, they jumped at the chance to take advantage of being at the same place at the same time; they did*

*everything for me they could think of doing, as if they had to hurry
or I'd be gone. Throw me out? Why, you old fool!* "I left home my
own self," she said. "Because I had to, like—" But here words
failed her, and she determined not to cry, and she determined not
to cry, and she cried.

"Better drink your coffee."

She did, and then she wanted something to eat with it, but
couldn't bear to sit with these people any longer. She sniffed
angrily. "I don't know what's the matter with me," she said. "I
never overslept before."

"Long as you know what you want," said Sam, and whether
that was the stupid, non-sequitur remark of a doddering dotard,
or something quite different, she did not know. "Well," she said,
rising abruptly; and then felt foolish because there was nothing
else to say. She escaped back to her room and to bed, and huddled
there most of the day dully regarding the two coddled ends of her
life, pampering in the past and pampering in the future, while trying to ignore today with its empty stomach and its buzzing head.

VII

During Prohibition it had been a restaurant, in that category
which is better than just "nice" but not as good as "exclusive"; the
town was too small then to have anything exclusive. Now it was a
bar as well, and although there was imitation Carrara on some
walls, and a good deal of cove-lighting, the balcony had never
been altered and still boasted the turned-spoke railing all the way
around, looking like a picket fence that had gone to heaven. There
was a little service bar up there, and a man could stay all evening
watching what went on down below without being seen. This was
what Tony O'Banion was doing, and he was doing it because he
had felt like a drink and had never been to the club before, and he
wanted to see what kind of place it was and what Sue Martin did
there; and every one of these reasons were superficial—if he preceded them with "Why," he felt lost. Within him were the things he
believed, about the right sort of people, about background, breeding, and blood. Around him was this place, as real as the things he
believed in. *Why* he was here, why he wanted a drink just now, why

he wanted to see the place and what happened in it—this was a bridge between one reality and the other, and a misty, maddening, nebulous bridge it was. He drank, and waited to see her emerge from the small door by the bandstand, and when she did he watched her move to the piano and help the pianist, a disheveled young man, stack and restack and shuffle his music, and he drank. He drank, and watched her go to the cashier and spend a time over a ledger and a pile of checks. She disappeared through the swinging doors into the kitchen, and he drank; he drank and she came out talking to a glossy man in a tuxedo, and he winced when they laughed.

At length the lights dimmed and the glossy man introduced her and she sang in a full, pleasant voice something about a boy next door, and someone else played an accordion which was the barest shade out of tune with the piano. Then the piano had a solo, and the man sang the last chorus, after which the lights came up again and he asked the folks to stick around for the main show at ten sharp. Then the accordion and the piano began to make dance music. It was all unremarkable, and Tony didn't know why he stayed. He stayed, though: "Waiter! Do it again."

"Do it twice."

Tony spun around. "Time someone else bought, hm?" said Sam Bittelman. He sat down.

"Sam! Well, sit down. Oh, you *are.*" Tony laughed embarrassedly. His tongue was thick and he was immeasurably glad to see the old man. He was going to wonder why until he remembered that he'd sworn off wondering why just now. He was going to ask what Sam was doing there and then decided Sam would only ask him the same, and it was a question he didn't want to fool with just now. Yes he did.

"I'm down here slumming in the fleshpots and watching the lower orders cavorting and carousing," he blurted, making an immense effort to be funny. He wasn't funny. He sounded like a little snob, and a tight little snob at that.

Sam regarded him gravely, not disapproving, not approving. "Sue Martin know you're here?"

"No."

"Good."

The waiter came just in time; Sam's single syllable had given him a hard hurt; but for all the pain, it was an impersonal thing, like getting hit by a golfer on his backswing. When the waiter had gone Sam asked quietly, "Why don't you marry the girl?"

"What're ya—kidding?"

Sam shook his head. O'Banion looked into his eyes and away, then down at Sue Martin where she leaned against the piano, leafing through some music, *Why don't you marry the girl?* "You mean if she'd have me?" It was not the way he felt, but it was something to say. He glanced at Sam's face, which was still waiting for a real answer. All right then. "It wouldn't be right."

"'Right'?" Sam repeated.

O'Banion nipped his thick tongue in the hope it might wake his brains up. The rightness of it . . . vividly he recalled his Mother's words on the subject: "Aside from the amount of trouble you'll save yourself, Anthony, you must remember that it's not only your right, it's your *duty* not to marry beneath your class. Fine hounds, fine horses, fine humans, my dear; it's breeding that matters." That was all very well, but how to say it to the kind old man, himself obviously a manual worker all his life? O'Banion was not a cruel man, and he was well aware that coarse origins did not always mean dull sensibilities. Actually, some of these people were very sensitive. So he made a genuinely noble try at simultaneous truth and kindness: "I've always felt it's wiser to form relationships like that with—uh—people of one's own kind."

"You mean, people with as much money as you got?"

"No!" O'Banion was genuinely shocked. "That's no longer a standard to go by, and it probably never was, not by itself." He laughed ruefully and added, "Besides, there hasn't been any money in my family since I can remember. Not since 1929."

"Then what's your kind of people?"

How? How? "It's . . . a way of life," he said at length. That pleased him. "A way of life," he repeated, and took a drink. He hoped Sam wouldn't pursue the subject any further. Why examine something when you're content with it the way it is?

"Why are you here anyway, boy?" Sam asked. "I mean, in this town instead of in the city, or New York or some place?"

"I'm good for a junior partnership in another year or so. Then I can transfer as a junior partner to a big firm. If I'd gone straight to the city it would take me twice as long to get up there."

Sam nodded. "Pretty cute. Why the law? I always figured lawyer's work was pretty tough and pretty dusty for a young man."

His Mother had said, "Of course the law field's being invaded by all sorts of riffraff now—but what isn't? However, it's still possible for a gentleman to do a gentleman's part in law." Well, that wouldn't do. He'd have to go deeper. He averted his eyes from old Sam's casual penetration and said, "Tough, yes. But there's something about law work . . ." He wondered if the old man would follow this. "Look, Sam, did it ever occur to you that the law is the biggest thing ever built? It's bigger'n bridges, bigger'n buildings— because they're all built *on* it. A lawyer's a part of the law, and the law is part of everything else—everything we own, the way we run governments, everything we make and carry and use. Ever think of that?"

"Can't say I did," said Sam. "Tell me something—the law, is it finished?"

"Finished?"

"What I mean, this rock everything's built on, how solid is it? Is it going to change much? Didn't it change a whole lot to get the way it is?"

"Well, sure! Everything changes a lot while it's growing up."

"Ah. It's grown up."

"Don't you think it has?" O'Banion asked with sudden truculence.

Sam grinned easily. "Shucks, boy, I don't think. I just ask questions. You were saying about 'your sort of people': you think you-all *belong* in the law?"

"Yes!" said O'Banion, and saw immediately that Sam would not be satisfied with so little. "We do in this sense," he said earnestly. "All through the ages men have worked and built and—and owned. And among them there rose a few who were born and bred and trained to—to—" He took another drink, but it and the preceding liquor seemed not to be helping him. He wanted to say *to rule* and he wanted to say *to own,* but he had wit enough about him to recognize that Sam would misunderstand. So he tried again. "Born and bred to—live that—uh—way of life I mentioned before. It's to the interest of those few people to invest their lives in things as they are, to keep them that way; in other words, to work

for and uphold the law." He leaned back with a flourish that somehow wasn't as eloquent as he had hoped and very nearly upset his
glass to boot.

"Don't the law contradict itself once in a while?"

"Naturally!" O'Banion's crystallizing concept of the nobility
of his work was beginning to intoxicate him more than anything
else. "But the very nature of our courts is a process of refinement,
constant purification." He leaned forward excitedly. "Look, laws
are dreams, when they're first thought of—inspirations! There's
something ... uh ... holy about that, something beyond the
world of men. And that's why when the world of men comes into
contact with it, the wording of the inspiration has to be redone in
the books, or interpreted in the courtroom. That's what we mean
by 'precedents'—that's what the big dusty books are for, to create
and maintain consistency under the law."

"What about justice?" murmured Sam, and then quickly, as if
he hadn't meant to change the subject, "That's not what I meant
by contradictin', counselor. I mean all laws that all men have
dreamed up and lived by and got theirselves killed over. Tell me
something, counselor, is there even one single law so right for men
that it shows up in every country that is or was?"

O'Banion made a startled sound, as half a dozen excellent
examples flashed into his mind at once, collided, and, under the
first examination, faded away.

"Because," said Sam in a voice which was friendly and almost
apologetic, "if there ain't such a law, you might say every set of
laws ever dreamed up, even the sets that were bigger and older and
lasted longer than the one you practice, even any set you can imagine for the future—they're all goin' to contradict one another
some way or other. So, who's really to say whose set of laws are
right—or fit to build anything on, or breed up a handful of folks fit
to run it?"

O'Banion stared at his glass without touching it. For an awful
moment he was totally disoriented; a churning pit yawned under
his feet and he must surely topple into it. He thought wildly, you
can't leave me here, old man! You'd better say something else, and
fast, or I ... or I ...

There was a sort of pressure in his ears, like sound too high-pitched for humans. Sam said softly, "You really think Sue Martin ain't good enough for you?"

"I didn't say that, I didn't say that!" O'Banion blurted, hoarse with indignation, and fright, and relief as well. He shuddered back and away from the lip of this personal precipice and looked redly at the composed old face. "I said different, too different, that's all. I'm thinking of her as well as—"

For once Sam bluntly interrupted, as if he had no patience with what O'Banion was saying. "What's different?"

"Background, I told you. Don't you know what that is?"

"You mean the closer a girl's background is to yours, the better chance you'd have bein' happy the rest of your life?"

"Isn't it obvious?" The perfect example popped into his mind, and he speared a finger out and downward toward the piano. "Did you hear what she was singing just before you got here? 'The boy next door.' Don't you understand what that really means, why that song, that idea, hits home to so many people? Everybody understands that; it's the appeal of what's familiar, close by—the similar background I'm talking about!"

"You have to shout?" chuckled Sam. Sobering, he said, "Well, counselor, if you're goin' to think consistently, like you said, couldn't you dream up a background even more sim'lar than your next-door neighbor?"

O'Banion stared at him blankly, and old Sam Bittelman asked, "Are you an only child, counselor?"

O'Banion closed his eyes and saw the precipice there waiting; he snapped them open in sheer self-defense. His hands hurt and he looked down, and slowly released them from the edge of the table. He whispered, "What are you trying to tell me?"

His bland face the very portrait of candor, Sam said, "Shucks, son, I couldn't tell you a thing, not a blessed thing. Why, I don't know anything you don't know to tell you! I ain't asked you a single question you couldn't've asked yourself, and the answers were all yours, not mine. Hey . . ." he breathed, "you better come along home. You wouldn't want Miz Martin to see you looking the way you do right now."

Numbly, Anthony Dunglass O'Banion followed him out.

VIII

It was hot, so hot that apparently even Bitty felt it, and after supper went to sit on the verandah. It was very late when at last she came in to do the dishes, but she went ahead without hurrying, doing her usual steady, thorough job. Sam had gone to bed, Mary Haunt was sulking in her room after yet another of those brief, violent brushes with Miss Schmidt. O'Banion was crouching sweatily over some law-books in the parlor, and Halvorsen—

Halvorsen was standing behind her, just inside the kitchen. On his face was a mixture of expressions far too complicated to analyze, but simple in sum—a sort of anxious wistfulness. In his hands was a paper sack, the mouth of which he held as if it were full of tarantulas. His stance was peculiar, strained, and off-balance, one foot advanced, his shoulders askew; his resolution had equated with his diffidence and immobilized him, and there he stayed like a bee in amber.

Bitty did not turn. She went right on working steadily, her back to him, until she finished the pot she was scouring. Still without turning, she reached for another and said, "Well, come on in, Philip."

Halvorsen literally sagged as her flat, matter-of-fact voice reached him, shattering with its exterior touch his interior deadlock. He grinned, or just bared his teeth, and approached her. "You *do* have eyes in the back of your head."

"Nup." She rapped once with her knuckle on the windowpane over the sink. Night had turned it to black glass. Halvorsen watched the little cone of suds her hand had left, then refocused his eyes on the image in the glass—vivid, the kitchen and everything in it. Hoarsely, he said, "I'm disappointed."

"I don't keep things I don't need," she said bluntly, as if they'd been talking about apple-corers. "What's on your mind? Hungry?"

"No." He looked down at his hands, tightened them still more on the bag. "No," he said again, "I have, I wanted . . ." He noticed that she had stopped working and was standing still, inhumanly still, with her hands in the dishwater and her eyes on the windowpane. "Turn around, Bitty."

When she would not, he supported the bottom of the paper bag with one hand and with the other scrabbled it open. He put his hands down inside it. "Please," he tried to say, but it was only a hiss.

She calmly shook water off her hands, wiped them on a paper towel. When she turned around her face was eloquent—as always, and only because it always was. Its lines were eloquent, and the shape of her penetrating eyes, and the light in them. As a photograph or a painting such a face is eloquent. It is a frightening thing to look into one and realize for the first time that behind it nothing need be moving. Behind the lines of wisdom and experience and the curved spoor of laughter, something utterly immobile could be waiting. Only waiting.

Halvorsen said, "I think all the time." He wet his lips. "I never stop thinking, I don't know how. It's . . . there's something wrong."

Flatly, "What's wrong?"

"You, Sam," said Halvorsen with difficulty. He looked down at the bag over his hand. She did not. "I've had the . . . feeling . . . for a long time now. I didn't know what it was. Just something wrong. So I talked to O'Banion. Miss Schmidt too. Just, you know, talk." He swallowed. "I found out. What's wrong, I mean. It's the way you and Sam talk to us, all of us." He gestured with the paper bag. "*You never say anything!* You only ask questions!"

"Is that all?" asked Bitty good-humoredly.

"No," he said, his eyes fixed on hers. He stepped back a pace.

"Aren't you afraid that paper bag'll spoil your aim, Philip?" He shook his head. His face turned the color of putty.

"You didn't go out and buy a gun just for me, did you?"

"You see?" he breathed. "Questions. You see?"

"You already had it, didn't you, Philip? Bought it for something else?"

"Stay away from me," he whispered, but she had not moved. He said, "Who are you? What are you after?"

"Philip," she said gently—and now she smiled. "Philip—*why do you want to be dead?*"

PART TWO

SPECIAL ENTRY IN FIELD EXPEDITION [NOTEBOOK]: Since it is now [my] intention to prefer charges against [my] [partner-teammate] [Smith] and to use these [notes] as a formal [document] in the matter, [I] shall now summarize in detail the particulars of the case: [We] have been on Earth for [expression of time-units] on a field expedition to determine whether or not the dominant species here possesses the Synapse known to our [catalog] as Beta sub Sixteen, the master [computer] [at home] having concluded that without the Synapse, this Earth culture must become extinct. Needless to [say] [we] are here to observe and not to interfere; to add to the [memory-banks] of the master [computer] only, it being a matter of no significance otherwise.

On arrival [we] set up the usual [detectors], expecting to get our information in a [expression of very short time-unit] or so; but to our [great astonishment] the readings on the [kickshaw], the [gimmick] and our high-sensitivity [snivvy] were mixed; it appears that this culture possessed the Synapse but did not use it. [!!!]

[We] therefore decided to conduct a [microcosmic] observation on each of the specimens in a small group, under [laboratory] conditions, to discover to what extent the Synapse exists in them, and under what circumstances it might become functional. We have set up for this purpose [the analog of] a [   ], or [residence], called, in Terrestrial terms, *small town boarding house*, and have attracted to it:

PHILIP HALVORSEN, a young vocational guidance expert, who has a ceaselessly active analytical mind, and a kind of instinct for illogic: he knows when a person or situation is, in some way, wrong, and will not rest until he finds out why. He has recently followed his own logic to the conclusion that he wants to be dead—and he can't find out why! ... MARY HAUNT, a beautiful girl who claims to be twenty-two [and lies], and who wants to be a movie star with an ambition transcending all reason. She is employed in a very minor capacity at the local radio station, and is always angry at everyone.... ANTHONY DUNGLASS O'BANION, a young lawyer, deeply convinced that his family background, "breeding," "culture" and occupation set him apart from everyone else in town; he is desperately fighting a growing conviction that he is in love with ... SUE MARTIN, young widowed night-club hostess (whom O'Banion's Mother, if she were here, would certainly refer to as a "woman of that sort"). Sue Martin, a woman of unusual equilibrium, loves O'Banion but will not submit herself to his snobbery and therefore keeps her feelings very much to herself.... Her young son ROBIN, who is three, and is friends with everyone everywhere including his invisible, "imaginary" playmates Boff and Googie. Robin's special friend is the lawyer O'Banion; they get along very well indeed.... Finally, MISS SCHMIDT, the high-school librarian, who is a soft-voiced, timid little rabbit of a woman, afraid of the world and abjectly obedient to propriety.

The retired couple who run the boarding house are SAM and BITTY BITTELMAN, wise, relaxed, helpful, observant. They are available always except for one day a month when they go out "for a ride."

That, in Terrestrial terms, is [our] laboratory setup. [We] installed a [widget] and [rigged-up] a [wadget] as complementary [observation-and-control] even though it meant using a [miserable] [inefficient] [old-fashioned] power supply on the [wadget], which has to be re[charged] every [equivalent of Earth month]. Everything proceeded satisfactorily until [Smith], plagued by what [I] can only, in the most cosmic breadth of generosity, call an excess of enthusiasm, insisted that [we] speed up our research by stimulating the Synapse in these specimens. In spite of [my] warnings and [my] caution, [he] [bulled] ahead giving [me] no choice but to assist [him] in re[wiring] the [machines] for this purpose. But let it be on the [record] that [I] specifically warned [him] of the dangers of revealing [our] presence here. [I] for [one] dread the idea of being responsible for the destruction of organized life. Even if only one of the specimens should detect [us], there is so much intercommunication in this small group that it would be virtually impossible to remove or destroy one without alerting and disturbing all. The least effect would be to negate all [our] efforts so far; the most is something [I] cannot [ethically] live with.

Under these [unhappy] circumstances [we] proceeded with the stimulation; Old Sam Bittelman went to Miss Schmidt's room when she reported her venetian blind broken and unable to close. She suddenly found it impossible not to answer Sam's questions, which probed at the very roots of her timidity. Shocked to these roots, but more thoughtful than she had ever been in her life, before, she went to bed forgetting the blind and thinking about the fact that her conditioning to keep her body covered was more deeply instilled into her than *Thou shalt not kill*—and other, equally unsettling concepts.

Mary Haunt overslept, for the very first time, and went into the kitchen, furious. Sam and Bitty were there, and suddenly the girl *had* to answer the questions they shot at her. She escaped quickly, but spent the rest of the day in bed, miserable and disoriented, wondering if, after all, she did want Hollywood. . . .

Anthony O'Banion went down to the night club where Sue Martin worked, and sat out of sight on the balcony. Suddenly Sam Bittelman was at the table with him, asking him deeply troubling questions about the law and why he practiced it, about his convictions of blood and breeding, and about his feelings for Sue Martin. Dizzied and speechless, O'Banion was led home by kind old Sam.

Bitty found Sue Martin alone in her room one morning, and asked her some pointed questions, all of which Sue answered with ease, quite undisturbed, quite willing. Yes, she loved O'Banion. No, she wouldn't do anything about it; that was O'Banion's problem. Sue Martin was no trouble at all to Bitty. . . .

Late one hot evening Halvorsen walked into the

kitchen with a gun in his hand, saying there was something wrong, something he couldn't name . . . but *"Who are you and what do you want?"* Bitty calmly asked him why he had bought a gun: "It was for yourself, wasn't it, Philip? *Why do you want to be dead?"* [I] submit that [Smith] is guilty of carelessness and [unethical] conduct. [I] see no solution but to destroy this specimen and perhaps the others. [I] declare that this situation has arisen only because [Smith] ignored [my] clearly [stated] warning. As [I] [write], this alerted, frightened specimen stands ready to commit violence on [our] [equipment] and thereby itself. [I] hereby serve notice on [Smith] that [he] got [us] into this and [he] can [   ]ing well get [us] out.

IX

"Why do you want to be dead?"

Phil Halvorsen stood gaping at the old woman, and the gun, still shrouded in its silly paper bag, began whispering softly as he trembled. The butt fitted his hand as his hand fitted the butt; *It's holding me,* he thought hysterically, knowing clearly that his hysteria was a cloud, a cloak, a defense against that which he was not equipped to think about . . . well, maybe not ready to think about; but how had she known?

For nearly two days he had been worrying and gnawing at this sense of wrongness about him. Back and back he would come to it, only to reach bafflement and kick it away angrily; not eating enough, hardly sleeping at all; *let me sleep first!* something wailed within him, and as he sensed it he kicked it away again: more hysteria, not letting him think. And then a word from O'Banion, a phrase from Miss Schmidt, and his own ragbag memory: The Bittelmans never said—they always asked. It was as if they could reach into a man's mind, piece together questions from the unused lumber stored there, and from it build shapes he couldn't bear to look at. *How many terrible questions have I locked away?* And has she broken the lock? He said, "Don't . . . ask me that . . . why did you ask me that?"

"Well, why ever not?"

"You're a . . . you can read my mind."

"Can I?"

"*Say* something!" he shouted. The paper bag stopped whispering. He thought she noticed it.

"Am I reading your mind," she asked reasonably, "if I see you walk in here the way you did looking like the wrath o' God, holding that thing out in front of you and shying away from it at the same time, and then tell you that if you accidentally pull the trigger you might have to die for it? Read minds? Isn't it enough to read the papers?"

Oh, he thought. . . . Oh-h. He looked at her sharply. She was quite calm, waiting, leaving it to him. He knew, suddenly and certainly, that this woman could outthink him, outtalk him, seven ways from Sunday without turning a hair. This meant either that he was completely and embarrassingly wrong, or that her easy explanations weren't true ones . . . which was the thing that had been bothering him in the first place. "Why did you say I bought the gun for something else?" he snapped.

She gave him that brief, very-warm smile. "Didn't say; I asked you, right? How could I really know?"

For one further moment he hesitated, and it came to him that if this flickering doubt about her was justified, the chances were that a gun would be as ineffective as an argument. And besides . . . it was like a silent current in the room, a sort of almost-sound, or the aural pressure he could feel sometimes when a car was braking near him; but here it came out feeling like comfort.

He let the bag fall until it swung from its mouth. He twisted it closed. "Will you—I mean," he bumbled, "I don't want it."

"Now what would I do with a gun?" she asked.

"I don't know. I just don't want it around. I can throw it away. I don't want to have anything to do with it. I thought maybe you could put it away somewhere."

"You know, you'd better sit down," said Bitty. She didn't exactly push him but he had to move back to get out of her way as she approached, and when the back of his knees hit a chair he had to sit down or fall down. Bitty continued across the kitchen, opened a high cupboard and put the bag on the topmost shelf. "Only place in the house Robin can't climb into."

"Robin. Oh yes," he said, seeing the possibilities. "I'm sorry. I'm sorry."

"You'd better talk it out, Philip," she said in her flat, kind way. "You're fixing to bust wide open. I won't have you messing up my kitchen."

"There's nothing to talk about."

She paused on her way back to the sink, in a strange hesitation like one listening. Suddenly she turned and sat down at the table with him. "What did you want with a gun, Philip?" she demanded; and just as abruptly, he answered her, as if she had hurled something at him and it had bounced straight back into her waiting hands, "I was thinking about killing myself."

If he thought this would elicit surprise, or an exclamation, or any more questions, he was disappointed. She seemed only to be waiting, so he said, with considerably more care, "I don't know why I told you that but it came out right. I said I was thinking about doing it. I didn't say I was going to do it." He looked at her. Not enough? Okay then: "I couldn't be sure exactly what I was thinking until I bought a gun. Does that make any sense to you?"

"Why not?"

"I don't ever know exactly what I think unless I try it out. Or get all the pieces laid out ready to try."

"Or tell somebody?"

"I couldn't tell anybody about this."

"Did you try?"

"*Damn* it!" It was a whisper, but it emerged under frightening pressure. Then normally, "I'm sorry, Bitty, I'm real sorry. I suddenly got mad at the language, you know what I mean? You say something in words of one syllable and it comes out meaning something you never meant. I told you, 'I couldn't tell anybody about this.' That sounds as if I knew all about it and was just shy or something. So you ask me, 'Did you try?' But what I really mean was that this whole thing, everything about it, is a bunch of—of feelings, and—well, crazy ideas *that I couldn't tell anyone about.*"

Bitty's rare smile flickered. "Did you try?"

"Well I'll be. You're worse than ever," he said, this time without anger. "You *do* know what I'm thinking."

"So what were you thinking?"

He sobered immediately. "Things . . . all crazy. I think all the time, Bitty, like a radio was playing all day, all night, and I can't turn it off. Wouldn't want to; wouldn't know how to live without it. Ask me is it going to rain and off I go, thinking about rain, where it comes from, about clouds, how many different kinds there are; about air-currents and jet-streams and everything else you pick up reading those little paragraphs at the bottom of newspaper columns; about—"

"About why you bought a gun?"

"Huh? Oh . . . all right, all right, I won't ramble." He closed his eyes to hear his thoughts, and frowned at them. "Anyway, at the tail end of these run-downs is always some single thing that stops the chain—for the time. It might be the answer to some question I asked myself, or someone asks me, or it might just be as far as the things I know will take me.

"So one day a few weeks ago I got to thinking about guns, and never mind the way I went, but what I arrived at was the idea of a gun killing me, and then just the idea of being dead. And the more I thought, the more scared I got."

After waiting what seemed to be long enough, Bitty said, "Scared."

"It wasn't kil—being dead that scared me. It was the feeling I had about it. I was glad about it. I wanted it. That's what scared me."

"Why do you want to be dead?"

"That's what I don't know." His voice fell. "Don't know, I just don't know," he mumbled. "So I couldn't get it out of my head and I couldn't make any sense out of it, and I thought the only thing I could do was to get a gun and load it and—get everything ready, to see how I felt then." He looked up at her. "That sounds real crazy, I bet."

Bitty shrugged. Either she denied the statement or it didn't matter. Halvorsen looked down again and said to his clenched hands, "I sat there in my room with the muzzle in my mouth and all the safeties off, and hooked my thumb around the trigger."

"Learn anything?"

His mouth moved but he couldn't find words to fit the movement. "Well," said Bitty sharply, "why didn't you pull it?"

"I just—" He closed his eyes in one of those long, inward-reading pauses. "—couldn't. I mean, *didn't*. I wasn't afraid, if that's what you want to know." He glanced at her and couldn't tell what she wanted to know. "Sitting there, that way, I came to real-ize that this wasn't the way it should happen," he said with some difficulty.

"What is the way?"

"Like this: if ever there was an earthquake, or I looked up and saw a safe falling on me, or some other thing like that, something from outside myself—I wouldn't move aside. I'd let it happen."

"Is there a difference between that and shooting yourself?"

"Yes!" he said, with more animation than he had shown so far. "Put it like this: there's part of me that's dead, and wants the rest of me dead. There's a part of me that's alive, and wants all of me alive." He looked that over and nodded at it. "My hand, my arm, my thumb on the trigger—they're alive. All the live parts of me want to help me go on living, d'you see? No live part should help the dead part get what it wants. The way it'll happen, the way it should happen, is not when I do something to make it happen. It'll be when I don't do something. I won't get out of the way, and that's it, and thanks for keeping the gun for me, it's no use to me." He stood up and found his eyes locked with hers, and sat right down again, breathing hard.

"Why do you want to be dead?" she asked flatly.

He put his head down on his hands and began to rock it slowly to and fro.

"Don't you want to know?"

Muffled, his voice came up from the edge of the table. "No." Abruptly he sat up, staring. "No? What made me say no? Bitty," he demanded, "what made me say that?"

She shrugged. He jumped up and began pacing swiftly up and down the kitchen. "I'll be dogged," he murmured once, and "Well, what d'ye kn—"

Bitty watched him, and catching him on a turn when their eyes could meet, she asked, "Well—why do you want to—"

"Shut up," he said. He said it, not to her, but to any interrup-tion. His figmentary signal-light, which indicated dissatisfaction, unrightness, was casting its glow all over his interior landscape. To be hounded half to death by something like this, then to discover that basically he didn't want to investigate it. . . . He sat down and faced her, his eyes alight. "I don't know yet," he said, "but I will, I will." He took a deep breath. "It's like being chased by something that's gaining on you, and you duck into an alley, and then you find it's blind, there's only a brick wall; so you sit down to wait, it's all you can do. And all of a sudden you find a door in the wall. Been there all the time. Just didn't look."

"Why do you want to be dead?"

"B-because I—I shouldn't be alive. Because the average guy— Different, that's what I am, different, unfit."

"Different, unfit." Bitty's eyebrows raised slightly. "They the same thing, Philip?"

"Well, sure."

"You can't jump like a kangaroo, you can't eat grass raw like a cow—different. You unfit because you can't do those things?"

He made an annoyed laugh. "Not that, not that. People, I mean."

"You can't fly a plane. You can't sing like Sue Martin. You can't spout law like Tony O'Banion. That kind of different?"

"No," he said, and in a surge of anguish, "No, no! I can't talk about it, Bitty!" He looked at her and again saw that rare, deep smile. He answered it in kind, but weakly, remembering that he had said that to her before. "This time I mean I can't talk about such things to you. To a lady," he said in abrupt, unbearable confusion.

"I'm no lady," said Bitty with conviction. Suddenly she punched his forearm; he thought it was the first time she had ever touched him. "To you I'm not even a human being. Not even another person. I mean it," she said warmly. "Have I asked you a single question you couldn't've asked yourself? Have I told you anything you didn't know?"

His peculiar linear mind cast rapidly back and up again. He felt an odd instant of disorientation. It was not unpleasant. Bitty said gently, "Go on talking to yourself, boy. Who knows—you might find yourself in good company."

"Aw . . . thanks, Bitty," he mumbled. His eyes stung and he shook his head. "All right, all *right,* then . . . it just came to me, one big flash, and I guess I couldn't sit here—here," he said, waving his arm to include the scrubbed, friendly kitchen, "and look at you, and think about these—uh this—all at once." He swallowed heavily. "Well, that time I told you about, that day I found out I wanted to be dead, it was like getting hit on the head. Right after that, only a couple of minutes, I got hit on the head just as hard by something else. I didn't know—want to know till now that they were connected, some way." He closed his eyes. "It was a theater, that rathole down across the Circle. You know. It—it hit out at me when I wasn't looking. It was all covered with . . . pictures and—and it said SEE this and SEE that and SEE some dirty other thing, adults only, you know what I mean." He opened his eyes to see what Bitty was doing, but Bitty was doing nothing at all. Waiting. He turned his face away from her, and said indistinctly into his shoulder, "All my life those things meant nothing to me. *There!*" he shouted, "you see? Different, different!"

But she wouldn't see. Or she wouldn't see until he did, himself, more clearly. She still waited.

He said, "Down at work, there's a fellow, Scodie. This Scodie, he's a good man, really can turn out a day's work. I mean, he likes what he's doing, he cares. Except every time a girl goes by, everything stops. He snaps up out of what he's doing, he watches her. I mean, *every* time. It's like he can't help himself. He does it the way a cadet salutes an officer on the street. He does it like that crossing-guard on the toy train, that pops out of his little house every time his little light goes on. He watches until the girl's gone by, and then he says 'mmm*yuh*!' and looks over at me and winks."

"What do you do, every time?"

"Well, I—" He laughed uncertainly. "I guess I wink back at him and I say, mm-*hm*! But I know why I do it, it's because he expects me to; he'd think it was sort of peculiar if I didn't. But he doesn't do it for me; I don't expect anything of him one way or the other. He does it—" Words failed him, and he tried again. "Doing that, he's part of—everybody. What he does is the same thing every song on every radio says every minute. Every ad in every magazine does it if it possibly can, even if it means a girl in her underwear with stillson wrenches for sale." He leapt to his feet and began to pace excitedly. "You got to back off a little to see it," he told Bitty, who smiled behind his back. "You got to look at the whole thing all at once, to see how *much* there is of it, the jokes people tell—yeah, you got to laugh at them, whatever, you even have to know a couple, or they'll ... The window displays, the television, the movies ... somebody's writing an article about transistors or termites or something, and every once in a while he figures he's been away from it long enough and he has to say something about the birds and the bees and 'Gentlemen prefer.' Everywhere you turn the whole world's at it, chipping and chipping away at it—"

He stamped back to the table and looked into Bitty's face intently. "You got to back away and look at it all at once," he cautioned again. "I'm not in kindergarten, I know what it's all about. I'm not a woman-hater. I've been in love. I'll get married, some day. Go ahead and tell me I'm talking about one of the biggest, strongest, down-deep urges we have—I'll buy that. That's what I *mean,* that's what I'm *talking* about." His forehead was pink and shiny; he took out a crumpled handkerchief and batted at it. "So much of it, all around you, all the time, filling a big hungry need in average people. I don't mean the urge itself; I mean all this *reminding,* this what do you call it, indoctrination. It's a need or folks wouldn't stand for so much of it, comic books, lipstick, that air-jet in the floor at the funny house at the Fair." He thumped into his chair, panting. "Do you begin to see what I mean about *'different'?*"

"Do you?" asked Bitty, but Halvorsen didn't hear her; he was talking again. "Different, because I don't feel that hunger to be reminded, I don't need all that high-pressure salesmanship, I don't want it. Every time I tell one of my jokes, every time I wink back at old Scodie, I feel like a fool, like some sort of liar. But you got to protect yourself; you can't let anyone find out. You know why? Because the average guy, the guy-by-the-millions that needs all that noise so much, he'll let you be the way he is, or he'll let you be ... I'm sorry, Bitty. Don't make me go into a lot of dirty details. You see what I mean, don't you?

"What do you mean?"

Irritated, he blew a single sharp blast from his nostrils. "Well, what I mean is, they'll let you be the way they are, or you have to be ... sick, crippled. You can't be anything else! You can't be Phil Halvorsen who isn't sick and who isn't crippled but who just doesn't naturally go around banging his antlers against the rocks so the whole world can hear it."

"So—that's what you mean by unfit?"

"That's why I wanted to be dead. I just don't think the way other people do; if I act the way other people do I feel . . . feel guilty. I guess I had this piling up in me for years, and that day with the guns, when I found out what I wanted to do . . . and then that theater-front, yawping over me like a wet mouth full of dirty teeth . . ." He giggled foolishly. "Listen to me, will you . . . Bitty, I'm sorry."

She utterly ignored this. "High-pressure salesmanship," she said.

"What?"

"You said it, I didn't . . . Isn't hunger one of those big deep needs, Philip? Suppose you had a bunch of folks starving on an island and dropped them a ton of food—would they need high-pressure salesmanship?"

It was as if he stood at the edge of a bottomless hole—more, the very outer edge of the world, so close his very toes projected over the emptiness. It filled him with wonder; he was startled, but not really afraid, because it might well be that to fall down and down into that endless place might be a very peaceful thing. He closed his eyes and slowly, very slowly, came back to reality, the kitchen. Bitty, Bitty's words. "You mean . . . the av—the ordin— you mean, people aren't really interested?"

"Not that interested."

He blinked; he felt as if he had ceased to exist in his world and had been plunked down in a very similar, but totally new one. It was far less lonely here.

He hit the table and laughed into Bitty's calm face. "I'm going to sleep," he said, and got up; and he knew she had caught his exact shade of meaning when she said gently, "Sure you can."

EXCERPT FROM FIELD EXPEDITION [NOTEBOOK]: [I] had thought up to now that in [Smith]'s [immorally] excessive enthusiasm and [bullheadedness] [I] had encountered the utmost in [irritants]. [I] was in [error]; [he] now surpasses these, and without effort. In the first place, having placated and outwitted the alerted specimen, [he] has destroyed [my] preliminary detailed [report] on him; this

is [irritat]ing not only because it was done without con-
sulting [me], not only because of the trouble [I] went to
[write] it all up, but mostly because [he] is technically
within [his] [ethics-rights]—the emergency created by
[his] [bumbling mismanagement] no longer exists. [I]
have [force]fully pointed out to [him] that it was only by
the application of [my] kind of cautious resourcefulness
that [he] succeeded, but [he] just [gloats]. [I] [most
strongly affirm-and-bind-myself], the instant [we] get
back home and are released from Expeditionary [ethic-
discipline], [I] shall [bend] [his] [   ]s over [his] [   ]
and [tie a knot in] them.

[We] have now, no [credit-thanks] to [Smith],
reached a point where all our specimens are in a state of
[heavy] preconditioning of their unaccountably random
Synapse Beta sub Sixteen. Being a synapse, it will of
course come into full operation only on a reflexive level
and in an extreme emergency, which [we] are now setting up.

Unless [Smith] produces yet more [stupidities], the
specimens should live through this.

X

It had become impossibly hot, and very still. Leaves dropped at
impossible angles, and still the dust lay on them. Sounds seemed
too enervated to travel very far. The sky was brass all day, and at
night, for want of ambition, the overcast was no more than a
gauzy hood of haze.

It was the Bittelmans' "day off" again, and without them the
spine had been snatched out of the household. The boarders ate
pokily, lightly, at random, and somehow got through the time
when there was nothing to do but sit up late enough to get tired
enough to get whatever rest the temperature would permit. It was
too hot, even, to talk, and no one attempted it. They drifted to
their rooms to wait for sleep; they slumped in front of the fans and
took cold showers which generated more heat than they dissi-

pated. When at last darkness came, it was a relief only to the eyes. The household pulse beat slowly and slower; by eight o'clock it was library-quiet, by nine quite silent, so that the soft brushing of knuckles on Miss Schmidt's door struck her like a shout.

"Wh-who is it?" she quavered, when she recovered her breath.

"Sue."

"Oh—oh. Oh, do come in." She pulled the damp sheet tight up against her throat.

"Oh, you're in bed already. I'm sorry."

"*I'm* sorry. It's all right."

Sue Martin swung the door shut and came all the way in. She was wearing an off-the-shoulder peasant blouse and a pleated skirt with three times more filmy nylon in it than one would guess until she turned, when it drifted like smoke. "My," said Miss Schmidt enviously. "You look cool."

"State of mind," Sue smiled. "I'm about to go to work and I wish I didn't have to."

"And Bitty's out. I'm honorary baby-sitter again."

"You're an angel."

"No, oh, no!" cried Miss Schmidt. "I wish everything I had to do was that easy. Why, in all the time I've known you, every time I've done it, I—I've had nothing to do!"

"He sleeps pretty soundly. Clear conscience, I guess."

"I think it's because he's happy. He smiles when he sleeps."

"Smiles? Sometimes he laughs out loud," said Sue Martin. "I was a little worried tonight, for a while. He was so flushed and wide-awake—"

"Well, it's *hot*."

"It wasn't that." Sue chuckled. "His precious Boff was all over the place, 'fixin' things,' Robin said. What he was fixing all over the walls and ceiling, Robin didn't say. Whatever it was, it's finished now, though, and Robin's sound asleep. I'm sure you won't even have to go in. And Bitty ought to be home soon."

"You'll leave your door open?"

Sue Martin nodded and glanced up at the large open transom over Miss Schmidt's door. "You'll hear him if he so much as blinks. . . . I've got to run. Thanks *so* much."

"Oh, really, Mrs. M—uh, Sue. Don't thank me. Just run along."

"Good night."

Sue Martin slipped out, silently closing the door behind her. Miss Schmidt sighed and looked up at the transom. After Sue's light footsteps had faded away, she listened, listened as hard as she could, trying to pour part of herself through the transom, across the hall, through Sue Martin's open door. A light sleeper at any time, she knew confidently that she was on guard now and would wake if anything happened. If she slept at all in this sticky heat.

She might sleep, at that, she thought after a while. She shifted herself luxuriously, and edged to a slightly cooler spot on the bed. "That wicked Sam," she murmured, and blushed in the dark. But he had been right. A *nightgown* in weather like this?

Suddenly, she slept.

In O'Banion's room, there was a soft sound. He had put off taking a shower until suddenly he had used up his energy, and could hardly stir. I'll just rest my eyes, he thought, and bowed his head. The soft sound was made by his forehead striking the book.

Halvorsen lay rigid on his bed, staring at the ceiling. There, almost as if it was projected, was the image of a flimsy cylinder vomiting smoke. Go ahead, he thought, detachedly. Or go away. I don't care which. Before I talked to Bitty, I wanted you. Now, I don't care. Is that better? He closed his eyes, but the image was still there. He lay very quietly, watching the insides of his eyelids. It was like being asleep. When he was asleep the thing was there too.

Mary Haunt sat by her window, pretending it was cooler there than in bed. There was no anger in her, just now as she lay back and dreamed. The Big Break, the pillars of light at her première, her name two stories tall over a Broadway marquee—these had no place in this particular favorite dream. I'll do over Mom's room, she thought, dimity, this time, and full, full skirts on the vanity and the night table. She closed her eyes, putting herself in Mom's room with such vividness that she could almost smell the cool faint odor of lavender sachets and the special freshness of sheets dried in the sun. Yes, and something else, outside the room, barely, just barely she knew bread was baking, so that the kitchen would be heavenly with it; the bread would dominate the spice-shelf for a while, until it was out of the oven and cooled. "Oh, Mom . . ." she whispered. She lay still in her easy-chair, holding and holding to the vision until this room, this house, this town didn't matter any more.

Some hours went by.

Robin floated in a luminous ocean of sleep where there was nothing to fear and where, if he just turned to look, there were love and laughter waiting for him. His left hand uncurled and he thrust the second and third fingers into his mouth. Somehow he was a big bulldozer with a motor that sounded like Mitster and tracks that clattered along like Coffeepot, and Boff and Googie were riding along with him and laughing. Then without effort he was a glittery Ferris wheel, but he could watch himself too in one of the cars, screaming his delight and leaning against Tonio's hard arm. All this, yet he was still afloat in that deep bright place where there was no fear, where love and laughter hid around some indescribable corner, waiting. Brighter, brighter. Warm, warm, warmer . . . oh, hot *hot!*

XI

Miss Schmidt opened her eyes to an impossible orange glare and a roar like the end of the world. For one full second she lay still, paralyzed by an utter disbelief; no light could have become so bright, no sound could have risen to this volume, without waking her as it began. Then she found a way to focus her eyes against the radiance, and saw the flames, and in what was left to her of her immobile second, she explained the whole thing to herself and said redly, of course, of course; it's only a nightmare and *suppose there's a fire?*—and that's so *silly,* Sam—

And then she was out of bed in a single bound, standing in the center of the room, face to flaming face with reality. Everything was burning—everything! The drapes had already gone and the slats of the venetian blind, their cords gone, were heaped on the floor, going like a campfire. Even as she watched the screen sagged and crumpled, its pine frame glaring and spitting pitch through blistering paint. It fell outside.

Outside, outside! The window's open, you're on the ground floor; yes, and there on the chair, not burning yet, your bathrobe; take the robe and jump, quick!

Then, beyond belief, there was a second louder than the earth-filling roar, and different; fine hot powder and a hot hail of plaster showered on her shoulders; she looked up to see the main beam, right over her head, sag toward her and hang groaning, one part reaching to the other with broken flat fingers of splintered wood which gloved themselves in flame as she saw them. She cowered, and just then the handle of the door turned and a gout of smoke slammed it open and whisked out of sight in the updraft; and there in the hall stood Robin, grinding a fat little fist into one abruptly wakened eye. She could see his lips move, though she could hear nothing in this mighty bellow of sound. She knew it, though, and heard it clearly in her mind: "What's 'at noice?"

The beam overhead grumbled and again she was showered with plaster. She batted it off her shoulders, and whimpered. A great flame must have burst from the roof above her just then, for through the window she saw a brilliant glare reflected from the white clapboards of the garage wall outside. The glare tugged at her—*jump!*—and besides, her robe . . .

The beam thundered and began to fall. Now she must make a choice, in microseconds. The swiftest thought would not be fast enough to weigh and consider and decide; all that could matter now was what was inside her, throwing switches (some so worn and easy to move!). A giant was throwing them, and he was strong; his strength was a conditioning deeper than *thou shalt not kill;* he was a lesson learned before she had learned to love God, or to walk, or to talk. He was her mother's authority and the fear of all the hairy, sweaty, dangerous mysteries from which she had shielded herself all her life; and his name and title were Cover Thyself! With him, helping him, was the reflexive Save Thyself! and against these—Robin, whom she loved (but love is what she felt, once, for a canary, and once for a Raggedy Ann doll) and her sense of duty to Sue Martin (but so lightly promised, and at the time such a meaningless formality). There could be no choice in such a battle, though she must live with the consequences for all her years.

Then—

—it was as if a mighty voice had called *Stop!* and the very flames froze. Half a foot above her hung the jagged end of the burning beam, and chunks of plaster, splinters and scraps of shattered lath and glowing joist stopped in midair. Yet during this sliver of a fraction of time, she knew that the phenomenon was a mental something, a figment, and the idea of time-cessation only a clumsy effort of her mind's to account for what was happening.

Save Thyself was still there, hysterical hands clutching for the controls, but *Cover Thyself* disappeared into the background. Save herself she would, but it would be on new terms. She was in the grip of a reflex of reflexes, one which took into consideration all the factors a normal reflex would, to the end goal of survival. But along with these, it called up everything Reta Schmidt had ever done, everything she had been. In a single soundless flash, a new kind of light was thrown into every crevice and cranny of her existence. It was her total self now, reacting to a total situation far wider than that which obtained here in this burning room. It illuminated even the future—that much of it which depended upon these events, between them and the next probable major "crossroads." It canceled past misjudgments and illogics and replaced them with rightness, even for the times she had known what was right and had done otherwise. It came and was gone even while she leaped, while she took two bounding steps across the floor and the beam crashed and crushed and showered sparks where she had been standing.

She scooped up the child and ran down the hall, through the foyer, into the kitchen. It was dark there, thick with swirling smoke, but the glass panels on the kitchen door glared with some unfamiliar light from outdoors. She began to cough violently, but grimly aimed at the light and drove ahead. It was eclipsed suddenly by a monstrous shadow, and suddenly it exploded inward. There were lights out there she had never seen before, and half-silhouetted in the broken doorway was a big man with a gleaming helmet and an axe. She tried to call, or perhaps it was only a scream, but instead she went into a spasm of coughing.

"Somebody in here?" asked the man. A beam of light, apparently from the street, lit up the shield on the front of his helmet as he leaned forward. He stepped inside. "Whew! Where are you?"

She went blindly to him and pushed Robin against his coat. "The baby," she croaked. "Get him out of this smoke."

He grunted and suddenly Robin was gone from her arms. "You all right?" He was peering into the black and the smoke.

"Take him out," she said. "Then I'll want your coat."

He went out. Miss Schmidt could hear Robin's clear voice: "You a fireman?"

"I sure am," rumbled the man. "Want to see my fire engine? Then sit right there on the grass and wait one second. Okay?"

"Okay."

The coat flew through the doorway.

"Got it?"

"Thank you." She put the huge garment on and went out. The fireman waited there, again holding Robin in his arms. "You all right, ma'am?"

Her lungs were an agony and she had burns on her feet and shoulders. Her hair was singed and one of her hands was flayed across its back. "I'm just fine," she said.

They began to walk up the road. Robin squirmed around in the man's arms and popped his head out to look back at the brightly burning house.

"'Bye, Boff," he said happily, and then gave his heart to the fire engine.

XII

"Mother, the bread's burning!"

Mary Haunt opened her eyes to an impossible glare and a great roaring. She shrieked and flailed out blindly, as if she could frighten it away, whatever it was; and then she came enough to her senses to realize that she still sat in her chair by the window, and that the house was on fire. She leaped to her feet, sending the heavy chair skittering across the room where it toppled over against the clothespress. As it always did when it was bumped, the clothespress calmly opened its doors.

But Mary Haunt didn't wait for that or anything else. She struck the screen with the flat of her hand. It popped out easily, and she hit the ground almost at the same time it did. She ran off a few steps, and then, like Lot's wife, curiosity overtook her and she stopped. She turned around in fascination.

Great wavering flames leapt fifty and sixty feet in the air and all the windows were alight. From the town side she could hear the

shriek and clang of fire engines, and the windows and doors opening, and running feet. But the biggest sound of all was the roar of
the fire, like a giant's blowtorch.

She looked back at her own window. She could see into the
room easily, the chair on its side, the bed with its chenille top-
spread sprouting measles of spark and char, and the gaping doors
of the—"My clothes! My clothes!"

Furiously she ran back to the window, paused a moment in
horror to see fire run along the picture-molding of the inside wall
like a nightmare caterpillar. "My clothes," she whispered. She
didn't make much money at her job, but every cent that wasn't
used in bed and board went on her back. She mouthed something,
and from her throat came that animal growl of hers; she put both
hands on the sill and leaped, and tumbled back into the house.

She was prepared for the heat but not for that intensity of
light, and the noise was worst of all. She recoiled from it and
stood for a moment with her hands over her eyes, swaying with the
impact of it. Then she ground her teeth and made her way across
to the clothespress. She swept open the bottom drawer and turned
out the neatly folded clothes. Down at the bottom was a cotton
print dress, wrapped around a picture frame. She lifted it out and
hugged it, and ran across to the window with it. She leaned far out
and dropped it gently on the grass, then turned back in again.

The far wall, by the door, began to buckle high up, and suddenly there was fire up there. The corner near the ceiling toppled
into the room with a crash and a cloud of white dust and greasy-
looking smoke, and then the whole wall fell, not toward her, but
away, so that her room now included a section of the corridor outside. As the dust settled somebody, a man, came roaring inarticu-
lately and battering through the rubble. She could not know who
it was. He apparently meant to travel the corridor whether it was
all there or not, and he did, disappearing again into the inferno.

She staggered back toward the clothespress. She felt mad,
drunk, crazy. Maybe it was the de-oxygenated atmosphere and
maybe it was fear and reaction, but it was sort of wonderful, too;
she felt her face writhing and part of her was numb with astonishment at what the rest of her was doing; she was laughing. She
slammed into the clothespress, gasping for breath, filled her lungs
and delivered up a shrill peal of laughter. Almost helpless from it,

she fumbled down a dull satin evening gown with a long silver sash. She held it up in front of her and laughed again, doubling over it, and then straightened up, rolling the dress up into a ball as she did so. With all her might she hurled it into the rubble of the hallway. Next was a simple black dress with no back and a little bolero; with an expression on her face that can only be described as cheerful, she threw it after the evening gown. Then the blue, and the organdy with the taffeta underskirt, and the black and orange one she used to call her Hallowe'en dress; each one she dragged out, held up, and hurled: "You," she growled between her convulsions of laughter, "you, and you, and *you*." When the press was empty, she ran to the bureau and snatched open her scarf drawer, uncovering a flowerbed of dainty, filmy silk and nylon and satin shawls, scarves, and kerchiefs. She whipped out an over-sized babushka, barely heavier than the air that floated it, and ran with it to the flaming mass where her door once was. She dipped and turned like a dancer, fluttering it through flame, and when it was burning she bounced back to the bureau and put it in the drawer with the others. Fire streamed out of the drawer and she laughed and laughed . . .

And something nipped her sharply on the calves; she yelped and turned and found the lace of her black negligee was on fire. She twisted back and gathered the cloth and ripped it away. The pain had sobered her and she was bewildered now, weak and beginning to be frightened. She started for the window and tripped and fell heavily, and when she got up the smoke was suddenly like a scalding blanket over her head and shoulders and she didn't know which way to go. She knelt and peered and found the window in an unexpected direction, and made for it. As she tumbled through, the ceiling behind her fell, and the roof after it.

On her belly she clawed away from the house, sobbing, and at last rose to her knees. She smelt of smoke and burned hair and all her lovely fingernails were broken. She squatted on the ground, staring at the flaming shell of the house, and cried like a little girl. But when her swollen eyes rested on that square patch in the grass, she stopped crying and got up and limped over to it. Her cotton print, and the picture . . . she picked the tidy package up and went tiredly away with it into the shadows where the hedge met the garage.

XIII

O'Banion raised his head groggily from the fly-leaf of his *Blackstone* and the neat inscription written there:

The law doth punish man or woman
That steals the goose from off the common,
But let the greater felon loose,
That steals the common from the goose,

—a piece of eighteenth-century japery which O'Banion deplored. However, it had been written there by Opdycke when he was in law school, and the Opdyckes were a darn fine family. Princeton people, of course, but nobody minded.

All this flickered through his mind as he swam up out of sleep, along with "What's the matter with my head?" because any roaring that loud must be in his ears; it would be too incredible anywhere else, and "What's the matter with the light?"

Then he was fully awake, and on his feet. "My *God!*"

He ran to the door and snatched it open. Flame squirted at him as if from a hose; in a split second he felt his eyebrows disappear. He yelled and staggered back from it, and it pursued him. He turned and dove out the window, landing clumsily on his stomach with his fists clenched over his solar plexus. His own weight drove the fists deep, and for a full minute he lay groaning for air. At last he got up, shook himself, and pelted around the house to the front. One fire engine was already standing by the curb. There was a police car and the knot of bug-eyed spectators who spring apparently out of the ground at the scene of any accident anywhere at any hour. At the far end of the Bittelman lot, there was a sharp scream of rubber and a glare of lights as a taxicab pulled in as close to the police barrier as it could get. The door was already open; a figure left it, half running, half thrown out by the sudden stop.

"Sue!" But no one heard him—everyone else was yelling too: "Look!" "Somebody stop her!" "Hey!" "Hey, you!"

O'Banion backed off a little to cup his hands and yell again, when directly over his head a cheerful small voice said, "Mommy runs *fast!*"

"Robin! You're all right—" He was perched on top of the fire engine with one arm around the shining brass bell, looking like a Botticelli seraph. Someone beside him—good heavens, it was Miss Schmidt, disheveled and bright-eyed, wrapped up in some tentlike garment—Miss Schmidt screamed, "Stop her, stop her, I've got the baby here!"

Robin said to Miss Schmidt, "Tonio runs fast too, shall we?"

Now they were all yelling at O'Banion, but in four paces he could hear nothing but the roar ahead of him. He had never seen a house burn like this, all over, all at once. He took the porch steps in one bound and had just time to turn his shoulder to the door. It was ajar, but couldn't swing fast enough under such an impact. It went down flat and slid, and for one crazy moment O'Banion was riding it like an aquaplane in a sea of fire, for the foyer floor was ablaze. Then the leading edge of the door caught on something and spilled him off. He rolled over twice in fuming debris and then got his feet under him. It was like a particularly bad dream, so familiar, so confusing. He turned completely around to orient himself, found the corridor, and started up it, yelling for Sue at the top of his voice. He saw a left-hand wall lean down toward him and had to scamper back out of the way. It had barely poured its rubble down when he was on, in, and through it. Over the crash and roar, over his own hoarse bellowing, he thought he heard a crazy woman laughing somewhere in the fire. Even in his near-hysteria, he could say, "Not Sue, that's not Sue Martin. . . ." And he was, before he knew it, at and past Sue Martin's room. He flung out a hand. He bounced off the end wall and turned as he did so, like a sprint swimmer, and swung into Sue Martin's room. "Sue! Sue!"

Was he mistaken? Did someone call, "Robin—Robin honey . . . "?

He dropped to his knees, where he could see in relatively clearer air. "Sue, oh Sue!"

She lay half buried in rubble from the fallen ceiling. He threw off scorched and broken two-by-fours and burning lath, took her by the shoulders and lifted her out of the heap of broken plaster—thank the powers for that! it had protected her to some degree. "Sue?"

"Robin," she croaked.

He shook her. "He's all right, he's outside, I saw him."

She opened her eyes and frowned at him. Not at him; at what he had said. "He's here somewhere."

"I saw him. Come on!" He lifted her to her feet, and as she dragged, "It's the truth; do you think *I* would lie to you?"

He felt strength surge into her body. "You forgot to say, 'I, an O'Banion,'" she said, but it didn't hurt. They stumbled to the window and he pushed her through it and leaped after her. For two painful breaths they lay gulping clean air, and then O'Banion got to his feet. His head was spinning and he almost lay down again. He set his jaw and helped Sue Martin up. "Too close!" he shouted. Holding her up, he half-dragged her no more than a step when she suddenly straightened, and with unexpected and irresistible strength leapt back toward the burning wall, pulling him with her. He caught at her to regain his balance, and she put her arms tight around him. "The wall!" he screamed, as it leaned out over them. She said nothing, but her arms tightened even more, and he could have moved more easily if he had been bound to a post with steel chains. The wall came down then, thunder and sparks, like the end of the world; madly, it occurred to him just then that he could solve one of his problem cases by defining the unorthodox contract under suit as a stock certificate.

But instead of dying he took a stinging blow on his right shoulder, and that was all. He opened his eyes. He and Sue Martin still stood locked together, and all around them was flame like a flower-bed with the rough outline of the house wall and its peaked roof. Around their feet was the four-foot circular frame of the attic vent, which had ringed them like a quoit.

The woman slumped in his arms, and he lifted her and picked his way, staggering, into the friendly dark and the welcome hands of the firemen. But when they tried to lift her away from him she held his arm and would not let go. "Put me down, just put me down," she said. "I'm all right. Put me down."

They did and she leaned against O'Banion. He said, "We're okay now. We'll go up to the road. Don't mind about us." The firemen hesitated, but when they began to walk, they were apparently reassured, and ran back to their work. Hopeless work, O'Banion amended. But for a few sagging studs and the two chimneys, the house was little more than a pit of flames.

"Is Robin really—"

"Shh. He's really. Miss Schmidt got him out, I think. Anyway, he's sitting on the fire engine enjoying every minute. He watched you going in. He approves of your speed."

"You—"

"I saw you too. I yelled."

"And then you came after me." They walked a slow pace or so. "Why?"

Robin was safe, of course, he was about to say, so you didn't have to—and then there was within him a soundless white flash that lit up all he had ever done and been, everything he had read, people and places and ideas. Where he had acted right, he felt the right proven; where he had been wrong, he could see now the right in full force, even when for years he had justified his wrong. He saw fully now what old Sam Bittelman had almost convinced him of intellectually with his searching questions. He had fought away Sam's suggestion that there was something ludicrous, contradictory about the law and its pretensions to permanence. Now he saw that the law, as he knew it, was not under attack at all. As long as a man treated the body of law like a great stone buttress, based in bedrock and propping up civilization, he was fortifying a dead thing which could only kill the thing it was built to uphold. But if he saw civilization as an intricate, *moving entity,* the function of law changed. It was governor, stabilizer, inhibitor, *control* of something dynamic and progressive, subject to the punishments and privileges of evolution like a living thing. His whole idea of the hair-splitting search for "precedent" as a refining process in law was wrong. It was an adaptive process instead. The suggestion that not one single law is common to all human cultures, past and present, was suddenly no insult to law at all, but a living compliment; to nail a culture to permanent laws now seemed as ridiculous a concept as man conventionally refusing to shed his scales and his gills.

And with this revelation of the viability of man and his works, O'Banion experienced a profound realignment in his (or was it really his) attitude toward himself, his effortful preoccupation to defend and justify his blood and breeding and his gentleman's place in the world. It came to him now that although the law may say here that men are born equal, and there that they must receive equal treatment before the law, no one but a complete fool would insist that men *are* equal. Men, wherever they come from, whatever they claim for themselves, are only what's in their heads and what's in their hearts. The purest royal blood that yields a weak king will yield a failure; a strong peasant can rise higher and accomplish more, and if what he accomplishes is compatible with human good, he is surely no worse than a beneficent king. Over and above anything else, however, shone the fact that a good man needs least of all to prove it by claiming that he comes from a line of good men. And for him to assume the privileges and postures of the landed gentry after the land is gone is pure buffoonery. Time enough for sharp vertical differentiations between men when the differences become so great that the highest may not cross-breed with the lowest; until then, in the broad view, differences are so subtle as to be negligible, and the concept "to marry out of one's class" belongs with the genesis of hippogriffs and gryphons—in mythology.

All this, and a thousand times more, unfolded and was clear to O'Banion in this illuminated instant, so short it took virtually no time at all, so bright it lit up all the days of his past and part of his future as well. And it had happened between pace and pace, when Sue Martin said, "You followed me. Why?"

"I love you," he said instantly.

"Why?" she whispered.

He laughed joyously. "It doesn't matter."

Sue Martin—*Sue Martin!*—began to cry.

XIV

Phil Halvorsen opened his eyes and saw that the house was on fire. He lay still, watching the flames feed, and thought, isn't this what I was waiting for?

Now there can be an end to it, he thought peacefully. Now I never need worry again that I'm wrong to be as I am, and other people's needs, the appetites and rituals of the great Average will no longer accuse me. I cannot be excluded unless I exist, so here's an end to being excluded. I cannot be looked down on when I can no longer be seen.

The ceiling began to develop a tan patch, and hot white powder fell from it to his face. He covered it with the pillow. He was resigned to later, final agonies because they would be final, but he saw no reason to put up with the preliminaries. Just then most of the plaster came down on him. It didn't hurt much, and it meant the thing would be over sooner than he thought.

He heard faintly, over the colossal roaring, a woman scream. He lay still. As much as anyone—perhaps more—he would ordinarily be concerned about the others. But not now. Not now. Such concern is for a man who expects to live with a conscience afterward.

Something—it sounded like an inside wall—went down very near. It jolted the foot of his bed and he felt its hot exhalation and the taste of its soot, but otherwise it did not reach him. "So come on," he said tightly, "get it over with, will you?" and hurled the pillow away.

As if in direct and obedient answer the ceiling over him opened up—*up;* apparently a beam had broken and was tipping down into an adjoining room, upward here. Then the tangle of stringers it carried fell away and started down. High above was blackness, suddenly rent by smoky orange light—inside of the roof, a section of which was falling in with the stringers.

"All right," said Halvorsen, as if someone had asked him a question. He closed his eyes.

He closed his eyes on a flash of something like an inner and unearthly light, and time stood still . . . or perhaps it was only that subjectively he had all the time in the world to examine this shadowless internal cosmos.

Most immediately, it laid out before him the sequence of events which had brought him here, awaiting death on a burning bed. In this sequence a single term smote him with that "well, of *course!*" revelation that rewarded his plodding, directive thoughts when they were successful for him. The term was "Average," and his revelation came like a burst of laughter: for anyone else this would have been a truism, an inarguable axiom; like a fool he had let his convoluted thinking breeze past "Average," use "Average," worry about "Average" without ever looking at it.

But "Average"—Average Appetite—was here for him to see, a line drawn from side to side on a huge graph. And all over the graph were spots—millions of them. (He was in a place where he could actually see and comprehend "millions.") On that line lived this creation, this demigod, to whom he had felt subservient for so long, whose hungers and whose sense of fitness ought to have been—*had* been—Halvorsen's bench-mark, his reference point. Halvorsen had always felt himself member of a minority—a minority which shrank as he examined it, and he was always examining it. All the world catered to Average Man and his "normal" urges, and this must be proper, for he was aware of the reciprocities: Average Man got these things because these things were what Average Man wanted and needed.

Want and need . . . and there was the extraordinary discovery he had made when Bitty asked him: if people really needed it, would there have to be so much high-pressure salesmanship?

This he threw on the graph like a transparent overlay; it too bore a line from side to side, but much lower down, indicating with much more accuracy just how interested Average Man was in the specific appetite about which he made so much noise. Now bend close and look at those millions of spots—individual people all, each with his true need for the kind of cultural pressure which was driving a man, here, to his death from guilt.

The first thing Halvorsen saw was that the dots were scattered so widely that the actual number falling on the line Average Man was negligible: there were countless millions more un-average people. It came to him that those who obey the gospel of Average Man are, in their efforts to be like the mass of humanity, obeying the dictates of one of the smallest minorities of all. The next thing to strike him was that it took the presence of *all* these dots to place that line just where it was; there was no question of better, or worse, or more or less fit. Except for the few down here and their opposite numbers up there, the handful of sick, insane, incomplete or distorted individuals whose sexual appetites were nonexistent or extreme, the vast majority above and below the true average were basically "normal." And here where he, Halvorsen might appear on the graph—he had plenty of company.

He'd never known that! The magazine covers, the advertisements, the dirty jokes—they hadn't let him know it.

He understood now, the mechanism of this cultural preoccupation; it came to him in the recollection that he had appeared at work for three hundred consecutive working days and nobody noticed his ears. And then one day a sebaceous cyst in his left lobe had become infected, and the doctor removed it and he showed up at work with a bandage covering his ear. *Everybody began to think about Halvorsen's ear!* Every interview had to begin with an explanation of his ear or the applicant would keep straying his attention to it. And he'd noticed, too, that after he explained about the cyst, the interviewee would always glance at Halvorsen's other ear before he got back to business. Now, in this silver place where all interrelationships were true ones, he could equate his covered and noticeable ear with a Bikini bathing suit, and see clearly how normal interest-disinterest—acceptance—can be put under forced draft.

It came to him also *why* this particular cultural matrix did this to itself. In its large subconscious, it probably knew quite clearly the true status of its sensual appetites. It must reason, then, that unless it kept these appetites whipped up to a froth at all times, it might not increase itself, and it felt it must increase. This was not a pretty thought, but neither is the pounce of a cat on a baby bird; yet one cannot argue with the drive behind it.

So it was that Halvorsen's reasons for not living ceased to be reasons; with the purest of truth he could say I am not unmanned; I am not unfit; I am not abnormal . . . I am not alone.

All this in no-time, as he closed his eyes to await the mass even now falling on him. And the reflex of reflexes acted just as eyelids met; he spun off the bed, bounced out of the nearby window, and was on the grass outside as the ceiling and walls together met the floor in a gout of flame.

XV

The girl climbed up to the front seat of the fire engine. "Move over."

Miss Schmidt swung her worried gaze away from the burning house, and said in a preoccupied tone, "I don't think you'd be allowed to, little girl. We're from that hou—why, it's Mary Haunt!"

"Didn't recognize me, huh?" said Mary Haunt. She swung a

hip and shunted Miss Schmidt over. "Can't say I blame you. What a mess!" she said, indicating the house.

"Mr. O'Banion is in there; he went after Mrs. Martin. And have you seen Mr. Halvorsen?"

"No."

"Tonio! Tonio!" Robin suddenly cried.

"Shh, dear. He'll be along."

"Dare he *iss!* Dare he *iss! Mom*ee*!*" he shrieked, "Come see my fire engine, shall we?"

"Oh, thank God, thank God they're safe," said Miss Schmidt. She hugged Robin until he grunted.

"I'm all choked up," growled Mary Haunt. Again she made the angry gesture at the house. "*What* a mess. Everything I own— the war-paint, the clothes, all my magazines—everything, gone. You know what that means. I—"

I've got to go home now. And it was here, on the slightest matter of phrasing that the strange flash of silver suffused Mary Haunt; not under the descending scythe of Death, nor under the impact of soul found, heart found: just for the nudge of a word, she had her timeless instant.

All her life and the meaning of her life and all the things in it: the dimity curtains and home-baked bread, Jackie and Seth whamming away at each other for the privilege of carrying her books, the spice-shelf and the daffodils under the parlor windows. She'd loved it so, and reigned over it; and mostly, she'd been a gentle princess and ruled kindly.

Did they throw you out, gal?

She'd never known where it started, how it came about, until now. Now, with astonishment, she did. Daddy started it, before she was old enough to walk, Daddy one of the millions who had applauded a child actress called Shirley Temple, one of the thousands who had idolized her, one of the hundreds who had deified her. "Little Mary Hollywood," he'd called his daughter, and it had been "When you're in pictures, honey—" Every morning was a fountain to empty the reservoir of his dreams; every night he filled again from the depthless well of his ambition for her.

And everyone believed him. Mom came to believe him, and her kid brother, and finally everyone in town. They had to; Daddy's unswerving, undoubting conviction overrode any alternatives, and she herself clinched it, just by being what she was, an exquisite child exquisitely groomed, who grew more beautiful (by Hollywood standards) every year. She wanted what every child wants: loving attention. She got it in fullest measure. She wanted to do what every child wants to do: gain the approval of her elders. She tried; and indeed, no other course was open to her.

Did they throw you out, gal?

Perhaps Daddy might have outgrown it; or if not, perhaps he'd have known, or found out, how to accomplish his dream in a real world. But Daddy died when she was six, and Mom took over his dream as if it had been a flower from his dead hand. She did not nourish it; she pressed it between the leaves of her treasured memories of him. It was a live thing, true, but arrested at the intensity and the formlessness of his hopes for her when she was six. She encouraged the child only to want to be in pictures, and to be sure she would be; it never occurred to her that there might be things for the child to learn. Her career was coming; it was coming like Christmas.

But no one knew when.

And when she cleaned house, they all thought it was sweet, so pretty to watch, but they'd rather take the broom away from her; and when she baked, it was pretty too but not what she was really *for;* and when she read the diet sections in the grocery magazines, that was all right, but the other features—how to make tangerine gravy for duck, how to remove spots from synthetic fibers—"Why, Mary! you'll have a little army worrying about those things for you!"

Movie magazines then, and movies, and waiting, until the day she left.

Did they throw you out, gal?

Screen Society had a feature on Hollywood High School, and it mentioned how many stars and starlets had come from there, and the ages some of them had been when they signed contracts. And suddenly she wasn't the Shirley Temple girl at all, she was older, years older than two girls in the article, the same age as five of them. Yet here she was still, while the whole town waited . . . suppose she never made it? Suppose nothing happened here? And she began to interpret this remark, that look, the other silence, in ways that troubled her, until she wanted to hide, or to drop dead, or leave.

Just like that, leaving was the answer. She told no one, she took what clothes she had that were good, she bought a ticket for just anywhere and wrote thrilling, imaginative, untrue letters at wider and wider intervals. Naïvely she got a job which might mean her Big Break and which actually never would. And at last she reached a point where she would not look back, for wanting home so much; she would not look forward, for knowing there was nothing there; she held herself in a present of futility and purposive refusal to further the ambition she insisted she had; and she had no pleasure and no outlet but anger. She took refuge in her furies; she scorned people and what they did and what they wanted, and told them all so. And she took the picture of Mom standing in front of the house in the spring, with the jonquils all about and the tulips coming, and she wrapped it up in the cotton print Mom had made for her fourteenth birthday and never given her because *Screen Society* had said princess-style for teeners was corny.

Did they throw you out, gal?

Old Sam had asked her that; he knew, even when she didn't. But now, in this strange silver moment, she knew; she knew it all. Yes, they had thrown her out. They had let her be a dead man's dream until she was nearly dead herself. They never let her be Mary Haunt who wanted to fix the new curtains or bake a berry pie, and have a square hedge along the Elm Street side and go to meeting on Sundays. They had marked her destiny on her face and body and on the clothes she wore, and stamped it into her speech and fixed her hair the way they wanted it, and to the bottom of her heart she was angry.

And now, all of a sudden, and for the very first time, it occurred to her that she could, if she wanted, be Mary Haunt her own self, and be it right there at home; that home was the best place to be that very good thing, and she could replace their disappointment with a very real pride. She could be home before the Strawberry Festival at the church; she would wear an apron and get suds on her forehead when she pushed her hair back, the way Bitty did sometimes.

So Mary Haunt sat on a fire engine, next to the high-school librarian who was enveloped in a tremendous raincoat, saying that everything was burned up, lost; and about to say, "I've got to go home now." But she said, "I can go home now." She looked into Miss Schmidt's eyes and smiled a smile the older woman had never seen before. "I can, I can! I can go home now!" Mary Haunt sang. Impulsively she took Miss Schmidt's hand and squeezed it. She looked into her face and laughed, "I'm not mad any more, not at you or anybody . . . and I've been a little stinker and I'm sorry; I'm going *home!*" And Miss Schmidt looked at the smudged face, the scorched hair drawn back into a childish ponytail and held by a rubber band, the spotless princess dress. "Why," said Miss Schmidt, "you're beautiful, just beautiful!" "I'm not. I'm seventeen, only seventeen," Mary Haunt said out of a wild happiness, "and I'm going home and bake a cake." And she hugged her mother's picture and smiled; even the ruined house did not glow quite this way.

EXCERPT FROM FIELD EXPEDITION [NOTEBOOK]: [! ! !] Did it ever work! [You]'d think these specimens had used Synapse Beta sub Sixteen all their lives! If [we] had a [tenth] as much stamina [we] could [lie down] in a [bed] of paradoxes and go to [sleep].

[We] will observe for a [short period] longer, and then pack up and leave. This is a [fascinating] place to visit, but [I] wouldn't want to [live] here.

XVI

It was October, and possibly the last chance they'd have for a picnic, and the day agreed and was beautiful for them. They found a fine spot where a stand of birch grew on both sides of an old split-rail fence, and a brook went by just out of sight. After they were finished O'Banion lay on his stomach in the sun, and thoughtfully scratched his upper lip with a bit of straw.

His wife laughed softly.

"Hm?"

"You're thinking about the Bittelmans again."

"How'd you know?"

"Just used to it. When you go off into yourself and look astonished and mystified and annoyed all at once, it's the Bittelmans again."

"Harmless hobby," said Halvorsen, and smiled.

"Is it, Phil? Tonio, how would you like me to go all pouty and coy and complain that you've spent more time thinking about them than about me?"

"Do by all means go all pouty and coy. I'll divorce you."

"Tony!"

"Well," he said lazily, "I had so much fun marrying you in the first place that it might be worth doing again. Where's Robin?"

"Right h—Oh, dear, *Robin!*"

Down in the cleft, where the brook gurgled, Robin's voice answered instantly. "Frogs here, Mommy. Deelicious!"

"Does he eat 'em raw?" asked Halvorsen mildly.

Sue laughed. "That just means 'pretty' or 'desirable' or even 'bright green.' Robin, don't you dare get wet, you promise me?"

"I promise me," said the voice.

"And don't go away!"

"I don't."

"Why don't they show up?" demanded O'Banion. "Just once, that's all I'd ever want. Just show their faces and answer two questions."

"Why don't who—oh, Sam and Bitty. What two questions?"

"What they did to us, how and why."

"That's one question, counselor?" asked Halvorsen.

"Yes. Two: What they are."

"Now, why'd you say 'what' instead of 'who'?"

"It comes to that." He rolled over and sat up. "Honey, would you mind if I ran down everything we've found out so far, just once more?"

"Summarize and rest your case?"

"I don't know about resting it . . . reviewing the brief."

"I often wonder why you call it a brief," Halvorsen chuckled.

O'Banion rose and went to the fence. Putting one hand on a slender birch trunk, he hopped upward, turning, to come to rest sitting on the top rail. "Well, one thing I'm sure of: Sam and Bitty could *do* things to people, and they did it to all of us. And I refuse to believe that they did it with logic and persuasion."

"They could be pretty persuasive."

"It was more than that," O'Banion said impatiently. "What they did to me changed everything about me."

"How very intriguing."

"Everything about the way I *think,* hussy. I can look back on that now and realize that I was roped, thrown, and notched. When he wanted me to answer questions I had to answer them, no matter what I was thinking. When he was through with me he turned me loose and made me go back to my business as if nothing had happened. Miss Schmidt told me the same thing." He shifted his weight on the rail and said excitedly, "Now there's our prize exhibit. All of us were—changed—by this thing, but Reta—she's a *really* different person."

"She wasn't more changed than the others," said Sue soberly. "She's thirty-eight years old. It's an interesting age because when you're there and look five years older, and then spruce up the way she did and look five years younger, it looked like twenty years' difference, not ten. That's all cosmetics and clothes, though. The real difference is as quiet and deep as—well, Phil here."

Again Halvorsen found a smile. "Perhaps you're right. She shifted from library to teaching. It was a shift from surrounding herself with other people's knowledge to surrounding other people with hers. She's alive."

"I'll say. Boyfriend too."

"Quiet and deep," said O'Banion thoughtfully, swinging his feet. "That's right. All you get out of Halvorsen when you ask him about it is a smile like a light going on and, 'Now it's right for me to be me.'"

"That's it—all of it," chuckled Halvorsen happily.

"And Mary Haunt, bless her. Second happiest child I ever saw. *Robin! Are you all right?*"

"Yis!" came the voice.

"I'm still not satisfied," said O'Banion. "I have the feeling we're staring at very petty and incidental results of some very important cause. In a moment of acute stress I made a decision which affected my whole life."

"*Our.*"

He blew her a kiss. "Reta Schmidt says the same thing, though she wouldn't go into detail. And maybe that's what Halvorsen means when he says, '*Now,* it's right for me . . .' *You* annoy me."

"Sir!" she cried with mock horror.

He laughed. "You know what I mean. Only you got exposed to the Bittelmans and didn't change. Everybody else got wonderful," he smiled, "You just stayed wonderful. Now what's so special about you?"

"Must we sit here and be—"

"Shush. Think back. Was there any *different* kind of thing that happened to you that night, some kind of emergency thinking you did that was above and beyond anything you thought you could do?"

"Not that I remember."

Suddenly he brought his fist down on his thigh. "There *was!* Remember right after we got out of the house, the wall fell on us? You dragged me back and held me still and that attic vent dropped right around us?"

"That. Yes, I remember. But it wasn't special. It just made sense."

"*Sense?* I'd like to put a computer on that job—after scorching it half through and kicking it around a while. Somehow you calculated how fast that thing was falling and how much ground it would cover when it hit. You computed that against our speed outward. You located the attic vent opening and figured where it would land, and whether or not it could contain us both. Then you estimated our speed *if* we went toward the safe spot and concluded that we could make it. *Then* you went into action, more or less over my dead body to boot. All that in—" He closed his eyes to relive the moment. "—all of one and a half seconds absolute tops. It wasn't *special?*"

"No, it wasn't," she said positively. "It was an emergency, don't you see? A real emergency, not only because we might get hurt, but in terms of all we were to each other and all we could be if only you—"

"Well, I did," he smiled. "But I still don't understand you. You mean you think more, not less—widen your scope instead of narrowing your focus when it's that kind of emergency? You can think of all those things at once, better and faster and more accurately?"

Halvorsen suddenly lunged and caught O'Banion's foot, pulling it sharply upward. He shouted *"Yoop!"* His right hand whipped up and back and scrabbled at the tree-trunk; his torso twisted and his left hand shot straight down. His legs flailed and straightened; for a moment he see-sawed on the rail on his kidneys. At last he got his left hand on the rail and pulled himself upward to sit again. "Hey! What do you think you're—"

"Proving a point," said Halvorsen. "Look, Tony: without warning you were thrown off balance. What did you do? You reached out for that tree-trunk without looking—got it, too; you knew just how fast and how far to go. But at the same time you put your left hand straight down, ready to catch your weight if you went down to the ground. Meantime you banged around with your legs and shifted your weight this way just enough to make a new balance on top. Now tell me: did you sit there after I pushed you and figure all those things out, one by one?"

"By golly no. Snop—snap—synapses."

"What?"

"Synapses. Sort of pathways in the brain that get paved better and better as you do something over and over. After a while they happen without conscious thought. Keeping your balance is that kind of thing, on the motor level. But don't tell me you have a sort of . . . personal-cultural inner ear—something that makes you reach reflexively in terms of your past and your future and . . . but that's what happened to me that night!" He stared at Halvorsen. "You figured that out long ago, you and your IBM head!"

"It always happens if the emergency's a bad one," Sue said composedly. "Sometimes when you don't even know it is an emergency. But what's remarkable? Aren't drowning men supposed to see their whole lives pass before them?"

"Did you say that always happens with your emergencies?"

"Well, doesn't it?"

Suddenly he began to chuckle softly, and at her questioning look he said, "You remind me of something a psychologist told me once. A man was asked to describe his exact sensations on getting drunk. 'Just like anybody else,' he says 'Well, describe it,' says the doctor. The man says, 'Well, first your face gets a little flushed and your tongue gets thick, and after a while your ears begin to wiggle—' Sue, honey, I've got news for you. Maybe you react like that in important moments, a great big shiny flash of truth and proportional relationships, but believe me, other people don't. I never did until that night. *That's it!*" he yelled at that top of his voice.

From down the slope came a clear little voice, "Wash 'at noice?"

Sue and Halvorsen smiled at one another and then O'Banion said earnestly, "That's what Bitty and Sam gave us—a synaptic reflex like the equilibrium mechanisms, but bigger—much bigger. A human being is an element in a whole culture, and the culture itself is alive . . . I suppose the species could be called, as a whole, a living thing. And when we found ourselves in a stress situation which was going to affect us signally—dangerously, or just importantly—we reacted to it in the way I did just now when you pushed me—only on a cultural level. It's as if Sam and Bitty had found a way to install or develop that 'balancing' mechanism in us. It resolved some deep personal conflict of Halvorsen's; it snapped Mary out of a dangerous delusion and Miss Schmidt out of a dangerous retreat. And, well, you know about me."

"I can't believe people don't think that way in emergencies!" she said, dazed.

"Maybe some do," said Halvorsen. "Come to think of it, people do some remarkable things under sudden stress; they make not-obvious but very right choices under pressure, like the man who cracks a joke and averts a panic or the boy who throws himself on a grenade to save his squad. They've surveyed themselves in terms of all they are and measured that against their surroundings and all it is—all in a split fraction of a second. I guess everyone has it. Some of it."

"Whatever this synapse is, the Bittelmans gave it to us . . . yes, and maybe set the house on fire too . . . why? Testing? Testing what—just us, or human beings? *What are they?*" demanded the lawyer.

"Gone, that's what," said Halvorsen.

For a very brief time, he was wrong to say that.

EXCERPT FROM FIELD EXPEDITION [NOTEBOOK]: [Our] last [hour] here, so [we] [induced] three of the test specimens to [locus B] for final informal observation. [Smith] pretends to a certain [chagrin]. After all, [he] [says] all [we] did was to come [sizable abstract number] of [terrestrially immeasurable distance unit]s, forgoing absolutely the company of [our] [   ] and the pleasures of the [   ]; strain [our] ingenuity and our [technical equipment] to the [break]ing point, even getting trapped into using that [miserable impractical] power supply and [charge]ing it up every [month]—all to detect and analyze the incidence of Synapse Beta sub Sixteen. And here these specimens sit, locating and defining the Synapse during a brief and idle conversation! Actually, [I] [think] [Smith] is [pleased] with them for it. We shall now [dismantle] the [widget] and the [wadget] and [take off].

Robin was watching a trout.

"Tsst! Tsst!"

He was watching more than the trout, really; he was watching its shadow. It had occurred to him that perhaps the shadow wasn't a shadow, but another and fuzzier kind of fish which wouldn't let the more clear-cut one get away from over it, so maybe that was why the trout kept hanging into the current, hanging and *zoom!* darting forward. But he never was fast enough for the fuzzy one, which stayed directly under him no matter what.

"Tsst! Robin!"

He looked up, and the trout was forgotten. He filled his powerful young lungs with air and his face with joy, and then made a heroic effort and stifled his noisy delight in obedience to that familiar finger-on-lips and its explosive *"Shh!"*

Barely able to contain himself, he splashed straight across the brook, shoes and all, and threw himself into Bitty's arms. "Ah Robin!" said the woman, "wicked little boy. Are you a wicked little boy!"

"Yis. Bitty-bitty-BITTY!"

"Shh. Look who's with me." She put him down, and there stood old Sam. "Hey-y-y-y, boy?"

"Ah Sam!" Robin clasped his hands together and got them between his knees, bending almost double in delight. "Ware you *been*, Sam?"

"Around," said Sam. "Listen, Robin, we came to say goodbye. We're going away now."

"Don't go 'way."

"We have to," said Bitty. She knelt and hugged him. "Goodbye, darling."

"Shake," said Sam gravely.

"Shake, rattle an' roll," said Robin with equal sobriety.

"Ready, Sam?"

"All set."

Swiftly they took off their bodies, folded them neatly and put them in two small green plastic cases. On one was lettered [WIDGET] and on the other [WADGET], but of course Robin was too young to read. Besides, he had something else to astonish him. "Boff!" he cried. "Googie!"

Boff and Googie [waved] at him and he waved back. They picked up the plastic cases and threw them into a sort of bubble that was somehow there, and [walked] in after them. Then they [went].

Robin turned away and without once looking back, climbed the slope and ran to Sue. He flung himself into her lap and uttered the long, whistle-like wail that preceded his rare bouts with bitter tears.

"Why *darling*, whatever happened? What *is* it? Did you bump your—"

He raised a flushed and contorted face to her. "Boff gone," he said wetly. "Oh, oh-h-h, Boff an' Googie gone."

He cried most of the way home, and never mentioned Boff again.

INCIDENTAL [NOTES] ON FIELD REPORT: **The discovery of total incidence and random use of Synapse Beta sub Sixteen in a species is unique in the known [cosmos]; yet introduction of the mass of data taken on the Field**

Expedition into the [master] [computer] alters its original [dictum] not at all: the presence of this Synapse in a species ensures its survival.

In the particular case at hand, the species undoubtedly bears, and will always bear, the [curse] of interpersonal and intercultural frictions, due to the amount of paradox possible. Where so many actions, decisions, and organizational activities can occur uncontrolled by the Synapse and its [universal-interrelational] modifying effect, paradox must result. On the other [hand], any species with such a concentration of the Synapse, even in partial use, will not destroy itself and very probably cannot be destroyed by anything.

Prognosis positive.

Their young are delightful. [I] [feel good]. [Smith], [I] [forgive] [you].

IT

It walked in the woods.

It was never born. It existed. Under the pine needles the fires burn, deep and smokeless in the mold. In heat and in darkness and decay there is growth. There is life and there is growth. It grew, but it was not alive. It walked unbreathing through the woods, and thought and saw and was hideous and strong, and it was not born and it did not live. It grew and moved about without living.

It crawled out of the darkness and hot damp mold into the cool of a morning. It was huge. It was lumped and crusted with its own hateful substances, and pieces of it dropped off as it went its way, dropped off and lay writhing, and stilled, and sank putrescent into the forest loam.

It had no mercy, no laughter, no beauty. It had strength and great intelligence. And—perhaps it could not be destroyed. It crawled out of its mound in the wood and lay pulsing in the sunlight for a long moment. Patches of it shone wetly in the golden glow, parts of it were nubbled and flaked. And whose dead bones had given it the form of a man?

It scrabbled painfully with its half-formed hands, beating the ground and the bole of a tree. It rolled and lifted itself up on its crumbling elbows, and it tore up a great handful of herbs and shredded them against its chest, and it paused and gazed at the gray-green juices with intelligent calm. It wavered to its feet, and seized a young sapling and destroyed it, folding the slender trunk back on itself again and again, watching attentively the useless, fibered splinters. And it snatched up a fear-frozen field creature, crushing it slowly, letting blood and pulpy flesh and fur ooze from between its fingers, run down and rot on the forearms.

It began searching.

Kimbo drifted through the tall grasses like a puff of dust, his bushy tail curled tightly over his back and his long jaws agape. He ran with an easy lope, loving his freedom and the power of his flanks and furry shoulders. His tongue lolled listlessly over his lips. His lips were black and serrated, and each tiny pointed liplet swayed with his doggy gallop. Kimbo was all dog, all healthy animal.

He leaped high over a boulder and landed with a startled yelp as a longeared cony shot from its hiding place under the rock. Kimbo hurtled after it, grunting with each great thrust of his legs. The rabbit bounced just ahead of him, keeping its distance, its ears flattened on its curving back and its little legs nibbling away at distance hungrily. It stopped, and Kimbo pounced, and the rabbit shot away at a tangent and popped into a hollow log. Kimbo yelped again and rushed snuffling at the log, and knowing his failure, curvetted but once around the stump and ran on into the forest. The thing that watched from the wood raised its crusted arms and waited for Kimbo.

Kimbo sensed it there, standing dead-still by the path. To him it was a bulk which smelled of carrion not fit to roll in, and he snuffled distastefully and ran to pass it.

The thing let him come abreast and dropped a heavy twisted fist on him. Kimbo saw it coming and curled up tight as he ran, and the hand clipped stunningly on his rump, sending him rolling and yipping down the slope. Kimbo straddled to his feet, shook his head, shook his body with a deep growl, came back to the silent thing with green murder in his eyes. He walked stiffly, straight-legged, his tail as low as his lowered head and a ruff of fury round his neck. The thing raised its arms again, waited.

Kimbo slowed, then flipped himself through the air at the

monster's throat. His jaws closed on it; his teeth clicked together through a mass of filth, and he fell choking and snarling at its feet. The thing leaned down and struck twice, and after the dog's back was broken, it sat beside him and began to tear him apart.

"Be back in an hour or so," said Alton Drew, picking up his rifle from the corner behind the wood box. His brother laughed.

"Old Kimbo 'bout runs your life, Alton," he said.

"Ah, I know the ol' devil," said Alton. "When I whistle for him for half an hour and he don't show up, he's in a jam or he's treed something wuth shootin' at. The ol' son of a gun calls me by not answerin'."

Cory Drew shoved a full glass of milk over to his nine-year-old daughter and smiled. "You think as much o' that houn'-dog o' yours as I do of Babe here."

Babe slid off her chair and ran to her uncle. "Gonna catch me the bad fella, Uncle Alton?" she shrilled. The "bad fella" was Cory's invention—the one who lurked in corners ready to pounce on little girls who chased the chickens and played around mowing machines and hurled green apples with a powerful young arm at the sides of the hogs, to hear the synchronized thud and grunt; little girls who swore with an Austrian accent like an ex-hired man they had had; who dug caves in haystacks till they tipped over, and kept pet crawfish in tomorrow's milk cans, and rode work horses to a lather in the night pasture.

"Get back here and keep away from Uncle Alton's gun!" said Cory. "If you see the bad fella, Alton, chase him back here. He has a date with Babe here for that stunt of hers last night." The preceding evening, Babe had kindheartedly poured pepper on the cows' salt block.

"Don't worry, kiddo," grinned her uncle, "I'll bring you the bad fella's hide if he don't get me first."

Alton Drew walked up the path toward the wood, thinking about Babe. She was a phenomenon—a pampered farm child. Ah well—she had to be. They'd both loved Clissa Drew, and she'd married Cory, and they had to love Clissa's child. Funny thing, love. Alton was a man's man, and thought things out that way; and his reaction to love was a strong and frightened one. He knew what love was because he felt it still for his brother's wife and would feel it as long as he lived for Babe. It led him through his life, and yet he embarrassed himself by thinking of it. Loving a dog was an easy thing, because you and the old devil could love one another completely without talking about it. The smell of gun smoke and wet fur in the rain were perfume enough for Alton Drew, a grunt of satisfaction and the scream of something hunted and hit were poetry enough. They weren't like love for a human, that choked his throat so he could not say words he could not have thought of anyway. So Alton loved his dog Kimbo and his Winchester for all to see, and let his love for his brother's women, Clissa and Babe, eat at him quietly and unmentioned.

His quick eyes saw the fresh indentations in the soft earth behind the boulder, which showed where Kimbo had turned and leaped with a single surge, chasing the rabbit. Ignoring the tracks, he looked for the nearest place where a rabbit might hide, and strolled over to the stump. Kimbo had been there, he saw, and had been there too late. "You're an ol' fool," muttered Alton. "Y' can't catch a cony by chasin' it. You want to cross him up some way." He gave a peculiar trilling whistle, sure that Kimbo was digging frantically under some nearby stump for a rabbit that was three counties away by now. No answer. A little puzzled, Alton went back to the path. "He never done this before," he said softly.

He cocked his .32–40 and cradled it. At the county fair someone had once said of Alton Drew that he could shoot at a handful of corn and peas thrown in the air and hit only the corn. Once he split a bullet on the blade of a knife and put two candles out. He had no need to fear anything that could be shot at. That's what he believed.

The thing in the woods looked curiously down at what it had done to Kimbo, and tried to moan the way Kimbo had before he died. It stood a minute storing away facts in its foul, unemotional mind. Blood was warm. The sunlight was warm. Things that moved and bore fur had a muscle to force the thick liquid through tiny tubes in their bodies. The liquid coagulated after a time. The liquid on rooted green things was thinner and the loss of a limb did not mean loss of life. It was very interesting, but the thing, the mold with a mind, was not pleased. Neither was it displeased. Its accidental urge was a thirst for knowledge, and it was only—interested.

It was growing late, and the sun reddened and rested awhile on the hilly horizon, teaching the clouds to be inverted flames. The thing threw up its head suddenly, noticing the dusk. Night was ever a strange thing, even for those of us who have known it in life. It would have been frightening for the monster had it been capable of fright, but it could only be curious; it could only reason from what it had observed.

What was happening? It was getting harder to see. Why? It threw its shapeless head from side to side. It was true—things were dim, and growing dimmer. Things were changing shape, taking on a new and darker color. What did the creatures it had crushed and torn apart see? How did they see? The larger one, the one that had attacked, had used two organs in its head. That must have been it, because after the thing had torn off two of the dog's legs it had struck at the hairy muzzle; and the dog, seeing the blow coming, had dropped folds of skin over the organs—closed its eyes. Ergo, the dog saw with its eyes. But then after the dog was dead, and its body still, repeated blows had had no effect on the eyes. They remained open and staring. The logical conclusion was, then, that a being that had ceased to live and breathe and move about lost the use of its eyes. It must be that to lose sight was, conversely, to die. Dead things did not walk about. They lay down and did not move. Therefore the thing in the wood concluded that it must be dead, and so it lay down by the path, not far away from Kimbo's scattered body, lay down and believed itself dead.

Alton Drew came up through the dusk to the wood. He was frankly worried. He whistled again, and then called, and there was still no response, and he said again, "The ol' fleabus never done this before," and shook his heavy head. It was past milking time, and Cory would need him. "Kimbo!" he roared. The cry echoed through the shadows, and Alton flipped on the safety catch of his rifle and put the butt on the ground beside the path. Leaning on it, he took off his cap and scratched the back of his head, wondering. The rifle butt sank into what he thought was soft earth; he staggered and stepped into the chest of the thing that lay beside the path. His foot went up to the ankle in its yielding rottenness, and he swore and jumped back.

"*Whew!* Somp'n sure dead as hell there! Ugh!" He swabbed at his boot with a handful of leaves while the monster lay in the growing blackness with the edges of the deep footprint in its chest sliding into it, filling it up. It lay there regarding him dimly out of its muddy eyes, thinking it was dead because of the darkness, watching the articulation of Alton Drew's joints, wondering at this new uncautious creature.

Alton cleaned the butt of his gun with more leaves and went on up the path, whistling anxiously for Kimbo.

Clissa Drew stood in the door of the milk shed, very lovely in red-checked gingham and a blue apron. Her hair was clean yellow, parted in the middle and stretched tautly back to a heavy braided knot. "Cory! Alton!" she called a little sharply.

"Well?" Cory responded gruffly from the barn, where he was stripping off the Ayrshire. The dwindling streams of milk plopped pleasantly into the froth of a full pail.

"I've called and called," said Clissa. "Supper's cold, and Babe won't eat until you come. Why—where's Alton?"

Cory grunted, heaved the stool out of the way, threw over the stanchion lock, and slapped the Ayrshire on the rump. The cow backed and filled like a towboat, clattered down the line and out into the barnyard. "Ain't back yet."

"Not back?" Clissa came in and stood beside him as he sat by the next cow, put his forehead against the warm flank. "But, Cory, he said he'd—"

"Yeh, yeh, I know. He said he'd be back fer the milkin'. I heard him. Well, he ain't."

"And you have to— Oh, Cory, I'll help you finish up. Alton would be back if he could. Maybe he's—"

"Maybe he's treed a blue jay," snapped her husband. "Him an' that damn dog." He gestured hugely with one hand while the other went on milking. "I got twenty-six head o' cows to milk. I got pigs to feed an' chickens to put to bed. I got to toss hay for the mare and turn the team out. I got harness to mend and a wire down in the night pasture. I got wood to split an' carry." He milked for a moment in silence, chewing on his lip. Clissa stood twisting her hands together, trying to think of something to stem the tide. It wasn't the first time Alton's hunting had interfered with the chores. "So I got to go ahead with it. I can't interfere with Alton's spoorin'. Every damn time that hound o' his smells out a squirrel I go without my supper. I'm gettin' sick and—"

"Oh, I'll help you!" said Clissa. She was thinking of the spring, when Kimbo had held four hundred pounds of raging black bear at bay until Alton could put a bullet in its brain, the time Babe had found a bearcub and started to carry it home, and had fallen into a freshet, cutting her head. You can't hate a dog that has saved your child for you, she thought.

"You'll do nothin' of the kind!" Cory growled. "Get back to the house. You'll find work enough there. I'll be along when I can. Dammit, Clissa, don't cry! I didn't mean to— Oh, shucks!" He got up and put his arms around her. "I'm wrought up," he said. "Go on now. I'd no call to speak that way to you. I'm sorry. Go back to Babe. I'll put a stop to this for good tonight. I've had enough. There's work here for four farmers an' all we've got is me an' that . . . that huntsman.

"Go on now, Clissa."

"All right," she said into his shoulder. "But, Cory, hear him out first when he comes back. He might be unable to come back. He might be unable to come back this time. Maybe he . . . he—"

"Ain't nothin' kin hurt my brother that a bullet will hit. He can take care of himself. He's got no excuse good enough this time. Go on, now. Make the kid eat."

Clissa went back to the house, her young face furrowed. If Cory quarreled with Alton now and drove him away, what with the drought and the creamery about to close and all, they just couldn't manage. Hiring a man was out of the question. Cory'd have to work himself to death, and he just wouldn't be able to make it. No one man could. She sighed and went into the house. It was seven o'clock, and the milking not done yet. Oh, why did Alton have to—

Babe was in bed at nine when Clissa heard Cory in the shed, slinging the wire cutters into a corner. "Alton back yet?" they both said at once as Cory stepped into the kitchen; and as she shook her head he clumped over to the stove, and lifting a lid, spat into the coals. "Come to bed," he said.

She laid down her stitching and looked at his broad back. He was twenty-eight, and he walked and acted like a man ten years older, and looked like a man five years younger. "I'll be up in a while," Clissa said.

Cory glanced at the corner behind the wood box where Alton's rifle usually stood, then made an unspellable, disgusted sound and sat down to take off his heavy muddy shoes.

"It's after nine," Clissa volunteered timidly. Cory said nothing, reaching for house slippers.

"Cory, you're not going to—"

"Not going to what?"

"Oh, nothing. I just thought that maybe Alton—"

"Alton!" Cory flared. "The dog goes hunting field mice. Alton goes hunting the dog. Now you want me to go hunting Alton. That's what you want?"

"I just— He was never this late before."

"I won't do it! Go out lookin' for him at nine o'clock in the night? I'll be damned! He has no call to use us so, Clissa."

Clissa said nothing. She went to the stove, peered into the wash boiler, set it aside at the back of the range. When she turned around, Cory had his shoes and coat on again.

"I knew you'd go," she said. Her voice smiled though she did not.

"I'll be back durned soon," said Cory. "I don't reckon he's strayed far. It is late. I ain't feared for him, but—" He broke his 12-gauge shotgun, looked through the barrels, slipped two shells in the breech and a box of them into his pocket. "Don't wait up," he said over his shoulder as he went out.

"I won't," Clissa replied to the closed door, and went back to her stitching by the lamp.

The path up the slope to the wood was very dark when Cory went up it, peering and calling. The air was chill and quiet, and a fetid odor of mold hung in it. Cory blew the taste of it out through impatient nostrils, drew it in again with the next breath, and swore. "Nonsense," he muttered. "Houn' dawg. Huntin', at ten in th' night, too. Alton!" he bellowed. "Alton Drew!" Echoes answered him, and he entered the wood. The huddled thing he passed in the dark heard him and felt the vibrations of his footsteps and did not move because it thought it was dead.

Cory strode on, looking around and ahead and not down since his feet knew the path.

"Alton!"

"That you, Cory?"

Cory Drew froze. That corner of the wood was thickly set and as dark as a burial vault. The voice he heard was choked, quiet, penetrating.

"Alton?"

"I found Kimbo, Cory."

"Where the hell have you been?" shouted Cory furiously. He disliked this pitch-darkness; he was afraid at the tense hopelessness of Alton's voice, and he mistrusted his ability to stay angry at his brother.

"I called him, Cory. I whistled at him, an' the ol' devil didn't answer."

"I can say the same for you, you ... you louse. Why weren't you to milkin'? Where are you? You caught in a trap?"

"The houn' never missed answerin' me before, you know," said the tight, monotonous voice from the darkness.

"Alton! What the devil's the matter with you? What do I care if your mutt didn't answer? Where—"

"I guess because he ain't never died before," said Alton, refusing to be interrupted.

"You *what*?" Cory clicked his lips together twice and then said, "Alton, you turned crazy? What's that you say?"

"Kimbo's dead."

"Kim ... oh! Oh!" Cory was seeing that picture again in his mind—Babe sprawled unconscious in the freshet, and Kimbo raging and snapping against a monster bear, holding her back until Alton could get there. "What happened, Alton?" he asked more quietly.

"I aim to find out. Someone tore him up."

"Tore him up?"

"There ain't a bit of him left tacked together, Cory. Every damn joint in his body tore apart. Guts out of him."

"Good God! Bear, you reckon?"

"No bear, nor nothin' on four legs. He's all here. None of him's been et. Whoever done it just killed him an'—tore him up."

"Good God!" Cory said again. "Who could've—" There was a long silence, then. "Come 'long home," he said almost gently. "There's no call for you to set up by him all night."

"I'll set. I aim to be here at sunup, an' I'm goin' to start trackin', an' I'm goin' to keep trackin' till I find the one done this job on Kimbo."

"You're drunk or crazy, Alton."

"I ain't drunk. You can think what you like about the rest of it. I'm stickin' here."

"We got a farm back yonder. Remember? I ain't going to milk twenty-six head o' cows again in the mornin' like I did jest now, Alton."

"Somebody's got to. I can't be there. I guess you'll just have to, Cory."

"You dirty scum!" Cory screamed. "You'll come back with me now or I'll know why!"

Alton's voice was still tight, half-sleepy. "Don't you come no nearer, bud."

Cory kept moving toward Alton's voice.

"I said"—the voice was very quiet now—"*stop where you are.*" Cory kept coming. A sharp click told of the release of the .32–40's safety. Cory stopped.

"You got your gun on me, Alton?" Cory whispered.

"Thass right, bud. You ain't a-trompin' up these tracks for me. I need 'em at sunup."

A full minute passed, and the only sound in the blackness was that of Cory's pained breathing. Finally:

"I got my gun, too, Alton. Come home."

"You can't see to shoot me."

"We're even on that."

"We ain't. I know just where you stand, Cory. I been here four hours."

"My gun scatters."

"My gun kills."

Without another word Cory Drew turned on his heel and stamped back to the farm.

———

Black and liquidescent it lay in the blackness, not alive, not understanding death, believing itself dead. Things that were alive saw
and moved about. Things that were not alive could do neither. It
rested its muddy gaze on the line of trees at the crest of the rise,
and deep within it thoughts trickled wetly. It lay huddled, dividing
its newfound facts, dissecting them as it had dissected live things
when there was light, comparing, concluding, pigeonholing.

The trees at the top of the slope could just be seen, as their
trunks were a fraction of a shade lighter than the dark sky behind
them. At length they, too, disappeared, and for a moment sky and
trees were a monotone. The thing knew it was dead now, and like
many a being before it, it wondered how long it must stay like this.
And then the sky beyond the trees grew a little lighter. That was a
manifestly impossible occurrence, thought the thing, but it could
see it and it must be so. Did dead things live again? That was curious. What about dismembered dead things? It would wait and see.

The sun came hand over hand up a beam of light. A bird
somewhere made a high yawning peep, and as an owl killed a
shrew, a skunk pounced on another, so that the night shift deaths
and those of the day could go on without cessation. Two flowers
nodded archly to each other, comparing their pretty clothes. A
dragonfly nymph decided it was tired of looking serious and
cracked its back open, to crawl out and dry gauzily. The first
golden ray sheared down between the trees, through the grasses,
passed over the mass in the shadowed bushes. "I am alive again,"
thought the thing that could not possibly live. "I am alive, for I see
clearly." It stood up on its thick legs, up into the golden glow. In a
little while the wet flakes that had grown during the night dried in
the sun, and when it took its first steps, they cracked off and a
small shower of them fell away. It walked up the slope to find
Kimbo, to see if he, too, were alive again.

Babe let the sun come into her room by opening her eyes. Uncle
Alton was gone—that was the first thing that ran through her
head. Dad had come home last night and had shouted at mother
for an hour. Alton was plumb crazy. He'd turned a gun on his own
brother. If Alton ever came ten feet into Cory's land, Cory would
fill him so full of holes he'd look like a tumbleweed. Alton was
lazy, shiftless, selfish, and one or two other things of questionable

taste but undoubted vividness. Babe knew her father. Uncle Alton would never be safe in this country.

She bounced out of bed in the enviable way of the very young, and ran to the window. Cory was trudging down to the night pasture with two bridles over his arm, to get the team. There were kitchen noises from downstairs.

Babe ducked her head in the washbowl and shook off the water like a terrier before she toweled. Trailing clean shirt and dungarees, she went to the head of the stairs, slid into the shirt, and began her morning ritual with the trousers. One step down was a step through the right leg. One more, and she was into the left. Then, bouncing step by step on both feet, buttoning one button per step, she reached the bottom fully dressed and ran into the kitchen.

"Didn't Uncle Alton come back a-tall, Mum?"

"Morning, Babe. No, dear." Clissa was too quiet, smiling too much, Babe thought shrewdly. Wasn't happy.

"Where'd he go, Mum?"

"We don't know, Babe. Sit down and eat your breakfast."

"What's a misbegotten, Mum?" the Babe asked suddenly. Her mother nearly dropped the dish she was drying. "Babe! You must never say that again!"

"Oh. Well, why is Uncle Alton, then?"

"Why is he what?"

Babe's mouth muscled around an outsize spoonful of oatmeal. "A misbe—"

"Babe!"

"All right, Mum," said Babe with her mouth full. "Well, why?"

"I told Cory not to shout last night," Clissa said half to herself.

"Well, whatever it means, he isn't," said Babe with finality. "Did he go hunting again?"

"He went to look for Kimbo, darling."

"Kimbo? Oh Mummy, is Kimbo gone, too? Didn't he come back either?"

"No dear. Oh, please, Babe, stop asking questions!"

"All right. Where do you think they went?"

"Into the north woods. Be quiet."

Babe gulped away at her breakfast. An idea struck her; and as she thought of it she ate slower and slower, and cast more and more glances at her mother from under the lashes of her tilted eyes. It would be awful if Daddy did anything to Uncle Alton. Someone ought to warn him.

Babe was halfway to the woods when Alton's .32–40 sent echoes giggling up and down the valley.

Cory was in the south thirty, riding a cultivator and cussing at the team of grays when he heard the gun. "Hoa," he called to the horses, and sat a moment to listen to the sound. "One-two-three. Four," he counted. "Saw someone, blasted away at him. Had a chance to take aim and give him another, careful. My God!" He threw up the cultivator points and steered the team into the shade of three oaks. He hobbled the gelding with swift tosses of a spare strap, and headed for the woods. "Alton a killer," he murmured, and doubled back to the house for his gun. Clissa was standing just outside the door.

"Get shells!" he snapped and flung into the house. Clissa followed him. He was strapping his hunting knife on before she could get a box off the shelf. "Cory—"

"Hear that gun, did you? Alton's off his nut. He don't waste lead. He shot at someone just then, and he wasn't fixin' to shoot pa'tridges when I saw him last. He was out to get a man. Gimme my gun."

"Cory, Babe—"

"You keep her here. Oh, God, this is a helluva mess. I can't stand much more." Cory ran out the door.

Clissa caught his arm: "Cory, I'm trying to tell you. Babe isn't here. I've called, and she isn't here."

Cory's heavy, young-old face tautened. "Babe— Where did you last see her?"

"Breakfast." Clissa was crying now.

"She say where she was going?"

"No. She asked a lot of questions about Alton and where he'd gone."

"Did you say?"

Clissa's eyes widened, and she nodded, biting the back of her hand.

"You shouldn't ha' done that, Clissa," he gritted, and ran

toward the woods. Clissa stood looking after him, and in that moment she could have killed herself.

Cory ran with his head up, straining with his legs and lungs and eyes at the long path. He puffed up the slope to the woods, agonized for breath after the forty-five minutes' heavy going. He couldn't even notice the damp smell of mold in the air.

He caught a movement in a thicket to his right, and dropped. Struggling to keep his breath, he crept forward until he could see clearly. There was something in there, all right. Something black, keeping still. Cory relaxed his legs and torso completely to make it easier for his heart to pump some strength back into them, and slowly raised the 12-gauge until it bore on the thing hidden in the thicket.

"Come out!" Cory said when he could speak.

Nothing happened.

"Come out or by God I'll shoot!" rasped Cory.

There was a long moment of silence, and his finger tightened on the trigger.

"You asked for it," he said, and as he fired the thing leaped sideways into the open, screaming.

It was a thin little man dressed in sepulchral black, and bearing the rosiest baby-face Cory had ever seen. The face was twisted with fright and pain. The man scrambled to his feet and hopped up and down saying over and over, "Oh, my hand. Don't shoot again! Oh, my hand. Don't shoot again!" He stopped after a bit, when Cory had climbed to his feet, and he regarded the farmer out of sad china-blue eyes. "You shot me," he said reproachfully, holding up a little bloody hand. "Oh, my goodness."

Cory said, "Now, who the hell are you?"

The man immediately became hysterical, mouthing such a flood of broken sentences that Cory stepped back a pace and half raised his gun in self-defense. It seemed to consist mostly of "I lost my papers," and "I didn't do it," and "It was horrible. Horrible. Horrible," and "The dead man," and "Oh, don't shoot again."

Cory tried twice to ask him a question, and then he stepped over and knocked the man down. He lay on the ground writhing and moaning and blubbering and putting his bloody hand to his mouth where Cory had hit him.

"Now what's going on around here?"

The man rolled over and sat up. "I didn't do it!" he sobbed. "I didn't. I was walking along and I heard the gun and I heard some swearing and an awful scream and I went over there and peeped and I saw the dead man and I ran away and you came and I hid and you shot me and—"

"Shut up!" The man did, as if a switch had been thrown. "Now," said Cory, pointing along the path, "you say there's a dead man up there?"

The man nodded and began crying in earnest. Cory helped him up. "Follow this path back to my farmhouse," he said. "Tell my wife to fix up your hand. *Don't* tell her anything else. And wait there until I come. Hear?"

"Yes. Thank you. Oh, thank you. *Snff.*"

"Go on now." Cory gave him a gentle shove in the right direction and went alone, in cold fear, up the path to the spot where he had found Alton the night before.

He found him here now, too, and Kimbo. Kimbo and Alton had spent several years together in the deepest friendship; they had hunted and fought and slept together, and the lives they owed each other were finished now. They were dead together.

It was terrible that they died the same way. Cory Drew was a strong man, but he gasped and fainted dead away when he saw what the thing of the mold had done to his brother and his brother's dog.

The little man in black hurried down the path, whimpering and holding his injured hand as if he rather wished he could limp with it. After a while the whimper faded away, and the hurried stride changed to a walk as the gibbering terror of the last hour receded. He drew two deep breaths, said: "My goodness!" and felt almost normal. He bound a linen handkerchief around his wrist, but the hand kept bleeding. He tried the elbow, and that made it hurt. So he stuffed the handkerchief back in his pocket and simply waved the hand stupidly in the air until the blood clotted. He did not see the great moist horror that clumped along behind him, although his nostrils crinkled with is foulness.

The monster had three holes close together on its chest, and one hole in the middle of its slimy forehead. It had three close-set pits in its back and one on the back of its head. These marks were where Alton Drew's bullets had struck and passed through. Half of the monster's shapeless face was sloughed away, and there was a deep indentation on its shoulder. This was what Alton Drew's gun butt had done after he clubbed it and struck at the thing that would not lie down after he put his four bullets through it. When these things happened the monster was not hurt or angry. It only wondered why Alton Drew acted that way. Now it followed the little man without hurrying at all, matching his stride step by step and dropping little particles of muck behind it.

The little man went on out of the wood and stood with his back against a big tree at the forest's edge, and he thought. Enough had happened to him here. What good would it do to stay and face a horrible murder inquest, just to continue this silly, vague search? There was supposed to be the ruin of an old, old hunting lodge deep in this wood somewhere, and perhaps it would hold the evidence he wanted. But it was a vague report—vague enough to be forgotten without regret. It would be the height of foolishness to stay for all the hick-town red tape that would follow that ghastly affair back in the wood. Ergo, it would be ridiculous to follow that farmer's advice, to go to his house and wait for him. He would go back to town.

The monster was leaning against the other side of the big tree.

The little man snuffled disgustedly at a sudden overpowering odor of rot. He reached for his handkerchief, fumbled and dropped it. As he bent to pick it up, the monster's arm *whuffed* heavily in the air where his head had been—a blow that would certainly have removed that baby-faced protuberance. The man stood up and would have put the handkerchief to his nose had it not been so bloody. The creature behind the tree lifted its arm again just as the little man tossed the handkerchief away and stepped out into the field, heading across country to the distant highway that would take him back to town. The monster pounced on the handkerchief, picked it up, studied it, tore it across several times and inspected the tattered edges. Then it gazed vacantly at the disappearing figure of the little man, and finding him no longer interesting, turned back into the woods.

Babe broke into a trot at the sound of the shots. It was important to warn Uncle Alton about what her father had said, but it was more interesting to find out what he had bagged. Oh, he'd bagged it, all right. Uncle Alton never fired without killing. This was about the first time she had ever heard him blast away like that. Must be a bear, she thought excitedly, tripping over a root, sprawling, rolling to her feet again, without noticing the tumble. She'd love to have another bearskin in her room. Where would she put it? Maybe they could line it and she could have it for a blanket. Uncle Alton could sit on it and read to her in the evening— Oh, no. No. Not with this trouble between him and Dad. Oh, if she could only do something! She tried to run faster, worried and anticipating, but she was out of breath and went more slowly instead.

At the top of the rise by the edge of the woods she stopped and looked back. Far down in the valley lay the south thirty. She scanned it carefully, looking for her father. The new furrows and the old were sharply defined, and her keen eyes saw immediately that Cory had left the line with the cultivator and had angled the team over to the shade trees without finishing his row. That wasn't like him. She could see the team now, and Cory's pale-blue denim was nowhere in sight. She giggled lightly to herself as she thought of the way she would fool her father. And the little sound of laughter drowned out, for her, the sound of Alton's hoarse dying scream.

She reached and crossed the path and slid through the brush beside it. The shots came from up around here somewhere. She stopped and listened several times, and then suddenly heard something coming toward her, fast. She ducked under cover, terrified, and a little baby-faced man in black, his blue eyes wide with horror, crashed blindly past her, the leather case he carried catching on the branches. It spun a moment and then fell right in front of her. The man never missed it.

Babe lay there for a long moment and then picked up the case and faded into the woods. Things were happening too fast for her. She wanted Uncle Alton, but she dared not call. She stopped again and strained her ears. Back toward the edge of the wood she heard her father's voice, and another's—probably the man who had dropped the briefcase. She dared not go over there. Filled with enjoyable terror, she thought hard, then snapped her fingers in triumph. She and Alton had played Injun many times up here; they had a whole repertoire of secret signals. She had practiced birdcalls until she knew them better than the birds themselves. What would it be? Ah—blue jay. She threw back her head and by some youthful alchemy produced a nerve-shattering screech that would have done justice to any jay that ever flew. She repeated it, and then twice more.

The response was immediate—the call of a blue jay, four times, spaced two and two. Babe nodded to herself happily. That was the signal that they were to meet immediately at The Place. The Place was a hide-out that he had discovered and shared with her, and not another soul knew of it; an angle of rock beside a stream not far away. It wasn't exactly a cave, but almost. Enough so to be entrancing. Babe trotted happily away toward the brook. She had just known that Uncle Alton would remember the call of the blue jay, and what it meant.

In the tree that arched over Alton's scattered body perched a large jay bird, preening itself and shining in the sun. Quite unconscious of the presence of death, hardly noticing the Babe's realistic cry, it screamed again four times, two and two.

It took Cory more than a moment to recover himself from what he had seen. He turned away from it and leaned weakly against a pine, panting. Alton. That was Alton lying there, in—parts.

"God! God, God, God—"

Gradually his strength returned, and he forced himself to turn again. Stepping carefully, he bent and picked up the .32–40. Its barrel was bright and clean, but the butt and stock were smeared with some kind of stinking rottenness. Where had he seen the stuff before? Somewhere—no matter. He cleaned it off absently, throwing the befouled bandanna away afterward. Through his mind ran Alton's words—was that only last night?—*"I'm goin' to start trackin'. An' I'm goin' to keep trackin' till I find the one done this job on Kimbo."*

Cory searched shrinkingly until he found Alton's box of shells. The box was wet and sticky. That made it—better, somehow. A bullet wet with Alton's blood was the right thing to use. He went away a short distance, circled around till he found heavy footprints, then came back.

"I'm a-trackin' for you, bud," he whispered thickly, and began. Through the brush he followed its wavering spoor, amazed at the amount of filthy mold about, gradually associating it with the thing that had killed his brother. There was nothing in the world for him any more but hate and doggedness. Cursing himself for not getting Alton home last night, he followed the tracks to the edge of the woods. They led him to a big tree there, and there he saw something else—the footprints of the little city man. Nearby lay some tattered scraps of linen, and—what was that?

Another set of prints—small ones. Small, stub-toed ones.

"Babe!"

No answer. The wind sighed. Somewhere a blue jay called.

Babe stopped and turned when she heard her father's voice, faint with distance, piercing.

"Listen at him holler," she crooned delightedly. "Gee, he sounds mad." She sent a jay bird's call disrespectfully back to him and hurried to The Place.

It consisted of a mammoth boulder beside the brook. Some upheaval in the glacial age had cleft it, cutting out a huge V-shaped chunk. The widest part of the cleft was at the water's edge, and the narrowest was hidden by bushes. It made a little ceilingless room, rough and uneven and full of pot-holes and cavelets inside, and yet with quite a level floor. The open end was at the water's edge.

Babe parted the bushes and peered down the cleft.

"Uncle Alton!" she called softly. There was no answer. Oh, well, he'd be along. She scrambled in and slid down to the floor.

She loved it here. It was shaded and cool, and the chattering stream filled it with shifting golden lights and laughing gurgles. She called again, on principle, and then perched on an outcropping to wait. It was only then she realized that she still carried the little man's briefcase.

She turned it over a couple of times and then opened it. It was divided in the middle by a leather wall. On one side were a few papers in a large yellow envelope, and on the other some sandwiches, a candy bar, and an apple. With a youngster's complacent acceptance of manna from heaven, Babe fell to. She saved one sandwich for Alton, mainly because she didn't like its highly spiced bologna. The rest made quite a feast.

She was a little worried when Alton hadn't arrived, even after she had consumed the apple core. She got up and tried to skim some flat pebbles across the roiling brook, and she stood on her hands, and she tried to think of a story to tell herself, and she tried just waiting. Finally, in desperation, she turned again to the brief-case, took out the papers, curled up by the rocky wall and began to read them. It was something to do, anyway.

There was an old newspaper clipping that told about strange wills that people had left. An old lady had once left a lot of money to whoever would make the trip from the Earth to the Moon and back. Another had financed a home for cats whose masters and mistresses had died. A man left thousands of dollars to the first man who could solve a certain mathematical problem and prove his solution. But one item was blue-penciled. It was:

> One of the strangest wills still in force is that of Thaddeus M. Kirk, who died in 1920. It appears that he built an elaborate mausoleum with burial vaults for all the remains of his family. He collected and removed caskets from all over the country to fill the designated niches. Kirk was the last of his line; there were no relatives when he died. His will stated that the mausoleum was to be kept in repair permanently, and that a certain sum was to be set aside as a reward for whoever who could produce the body of his grandfather, Roger Kirk, whose niche is still empty. Anyone finding his body is eligible to receive a substantial fortune.

Babe yawned vaguely over this, but kept on reading because there was nothing else to do. Next was a thick sheet of business correspondence, bearing the letterhead of a firm of lawyers. The body of it ran:

> In regard to your query regarding the will of Thaddeus Kirk, we are authorized to state that his grandfather was a man about five feet, five inches, whose left arm had been broken and who had a triangular silver plate set into his

skull. There is no information as to the whereabouts of his death. He disappeared and was declared legally dead after the lapse of fourteen years.

The amount of the reward as stated in the will, plus accrued interest, now amounts to a fraction over sixty-two thousand dollars. This will be paid to anyone who produces the remains, providing that said remains answer descriptions kept in our private files.

There was more, but Babe was bored. She went on to the little black notebook. There was nothing in it but penciled and highly abbreviated records of visits to libraries; quotations from books with titles like "History of Angelina and Tyler Counties: and "Kirk Family History." Babe threw that aside, too. Where could Uncle Alton be?

She began to sing tunelessly, "Tumalumalum tum, ta ta ta," pretending to dance a minuet with flowing skirts like a girl she had seen in the movies. A rustle of the bushes at the entrace to The Place stopped her. She peeped upward, saw them being thrust aside. Quickly she ran to a tiny cul-de-sac in the rock wall, just big enough for her to hide in. She giggled at the thought of how surprised Uncle Alton would be when she jumped out at him.

She heard the newcomer come shuffling down the steep slope of the crevice and land heavily on the floor. There was something about the sound— What was it? It occurred to her that though it was a hard job for a big man like Uncle Alton to get through the little opening in the bushes, she could hear no heavy breathing. She heard no breathing at all!

Babe peeped out into the main cave and squealed in utmost horror. Standing there was, not Uncle Alton, but a massive caricature of a man: a huge thing like an irregular mud doll, clumsily made. It quivered and parts of it glistened and parts of it were dried and crumbly. Half of the lower left part of its face was gone, giving it a lopsided look. It had no perceptible mouth or nose, and its eyes were crooked, one higher than the other, both a dingy brown with no whites at all. It stood quite still looking at her, its only movement a steady unalive quivering.

It wondered about the queer little noise Babe had made.

Babe crept far back against a little pocket of stone, her brain running round and round in tiny circles of agony. She opened her mouth to cry out, and could not. Her eyes bulged and her face flamed with the strangling effort, and the two golden ropes of her braided hair twitched and twitched as she hunted hopelessly for a way out. If only she were out in the open—or in the wedge-shaped half-cave where the thing was—or home in bed!

The thing clumped toward her, expressionless, moving with a slow inevitability that was the sheer crux of horror. Babe lay wide-eyed and frozen, mounting pressure of terror stilling her lungs, making her heart shake the whole world. The monster came to the mouth of the little pocket, tried to walk to her and was stopped by the sides. It was such a narrow little fissure, and it was all Babe could do to get in. The thing from the wood stood straining against the rock at its shoulders, pressing harder and harder to get to Babe. She sat up slowly, so near to the thing that its odor was almost thick enough to see, and a wild hope burst through her voiceless fear. It couldn't get in! It couldn't get in because it was too big!

The substance of its feet spread slowly under the tremendous strain and at its shoulder appeared a slight crack. It widened as the monster unfeelingly crushed itself against the rock, and suddenly a large piece of the shoulder came away and the being twisted slushily three feet farther in. It lay quietly with its muddy eyes fixed on her, and then brought one thick arm up over its head and reached.

Babe scrambled in the inch farther she had believed impossible, and the filthy clubbed hand stroked down her back, leaving a trail of muck on the blue denim of the shirt she wore. The monster surged suddenly and, lying full length now, gained that last precious inch. A black hand seized one of her braids, and for Babe the lights went out.

When she came to, she was dangling by her hair from that same crusted paw. The thing held her high, so that her face and its featureless head were not more than a foot apart. It gazed at her with a mild curiosity in its eyes, and it swung her slowly back and forth. The agony of her pulled hair did what fear could not do—gave her a voice. She screamed. She opened her mouth and puffed up her powerful young lungs, and she sounded off. She held her throat in the position of the first scream, and her chest labored and

pumped more air thorugh the frozen throat. Shrill and monotonous and infinitely piercing, her screams.

The thing did not mind. It held her as she was, and watched.
When it had learned all it could from this phenomenon, it
dropped her jarringly, and looked around the half-cave, ignoring
the stunned and huddled Babe. It reached over and picked up the
leather briefcase and tore it twice across as if it were tissue. It saw
the sandwich Babe had left, picked it up, crushed it, dropped it.

Babe opened her eyes, saw that she was free, and just as the
thing turned back to her she dove between its legs and out into the
shallow pool in front of the rock, paddled across and hit the other
bank screaming. A vicious little light of fury burned in her; she
picked up a grapefruit-sized stone and hurled it with all her fren-
zied might. It flew low and fast, and struck squashily on the monster's ankle. The thing was just taking a step toward the water; the
stone caught it off balance, and its unpracticed equilibrium could
not save it. It tottered for a long, silent moment at the edge and
then splashed into the stream. Without a second look Babe ran
shrieking away.

Cory Drew was following the little gobs of mold that somehow indicated the path of the murderer, and he was nearby when
he first heard her scream. He broke into a run, dropping his shotgun and holding the .32–40 ready to fire. He ran with such deadly
panic in his heart that he ran right past the huge cleft rock and was
a hundred yards past it before she burst out through the pool and
ran up the bank. He had to run hard and fast to catch her, because
anything behind her was that faceless horror in the cave, and she
was living for the one idea of getting away from there. He caught
her in his arms and swung her to him, and she screamed on and on
and on.

Babe didn't see Cory at all, even when he held her and quieted
her.

The monster lay in the water. It neither liked nor disliked this new
element. It rested on the bottom, its massive head a foot beneath
the surface, and it curiously considered the facts it had garnered.
There was the little humming noise of Babe's voice that sent the
monster questing into the cave. There was the black material of
the briefcase that resisted so much more than green things when

he tore it. There was the two-legged one who sang and brought him near, and who screamed when he came. There was this new cold moving thing he had fallen into. It was washing his body away. That had never happened before. That was interesting. The monster decided to stay and observe this new thing. It felt no urge to save itself; it could only be curious.

The brook came laughing down out of its spring, ran down from its source beckoning to the sunbeams and embracing freshets and helpful brooklets. It shouted and played with streaming little roots, and nudged the minnows and pollywogs about in its tiny backwaters. It was a happy brook. When it came to the pool by the cloven rock it found the monster there, and plucked at it. It soaked the foul substances and smoothed and melted the molds, and the waters below the thing eddied darkly with its diluted matter. It was a thorough brook. It washed all it touched, persistently. Where it found filth, it removed filth; if there were layer on layer of foulness, then layer by foul layer it was removed. It was a good brook. It did not mind the poison of the monster, but took it up and thinned it and spread it in little rings round rocks downstream, and let it drift to the rootlets of water plants, that they might grow greener and lovelier. And the monster melted.

"I am smaller," the thing thought. "That is interesting. I could not move now. And now this part of me which thinks is going, too. It will stop in just a moment, and drift away with the rest of the body. It will stop thinking and I will stop being, and that, too, is a very interesting thing."

So the monster melted and dirtied the water, and water was clean again, washing and washing the skeleton that the monster had left. It was not very big, and there was a badly healed knot on the left arm. The sunlight flickered on the triangular silver plate set into the pale skull, and the skeleton was very clean now. The brook laughed about it for an age.

They found the skeleton, six grimlipped men who came to find a killer. No one had believed Babe, when she told her story days later. It had to be days later because Babe had screamed for seven hours without stopping, and had lain like a dead child for a day. No one believed her at all, because her story was all about the bad fella, and they knew that the bad fella was simply a thing that her father had made up to frighten her with. But it was through her that the skeleton was found, and so the men at the bank sent a check to the Drews for more money than they had ever dreamed about. It was old Roger Kirk, sure enough, that skeleton, though it was found five miles from where he had died and sank into the forest floor where the hot molds builded around his skeleton and emerged—a monster.

So the Drews had a new barn and fine new livestock and they hired four men. But they didn't have Alton. And they didn't have Kimbo. And Babe screams at night and has grown very thin.

A WAY OF THINKING

I'll have to start with an anecdote or two that you may have heard from me before, but they'll bear repeating, since it's Kelley we're talking about.

I shipped out with Kelley when I was a kid. Tankships, mostly coastwise: load somewhere in the oil country—New Orleans, Aransas Pass, Port Arthur, or some such—and unload at ports north of Hatteras. Eight days out, eighteen hours in, give or take a day or six hours. Kelley was ordinary seaman on my watch, which was a laugh; he knew more about the sea than anyone aft of the galley. But he never ribbed me, stumbling around the place with my blue A.B. ticket. He had a sense of humor in his peculiar quiet way, but he never gratified it by proofs of the obvious—that he was twice the seaman I could ever be.

There were a lot of unusual things about Kelley, the way he looked, the way he moved; but most unusual was the way he thought. He was like one of those extra-terrestrials you read about, who can think as well as a human being but not *like* a human being.

Just for example, there was that night in Port Arthur. I was sitting in a honkytonk up over a bar with a red-headed girl called

Red, trying to mind my own business while watching a chick known as Boots, who sat alone over by the juke-box. This girl Boots was watching the door and grinding her teeth, and I knew why, and I was worried. See, Kelley had been seeing her pretty regularly, but this trip he'd made the break and word was around that he was romancing a girl in Pete's place—a very unpopular kind of rumor for Boots to be chewing on. I also knew that Kelley would be along any minute because he'd promised to meet me here.

And in he came, running up that long straight flight of steps easy as a cat, and when he got in the door everybody just hushed, except the juke-box, and it sounded scared.

Now, just above Boots' shoulder on a little shelf was an electric fan. It had sixteen-inch blades and no guard. The very second Kelley's face showed in the doorway Boots rose up like a snake out of a basket, reached behind her, snatched that fan off the shelf and threw it.

It might as well have been done with a slow-motion camera as far as Kelley was concerned. He didn't move his feet at all. He bent sideways, just a little, from the waist, and turned his wide shoulders. Very clearly I heard three of those whining blade-tips touch a button on his shirt *bip-bip-bip!* and then the fan hit the doorpost.

Even the juke-box shut up then. It was *so* quiet. Kelley didn't say anything and neither did anyone else.

Now, if you believe in do-as-you-get-done-to, and someone heaves an infernal machine at you, you'll pick it right up and heave it back. But Kelley doesn't think like you. He didn't look at the fan. He just watched Boots, and she was white and crazed-looking, waiting for whatever he might have in mind.

He went across the room to her, fast but not really hurrying, and he picked her out from behind that table, and he threw her.

He threw her at the fan.

She hit the floor and slid, sweeping up the fan where it lay, hitting the doorjamb with her head, spinning out into the stairway. Kelley walked after her, stepped over her, went on downstairs and back to the ship.

And there was the time we shipped a new main spur gear for the starboard winch. The deck engineer used up the whole morning watch trying to get the old gear-wheel off its shaft. He heated the hub. He pounded it. He put in wedges. He hooked on with a handybilly—that's a four-sheave block-and-tackle to you—and all he did with that was break a U-bolt.

Then Kelley came on deck, rubbing sleep out of his eyes, and took one brief look. He walked over to the winch, snatched up a crescent wrench, and relieved the four bolts that held the housing tight around the shaft. He then picked up a twelve-pound maul, hefted it, and swung it just once. The maul hit the end of the shaft and the shaft shot out of the other side of the machine like a torpedo out of its tube. The gearwheel fell down on the deck. Kelley went forward to take the helm and thought no more about it, while the deck crew stared after him, wall-eyed. You see what I mean? Problem: Get a wheel off a shaft. But in Kelley's book it's: Get the shaft out of the wheel.

I kibitzed him at poker one time and saw him discard two pair and draw a winning straight flush. Why that discard? Because he'd just realized the deck was stacked. Why the flush? God knows. All Kelley did was pick up the pot—a big one—grin at the sharper, and leave.

I have plenty more yarns like that, but you get the idea. The guy had a special way of thinking, that's all, and it never failed him.

I lost track of Kelley. I came to regret that now and then; he made a huge impression on me, and sometimes I used to think about him when I had a tough problem to solve. What would Kelley do? And sometimes it helped, and sometimes it didn't; and when it didn't, I guess it was because I'm not Kelley.

I came ashore and got married and did all sorts of other things, and the years went by, and a war came and went, and one warm spring evening I went into a place I know on West 48th St. because I felt like drinking *tequila* and I can always get it there. And who should be sitting in a booth finishing up a big Mexican dinner but—no, not Kelley.

It was Milton. He looks like a college sophomore with money. His suits are always cut just so, but quiet; and when he's relaxed he looks as if he's just been tapped for a fraternity and it matters to him, and when he's worried you want to ask him has he been cutting classes again. It happens he's a damn good doctor.

He was worried, but he gave me a good hello and waved me

into the booth while he finished up. We had small talk and I tried
to buy him a drink. He looked real wistful and then shook his
head. "Patient in ten minutes," he said, looking at his watch.

"Then it's nearby. Come back afterward."

"Better yet," he said, getting up, "come with me. This might
interest you, come to think of it."

He got his hat and paid Rudy, and I said, *"Luego,"* and Rudy
grinned and slapped the *tequila* bottle. Nice place, Rudy's.

"What about the patient?" I asked as we turned up the avenue.
I thought for a while he hadn't heard me, but at last he said, "Four
busted ribs and a compound femoral. Minor internal hemorrhage
which might or might not be a ruptured spleen. Necrosis of the
oral frenum—or was while there was any frenum left."

"What's a frenum?"

"That little strip of tissue under your tongue."

"Ongk," I said, trying to reach it with the tip of my tongue.
"What a healthy fellow."

"Pulmonary adhesions," Milton ruminated. "Not serious, certainly not tubercular. But they hurt and they bleed and I don't like
'em. And acne rosacea."

"That's the nose like a stop light, isn't it?"

"It isn't as funny as that to the guy that has it."

I was quelled. "What was it—a goon-squad?"

He shook his head.

"A truck?"

"No."

"He fell off something."

Milton stopped and turned and looked me straight in the eye.
"No," he said. "Nothing like anything. Nothing," he said, walking
again, "at all."

I said nothing to that because there was nothing to say.

"He just went to bed," said Milton thoughtfully, "because he
felt off his oats. And one by one these things happened to him."

"In *bed?*"

"Well," said Milton, in a to-be-absolutely-accurate tone,
"when the ribs broke he was on his way back from the bathroom."

"You're kidding."

"No I'm not."

"He's lying."

Milton said, "I believe him."

I know Milton. There's no doubt that he believed the man. I said, "I keep reading things about psychosomatic disorders. But a broken—what did you say it was?"

"Femur. Thigh, that is. Compound. Oh, it's rare, all right. But it can happen, has happened. These muscles are pretty powerful, you know. They deliver two-fifty, three hundred pound thrusts every time you walk up stairs. In certain spastic hysteriae, they'll break bones easily enough."

"What about al those other things?"

"Functional disorders, every one of 'em. No germ disease."

"Now this boy," I said, "*really* has something on his mind."

"Yes, he has."

But I didn't ask what. I could hear the discussion closing as if it had a spring latch on it.

We went into a door tucked between store fronts and climbed three flights. Milton put out his hand to a bell-push and then dropped it without ringing. There was a paper tacked to the door. DOC I WENT FOR SHOTS COME ON IN.

It was unsigned. Milton turned the knob and we went in.

The first thing that hit me was the smell. Not too strong, but not the kind of thing you ever forget if you ever had to dig a slit trench through last week's burial pit. "That's the necrosis," muttered Milton. "Damn it." He gestured. "Hang your hat over there. Sit down. I'll be out soon." He went into an inner room, saying, "Hi, Hal," at the doorway. From inside came an answering rumble, and something twisted in my throat to hear it, for no voice which is that tired should sound that cheerful.

I sat watching the wallpaper and laboriously un-listening to those clinical grunts and the gay-weary responses in the other room. The wallpaper was awful. I remember a night-club act where Reginald Gardiner used to give sound-effect renditions of wallpaper designs. This one, I decided, would run "Body to *weep* . . . yawp, yawp; body to weep . . . yawp, yawp," very faintly, with the final syllable a straining retch. I had just reached a particularly clumsy join where the paper utterly demolished its own rhythm and went "Yawp yawp body to *weep*" when the outer door opened and I leaped to my feet with the rush of utter guilt one feels when caught in an unlikely place with no curt and lucid explanation.

He was two long strides into the room, tall and soft-footed, his face and long green eyes quite at rest, when he saw me. He stopped as if on leaf springs and shock absorbers, not suddenly, completely controlled, and asked, "Who are you?"

"I'll be damned," I answered. "Kelley!"

He peered at me with precisely the expression I had seen so many times when he watched the little square windows on the one-arm bandits we used to play together. I could almost hear the tumblers, see the drums; not lemon . . . cherry . . . cherry . . . and *click!* this time but tankship . . . Texas . . . him! . . . and *click!* "I be *god*dam," he drawled, to indicate that he was even more surprised than I was. He transferred the small package he carried from his right hand to his left and shook hands. His hand went one and a half times around mine with enough left over to tie a half-hitch. "Where in time you been keepin' yourse'f? How'd you smoke me out?"

"I never," I said. (Saying it, I was aware that I always fell into the idiom of people who impressed me, to the exact degree of that impression. So I always found myself talking more like Kelley than Kelley's shaving mirror.) I was grinning so wide my face hurt. "I'm glad to see you." I shook hands with him again, foolishly. "I came with the doctor."

"You a doctor now?" he said, his tone prepared for wonders.

"I'm a writer," I said deprecatingly.

"Yeah, I heard," he reminded himself. His eyes narrowed; as of old, it had the effect of sharp-focusing a searchlight beam. "I heard!" he repeated, with deeper interest. "Stories. Gremlins and flyin' saucers an' all like that." I nodded. He said, without insult, "Hell of a way to making a living."

"What about you?"

"Ships. Some drydock. Tank cleaning. Compass 'djustin'. For a while had a job holdin' an insurance inspector's head. You know."

I glanced at the big hands that could weld or steer or compute certainly with the excellence I used to know, and marveled that he found himself so unremarkable. I pulled myself back to here and now and nodded toward the inner room. "I'm holding you up."

"No you ain't. Milton, he knows what he's doin'. He wants me, he'll holler."

"Who's sick?"

His face darkened like the sea in scud-weather, abruptly and deep down. "My brother." He looked at me searchingly. "He's . . ." Then he seemed to check himself. "He's sick," he said unnecessarily, and added quickly, "He's going to be all right, though."

"Sure," I said quickly.

I had the feeling that we were both lying and that neither of us knew why.

Milton came out, laughing a laugh that cut off as soon as he was out of range of the sick man. Kelley turned to him slowly, as if slowness were the only alternative to leaping on the doctor, pounding the news out of him. "Hello, Kelley. Heard you come in."

"How is he, Doc?"

Milton looked up quickly, his bright round eyes clashing with Kelley's slitted fierce ones. "You got to take it easy, Kelley. What'll happen to him if you crack up?"

"Nobody's cracking up. What do you want me to do?"

Milton saw the package on the table. He picked it up and opened it. There was a leather case and two phials. "Ever use one of these before?"

"He was a pre-med before he went to sea," I said suddenly.

Milton stared at me. "You two know each other?"

I looked at Kelley. 'Sometimes I think I invented him."

Kelley snorted and thumped my shoulder. Happily I had one hand on a built-in china shelf. His big hand continued the motion and took the hypodermic case from the doctor. "Sterilize the shaft and needle," he said sleepily, as if reading. "Assemble without touching needle with fingers. To fill, puncture diaphragm and withdraw plunger. Squirt upward to remove air an' prevent embolism. Locate major vein in—"

Milton laughed. "Okay, okay. But forget the vein. Any place will do—it's subcutaneous, that's all. I've written the exact amounts to be used for exactly the symptoms you can expect. Don't jump the gun, Kelley. And remember how you salt your stew. Just because a little is good, it doesn't figure that a lot has to be better."

Kelley was wearing that sleepy inattention which, I remembered, meant only that he was taking in every single word like a tape recorder. He tossed the leather case gently, caught it. "Now?" he said.

"Not now," the doctor said positively. "Only when you have to."

Kelley seemed frustrated. I suddenly understood that he wanted to do something, build something, fight something. Anything but sit and wait for therapy to bring results. I said, "Kelley, any brother of yours is a—well, you know. I'd like to say hello, if it's all—"

Immediately and together Kelley and the doctor said loudly, "Sure, when he's on his feet," and "Better not just now, I've just given him a sedat—" And together they stopped awkwardly.

"Let's go get that drink," I said before they could flounder any more.

"Now you're talking. You too, Kelley. It'll do you good."

"Not me," said Kelley. "Hal—"

"I knocked him out," said the doctor bluntly. "You'll cluck around scratching for worms and looking for hawks till you wake him up, and he needs his sleep. Come on."

Painfully I had to add to my many mental images of Kelley the very first one in which he was indecisive. I hated it.

"Well," said Kelley, "let me go see."

He disappeared. I looked at Milton's face, and turned quickly away. I was sure he wouldn't want me to see that expression of sick pity and bafflement.

Kelley came out, moving silently as always. "Yeah, asleep," he said. "For how long?"

"I'd say four hours at least."

"Well, all right." From the old-fashioned clothes tree he took a battered black engineer's cap with a shiny, crazed patent leather visor. I laughed. Both men turned to me, with annoyance, I thought.

On the landing outside I explained. "The hat," I said. "Remember? Tampico?"

"Oh," he grunted. He thwacked it against his forearm.

"He left it on the bar of this ginmill," I told Milton. "We got back to the gangplank and he missed it. Nothing would do but he has to go back for it, so I went with him."

"You was wearin' a *tequila* label on your face," Kelley said. "Kept tryin' to tell the taxi man you was a bottle."

"He didn't speak English."

Kelley flashed something like his old grin. "He got the idea."

"Anyway," I told Milton, "the place was closed when we got there. We tried the front door and the side doors and they were locked like Alcatraz. We made so much racket I guess if anyone was inside they were afraid to open up. We could see Kelley's hat in there on the bar. Nobody's *about* to steal that hat."

"It's a good hat," he said in an injured tone.

"Kelley goes into action," I said. "Kelley don't think like other people, you know, Milt. He squints through the window at the other wall, goes around the building, sets one foot against the corner stud, gets his fingers under the edge of that corrugated iron siding they use. 'I'll pry this out a bit,' he says. 'You slide in and get my hat.'"

"Corrugated was only nailed on one-by-twos," said Kelley.

"He gives one almighty pull," I chuckled, "and the whole damn side falls out of the building, I mean the second floor too. You never heard such a clap-o'-thunder in your life."

"I got my hat," said Kelley. He uttered two syllables of a laugh. "Whole second floor was a cathouse, an' the one single stairway come out with the wall."

"Taxi driver just took off. But he left his taxi. Kelley drove back. I couldn't. I was laughing."

"You was drunk."

"Well, *some,*" I said.

We walked together quietly, happily. Out of Kelley's sight, Milton thumped me gently on the ribs. It was eloquent and it pleased me. It said that it was a long time since Kelley had laughed. It was a long time since he had thought about anything but Hal.

I guess we felt it equally when, with no trace of humor . . . more, as if he had let my episode just blow itself out until he could be heard . . . Kelley said, "Doc, what's with the hand?"

"It'll be all right," Milton said.

"You put splints."

Milton sighed. "All right, all right. Three fractures. Two on the middle finger and one on the ring."

Kelley said, "I saw they were swollen."

I looked at Kelley's face and I looked at Milton's, and I didn't like either, and I wished to God I were somewhere else, in a uranium mine maybe, or making out my income tax. I said, "Here we are. Ever been to Rudy's, Kelley?"

He looked up at the little yellow-and-red marquee. "No."

"Come on," I said. *"Tequila."*

We went in and got a booth. Kelley ordered beer. I got mad then and started to call him some things I'd picked up on waterfronts from here to Tierra del Fuego. Milton stared wall-eyed at me and Kelley stared at his hands. After a while Milton began to jot some of it down on a prescription pad he took from his pocket. I was pretty proud.

Kelley gradually got the idea. If I wanted to pick up the tab and he wouldn't let me, his habits were those of *una puñeta sin cojones* (which a Spanish dictionary will reliably misinform you means "a weakling without eggs"), and his affections for his forebears were powerful but irreverent. I won, and soon he was lapping up a huge combination plate of beef *tostadas,* chicken *enchiladas,* and pork *tacos.* He endeared himself to Rudy by demanding salt and lemon with his *tequila* and dispatching same with flawless ritual: hold the lemon between left thumb and forefinger, lick the back of the left hand, sprinkle salt on the wet spot, lift the *tequila* with the right, lick the salt, drink the *tequila,* bite the lemon. Soon he was imitating the German second mate we shipped out of Puerto Barrios one night, who ate fourteen green bananas and lost them and all his teeth over the side, in gummed gutturals which had us roaring.

But after that question about fractured fingers back there in the street, Milton and I weren't fooled any more, and though everyone tried hard and it was a fine try, none of the laughter went deep enough or stayed long enough, and I wanted to cry.

We all had a huge hunk of the nesselrode pie made by Rudy's beautiful blond wife—pie you can blow off your plate by flapping a napkin . . . sweet smoke with calories. And then Kelley demanded to know what time it was and cussed and stood up.

"It's only been two hours," Milton said.

"I just as soon head home all the same," said Kelley. "Thanks."

"Wait," I said. I got a scrap of paper out of my wallet and wrote on it. "Here's my phone. I want to see you some more. I'm working for myself these days; my time's my own. I don't sleep much, so call me any time you feel like it."

He took the paper. "You're no good," he said. "You never were no good." The way he said it, I felt fine.

"On the corner is a newsstand," I told him. "There's a magazine called *Amazing* with one of my lousy stories in it."

"They print it on a roll?" he demanded. He waved at us, nodded to Rudy, and went out.

I swept up some spilled sugar on the table top and pushed it around until it was a perfect square. After a while I shoved in the sides until it was a lozenge. Milton didn't say anything either. Rudy, as is his way, had sense enough to stay away from us.

"Well, that did him some good," Milton said after a while.

"You know better than that," I said bitterly.

Milton said patiently, "Kelley thinks *we* think it did him some good. And thinking that does him good."

I had to smile at that contortion, and after that it was easier to talk. "The kid going to live?"

Milton waited, as if some other answer might spring from somewhere, but it didn't. He said, "No."

"Fine doctor."

"Don't kid like that!" he snapped. He looked up at me. "Look, if this was one of those—well, say pleurisy cases on the critical list, without the will to live, why I'd know what to do. Usually those depressed cases have such a violent desire to be reassured, down deep, that you can snap 'em right out of it if only you can think of the right thing to say. And you usually can. But Hal's not one of those. He wants to live. If he didn't want so much to live he'd've been dead three weeks ago. What's killing him is sheer somatic trauma—one broken bone after another, one failing or inflamed internal organ after another."

"Who's doing it?"

"Damn it, *no*body's doing it!" He caught me biting my lip. "If either one of us should say Kelley's doing it, the other one will punch him in the mouth. Right?"

"Right."

"Just so that doesn't have to happen," said Milton carefully,

"I'll tell you what you're bound to ask me in a minute: why isn't he in a hospital!"

"Okay, why?"

"He was. For weeks. And all the time he was there these things kept on happening to him, only worse. More, and more often. I got him home as soon as it was safe to get him out of traction for that broken thigh. He's much better off with Kelley. Kelley keeps him cheered up, cooks for him, medicates him—the works. It's all Kelley does these days."

"I figured. It must be getting tough."

"It is. I wish I had your ability with invective. You can't lend that man anything, give him anything . . . proud? God!"

"Don't take this personally, but have you had consultations?"

He shrugged. "Six ways from the middle. And nine-tenths of it behind Kelley's back, which isn't easy. The lies I've told him! Hal's just *got* to have a special kind of Persian melon that some-one is receiving in a little store in Yonkers. Out Kelley goes, and in the meantime I have to corral two or three doctors and whip 'em in to see Hal and out again before Kelley gets back. Or Hal has to have a special prescription, and I fix up with the druggist to take a good two hours compounding it. Hal saw Grundage, the osteo man, that way, but poor old Ancelowics the pharmacist got punched in the chops for the delay."

"Milton, you're all right."

He snarled at me, and then went on quietly, "None of it's done any good. I've learned a whole encyclopedia full of wise words and some therapeutic tricks I didn't know existed. But . . ." He shook his head. "Do you know why Kelley and I wouldn't let you meet Hal?" He wet his lips and cast about for an example. "Remember the pictures of Mussolini's corpse after the mob got through with it?"

I shuddered. "I saw 'em."

"Well, that's what he looks like, only he's alive, which doesn't make it any prettier. Hal doesn't know how bad it is, and neither Kelley nor I would run the risk of having him see it reflected in someone else's face. I wouldn't send a wooden Indian into that room."

I began to pound the table, barely touching it, hitting it harder and harder until Milton caught my wrist. I froze then, unhappily conscious of the eyes of everyone in the place looking at me. Gradually the normal sound of the restaurant resumed. "Sorry."

"It's all right."

"There's got to be some sort of reason!"

His lips twitched in a small acid smile. "That's what you get down to at last, isn't it? There's always a reason for everything, and if we don't know it, we can find it out. But just one single example of real unreason is enough to shake our belief in everything. And then the fear gets bigger than the case at hand and extends to a whole universe of concepts labelled 'unproven.' Shows you how little we believe in anything, basically."

"That's a miserable piece of philosophy!"

"Sure. If you have another arrival point for a case like this, I'll buy it with a bonus. Meantime I'll just go on worrying at this one and feeling more scared than I ought to."

"Let's get drunk."

"A wonderful idea."

Neither of us ordered. We just sat there looking at the lozenge of sugar I'd made on the table top. After a while I said, "Hasn't Kelley any idea of what's wrong?"

"You know Kelley. If he had an idea he'd be working on it. All he's doing is sitting by watching his brother's body stew and swell like yeast in a vat."

"What about Hal?"

"He isn't lucid much any more. Not if I can help it."

"But maybe he—"

"Look," said Milton, "I don't want to sound cranky or anything, but I can't hold still for a lot of questions like . . ." He stopped, took out his display handkerchief, looked at it, put it away. "I'm sorry. You don't seem to understand that I didn't take this case yesterday afternoon. I've been sweating it out for nearly three months now. I've already thought of everything you're going to think of. Yes, I questioned Hal, back and forth and sideways. Nothing. N-n-nothing."

That last word trailed off in such a peculiar way that I looked up abruptly. "Tell me," I demanded.

"Tell you what?" Suddenly he looked at his watch. I covered it with my hand. "Come on, Milt."

"I don't know what you're—damn it, leave me alone, will you? If it was anything important, I'd've chased it down long ago."

"Tell me the unimportant something."

"No."

"Tell me why you won't tell me."

"Damn you, I'll do that. It's because you're a crackpot. You're a nice guy and I like you, but you're a crackpot." He laughed suddenly, and it hit me like the flare of a flashbulb. "I didn't know you could look so astonished!" he said. "Now take it easy and listen to me. A guy comes out of a steak house and steps on a rusty nail, and ups and dies of tetanus. But your crackpot vegetarian will swear up and down that the man would still be alive if he hadn't poisoned his system with meat, and uses the death to prove his point. The perennial Dry will call the same casualty a victim of John Barleycorn if he knows the man had a beer with his steak. This one death can be ardently and whole-heartedly blamed on the man's divorce, his religion, his political affiliations or on a hereditary taint from his great-great-grandfather who worked for Oliver Cromwell. You're a nice guy and I like you," he said again, "and I am not going to sit across from you and watch you do the crackpot act."

"I do not know," I said slowly and distinctly, "what the hell you are talking about. And now you *have* to tell me."

"I suppose so," he said sadly. He drew a deep breath. "You believe what you write. No," he said quickly, "I'm not asking you, I'm telling you. You grind out all this fantasy and horror stuff and you believe every word of it. More basically, you'd rather believe in the *outré* and the so-called 'unknowable' than in what I'd call *real* things. You think I'm talking through my hat."

"I do," I said, "but go ahead."

"If I called you up tomorrow and told you with great joy that they'd isolated a virus for Hal's condition and a serum was on the way, you'd be just as happy about it as I would be, but way down deep you'd wonder if that was what was really wrong with him, or if the serum is what really cured him. If on the other hand I admitted to you that I'd found two small punctures on Hal's throat and a wisp of fog slipping out of the room—by God! see what I mean? You have a gleam in your eye already!"

I covered my eyes. "Don't let me stop you now," I said, coldly. "Since you are not going to admit Dracula's punctures, what are you going to admit?"

"A year ago Kelley gave his brother a present. An ugly little brute of a Haitian doll. Hal kept it around to make faces at for a while and then gave it to a girl. He had bad trouble with the girl. She hates him—really hates him. As far as anyone knows she still has the doll. Are you happy now?"

"Happy," I said disgustedly. "But Milt—you're not just ignoring this doll thing. Why, that could easily be the whole basis of . . . hey, sit down! Where are you going?"

"I told you I wouldn't sit across from a damn hobbyist. Enter hobbies, exit reason." He recoiled. "Wait—*you* sit down now."

I gathered up a handful of his well-cut lapels. "We'll both sit down," I said gently, "or I'll prove to your heart's desire that I've reached the end of reason."

"Yessir," he said good-naturedly, and sat down. I felt like a damn fool. The twinkle left his eyes and he leaned forward. "Perhaps now you'll listen instead of riding off like that. I suppose you know that in many cases the voodoo doll does work, and you know why?"

"Well, yes. I didn't think you'd admit it." I got no response from his stony gaze, and at last realized that a fantasist's pose of authority on such matters is bound to sit ill with a serious and progressive physician. A lot less positively, I said, "It comes down to a matter of subjective reality, or what some people call faith. If you believe firmly that the mutilation of a doll with which you identify yourself will result in your own mutilation, well, that's what will happen."

"That, and a lot of things even a horror story writer could find out if he researched anywhere else except in his projective imagination. For example, there are Arabs in North Africa today whom you dare not insult in any way really important to them. If they feel injured, they'll threaten to die, and if you call the bluff they'll sit down, cover their heads, and damn well *die*. There are psychosomatic phenomena like the stigmata, or wounds of the cross, which appear from time to time on the hands, feet and breasts of exceptionally devout people. I know you know a lot of this," he added abruptly, apparently reading something in my expression, "but I'm not going to get my knee out of your chest until you'll admit I'm at least capable of taking a thing like this into consideration and tracking it down."

"I never saw you before in my life," I said, and in an important way I meant it.

"Good," he said with considerable relief. "Now I'll tell you what I did. I jumped at this doll episode almost as wildly as you did. It came late in the questioning because apparently it *really didn't matter* to Hal."

"Oh, well, but the subconscious—"

"Shaddup!" He stuck a surprisingly sharp forefinger into my collarbone. "I'm telling you; you're not telling me. I won't disallow that a deep belief in voodoo might be hidden in Hal's subconscious, but if it is, it's where sodium amytal and word association and light and profound hypnosis and a half-dozen other therapies give not a smidgin of evidence. I'll take that as proof that he carries no such conviction. I guess from the looks of you I'll have to remind you again that I've dug into this thing in more ways for longer and with more tools than you have—and I doubt that it means any less to me than it does to you."

"You know, I'm just going to shut up," I said plaintively.

"High time," he said, and grinned. "No, in every case of voodoo damage or death, there has to be that element of devout belief in the powers of the witch or wizard, and through it a complete sense of identification with the doll. In addition, it helps if the victim knows what sort of damage the doll is sustaining— crushing, or pins sticking into it, or what. And you can take my word for it that no such news has reached Hal."

"What about the doll? Just to be absolutely sure, shouldn't we get it back?"

"I thought of that. But there's no way I know of getting it back without making it look valuable to the woman. And if she thinks it's valuable to Hal, we'll *never* see it."

"Hm. Who is she, and what's her royal gripe?"

"She's as nasty a piece of fluff as they come. She got involved with Hal for a little while—nothing serious, certainly not on his part. He was . . . he's a big good-natured kid who thinks the only evil people around are the ones who get killed at the end of the movie. Kelley was at sea at the time and he blew in to find this little

vampire taking Hal for everything she could, first by sympathy,
then by threats. The old badger game. Hal was just bewildered.
Kelley got his word that nothing had occurred between them, and
then forced Hal to lower the boom. She called his bluff and it went
to court. They forced a physical examination of her and she got
laughed out of court. She wasn't the mother of anyone's unborn
child. She never will be. She swore to get even with him. She's
without brains or education or resources, but that doesn't stop her
from being pathological. She sure can hate."

"Oh. You've seen her."

Milton shuddered. "I've seen her. I tried to get all Hal's gifts
back from her. I had to say all because I didn't dare to itemize. All
I wanted, it might surprise you to know, was that damned doll.
Just in case, you know . . . although I'm morally convinced that
the thing has nothing to do with it. Now do you see what I mean
about a single example of unreason?"

"'Fraid I do." I felt upset and quelled and sat upon and I
wasn't fond of the feeling. I've read too many stories where the scientist just hasn't the imagination to solve a haunt. It had been
great, feeling superior to a bright guy like Milton.

We walked out of there and for the first time I felt the mood of
a night without feeling that an author was ramming it down my
throat for story purposes. I looked at the clean-swept, star-reaching
cubism of the Radio City area and its living snakes of neon, and I
suddenly thought of an Evelyn Smith story the general idea of
which was "After they found out the atom bomb was magic, the
rest of the magicians who enchanted refrigerators and washing
machines and the telephone system came out into the open." I felt
a breath of wind and wondered what it was that had breathed. I
heard the snoring of the city and for an awesome second felt it
would roll over, open its eyes, and . . . *speak*.

On the corner I said to Milton, "Thanks. You've given me a
thumping around. I guess I needed it." I looked at him. "By the
Lord I'd like to find some place where you've been stupid in this
thing."

"I'd be happy if you could," he said seriously.

I whacked him on the shoulder. "See? You take all the fun out
of it."

He got a cab and I started to walk. I walked a whole lot that night, just anywhere. I thought about a lot of things. When I got home the phone was ringing. It was Kelley.

I'm not going to give you a blow-by-blow of that talk with Kelley. It was in that small front room of his place—an apartment he'd rented after Hal got sick, and not the one Hal used to have—and we talked the night away. All I'm withholding is Kelley's expression of things you already know: that he was deeply attached to his brother, that he had no hope left for him, that he would find who or what was responsible and deal with it his way. It is a strong man's right to break down if he must, with whom and where he chooses, and such an occasion is only an expression of strength. But when it happens in a quiet sick place, where he must keep the command of hope strongly in the air; when a chest heaves and a throat must he held wide open to sob silently so that the dying one shall not know; these things are not pleasant to describe in detail. Whatever my ultimate feeling for Kelley, his emotions and the expressions of them are for him to keep.

He did, however, know the name of the girl and where she was. He did not hold her responsible. I thought he might have a suspicion, but it turned out to be only a certainty that this was no disease, no subjective internal disorder. If a great hate and a great determination could solve the problem, Kelley would solve it. If research and logic could solve it, Milton would do it. If I could do it, I would.

She was checking hats in a sleazy club out where Brooklyn and Queens, in a remote meeting, agree to be known as Long Island. The contact was easy to make. I gave her my spring coat with the label outward. It's a good label. When she turned away with it I called her back and drunkenly asked her for the bill in the right-hand pocket. She found it and handed it to me. It was a hundred. "Damn taxis never got change," I mumbled and took it before her astonishment turned to sleight-of-hand. I got out my wallet, crowded the crumpled note into it clumsily enough to display the two other C-notes there, shoved it into the front of my jacket so that it missed the pocket and fell to the floor, and walked off. I walked back before she could lift the hinged counter and skin out after it. I picked it up and smiled foolishly at her. "Lose more business cards that way," I said. Then I brought her into focus. "Hey, you know, you're cute."

I suppose "cute" is one of the four-letter words that describe her. "What's your name?"

"Charity," she said. "But don't get ideas." She was wearing so much pancake makeup that I couldn't tell what her complexion was. She leaned so far over the counter that I could see lipstick stains on her brassiere.

"I don't have a favorite charity yet," I said. "You work here alla time?"

"I go home once in a while," she said.

"What time?"

"One o'clock."

"Tell you what," I confided, "let's both be in front of this place at a quarter after and see who stands who up, okay?" Without waiting for an answer I stuck the wallet into my back pocket so that my jacket hung on it. All the way into the dining room I could feel her eyes on it like two hot, glistening, broiled mushrooms. I came within an ace of losing it to the head waiter when he collided with me, too.

She was there all right, with a yellowish fur around her neck and heels you could have driven into a pine plank. She was up to the elbows in jangly brass and chrome, and when we got into a cab she threw herself on me with her mouth open. I don't know where I got the reflexes, but I threw my head down and cracked her in the cheekbone with my forehead, and when she squeaked indignantly I said I'd dropped the wallet again and she went about helping me find it quietly as you please. We went to a place and another place and an after-hours place, all her choice. They served her sherry in her whiskey-ponies and doubled all my orders, and tilted the checks something outrageous. Once I tipped a waiter eight dollars and she palmed the five. Once she wormed my leather notebook out of my breast pocket thinking it was the wallet, which by this time was safely tucked away in my knit shorts. She did get one enamel cuff link with a rhinestone in it, and my fountain pen. All in all it was quite a duel. I was loaded to the eyeballs with thiamin hydrochloride and caffeine citrate, but a most respectable amount of alcohol soaked through them, and it was all I could do to play it through. I made it, though, and blocked her at every turn until she had no further choice but to take me home. She was furious and made only the barest attempts to hide it.

We got each other up the dim dawnlit stairs, shushing each other drunkenly, both much soberer than we acted, each promising what we expected not to deliver. She negotiated her lock successfully and waved me inside.

I hadn't expected it to be so neat. Or so cold. "I didn't leave that window open," she said complainingly. She crossed the room and closed it. She pulled her fur around her throat. "This is awful."

It was a long low room with three windows. At one end, covered by a venetian blind was a kitchenette. A door at one side of it was probably a bathroom.

She went to the venetian blind and raised it. "Have it warmed up in a jiffy," she said.

I looked at the kitchenette. "Hey," I said as she lit the little oven, "coffee. How's about coffee?"

"Oh, all right," she said glumly. "But talk quiet, huh?"

"Sh-h-h-h." I pushed my lips around with a forefinger. I circled the room. Cheap phonograph and records. Small screen TV. A big double studio couch. A bookcase with no books in it, just china dogs. It occurred to me that her unsubtle approach was probably not successful as often as she might wish.

But where was the thing I was looking for?

"Hey, I wanna powder my nose," I announced.

"In there," she said. "Can't you talk quiet?"

I went into the bathroom. It was tiny. There was a foreshortened tub with a circular frame over it from which hung a horribly cheerful shower curtain, with big red roses. I closed the door behind me and carefully opened the medicine chest. Just the usual. I closed it carefully so it wouldn't click. A built-in shelf held towels.

Must be a closet in the main room, I thought. Hatbox, trunk, suitcase, maybe. Where would I put a devil-doll if I were hexing someone?

I wouldn't hide it away, I answered myself. I don't know why, but I'd sort of have it out in the open somehow . . .

I opened the shower curtain and let it close. Round curtain, square tub.

"Yup!"

I pushed the whole round curtain back, and there in the corner, just at eye level, was a triangular shelf. Grouped on it were four figurines, made apparently from kneaded wax. Three had wisps of hair fastened by candle-droppings. The fourth was hairless, but had slivers of a horny substance pressed into the ends of the arms. Fingernail parings.

I stood for a moment thinking. Then I picked up the hairless doll, turned to the door. I checked myself, flushed the toilet, took a towel, shook it out, dropped it over the edge of the tub. Then I reeled out. "Hey honey, look what I got, ain't it *cute?*"

"Shh!" she said. "Oh for crying out loud. Put that back, will you?"

"Well, what is it?"

"It's none of your business, that's what it is. Come on, put it back."

I wagged my finger at her. "You're not being nice to me," I complained.

She pulled some shreds of patience together with an obvious effort. "It's just some sort of toys I have around. Here."

I snatched it away. "All right, you don't wanna be nice!" I whipped my coat together and began to button it clumsily, still holding the figurine.

She sighed, rolled her eyes, and came to me. "Come on, Dadsy. Have a nice cup of coffee and let's not fight." She reached for the doll and I snatched it away again.

"You got to tell me," I pouted.

"It's pers'nal."

"I wanna be personal," I pointed out.

"Oh all right," she said. "I had a roommate one time, she used to make these things. She said you make one, and s'pose I decide I don't like you, I got something of yours, hair or toenails or something. Say your name is George. What is your name?"

"George," I said.

"All right, I call the doll George. Then I stick pins in it. That's all. Give it to me."

"Who's this one?"

"That's Al."

"Hal?"

"Al. I got one called Hal. He's in there. I hate him the most."

"Yeah, huh. Well, what happens to Al and George and all when you stick pins in 'em?"

"They're s'posed to get sick. Even die."

"Do they?"

"Nah," she said with immediate and complete candor. "I told you, it's just a game, sort of. If it worked believe me old Al would bleed to death. He runs the delicatessen." I handed her the doll, and she looked at it pensively. "I wish it did work sometimes. Sometimes I almost believe in it. I stick 'em and they just *yell.*"

"Introduce me," I demanded

"What?"

"Introduce me," I said. I pulled her toward the bathroom. She made a small irritated "oh-h," and came along.

"This is Fritz and this is Bruno and—where's the other one?"

"What other one?"

"Maybe he fell behind the—down back of—" She knelt on the edge of the tub and leaned over to the wall, to peer behind it. She regained her feet, her face red from effort and anger. "What are you trying to pull? You kidding around or something?"

I spread my arms. "What do you mean?"

"Come on," she said between her teeth. She felt my coat, my jacket. "You hid it some place."

"No I didn't. There was only four." I pointed. "Al and Fritz and Bruno and Hal. Which one's Hal?"

"That's Freddie. He give me twenny bucks and took twenny-three out of my purse, the dirty—. But Hal's gone. He was the best one of all. You *sure* you didn't hide him?" Then she thumped her forehead.

"The window!" she said, and ran into the other room. I was on my four bones peering under the tub when I understood what she meant. I took a last good look around and then followed her. She was standing by the window, shading her eyes and peering out. "What do you know. Imagine somebody would swipe a thing like that!"

A sick sense of loss was born in my solar plexus.

"Aw, forget it. I'll make another one for that Hal. But I'll never make another one that ugly," she added wistfully. "Come on, the coffee's—what's the matter? You sick?"

"Yeah," I said, "I'm sick."

"Of all the things to steal," she said from the kitchenette. "Who do you suppose would do such a thing?"

Suddenly I knew who would. I cracked my fist into my palm and laughed.

"What's the matter, you crazy?"

"Yes," I said. "You got a phone?"

"No. Where you going?"

"Out. Goodbye, Charity."

"Hey, now wait, honey. Just when I got coffee for you." I snatched the door open. She caught my sleeve.

"You can't go away like this! How's about a little something for Charity?"

"You'll get yours when you make the rounds tomorrow, if you don't have a hangover from those sherry highballs," I said cheerfully. "And don't forget the five you swiped from the tip plate. Better watch out for that waiter, by the way. I think he saw you do it."

"You're not drunk!" she gasped.

"You're not a witch," I grinned. I blew her a kiss and ran out.

I shall always remember her like that, round-eyed, a little more astonished than she was resentful, the beloved dollar signs fading from her hot brown eyes, the pathetic, useless little twitch of her hips she summoned up as a last plea.

Every try to find a phone booth at five A.M.? I half-trotted nine blocks before I found a cab, and I was on the Queens side of the Triboro Bridge before I found a gas station open.

I dialed. The phone said, "Hello?"

"Kelley?" I roared happily. "Why didn't you tell me? You'd 'a saved sixty bucks worth of the most dismal fun I ever—"

"This is Milton," said the telephone. "Hal just died."

My mouth was still open and I guess it just stayed that way. Anyway it was cold inside when I closed it. "I'll be right over."

"Better not," said Milton. His voice was shaking with incomplete control. "Unless you really want to . . . there's nothing you can do, and I'm going to be . . . busy."

"Where's Kelley?" I whispered.

"I don't know."

"Well," I said. "Call me."

I got back into my taxi and went home. I don't remember the trip.

Sometimes I think I dreamed I saw Kelley that morning.

A lot of alcohol and enough emotion to kill it, mixed with no sleep for thirty hours, makes for blackout. I came up out of it reluctantly, feeling that this was no kind of world to be aware of. Not today.

I lay looking at the bookcase. It was very quiet. I closed my eyes, turned over, burrowed into the pillow, opened my eyes again and saw Kelley sitting in the easy chair, poured out in his relaxed feline fashion, legs too long, arms too long, eyes too long and only partly open.

I didn't ask him how he got in because he was already in, and welcome. I didn't say anything because I didn't want to be the one to tell him about Hal. And besides I wasn't awake yet. I just lay there.

"Milton told me," he said. "It's all right."

I nodded.

Kelley said, "I read your story. I found some more and read them too. You got a lot of imagination."

He hung a cigarette on his lower lip and lit it. "Milton, he's got a lot of knowledge. Now, both of you think real good up to a point. Then too much knowledge presses him off to the no'theast. And too much imagination squeezes you off to the no'thwest."

He smoked a while.

"Me, I think straight through but it takes me a while."

I palmed my eyeballs. "I don't know what you're talking about."

"That's okay," he said quietly. "Look, I'm goin' after what killed Hal."

I closed my eyes and saw a vicious, pretty, empty little face. I said, "I was most of the night with Charity."

"Were you now."

"Kelley," I said, "if it's her you're after, forget it. She's a sleazy little tramp but she's also a little kid who never had a chance. She didn't kill Hal."

"I know she didn't. I don't feel about her one way or the other. I know what killed Hal, though, and I'm goin' after it the only way I know for sure."

"All right then," I said. I let my head dig back into the pillow. "What did kill him?"

"Milton told you about that doll Hal give her."

"He told me. There's nothing in that, Kelley. For a man to be a voodoo victim, he's got to believe that—"

"Yeh, yeh, yeh. Milton told me. For hours he told me."

"Well all right."

"You got imagination," Kelley said sleepily. "Now just imagine along with me a while. Milt tell you how some folks, if you point a gun at 'em and go bang, they drop dead, even if there was only blanks in the gun?"

"He didn't, but I read it somewhere. Same general idea."

"Now imagine all the shootings you ever heard of was like that, with blanks."

"Go ahead."

"You got a lot of evidence, a lot of experts, to prove about this believing business, ever' time anyone gets shot."

"Got it."

"Now imagine somebody shows up with live ammunition in his gun. Do you think those bullets going to give a damn who believes what?"

I didn't say anything.

"For a long time people been makin' dolls and stickin' pins in 'em. Wherever somebody believes it can happen, they get it. Now suppose somebody shows up with the doll all those dolls was copied from. The real one."

I lay still.

"You don't have to know nothin' about it," said Kelley lazily. "You don't have to be anybody special. You don't have to understand how it works. Nobody has to believe nothing. All you do, you just point it where you want it to work."

"Point it how?" I whispered.

He shrugged. "Call the doll by a name. Hate it, maybe."

"For God's sake, Kelley, you're crazy! Why, there can't be anything like that!"

"You eat a steak," Kelley said. "How's your gut know what to take and what to pass? Do *you* know?"

"Some people know."

"You don't. But your gut does. So there's lots of natural laws that are goin' to work whether anyone understands 'em or not. Lots of sailors take a trick at the wheel without knowin' how a steering engine works. Well, that's me. I know where I'm goin' and I know I'll get there. What do I care how does it work, or who believes what?"

"Fine, so what are you going to do?"

"Get what got Hal." His tone was just as lazy but his voice was very deep, and I knew when not to ask any more questions. Instead I said, with a certain amount of annoyance, "Why tell me?"

"Want you to do something for me."

"What?"

"Don't tell no one what I just said for a while. And keep something for me."

"What? And for how long?"

"You'll know."

I'd have risen up and roared at him if he had not chosen just that second to get up and drift out of the bedroom. "What gets me," he said quietly from the other room, "is I could have figured this out six months ago."

I fell asleep straining to hear him go out. He moves quieter than any big man I ever saw.

It was afternoon when I awoke. The doll was sitting on the mantelpiece glaring at me. Ugliest thing ever happened.

I saw Kelley at Hal's funeral. He and Milt and I had a somber drink afterward. We didn't talk about dolls. Far as I know Kelley shipped out right afterward. You assume that seamen do, when they drop out of sight. Milton was as busy as a doctor, which is very. I left the doll where it was for a week or two, wondering when Kelley was going to get around to his project. He'd probably call for it when he was ready. Meanwhile I respected his request and told no one about it. One day when some people were coming over I shoved it in the top shelf of the closet, and somehow it just got left there.

About a month afterward I began to notice the smell. I couldn't identify it right away; it was too faint; but whatever it was, I didn't like it. I traced it to the closet, and then to the doll. I took it down and sniffed it. My breath exploded out. It was that same smell a lot of people wish they could forget—what Milton called necrotic flesh. I came within an inch of pitching the filthy thing down the incinerator, but a promise is a promise. I put it down on the table, where it slumped repulsively. One of the legs was broken above the knee. I mean, it seemed to have two knee joints. And it was somehow puffy, sick-looking.

I had an old bell-jar somewhere, that once had a clock in it. I found it and a piece of inlaid linoleum, and put the doll under the jar at least so I could live with it.

I worked and saw people—dinner with Milton, once—and the days went by the way they do, and then one night it occurred to me to look at the doll again.

It was in pretty sorry shape. I'd tried to keep it fairly cool, but it seemed to be melting and running all over. For a moment I worried about what Kelley might say, and then I heartily damned Kelley and put the whole mess down in the cellar.

And I guess it was altogether two months after Hal's death that I wondered why I'd assumed Kelley would have to call for the little horror before he did what he had to do. He said he was going to get what got Hal, and he intimated that the doll was that something.

Well, that doll was being got, but good. I brought it up and put it under the light. It was still a figurine, but it was one unholy mess. "Attaboy, Kelley," I gloated. "Go get 'em, kid."

Milton called me up and asked me to meet him at Rudy's. He sounded pretty bad. We had the shortest drink yet.

He was sitting in the back booth chewing on the insides of his cheeks. His lips were gray and he slopped his drink when he lifted it.

"What in time happened to you?" I gasped.

He gave me a ghastly smile. "I'm famous," he said. I heard his glass chatter against his teeth. He said, "I called in so many consultants on Hal Kelley that I'm supposed to be an expert on that—on that . . . condition." He forced his glass back to the table with both hands and held it down. He tried to smile and I wished he wouldn't. He stopped trying and almost whispered, "I can't nurse one of 'em like that again. I can't."

"You going to tell what happened?" I asked harshly. That works sometimes.

"Oh, oh yes. Well they brought in a . . . another one. At General. They called me in. Just like Hal. I mean *exactly* like Hal. Only I won't have to nurse this one, no I won't, I won't have to. She died six hours after she arrived."

"She?"

"You know what you'd have to do to someone to make them look like that?" he said shrilly. "You'd have to tie off parts so they mortified. You'd have to use a wood rasp, maybe; a club; filth to rub into the wounds. You'd have to break bones in a vise."

"All right, all right, but nobody—"

"And you'd have to do that for about two months, every day, every night." He rubbed his eyes. He drove his knuckles in so hard that I caught at his wrists. "I *know* nobody did it; did I say anyone did it?" he barked. "Nobody did anything to Hal, did they?"

"Drink up."

He didn't. He whispered, "She just said the same thing over and over every time anyone talked to her. They'd say, 'What happened?' or 'Who did this to you?' or 'What's your name?' and she'd say, 'He called me Dolly.' That's all she'd say, just 'He called me Dolly.'"

I got up. "Bye, Milt."

He looked stricken. "Don't go, will you, you just got—"

"I got to go," I said. I didn't look back. I had to get out and ask myself some questions. Think.

Who's guilty of murder, I asked myself, the one who pulls the trigger, or the gun?

I thought of a poor damn pretty, empty little face with greedy hot brown eyes, and what Kelley said, "I don't care about her one way or the other."

I thought, when she was twisting and breaking and sticking, how did it look to the doll? Bet she never even wondered about that.

I thought, action: A girl throws a fan at a man. Reaction: The man throws the girl at the fan. Action: A wheel sticks on a shaft. Reaction: Knock the shaft out of the wheel. Situation: We can't get inside. Resolution: Take the outside off it.

It's a way of thinking.

How do you kill a person? Use a doll.

How do you kill a doll?

Who's guilty, the one who pulls the trigger, or the gun?

"He called me Dolly."
"He called me Dolly."
"He called me Dolly."
When I got home the phone was ringing.

"Hi," said Kelley.

I said, "It's all gone. The doll's all gone, Kelley." I said, "stay away from me."

"All right," said Kelley.

THE MAN WHO LOST THE SEA

Say you're a kid, and one dark night you're running along the cold sand with this helicopter in your hand, saying very fast *witchy-witchy-witchy*. You pass the sick man and he wants you to shove off with that thing. Maybe he thinks you're too old to play with toys. So you squat next to him in the sand and tell him it isn't a toy, it's a model. You tell him look here, here's something most people don't know about helicopters. You take a blade of the rotor in your fingers and show him how it can move in the hub, up and down a little, back and forth a little, and twist a little, to change pitch. You start to tell him how this flexibility does away with the gyroscopic effect, but he won't listen. He doesn't want to think about flying, about helicopters, or about you, and he most especially does not want explanations about anything by anybody. Not now. Now, he wants to think about the sea. So you go away.

The sick man is buried in the cold sand with only his head and his left arm showing. He is dressed in a pressure suit and looks like a man from Mars. Built into his left sleeve is a combination time-piece and pressure gauge, the gauge with a luminous blue indicator which makes no sense, the clock hands luminous red. He can hear the pounding of surf and the soft swift pulse of his pumps. One time long ago when he was swimming he went too deep and

407

stayed down too long and came up too fast, and when he came to it was like this: they said, "Don't move, boy. You've got the bends. Don't even *try* to move." He had tried anyway. It hurt. So now, this time, he lies in the sand without moving, without trying.

His head isn't working right. But he knows clearly that it isn't working right, which is a strange thing that happens to people in shock sometimes. Say you were that kid, you could say how it was, because once you woke up lying in the gym office in high school and asked what had happened. They explained how you tried something on the parallel bars and fell on your head. You understood exactly, though you couldn't remember falling. Then a minute later you asked again what had happened and they told you. You understood it. And a minute later . . . forty-one times they told you, and you understood. It was just that no matter how many times they pushed it into your head, it wouldn't stick there; but all the while you *knew* that your head would start working again in time. And in time it did. . . . Of course, if you were that kid, always explaining things to people and to yourself, you wouldn't want to bother the sick man with it now.

Look what you've done already, making him send you away with that angry shrug of the mind (which, with the eyes, are the only things that will move just now). The motionless effort costs him a wave of nausea. He has felt seasick before but he has never *been* seasick, and the formula for that is to keep your eyes on the horizon and stay busy. Now! Then he'd better get busy—now; for there's one place especially not to be seasick in, and that's locked up in a pressure suit. Now!

So he busies himself as best he can, with the seascape, landscape, sky. He lies on high ground, his head propped on a vertical wall of black rock. There is another such outcrop before him, whip-topped with white sand and with smooth flat sand. Beyond and down is valley, salt-free, estuary; he cannot yet be sure. He is sure of the line of footprints, which begin behind him, pass to his left, disappear in the outcrop shadows, and reappear beyond to vanish at last into the shadows of the valley.

Stretched across the sky is old mourning-cloth, with starlight burning holes in it, and between the holes the black is absolute— wintertime, mountaintop sky-black.

(Far off on the horizon within himself, he sees the swell and crest of approaching nausea; he counters with an undertow of weakness, which meets and rounds and settles the wave before it can break. Get busier. *Now.*)

Burst in on him, then, with the X-15 model. That'll get him. Hey, how about this for a gimmick? Get too high for the thin air to give you any control, you have these little jets in the wingtips, see? and on the sides of the empennage: bank, roll, yaw, whatever, with squirts of compressed air.

But the sick man curls his sick lip: oh, git, kid, git, will you?— that has nothing to do with the sea. So you git.

Out and out the sick man forces his view, etching all he sees with a meticulous intensity, as if it might be his charge, one day, to duplicate all this. To his left is only starlit sea, windless. In front of him across the valley, rounded hills with dim white epaulettes of light. To his right, the jutting corner of the black wall against which his helmet rests. (He thinks the distant moundings of nausea becalmed, but he will not look yet.) So he scans the sky, black and bright, calling Sirius, calling Pleiades, Polaris, Ursa Minor, calling that . . . that . . . Why, it *moves.* Watch it: yes, it moves! It is a fleck of light, seeming to be wrinkled, fissured, rather like a chip of boiled cauliflower in the sky. (Of course, he knows better than to trust his own eyes just now.) But that movement . . .

As a child he had stood on cold sand in a frosty Cape Cod evening, watching Sputnik's steady spark rise out of the haze (madly, dawning a little north of west); and after that he had sleeplessly wound special coils for his receiver, risked his life restringing high antennas, all for the brief capture of an unreadable *tweetle-eep-tweetle* in his earphones from Vanguard. Explorer, Lunik, Discoverer, Mercury. He knew them all (well, some people collect match-covers, stamps) and he knew especially that unmistakable steady sliding in the sky.

This moving fleck was a satellite, and in a moment, motionless, uninstrumented but for his chronometer and his part-brain, he will know which one. (He is grateful beyond expression— without that sliding chip of light, there were only those footprints, those wandering footprints, to tell a man he was not alone in the world.)

Say you were a kid, eager and challengeable and more than a little bright, you might in a day or so work out a way to measure

the period of a satellite with nothing but a timepiece and a brain;
you might eventually see that the shadow in the rocks ahead had
been there from the first only because of the light from the rising
satellite. Now if you check the time exactly at the moment when
the shadow on the sand is equal to the height of the outcrop, and
time it again when the light is at the zenith and the shadow gone,
you will multiply this number of minutes by 8—think why, now;
horizon to zenith is one-fourth of the orbit, give or take a little,
and halfway up the sky is half that quarter—and you will then
know this satellite's period. You know all the periods—ninety
minutes, two, two-and-a-half hours; with that and the appearance
of this bird, you'll find out which one it is.

But if you were that kid, eager or resourceful or whatever, you
wouldn't jabber about it to the sick man, for not only does he not
want to be bothered with you, he's thought of all that long since
and is even now watching the shadows for that triangular split second of measurement. *Now!* His eyes drop to the face of his
chronometer: 0400, near as makes no never mind.

He has minutes to wait now—ten? . . . thirty? . . . twenty-
three?—while this baby moon eats up its slice of shadowpie; and
that's too bad, the waiting, for though the inner sea is calm there
are currents below, shadows that shift and swim. Be busy. Be busy.
He must not swim near the great invisible amoeba, whatever happens: its first cold pseudopod is even now reaching for the vitals.

Being a knowledgeable young fellow, not quite a kid any
more, wanting to help the sick man too, you want to tell him
everything you know about that cold-in-the-gut, that reaching
invisible surrounding implacable amoeba. You know all about
it—listen, you want to yell at him, don't let that touch of cold
bother you. Just know what it is, that's all. Know what it is that is
touching your gut. You want to tell him, listen:

Listen, this is how you met the monster and dissected it. Listen,
you were skin-diving in the Grenadines, a hundred tropical shoal-
water islands; you had a new blue snorkel mask, the kind with
face-plate and breathing-tube all in one, and new blue flippers on
your feet, and a new blue spear-gun—all this new because you'd
only begun, you see; you were a beginner, aghast with pleasure at
your easy intrusion into this underwater otherworld. You'd been

out in a boat, you were coming back, you'd just reached the mouth of the little bay, you'd taken the notion to swim the rest of the way. You'd said as much to the boys and slipped into the warm silky water. You brought your gun.

Not far to go at all, but then beginners find wet distances deceiving. For the first five minutes or so it was only delightful, the sun hot on your back and the water so warm it seemed not to have any temperature at all and you were flying. With your face under the water, your mask was not so much attached as part of you, your wide blue flippers trod away yards, your gun rode all but weightless in your hand, the taut rubber sling making an occasional hum as your passage plucked it in the sunlit green. In your ears crooned the breathy monotone of the snorkel tube, and through the invisible disk of plate glass you saw wonders. The bay was shallow—ten, twelve feet or so—and sandy, with great growths of brain-, bone-, and fire-coral, intricate waving sea-fans, and fish—such fish! Scarlet and green and aching azure, gold and rose and slate-color studded with sparks of enamel-blue, pink and peace and silver. And that *thing* got into you, that . . . monster.

There were enemies in this otherworld: the sand-colored spotted sea-snake with his big ugly head and turned-down mouth, who would not retreat but lay watching the intruder pass; and the mottled moray with jaws like bolt-cutters; and somewhere around, certainly, the barracuda with his undershot face and teeth turned inward so that he must take away whatever he might strike. There were urchins—the plump white sea-egg with its thick fur of sharp quills and the black ones with the long slender spines that would break off in unwary flesh and fester there for weeks; and file-fish and stone-fish with their poisoned barbs and lethal meat; and the stingaree who could drive his spike through a leg bone. Yet these were not *monsters,* and could not matter to you, the invader churning along above them all. For you were above them in so many ways—armed, rational, comforted by the close shore (ahead the beach, the rocks on each side) and by the presence of the boat not too far behind. Yet you were . . . attacked.

At first it was uneasiness, not pressing, but pervasive, a contact quite as intimate as that of the sea; you were sheathed in it. And also there was the touch—the cold inward contact. Aware of it at last, you laughed: for Pete's sake, what's there to be scared of?

The monster, the amoeba.

You raised your head and looked back in air. The boat had edged in to the cliff at the right; someone was giving a last poke around for lobster. You waved at the boat; it was your gun you waved, and emerging from the water it gained its latent ounces so that you sank a bit, and as if you had no snorkel on, you tipped your head back to get a breath. But tipping your head back plunged the end of the tube under water; the valve closed; you drew in a hard lungful of nothing at all. You dropped your face under; up came the tube; you got your air, and along with it a bullet of seawater which struck you somewhere inside the throat. You coughed it out and floundered, sobbing as you sucked in air, inflating your chest until it hurt, and the air you got seemed no good, no good at all, a worthless devitalized inert gas.

You clenched your teeth and headed for the beach, kicking strongly and knowing it was the right thing to do; and then below and to the right you saw a great bulk mounding up out of the sand floor of the sea. You knew it was only the reef, rocks and coral and weed, but the sight of it made you scream; you didn't care what you knew. You turned hard left to avoid it, fought by as if it would reach for you, and you couldn't get air, couldn't get air, for all the unobstructed hooting of your snorkel tube. You couldn't bear the mask, suddenly, not for another second, so you shoved it upward clear of your mouth and rolled over, floating on your back and opening your mouth to the sky and breathing with a quacking noise.

It was then and there that the monster well and truly engulfed you, mantling you round and about within itself—formless, borderless, the illimitable amoeba. The beach, mere yards away, and the rocky arms of the bay, and the not-too-distant boat—these you could identify but no longer distinguish, for they were all one and the same thing . . . the thing called unreachable.

You fought that way for a time, on your back, dangling the gun under and behind you and straining to get enough warm sun-stained air into your chest. And in time some particles of sanity began to swirl in the roil of your mind, and to dissolve and tint it. The air pumping in and out of your square-grinned frightened mouth began to be meaningful at last, and the monster relaxed away from you.

You took stock, saw surf, beach, a leaning tree. You felt the new scent of your body as the rollers humped to become breakers. Only a dozen firm kicks brought you to where you could roll over and double up; your shin struck coral with a lovely agony and you stood in foam and waded ashore. You gained the wet sand, hard sand, and ultimately, with two more paces powered by bravado, you crossed high-water mark and lay in the dry sand, unable to move.

You lay in the sand, and before you were able to move or to think, you were able to feel a triumph—a triumph because you were alive and knew that much without thinking at all.

When you *were* able to think, your first thought was of the gun, and the first move you were able to make was to let go at last of the thing. You had nearly died because you had not let it go before; without it you would not have been burdened and you would not have panicked. You had (you began to understand) kept it because someone else would have had to retrieve it—easily enough—and you could not have stood the laughter. You had almost died because They might laugh at you.

This was the beginning of the dissection, analysis, study of the monster. It began then; it had never finished. Some of what you had learned from it was merely important; some of the rest—vital.

You had learned, for example, never to swim farther with a snorkel than you could swim back without one. You learned never to burden yourself with the unnecessary in an emergency: even a hand or a foot might be as expendable as a gun; pride was expendable, dignity was. You learned never to dive alone, even if They laugh at you, even if you have to shoot a fish yourself and say afterward "we" shot it. Most of all, you learned that fear has many fingers, and one of them—a simple one, made of too great a concentration of carbon dioxide in your blood, as from too-rapid breathing in and out of the same tube—is not really fear at all but feels like fear, and can turn into panic and kill you.

Listen, you want to say, listen, there isn't anything wrong with such an experience or with all the study it leads to, because a man who can learn enough from it could become fit enough, cautious enough, foresighted, unafraid, modest, teachable enough to be chosen, to be qualified for—

You lose the thought, or turn it away, because the sick man feels that cold touch deep inside, feels it right now, feels it beyond ignoring, above and beyond anything that you, with all your experience and certainty, could explain to him even if he would listen, which he won't. Make him, then; tell him the cold touch is some simple explainable thing like anoxia, like gladness even: some triumph that he will be able to appreciate when his head is working right again.

Triumph? Here he's alive after . . . whatever it is, and that doesn't seem to be triumph enough, though it was in the Grenadines, and that other time, when he got the bends, saved his own life, saved two other lives. Now, somehow, it's not the same: there seems to be a reason why just being alive afterward isn't a triumph.

Why not triumph? Because not twelve, not twenty, not even thirty minutes is it taking the satellite to complete its eighth-of-an-orbit: fifty minutes are gone, and still there's a slice of shadow yonder. It is this, *this* which is placing the cold finger upon his heart, and he doesn't know why, he doesn't know why, he *will* not know why; he is afraid he shall when his head is working again. . . .

Oh, where's the kid? Where is any way to busy the mind, apply it to something, anything else but the watchhand which outruns the moon? Here, kid: come over here—what you got there?

If you were the kid, then you'd forgive everything and hunker down with your new model, not a toy, not a helicopter or a rocket-plane, but the big one, the one that looks like an overgrown cartridge. It's so big, even as a model, that even an angry sick man wouldn't call it a toy. A giant cartridge, but watch: the lower four-fifths is Alpha—all muscle—over a million pounds thrust. (Snap it off, throw it away.) Half the rest is Beta—all brains—it puts you on your way. (Snap it off, throw it away.) And now look at the polished fraction which is left. Touch a control somewhere and see—see? it has wings—wide triangular wings. This is Gamma, the one with wings, and on its back is a small sausage; it is a moth with a sausage on its back. The sausage (click! it comes free) is Delta. Delta is the last, the smallest: Delta is the way home.

What will they think of next? Quite a toy. Quite a toy. Beat it, kid. The satellite is almost overhead, the sliver of shadow going—going—almost gone and . . . gone.

Check: 0459. Fifty-nine minutes? give or take a few. Times eight . . . 472 . . . is, uh, 7 hours 52 minutes.

Seven hours fifty-two minutes? Why, there isn't a satellite round earth with a period like that. In all the solar system there's only . . .

The cold finger turns fierce, implacable.

The east is paling and the sick man turns to it, wanting the light, the sun, an end to questions whose answers couldn't be looked upon. The sea stretches endlessly out to the growing light, and endlessly, somewhere out of sight, the surf roars. The paling east bleaches the sandy hilltops and throws the line of footprints into aching relief. That would be the buddy, the sick man knows, gone for help. He cannot at the moment recall who the buddy is, but in time he will, and meanwhile the footprints make him less alone.

The sun's upper rim thrusts itself above the horizon with a flash of green, instantly gone. There is no dawn, just the green flash and then a clear white blast of unequivocal sunup. The sea could not be whiter, more still, if it were frozen and snow-blanketed. In the west, stars still blaze, and overhead the crinkled satellite is scarcely abashed by the growing light. A formless jumble in the valley below begins to resolve itself into a sort of tent-city, or installation of some kind, with tubelike and sail-like buildings. This would have meaning for the sick man if his head were working right. Soon, it would. Will. (Oh . . .)

The sea, out on the horizon, just under the rising sun, is behaving strangely, for in that place where properly belongs a pool of unbearable brightness, there is instead a notch of brown. It is as if the white fire of the sun is drinking dry the sea—for look, look! the notch becomes a bow and the bow a crescent, racing ahead of the sunlight, white sea ahead of it and behind it a cocoa-dry stain spreading across and down toward where he watches.

Beside the finger of fear which lies on him, another finger places itself, and another, making ready for that clutch, that grip, that ultimate insane squeeze of panic. Yet beyond that again, past that squeeze when it comes, to be savored if the squeeze is only fear and not panic, lies triumph—triumph, and a glory. It is perhaps this which constitutes his whole battle: to fit himself, prepare himself to bear the utmost that fear could do, for if he can do that, there is a triumph on the other side. But . . . not yet. Please, not yet awhile.

Something flies (or flew, or will fly—he is a little confused on this point) toward him, from the far right where the stars still shine. It is not a bird and it is unlike any aircraft on earth, for the aerodynamics are wrong. Wings so wide and so fragile would be useless, would melt and tear away in any of earth's atmosphere but the outer fringes. He sees then (because he prefers to see it so) that it is the kid's model, or part of it, and for a toy it does very well indeed.

It is the part called Gamma, and it glides in, balancing, parallels the sand and holds away, holds away slowing, then settles, all in slow motion, throwing up graceful sheet-fountains of fine sand from its skids. And it runs along the ground for an impossible distance, letting down its weight by the ounce and stingily the ounce, until *look out* until a skid *look out* fits itself into a bridged crevasse, *look out, look out!* and still moving on, it settles down to the struts. Gamma then, tired, digs her wide left wingtip carefully into the racing sand, digs it in hard; and as the wing breaks off, Gamma slews, sidles, slides slowly, pointing her other triangular tentlike wing at the sky, and broadside crushes into the rocks at the valley's end.

As she rolls smashing over, there breaks from her broad back the sausage, the little Delta, which somersaults away to break its back upon the rocks, and through the broken hull spill smashed shards of graphite from the moderator of her power-pile. *Look out! Look out!* and at the same instant from the finally checked mass of Gamma there explodes a doll, which slides and tumbles into the sand, into the rocks and smashed hot graphite from the wreck of Delta.

The sick man numbly watches this toy destroy itself: what will they think of next?—and with a gelid horror prays at the doll lying in the raging rubble of the atomic pile: *don't stay there, man—get away! get away! that's hot, you know?* But it seems like a night and a day and half another night before the doll staggers to its feet and, clumsy in its pressure-suit, runs away up the valleyside, climbs a sand-topped outcrop, slips, falls, lies under a slow cascade of cold ancient sand until, but for an arm and the helmet, it is buried.

The sun is high now, high enough to show the sea is not a sea, but brown plain with the frost burned off it, as now it burns away from the hills, diffusing in air and blurring the edges of the sun's disk, so that in a very few minutes there is no sun at all, but only a glare in the east. Then the valley below loses its shadows, and, like an arrangement in a diorama, reveals the form and nature of the wreckage below: no tent city this, no installation, but the true real ruin of Gamma and the eviscerated hulk of Delta. (Alpha was the muscle, Beta the brain; Gamma was a bird, but Delta, Delta was the way home.)

And from it stretches the line of footprints, to and by the sick man, above to the bluff, and gone with the sandslide which had buried him there. Whose footprints?

He knows whose, whether or not he knows that he knows, or wants to or not. He knows what satellite has (give or take a bit) a period like that (want it exactly?—it's 7.66 hours). He knows what world has such a night, and such a frosty glare by day. He knows these things as he knows how spilled radioactives will pour the crash and mutter of surf into a man's earphones.

Say you were that kid: say, instead, at last, that you are the sick man, for they are the same; surely then you can understand why of all things, even while shattered, shocked, sick with radiation calculated (leaving) radiation computed (arriving) and radiation past all bearing (lying in the wreckage of Delta) you would want to think of the sea. For no farmer who fingers the soil with love and knowledge, no poet who sings of it, artist, contractor, engineer, even child bursting into tears at the inexpressible beauty of a field of daffodils—none of these is as intimate with Earth as those who live on, live with, breathe and drift in its seas. So of these things you must think; with these you must dwell until you are less sick and more ready to face the truth.

The truth, then, is that the satellite fading here is Phobos, that those footprints are your own, that there is no sea here, that you have crashed and are killed and will in a moment be dead. The cold hand ready to squeeze and still your heart is not anoxia or even fear, it is death. Now, if there is something more important than this, now is the time for it to show itself.

The sick man looks at the line of his own footprints, which testify that he is alone, and at the wreckage below, which states

that there is no way back, and at the white east and the mottled
west and the paling fleck-like satellite above. Surf sounds in his
ears. He hears his pumps. He hears what is left of his breathing.
The cold clamps down and folds him round past measuring, past
all limit.

Then he speaks, cries out: then with joy he takes his triumph
at the other side of death, as one takes a great fish, as one com-
pletes a skilled and mighty task, rebalances at the end of some great
daring leap; and as he used to say "we shot a fish" he uses no "I":

"God," he cries, dying on Mars, "God, we made it!"

SLOW SCULPTURE

She didn't know who he was when she met him; well, not many people did. He was in the high orchard doing something under a pear tree. The land smelled of late summer and wind: bronze, it smelled bronze. He looked up at a compact girl in her mid-twenties, with a fearless face and eyes the same color as her hair, which was extraordinary because her hair was red-gold. She looked down at a leather-skinned man in his forties with a gold-leaf electroscope in his hand, and felt she was an intruder. She said, "Oh," in what was apparently the right way, because he nodded once and said, "Hold this," and there could then be no thought of intrusion. She knelt down by him and took the instrument, holding it just where he positioned her hand, and then he moved a little away and struck a tuning fork against his kneecap. "What's it doing?" He had a good voice, the kind of voice strangers notice and listen to.

She looked at the delicate leaves of gold in the glass shield of the electroscope. "They're moving apart."

He struck the tuning fork again and the leaves pressed away from one another. "Much?"

"About forty-five degrees when you hit the fork."

"Good—that's about the most we'll get." From a pocket of his bush jacket he drew a sack of chalk-dust and dropped a small handful on the ground. "I'll move now. You stay right there and tell me how much the leaves separate."

He traveled around the pear tree in a zigzag course, striking his tuning fork while she called out numbers—ten degrees, thirty, five, twenty, nothing. Whenever the gold foil pressed apart to maximum, forty degrees or more, he dropped more chalk. When he was finished the tree was surrounded, in a rough oval, by the white dots of chalk. He took out a notebook and diagrammed them and the tree, and put away the book, and took the electroscope out of her hands. "Were you looking for something?" he asked her.

"No," she said. "Yes."

He could smile. Though it did not last long, she found it very surprising in a face like that. "That's not what is called, in a court of law, a responsive answer."

She glanced across the hillside, metallic in that late light. There wasn't much on it—rocks, weeds the summer was done with, a tree or so, and then the orchard. Anyone present had come a long way to get here. "It wasn't a simple question," she said, tried to smile, and burst into tears.

She was sorry and said so.

"Why?" he asked. This was the first time she was to experience this ask-the-next-question thing of his. It was unsettling. It always would be—never less, sometimes a great deal more. "Well—one doesn't have emotional explosions in public."

"*You* do. I don't know this 'one' you're talking about."

"I—guess I don't either, now that you mention it."

"Tell the truth then. No sense in going round and round about it, 'he'll think that I—' and the like. I'll think what I think, whatever you say. Or—go on down the mountain and just don't say any more." She did not turn to go, so he added, "Try the truth, then. If it's important, it's simple, and if it's simple it's easy to say."

"I'm going to die!" she cried.

"So am I."

"I have a lump in my breast."

"Come up to the house and I'll fix it."

Without another word he turned away and started through the orchard. Startled half out of her wits, indignant and full of insane hope, experiencing, even, a quick curl of astonished laugh-

ter, she stood for a moment watching him go, and then found herself (at what point did I decide?) running after him.

She caught up with him on the uphill margin of the orchard.
"Are you a doctor?"

He appeared not to notice that she had waited, had run.
"No," he said, and, walking on, appeared not to see her stand
again pulling on her lower lip, then run again to catch up.

"I must be out of my mind," she said, joining him on a garden
path. She said it to herself, which he must have known because he
did not answer. The garden was alive with defiant chrysanthemums and a pond in which she saw the flicker of a pair of redcap
imperials—silver, not gold fish—which were the largest she had
ever seen. Then—the house.

First it was part of the garden, with its colonnaded terrace,
and then, with its rock walls (too big to be called fieldstone) part
of the mountain. It was on and in the hillside, and its roofs paralleled the skylines, front and sides, and part of it was backed
against an outjutting cliff face. The door, beamed and studded
and with two archers' slits, was opened for them (but there was no
one there) and when it closed it was silent, a far more solid exclu-
sion of things outside than any click or clang of latch or bolt. She
stood with her back against it, watching him cross what seemed to
be the central well of the house, or at least this part of it. It was a
kind of small court in the center of which was an atrium, glazed
on all its five sides and open to the sky at the top. In it was a tree, a
cypress or juniper, gnarled and twisted and with the turned-back,
paralleled, sculptured appearance of what the Japanese call bonsai.

"Aren't you coming?" he called, holding open a door behind
the atrium.

"Bonsai just aren't fifteen feet tall," she said.

"This one is."

She came by it slowly, looking. "How long have you had it?"

His tone of voice said he was immensely pleased. It is a clum-
siness to ask the owner of a bonsai how old it is; you are then
demanding to know if it is his work or if he has acquired and continued the concept of another; you are tempting him to claim for
his own the concept and the meticulous labor of someone else,

and it becomes rude to tell a man he is being tested. Hence "How long have you had it?" is polite, forbearing, profoundly courteous. He answered, "Half my life." She looked at the tree. Trees can be found, sometimes, not quite discarded, not quite forgotten, potted in rusty gallon cans in not quite successful nurseries, unsold because they are shaped oddly or have dead branches here and there, or because they have grown too slowly in whole or part. These are the ones which develop interesting trunks and a resistance to misfortune that makes them flourish if given the least excuse for living. This one was far older than half this man's life, or all of it. Looking at it, she was terrified by the unbidden thought that a fire, a family of squirrels, some subterranean worm or termite could end this beauty—something working outside any concept of rightness or justice or . . . or respect. She looked at the tree. She looked at the man.

"Coming?"

"Yes," she said and went with him into his laboratory. "Sit down over there and relax," he told her. "This might take a little while."

"Over there" was a big leather chair by the bookcase. The books were right across the spectrum—reference works in medicine and engineering, nuclear physics, chemistry, biology, psychiatry. Also tennis, gymnastics, chess, the oriental war game Go, and golf. And then drama, the techniques of fiction, *Modern English Usage, The American Language* and supplement, Wood's and Walker's rhyming dictionaries and an array of other dictionaries and encyclopedias. A whole long shelf of biographies. "You have quite a library."

He answered her rather shortly: clearly he did not want to talk just now, for he was very busy. He said only, "Yes I have—perhaps you'll see it some time," which left her to pick away at his words to find out what on earth he meant by them. He could only have meant, she decided, that the books beside her chair were what he kept handy for his work—that his real library was elsewhere. She looked at him with a certain awe.

And she watched him. She liked the way he moved—swiftly, decisively. Clearly he knew what he was doing. He used some equipment that she recognized—a glass still, titration equipment, a centrifuge. There were two refrigerators, one of which was not a refrigerator at all, for she could see the large indicator on the door: it stood at 70°F. It came to her that a modern refrigerator is perfectly adaptable to the demand for controlled environment, even a warm one.

But all that, and the equipment she did not recognize, was only furniture. It was the man who was worth watching, the man who kept her occupied so that not once in all the long time she sat there was she tempted toward the bookshelves.

At last he finished a long sequence at the bench, threw some switches, picked up a tall stool and came over to her. He perched on the stool, hung his heels on the cross-spoke, and laid a pair of long brown hands over his knees. "Scared?"

"I s'pose I am."

"You don't have to stay."

"Considering the alternative," she began bravely, but the courage-sound somehow oozed out, "it can't matter much."

"Very sound," he said, almost cheerfully. "I remember when I was a kid there was a fire scare in the apartment house where we lived. It was a wild scramble to get out, and my ten-year-old brother found himself outside in the street with an alarm clock in his hand. It was an old one and it didn't work—but of all the things in the place he might have snatched up at a time like that, it turned out to be the clock. He's never been able to figure out why."

"Have you?"

"Not why he picked that particular thing, no. But I think I know why he did something obviously irrational. You see, panic is a very special state. Like fear and flight, or fury and attack, it's a pretty primitive reaction to extreme danger. It's one of the expressions of the will to survive. What makes it so special is that it's irrational. Now, why would the abandonment of reason be a survival mechanism?"

She thought about this seriously. There was that about this man which made serious thought imperative. "I can't imagine," she said finally. "Unless it's because, in some situations, reason just doesn't work."

"You *can* imagine," he said, again radiating that huge approval, making her glow. "And you just did. If you are in danger and you try reason, and reason doesn't work, you abandon it. You can't say it's unintelligent to abandon what doesn't work, right? So then you are in panic; then you start to perform random acts. Most of them—far and away most—will be useless; some might even be dangerous, but that doesn't matter—you're in danger already. Where the survival factor comes in is that away down deep you know that one chance in a million is better than no chance at all. So—here you sit—you're scared and you could run; something says you should run; but you won't."

She nodded.

He went on: "You found a lump. You went to a doctor and he made some tests and gave you the bad news. Maybe you went to another doctor and he confirmed it. You then did some research and found out what was to happen next—the exploratory, the radical, the questionable recovery, the whole long agonizing procedure of being what they call a terminal case. You then flipped out. Did some things you hope I won't ask you about. Took a trip somewhere, anywhere, wound up in my orchard for no reason." He spread the good hands and let them go back to their kind of sleep. "Panic. The reason for little boys in their pajamas standing at midnight with a broken alarm clock in their arms, and for the existence of quacks." Something chimed over on the bench and he gave her a quick smile and went back to work, saying over his shoulder: "I'm not a quack, by the way. To qualify as a quack you have to claim to be a doctor. I don't."

She watched him switch off, switch on, stir, measure, and calculate. A little orchestra of equipment chorused and soloed around him as he conducted, whirring, hissing, clicking, flickering. She wanted to laugh, to cry, and to scream. She did no one of these things for fear of not stopping, ever.

When he came over again, the conflict was not raging within her, but exerting steady and opposed tensions; the result was a terrible stasis, and all she could do when she saw the instrument in his hand was to widen her eyes. She quite forgot to breathe.

"Yes, it's a needle," he said, his tone almost bantering. "A long shiny sharp needle. Don't tell me you are one of those needle-shy people." He flipped the long power-cord which trailed from the black housing around the hypodermic, to get some slack, and straddled the stool. "Want something to steady your nerves?"

She was afraid to speak; the membrane containing her sane self was very thin, stretched very tight.

He said, "I'd rather you didn't, because this pharmaceutical stew is complex enough as it is. But if you need it . . ."

She managed to shake her head a little, and again she felt the wave of approval from him. There were a thousand questions she wanted to ask—had meant to ask—needed to ask: What was in the needle? How many treatments must she have? What would they be like? How long must she stay, and where? And most of all—oh could she live, could she live?

He seemed concerned with the answer to only one of these. "It's mostly built around an isotope of potassium. If I told you all I know about it and how I came on it in the first place, it would take—well, more time than we've got. But here's the general idea: Theoretically, every atom is electrically balanced (never mind ordinary exceptions). Likewise all electrical charges in the molecule are supposed to be balanced—so much plus, so much minus, total zero. I happened on the fact that the balance of charges in a wild cell is not zero—not quite. It's as if there was a submicroscopic thunderstorm going on at the molecular level, with little lightning bolts flashing back and forth and changing the signs. Interfering with communications—static—and that," he said, gesturing with the shielded hypo in his hand, "is what this is all about. When something interferes with communications—especially the RNA mechanism, which says, Read this blueprint and build accordingly, and stop when it's done—when that message gets garbled, lopsided things get built, off-balance things, things which do almost what they should, do it almost right: they're wild cells, and the messages they pass on are even worse.

"Okay: Whether these thunderstorms are caused by viruses or chemicals or radiation or physical trauma or even anxiety—and don't think anxiety can't do it—that's secondary. The important thing is to fix it so the thunderstorm can't happen. If you can do that, the cells have plenty of ability all by themselves to repair and replace what's gone wrong. And biological systems aren't like Ping-Pong balls with static charges waiting for the charge to leak away or to discharge into a grounded wire. They have a kind of resilience—I call it forgiveness—which enables them to take on a little more charge, or a little less, and do all right. Well then: Say a certain clump of cells is wild and say it carries an aggregate of a hundred units extra on the positive side. Cells immediately around it are affected, but not the next layer or the next.

"If they could be opened to the extra charge, if they could help to drain it off, they would, well, *cure* the wild cells of the surplus, you see what I mean? And they would be able to handle that little overage themselves, or pass it on to other cells and still others who could deal with it. In other words, if I can flood your body with some medium which can drain off and distribute a concentration of this unbalanced charge, the ordinary bodily processes will be free to move in and clear up the wild-cell damage. And that's what I have here."

He held the shielded needle between his knees and from a side pocket of his lab coat he took a plastic box, opened it and drew out an alcohol swab. Still cheerfully talking, he took her terror-numbed arm and scrubbed at the inside of her elbow. "I am not for one second implying that nuclear charges in the atom are the same thing as static electricity. They're in a different league altogether. But the analogy holds. I could use another analogy. I could liken the charge on the wild cells to accumulations of fat, and this gunk of mine to a detergent, which would break it up and spread it so far it couldn't be detected any more. But I'm led to the static analogy by an odd side effect—organisms injected with this stuff do build up one hell of a static charge. It's a by-product, and for reasons I can only theorize about at the moment, it seems to be keyed to the audio spectrum. Tuning forks and the like. That's what I was playing with when I met you. That tree is drenched with this stuff. It used to have a whorl of wild-cell growth. It hasn't any more." He gave her the quick surprising smile and let it click away as he held the needle point upward and squirted it. With his other hand wrapped around her left biceps, he squeezed gently and firmly. The needle was lowered and placed and slid into the big vein so deftly that she gasped—not because it hurt, but because it did not. Attentively he watched the bit of glass barrel protruding from a black housing as he withdrew the plunger a fraction and saw the puff of red into the colorless fluid inside, and then he bore steadily on the plunger again.

"Please don't move . . . I'm sorry; this will take a little time. I have to get quite a lot of this into you. Which is fine, you know," he said, resuming the tone of his previous remarks about audio spectra, "because side effect or no, it's consistent. Healthy bio systems develop a strong electrostatic field, unhealthy ones a weak one or none at all. With an instrument as primitive and simple as that little electroscope you can tell if any part of the organism has a community of wild cells, and if so, where it is and how big and how wild." Deftly he shifted his grip on the encased hypodermic without moving the point or varying the amount of plunger pressure. It was beginning to be uncomfortable, an ache turning into a bruise. "And if you're wondering why this mosquito has a housing on it with a wire attached (although I'll bet you're not and that you know as well as I do that I'm doing all this talking just to keep your mind occupied!) I'll tell you. It's nothing but a coil carrying a high-frequency alternating current. The alternating field sees to it that the fluid is magnetically and electrostatically neutral right from the start." He withdrew the needle suddenly and smoothly, bent her arm, and trapped in the inside of her elbow a cotton swab.

"Nobody ever told me that before after a treatment," she said.

"What?"

"No charge," she said.

Again that wave of approval, this time with words: "I like your style. How do you feel?"

She cast about for accurate phrases. "Like the owner of a large sleeping hysteria begging someone not to wake it up."

He laughed. "In a little while you are going to feel so weird you won't have time for hysteria." He got up and returned the needle to the bench, looping up the cable as he went. He turned off the AC field and returned with a large glass bowl and a square of plywood. He inverted the bowl on the floor near her and placed the wood on its broad base.

"I remember something like that," she said. "When I was in—in junior high school. They were generating artificial lightning with a . . . let me see . . . well, it had a long endless belt running over pulleys and some little wires scraping on it and a big copper ball on top."

"Van de Graaff generator."

"Right! And they did all sorts of things with it, but what I specially remember is standing on a piece of wood on a bowl like that and they charged me up with the generator, and I didn't feel much of anything except all my hair stood out from my head. Everyone laughed. I looked like a golliwog. They said I was carrying forty thousand volts."

"Good! I'm glad you remember that. This'll be a little different, though. By roughly another forty thousand."

"Oh!"

"Don't worry. Long as you're insulated, and as long as grounded, or comparatively grounded objects—me, for example—stay well away from you, there won't be any fireworks."

"Are you going to use a generator like that?"

"Not like that, and I already did. You're the generator."

"I'm—*oh!*" She had raised her hand from the upholstered chair arm and there was a crackle of sparks and the faint smell of ozone.

"Oh, you sure are, and more than I thought, and quicker. Get up!"

She started up slowly; she finished the maneuver with speed. As her body separated from the chair she was, for a fractional second, seated in a tangle of spitting blue-white threads. They, or she, propelled her a yard and a half away, standing. Literally shocked half out of her wits, she almost fell.

"Stay on your feet!" he snapped, and she recovered, gasping. He stepped back a pace. "Get up on the board. Quick, now!"

She did as she was told, leaving, for the two paces she traveled, two brief footprints of fire. She teetered on the board. Visibly, her hair began to stir. "What's happening to me?" she cried.

"You're getting charged after all," he said jovially, but at this point she failed to appreciate the extension of even her own witticism. She cried again, "What's happening to me?"

"It's all right," he said consolingly. He went to the bench and turned on a tone generator. It moaned deep in the one to three hundred cycle range. He increased the volume and turned the pitch control. It howled upward and as it did so her red-gold hair shivered and swept up and out, each hair attempting frantically to get away from all the others. He ran the tone up above ten thousand cycles and all the way back to a belly-bumping inaudible eleven; at the extremes her hair slumped, but at around eleven hundred it stood out in (as she had described it) golliwog style.

He turned down the gain to a more or less bearable level and picked up the electroscope. He came toward her, smiling. "You *are* an electroscope, you know that? And a living Van de Graaff generator as well. And a golliwog."

"Let me down," was all she could say.

"Not yet. Please hang tight. The differential between you and everything else here is so high that if you got near any of it you'd discharge into it. It wouldn't harm you—it isn't current electricity—but you might get a burn and a nervous shock out of it." He held out the electroscope; even at that distance, and in her distress, she could see the gold leaves writhe apart. He circled her, watching the leaves attentively, moving the instrument forward and back and from side to side. Once he went to the tone generator and turned it down some more. "You're sending such a strong field I can't pick up the variations," he explained, and returned to her, closer now.

"I can't, much more . . . I can't," she murmured; he did not hear, or he did not care. He moved the electroscope near her abdomen, up and from side to side.

"Yup. There you are!" he said cheerfully, moving the instrument close to her right breast.

"What?" she whimpered.

"Your cancer. Right breast, low, around toward the armpit." He whistled. "A mean one, too. Malignant as hell."

She swayed and then collapsed forward and down. A sick blackness swept down on her, receded explosively in a glare of agonizing blue-white, and then crashed down on her like a mountain falling.

Place where wall meets ceiling. Another wall, another ceiling. Hadn't seen it before. Didn't matter. Don't care.

Sleep.

Place where wall meets ceiling. Something in the way. His face, close, drawn, tired; eyes awake though and penetrating. Doesn't matter. Don't care.

Sleep.

———

Place where wall meets ceiling. Down a bit, late sunlight. Over a little, rusty-gold chrysanthemums in a goldgreen glass cornucopia.
Something in the way again: his face.

"Can you hear me?"

Yes, but don't answer. Don't move. Don't speak.

Sleep.

It's a room, a wall, a table, a man pacing; a nighttime window and
mums you'd think were alive, but don't you know they're cut right
off and dying?

Do they know that?

"How are you?" Urgent, urgent.

"Thirsty."

Cold and a bite to it that aches the hinges of the jaws. Grape-
fruit juice. Lying back on his arm while he holds the glass in the
other hand, oh, no, that's not . . . "Thank you. Thanks very—"
Try to sit up, the sheet, *my clothes!*

"Sorry about that," he said, the mindreader-almost. "Some
things that have to be done just aren't consistent with panty-hose
and a mini-dress. All washed and dried and ready for you, though—
any time. Over there."

The brown wool and the panty-hose and the shoes, on the
chair. He's respectful, standing back, putting the glass next to an
insulated carafe on the night-table.

"What things?"

"Throwing up. Bedpans," he said candidly.

Protective with the sheet, which can hide bodies but oh not
embarrassment. "Oh I'm sorry . . . Oh. I must've—" Shake head
and he slides back and forth in the vision.

"You went into shock, and then you just didn't come out of
it." He hesitated. It was the first time she had ever seen him hesitate over anything. She became for a moment an almost-mind-
reader: *Should I tell her what's in my mind?* Sure he should, and he
did: "You didn't *want* to come out of it."

"It's all gone out of my head."

"The pear tree, the electroscope. The injection, the electrostatic response."

"No," she said, not knowing, then, knowing: *"No!"*

"Hang on!" he rapped, and next thing she knew he was by the bed, over her, his two hands hard on her cheeks. "Don't slip off again. You can handle it. You can handle it because it's all right now, do you understand that? You're all right!"

"You told me I had cancer." It sounded pouty, accusing. He laughed at her, actually laughed.

"You told *me* you had it."

"Oh, but I didn't *know.*"

"That explains it, then," he said in a load-off-my-back tone. "There wasn't anything in what I did that could cause a three-day withdrawal like that; it had to be something in you."

"Three *days!*"

He simply nodded in response to that and went on with what he was saying. "I get a little pompous once in a while," he said engagingly. "Comes from being right so much of the time. Took a bit more for granted than I should have, didn't I? when I assumed you'd been to a doctor, maybe even had a biopsy. You didn't, did you?"

"I was afraid," she admitted. She looked at him. "My mother died of it, and my aunt, and my sister had a radical mastectomy. I couldn't bear it. And when you—"

"When I told you what you already knew, and what you never wanted to hear, you couldn't take it. You blacked right out, you know. Fainted away, and it had nothing to do with the seventy-odd thousand volts of static you were carrying. I caught you." He put out his arms and instinctively she shrank back, but he held the arms where they were, on display, until she looked at them and saw the angry red scorch marks on his forearms and the heavy biceps, as much of them as she could see from under his short-sleeved shirt. "About nine-tenths knocked me out too," he said, "but at least you didn't crack your head or anything."

"Thank you," she said reflexively, and then began to cry. "What am I going to *do?*"

"Do? Go back home, wherever that is—pick up your life again, whatever that might mean."

"But you said—"

"When are you going to get it into your head that what I did was not a diagnostic?"

"Are you—did you—you mean you cured it?"

"I mean you're curing it right now. I explained it all to you before—you remember that now, don't you?"

"Not altogether, but—yes." Surreptitiously (but not enough, because he saw her) she felt under the sheet for the lump. "It's still there."

"If I bopped you over the head with a bat," he said with slightly exaggerated simplicity, "there would be a lump on it. It would be there tomorrow and the next day. The day after that it might be smaller, and in a week you'd still be able to feel it, but it would be gone. Same thing here."

At last she let the enormity of it touch her. "A one-shot cure for cancer. . . ."

"Oh God," he said harshly, "I can tell by looking at you that I am going to have to listen to that speech *again*. Well, I won't."

Startled, she said, "What speech?"

"The one about my duty to humanity. It comes in two phases and many textures. Phase one has to do with my duty to humanity and really means we could make a classic buck with it. Phase two deals solely with my duty to humanity, and I don't hear that one very often. Phase two utterly overlooks the reluctance humanity has to accept good things unless they arrive from accepted and respectable sources. Phase one is fully aware of this but gets very rat-shrewd in figuring ways around it."

She said, "I don't—" but could get no farther.

"The textures," he overrode her, "are accompanied by the light of revelation, with or without religion and/or mysticism; or they are cast sternly in the ethical-philosophy mold and aim to force me to surrender through guilt mixed, to some degree all the way up to total, with compassion."

"But I only—"

"You," he said, aiming a long index finger at her, "have robbed yourself of the choicest example of everything I have just said. If my assumptions had been right and you had gone to your friendly local sawbones, and he had diagnosed cancer and referred you to a specialist, and he had done likewise and sent you to a colleague for consultation, and in random panic you had fallen into my hands and been cured, and had gone back to your various doctors to report a miracle, do you know what you'd have gotten from them?

'Spontaneous remission,' that's what you'd have gotten. And it wouldn't be only doctors," he went on with a sudden renewal of passion, under which she quailed in her bed. "Everybody has his own commercial. Your nutritionist would have nodded over his wheat germ or his macrobiotic rice cakes, your priest would have dropped to his knees and looked at the sky, your geneticist would have a pet theory about generation skipping and would assure you that your grandparents probably had spontaneous remissions too and never knew it."

"Please!" she cried, but he shouted at her. "Do you know what I am? I am an engineer twice over, mechanical and electrical, and I have a law degree. If you were foolish enough to tell anyone about what has happened here (which I hope you aren't, but if you are I know how to protect myself) I could be jailed for practicing medicine without a license, you could have me up for assault because I stuck a needle into you and even for kidnapping if you could prove I carried you in here from the lab. Nobody would give a damn that I had cured your cancer. You don't know who I am, do you?"

"No, I don't even know your name."

"And I won't tell you. I don't know your name, either—"

"Oh! It's—"

"Don't tell me! Don't tell me! I don't want to hear it! I wanted to be involved with your lump and I was. I want it and you to be gone as soon as you're both up to it. Have I made myself absolutely clear?"

"Just let me get dressed," she said tightly, "and I'll leave right now!"

"Without making a speech?"

"Without making a speech." And in a flash her anger turned to misery and she added, "I was going to say I was grateful. Would that have been all right?"

And his anger underwent a change too, for he came close to the bed and sat down on his heel, bringing their faces to a level, and said quite gently, "That would be fine. Although . . . you won't really be grateful for another ten days, when you get your 'spontaneous remission' reports, or maybe for six months or a year or two or five, when examinations keep on testing out negative."

She detected such a wealth of sadness behind this that she found herself reaching for the hand with which he steadied himself against the edge of the bed. He did not recoil, but he didn't seem to welcome it either. "Why can't I be grateful right now?"

"That would be an act of faith," he said bitterly, "and that just doesn't happen any more—if it ever did." He rose and went toward the door. "Please don't go tonight," he said. "It's dark and you don't know the way. I'll see you in the morning."

When he came back in the morning the door was open. The bed was made and the sheets were folded neatly on the chair, together with the pillow slips and the towels she had used. She wasn't there.

He came out into the entrance court and contemplated his bonsai.

Early sun gold-frosted the horizontal upper foliage of the old tree and brought its gnarled limbs into sharp relief, tough brown-gray and crevices of velvet. Only the companion of a bonsai (there are owners of bonsai, but they are a lesser breed) fully understands the relationship. There is an exclusive and individual tree-ness to the tree because it is a living thing, and living things change, and there are definite ways in which the tree desires to change. A man sees the tree and in his mind makes certain extensions and extrapolations of what he sees, and sets about making them happen. The tree in turn will do only what a tree can do, will resist to the death any attempt to do what it cannot do, or to do it in less time than it needs. The shaping of a bonsai is therefore always a compromise and always a cooperation. A man cannot create bonsai, nor can a tree; it takes both, and they must understand each other. It takes a long time to do that. One memorizes one's bonsai, every twig, the angle of every crevice and needle, and lying awake at night or in a pause a thousand miles away, one recalls this or that line or mass, one makes one's plans. With wire and water and light, with tilting and with the planting of water-robbing weeds or heavy root-shading ground cover, one explains to the tree what one wants, and if the explanation is well enough made, and there is great enough understanding, the tree will respond and obey—almost. Always there will be its own self-respecting, highly individual variation: *Very well, I shall do what you want, but I will do it my way.* And for these variations, the tree is always willing to present a clear and logical explanation, and more often than not (almost smiling) it will make clear to the man that he could have avoided it if his understanding had been better.

It is the slowest sculpture in the world, and there is, at times, doubt as to which is being sculpted, man or tree.

So he stood for perhaps ten minutes watching the flow of gold over the upper branches, and then went to a carved wooden chest, opened it, shook out a length of disreputable cotton duck, opened the hinged glass at one side of the atrium, and spread the canvas over the roots and all the earth to one side of the trunk, leaving the rest open to wind and water. Perhaps in a while—a month or two—a certain shoot in the topmost branch would take the hint, and the uneven flow of moisture up through the cambium layer would nudge it away from that upward reach and persuade it to continue this horizontal passage. And perhaps not, and it would need the harsher language of binding and wire. But then it might have something to say, too, about the rightness of an upward trend, and would perhaps say it persuasively enough to convince the man; altogether, a patient, meaningful, and rewarding dialogue.

"Good morning."

"Oh goddam!" he barked, "you made me bite my tongue. I thought you'd gone."

"I did." She knelt in the shadows with her back against the inner wall, facing the atrium. "But then I stopped to be with the tree for a while."

"Then what?"

"I thought a lot."

"What about?"

"You."

"Did you now!"

"Look," she said firmly, "I'm not going to any doctor to get this thing checked out. I didn't want to leave until I had told you that, and until I was sure you believed me."

"Come on in and we'll get something to eat."

Foolishly, she giggled. "I can't. My feet are asleep."

Without hesitation he scooped her up in his arms and carried her around the atrium. She said, her arm around his shoulders and their faces close, "Do you believe me?"

He continued around until they reached the wooden chest, then stopped and looked into her eyes. "I believe you. I don't know why you decided that, but I'm willing to believe you." He set her down on the chest and stood back.

"It's that act of faith you mentioned," she said gravely. "I thought you ought to have it, at least once in your life, so you can never say such a thing again." She tapped her heels gingerly against the slate floor. "Ow." She made a pained smile. "Pins and needles."

"You must have been thinking for a long time."

"Yes. Want more?"

"Sure."

"You are an angry, frightened man."

He seemed delighted. "Tell me about all that!"

"No," she said quietly. "You tell me. I'm very serious about this. Why are you angry?"

"I'm not!"

"Why are you so angry?"

"I tell you I'm not! Although," he added good-naturedly, "you're pushing me in that direction."

"Well then, why?"

He gazed at her for what, to her, seemed a very long time indeed. "You really want to know, don't you?"

She nodded.

He waved a sudden hand, up and out. "Where do you suppose all this came from—the house, the land, the equipment?"

She waited.

"An exhaust system," he said, with a thickening of the voice she was coming to know. "A way of guiding exhaust gases out of internal-combusion engines in such a way that they are given a spin. Unburned solids are embedded in the walls of the muffler in a glass-wool liner that slips out in one piece and can be replaced by a clean one every couple of thousand miles. The rest of the exhaust is fired by its own spark plug and what will burn, burns. The heat is used to preheat the fuel; the rest is spun again through a five-thousand mile cartridge. What finally gets out is, by today's standards at least, pretty clean; and because of the preheating, it actually gets better mileage out of the engine."

"So you've made a lot of money."

"I made a lot of money," he echoed. "But not because the thing is being used to cut down air pollution. I got the money because an automobile company bought it and buried it in a lockbox. They don't like it because it costs something to install in new cars. Some friends of theirs in the refining business don't like it because it gets high performance out of crude fuels. Well all right—I didn't know any better and I won't make the same mistake again. But yes—I'm angry. I was angry when I was a kid on a tankship and we were set to washing down bulkheads with chipped brown-soap and canvas, and I went ashore and bought a detergent and tried it and it was better, faster and cheaper so I took it to the bos'n, who gave me a punch in the mouth for pretending to know his job better than he did . . . well, he was drunk at the time, but the rough part was when the old shellbacks in the crew got wind of it and ganged up on me for being what they called a 'company man'—that's a dirty name in a ship. I just couldn't understand why people got in the way of something better.

"I've been up against that all my life. I have something in my head that just won't quit: it's a way I have of asking the next question: Why is so-and-so the way it is? Why can't it be such-and-such instead? There is always another question to be asked about any thing or any situation; especially you shouldn't quit when you like an answer because there's always another one after it. And we live in a world where people just don't want to ask the next question!

"I've been paid all my stomach will take for things people won't use, and if I'm mad all the time it's really my fault—I admit it; because I just can't stop asking that next question and coming up with answers. There's a half-dozen real blockbusters in that lab that nobody will ever see, and half a hundred more in my head; but what can you do in a world where people would rather kill each other in a desert even when they're shown it can turn green and bloom, where they'll fall all over themselves to pour billions into developing a new oil strike when it's been proved over and over again that the fossil fuels will kill us all?

"Yes, I'm angry. Shouldn't I be?"

She let the echoes of his voice swirl around the court and out through the hole in the top of the atrium, and waited a little longer to let him know he was here with her and not beside himself and his fury. He grinned at her sheepishly when he came to this, and she said:

"Maybe you're asking the next question instead of asking the right question. I think people who live by wise old sayings are trying not to think, but I know one worth paying some attention to. It's this: If you ask a question the right way, you've just given the answer." She paused to see if he was paying real attention. He was. She went on, "I mean, if you put your hand on a hot stove you might ask yourself, how can I stop my hand from burning? And the answer is pretty clear, isn't it? If the world keeps rejecting what you have to give, there's some way of asking why that contains the answer."

"It's a simple answer," he said shortly. "People are stupid."

"That isn't the answer and you know it," she said.

"What is?"

"Oh, I can't tell you that! All I know is that the way you do something, when people are concerned, is more important than what you do, if you want results. I mean . . . you already know how to get what you want with the tree, don't you?"

"I'll be damned."

"People are living growing things too. I don't know a hundredth part of what you do about bonsai, but I do know this: when you start one, it isn't often the strong straight healthy ones you take. It's the twisted sick ones that can be made the most beautiful. When you get to shaping humanity, you might remember that."

"Of all the—I don't know whether to laugh in your face or punch you right in the mouth!"

She rose. He hadn't realized she was quite this tall. "I'd better go."

"Come on now. You know a figure of speech when you hear one."

"Oh, I didn't feel threatened. But—I'd better go, all the same."

Shrewdly, he asked her, "Are you afraid to ask the next question?"

"Terrified."

"Ask it anyway."

"No!"

"Then I'll do it for you. You said I was angry—and afraid. You want to know what I'm afraid of."

"Yes."

"You. I am scared to death of you."

"Are you really?"

"You have a way of provoking honesty," he said with some difficulty. "I'll say what I know you're thinking: I'm afraid of any close human relationship. I'm afraid of something I can't take apart with a screwdriver or a mass spectroscope or a table of cosines and tangents." His voice was jocular but his hands were shaking.

"You do it by watering one side," she said softly, "or by turning it just so in the sun. You handle it as if it were a living thing, like a species or a woman or a bonsai. It will be what you want it to be if you let it be itself and take the time and the care."

"I think," he said, "that you are making me some kind of offer. Why?"

"Sitting there most of the night," she said, "I had a crazy kind of image. Do you think two sick twisted trees ever made bonsai out of one another?"

"What's your name?" he asked her.